When the Night Waves Crash on Clark's Harbor

They stayed as close to the high water line as they could, hurrying down the beach. The flashlight was almost useless, its beam refracting madly in the downpour, shattering into a thousand pinpoints of light that illuminated nothing, but made the darkness seem even blacker than it was.

Suddenly Missy stopped and yanked at her mother's hand.

"Someone's here," she said.

Rebecca flashed the light around with a shaking hand. "Robby?" she called. "Roobbeeeee!"

She turned so that her back was to the wind and called out again. There was no answer, but she suddenly felt the sharp sting of an electrical shock as a bolt of lightning flashed out of the sky and grounded itself in the nearby forest. And, she was sure, there was something behind her: an unfamiliar presence.

A presence she knew was not her son.

She dropped Missy's hand.

"Run, Missy! Run as fast as you can."

And then, as she watched Missy dash off into the darkness, she felt something slide around her neck.

No, she thought. *Not like this. Please, God, no . . .*

by John Saul

SUFFER THE CHILDREN
PUNISH THE SINNERS
CRY FOR THE STRANGERS

Cry for
the Strangers

John Saul

A DELL BOOK

For my parents

Published by
Dell Publishing Co., Inc.
1 Dag Hammarskjold Plaza
New York, New York 10017

Dell ® TM 681510, Dell Publishing Co., Inc.

ISBN: 0-440-11869-7

Printed in the United States of America

First printing—June 1979

Prologue

A clap of thunder awakened the boy, and he lay very still in his bed for a long time, wishing the storm would go away, yet, at the same time enjoying the excitement of it. As each flash of lightning briefly illuminated his bedroom, he began counting the seconds, waiting for the explosive roar of thunder. The storm bore down on the coast; the interval between the flash and the sound grew shorter.

When the moment separating sight and sound shrank to only seconds, and the boy knew the storm had reached the beach a mile away, he rose from his bed and began to dress.

A few minutes later he opened the door and stepped out into the driving rain. It slashed through his clothing, but he seemed not to notice. He began walking slowly away from his home, into the wrath of the storm.

He heard the roar of the surf when he was still a quarter of a mile from the beach. The rhythmic pounding of the waves, usually a soft, gentle sound, was amplified by the storm, its steady beat carried on the wind. The boy began to run toward the sound.

A sheet of lightning lit the sky as he left the road

and turned onto the path that would take him through a narrow strip of forest to the beach beyond. The thunder crashed in his ears as the white light faded from his eyes: the storm was all around him.

He approached the beach slowly, almost with reverence. Just beyond the woods a mound of driftwood lay tangled on the beach, blocking his way. He worked his way over it carefully but steadily, his feet finding the familiar toeholds almost without guidance from his eyes.

He was about to clamber over the last immense log when the storm suddenly broke and a full moon illuminated the beach. As if by instinct, the boy dropped to his knees, crouching as he surveyed the strip of sand and rocks in front of him.

He was not alone on the beach.

Directly in front of him he could see shapes, dark figures of dancers writhing in the moonlight as if in some sort of ceremony. He watched them in fascination. Then he realized there was something else. Something vaguely disturbing.

As he watched his eye was caught by a movement near the dancers. Two other forms were moving in the moonlight—not gracefully, purposefully, as the dancers did, but struggling, rolling about in the sand as they fought the ropes that bound them hand and foot. The boy remembered the legends, the stories his grandmother had told him about the beach, and with the memories came an electric surge of fear. He was watching a storm dance, and he knew what would happen. He crouched lower, concealing himself behind the log.

The dancers continued their strange rhythms for a little longer, then suddenly stopped.

As the boy looked on, the dancers surrounded the bound figures who lay squirming at their feet—a man and a woman, he realized now.

They put the man into the pit first, then the woman beside him. They seemed to be weakened, for their struggles were feeble and their voices could not be heard above the surf.

The dancers put them in the pit so that they faced the sea.

And then the dancers began refilling the pit.

They did it carefully, relentlessly. No sand fell into the faces of the victims, nor did the shovels strike them. But as the minutes passed, the pit filled. In a little while there was nothing left above the surface except the silhouettes of the two heads against the foaming surf beyond.

The dancers stared briefly at the results of their work, then burst into loud laughter—laughter that carried above the surf and sounded in the boy's ears, driving out memory of the thunder and the roar of the sea.

As the tide began to rise the dancers started walking toward the woods, toward the boy.

The moon disappeared as quickly as it had come, and the driving rain began again. The macabre scene on the beach disappeared into the gloom, remaining only in the boy's memory, where it would stay forever.

Under cover of the storm the boy left his hiding place behind the log and scurried back into the woods. By the time the dancers from the beach had made their way through the driftwood barrier, he was almost home.

The tide was rising.

The boy woke up early the next morning and stretched in the warm coziness of his bed. The sun poured through his window in bright denial of the recent storm, and the child smiled happily as he looked out at the clear blue sky. It would be a good day for the beach.

The beach.

The night came back to him, a dark confusion of shapes and sounds. He remembered the storm, and waking up. He remembered counting the seconds between the flashes of lightning and the thunderclaps. But the rest was all fuzzy, like a dream.

He dimly recalled going down to the beach and seeing something.

Dancers, burying two people in the sand.

And the tide coming in.

The boy shook himself. It must have been a dream. It had to be.

He began listening for the sounds of morning. His father would be gone already, working the woods. His grandmother would be bustling around the kitchen, and his grandfather would be sitting at the kitchen table, drinking coffee and reading out loud to nobody in particular.

But this morning there was silence.

He lay in bed for a long time, listening. He told himself that if he listened long enough, the familiar sounds would begin, and the nightmare would fade from his mind.

The silence terrified him.

At last he rose and started to dress. But his clothes, the clothes he had neatly placed on the chair the evening before, were scattered on the floor this morning, and wet.

It hadn't been a dream after all.

He put on clean clothes, dressing slowly, hoping every second that the morning sounds would begin, that he would hear his grandmother clattering dishes in the sink and his grandfather's voice droning steadily in the background. But when he was fully dressed the silence still resonated through the house.

He went to the kitchen. The remains of his father's breakfast were still on the table. That was all right, then. But where were his grandparents?

He made his way up the stairs, calling out to them as he went. They must have overslept. That was it—they were still in bed, sound asleep.

Their room was empty.

The dream came back to him.

He left the house and began running toward the beach.

He paused at the edge of the woods and stared into the trees as if hoping that somehow he would be able to see through them to whatever lay waiting for him on the beach.

His face tightened with worry as he stepped into the woods. He almost turned back when he came to the driftwood barrier.

But he had to know.

He picked his way carefully through the tangle of logs, not so much because the way was unfamiliar, but because he wanted to prolong it, wanted to put off reaching the crescent of the sand.

Minutes later he climbed slowly over the last log and stood on the beach.

The storm had covered the beach with debris: kelp lay in tangled heaps everywhere, and a new crop of driftwood was scattered helter-skelter across the expanse of sand and rock.

The boy looked quickly around. Nothing unusual. His heart surged with relief and the worry on his face gave way to a grin. There would be good beachcombing this morning. With a little luck he might even find some glass floats lying in the seaweed.

Near the water he saw a huge mound of kelp and headed toward it. He walked eagerly at first, but as he approached the dark brown tangle, he slowed, his apprehension flooding back.

He began pulling at the tangle.

Either it was buried deep in the sand or it was caught on something.

He pulled harder.

The kelp gave way.

It hadn't been a dream. From under the kelp, still buried in the sand up to their necks, two faces stared grotesquely up at the child, their features contorted with fear, the eyes bulging open.

His grandparents.

The boy stared helplessly back at them, frozen, his mind whirling.

He could see in their faces how they must have died, waiting helplessly, watching the surf creep inexorably toward them, lapping at their faces, licking at them, then withdrawing to mount another attack.

It must have been a slow death, and a terrifying one. They must have coughed and choked, holding their breaths and spitting out the brine, screaming, unheard, into the wind and rain.

The boy looked once more into the eyes of, first, his grandfather, then his grandmother. As he stared, grieving, into the finely planed, dark face of the old lady, he thought he heard something.

Softly at first, then louder.

"Cry . . ." the voice inside his head wailed. "Cry for them . . . and for me."

It was his grandmother's voice, but she was dead.

The boy screamed and turned away.

But he never forgot.

BOOK ONE

Clark's Harbor

1

Pete Shelling stared out at the sea, reading the swells like a map. Far off to the south the rest of the fleet was moving slowly toward the harbor, their running lights winking cheerfully in the night. Pete was tempted to alter his course and follow the fleet. He put the temptation down at once.

Following the fleet was not Shelling's way; it never had been, and wouldn't be now.

The wind freshened and Pete went aft to begin the back breaking task of hauling in his nets. Even with the power winch it was difficult work. He grimaced quietly, wishing he'd brought someone with him—he was getting too old to work alone, and the years were beginning to take their toll.

The nets began coming inexorably in, and he guided the thrashing fish into the hold, keeping the net neatly piled, ready to be reset. By the time he was finished, with the catch secure in the hold, Pete Shelling was alone on the sea.

The fleet was gone.

Once more he considered returning to harbor. He looked critically at the sea and remembered all the stories he'd heard about this part of the Pacific—about

15

the sudden storms that plagued this stretch of the Washington coast, storms that seemed to come up out of nowhere, whipping the sea into a frenzy of wrath that could pick up a boat the size of *Sea Spray* and spin it across the surface like a top. But he had never seen such a storm—they seemed to be a thing of the past, probably an exaggeration, tales built into legend more by the active imaginations of generations of local fishermen than by the storms' actual ferocity.

Pete Shelling's eyes swept the horizon and he made his decision. He would reset the nets and take in one more catch before calling it a night. The tide would be at its fullest and he would have to fight the beginning ebb on his way back into the harbor, but that was all right. Pete Shelling was used to fighting.

Not that he'd intended to fight, not at first. Years ago, when he'd first decided to put his roots down in Clark's Harbor, he'd planned to take life easy, join the fishing community, and spend the rest of his years in affable companionship.

But it hadn't worked out that way.

Clark's Harbor hadn't welcomed him, and he'd spent fifteen years feeling like a stranger. He'd become a fisherman, but not part of the fleet. The rumors of good fishing never came to him, nor did the easy banter over beers at the Harbor Inn. Instead, the fishermen of Clark's Harbor merely tolerated Pete Shelling, and he learned to live with it. But it had hardened him, made him as obstinate as they. Now, when the fleet went in, he stayed, waiting for the last catch, the catch that would prove to them that no matter what they thought of him, he was better than they were.

He moved the boat north now and began slowly letting the nets out again, bringing the trawler around in a sweeping arc so that the current would carry the richest harvest into the submerged mesh. Then, when the nets were fully out, he dropped anchor and lit his pipe. One, maybe two pipefuls, and he would start the last haul of the night. The last and the longest.

He was knocking the dottle out of his pipe, about to check the position of the nets, when he realized something was wrong. The wind, which had been blowing steadily, suddenly shifted, gusting against the boat. The face of the water was different. The swell had been running steadily shoreward; now, it turned choppy, and grew in front of Shelling's eyes.

Pete moved aft, intent on hauling in the nets. He threw a switch and the winch began humming steadily. The nets snaked slowly in. He worked quickly, gathering in the net, guiding the thrashing fish into the hold.

The swell increased and the wind began tearing at his slicker. He increased the speed of the winch and stopped worrying about stowing the net: there would be plenty of time in the morning to straighten it out. The important thing now was to get the catch in and head for the harbor before the full force of the storm broke over him. Pete Shelling worked furiously, hauling on the net, kicking at the fish, racing the elements.

Moments later, the storm broke with a flash of lightning and a clap of thunder. For a brief second the wild coastline was silhouetted in white light.

Disaster struck as the roar of the thunder died away. The humming of the winch stopped and the nets suddenly reversed themselves, pouring back into the sea.

17

Pete Shelling cursed loudly, realized the danger, and tried to leap aside.

But it was too late. A coil of net seemed to leap up at him, wrap itself around his foot, and twist. The fisherman was thrown violently from his feet and felt himself being pulled overboard. He grabbed at the gunwhale, held on for a split second, then was torn loose by the weight of the sea tugging mightily at the net. Before he could scream the cold water closed over his head.

Time seemed to slow down for him, and he resisted the panic building in him, struggling against the almost overpowering urge to thrash toward the surface. Instead, he forced himself still deeper, straining to reach the entangled foot. He opened his eyes, then closed them again immediately—there was nothing to see in the blackness. He felt the loop around his ankle and, with a terrible twist and thrust, managed to work it free. Now he began fighting his way upward.

He felt the net tangling his arms imprisoning him. He kicked harder, and suddenly his head broke the surface. He gasped desperately, sucking the icy air deep into his lungs, and sank back into the sea, the net pulling at him, his kicks barely holding up against its weight.

He tried to untangle his arms from the grasping cords, but soon had to give it up and use his arms to force his way once more to the surface. This time, as he broke free of the water, he opened his eyes and saw his boat. The net was still feeding swiftly over the side, the winch spinning free.

Shelling sank once more below the surface. The net

was all around him now and he no longer had room to kick. He thrashed his arms, but with his legs bound and useless in the grip of the heavy mesh, his struggles did no good.

Pete Shelling knew he was going to die.

Fear rose up in his gorge. He forced it back. Slowly, methodically, he began letting air out of his bursting lungs. He felt himself losing his buoyancy, and for an instant his fear left him. As soon as he breathed air in, the buoyancy would return. Then he remembered that there was no air to breathe. Only water.

He steeled himself to suck the sea into his lungs, and was mildly surprised to find that he couldn't do it. His muscles steadfastly refused to obey the messages he sent them. His throat closed. He began to feel himself dying.

When at last he relaxed and the sea found its way in, Pete Shelling changed his mind. He wouldn't die. He would fight back. The sea would not defeat him.

He thrashed again, thrashed wildly against the entangling nets, his weakening arms struggling against the bonds.

Then suddenly, almost miraculously, he broke the surface. But it was too late. His eyes searched wildly for help, but there was no one. He tried to scream, but was too choked with salt water for any sound to emerge. He sank back below the surface.

As Pete Shelling died, he tried to analyze the strange vision that was his last glimpse of the world. A boat. There seemed to be a boat. Not his own *Sea Spray*, but a smaller one. And a face. A dark face, almost like an Indian. But it couldn't have been, of course. He was alone on the sea, alone in a storm that had blown up from nowhere. He was dying alone. There was nothing—only the last desperate hope of a drowning man.

The sea drowned the hope, and the man.

When sunrise came, hours later, *Sea Spray* floated peacefully on a calm sea, her nets spread around her like the tired skirts of an exhausted woman who has stayed too late and danced too long.

Pete Shelling had long since disappeared. The *Sea Spray*, alone in the ocean, seemed to mourn him.

2

Brad Randall glanced at his watch and saw that his stomach and the instrument on his wrist were, as usual, perfectly synchronized.

"Lunchtime?" his wife asked, reading his mind.

"I can go another half hour, but then I'll get grouchy," Brad said. "Any place around here look promising?"

Elaine reached for the map that lay neatly folded on the dashboard. "Unfortunately, they don't put anything on road maps except the names of the towns," she said dryly. "No evaluations." She glanced at the map briefly, then looked out the window. "God, Brad, it's so beautiful out here."

They were driving south on Route 101 along the west coast of the Olympic Peninsula. For the last hour, ever since they had passed Crescent Lake, the road had wound through lush green forests, choked with underbrush so dense that Elaine had several times wondered aloud how anyone could have cut through it to build the highway. Then the forest had given way to beach, and just as they had arrived at the coast the cloud cover had broken. To their right the Pacific Ocean lay sparkling in the late morning sun, a stiff breeze frosting it with whitecaps. To the left the dense forest rose steeply to the towering heights of the Olympic Range, standing as a proud barrier between the ocean to the west and Puget Sound to the east.

"Let's stop," Elaine said suddenly. "Please? Just for a few minutes?"

Brad paused, considering, then looked once more at his watch. "Okay, but remember: just a few minutes. And remember that there is no more room in the trunk for driftwood."

He veered the car off the road and came to a stop, then turned his full attention to the beach. It was, indeed, beautiful. Between the road and the sand the ever-present tangle of driftwood formed a silvery barrier that promised hidden treasures for the persistent beachcomber. And Elaine Randall was persistent. Before Brad had even made his way around the car she was clambering over the driftwood, poking here and there, picking up pieces of flotsam, evaluating them against the memory of things she had already collected, then discarding them in the hope of finding something better in the next nook. Brad watched with amusement; during their two weeks on the peninsula Elaine had filled and emptied the trunk of their car at least three times—throwing away yesterday's "perfect" piece of driftwood in favor of today's, which would in turn be discarded tomorrow.

He began making his way toward her, knowing from experience that his help would be required to haul her finds back to the car. He was only a few yards from her when Elaine gave a whoop of victory.

"I found one!" she cried. "I finally found one!" She

held a sparkling blue object aloft and Brad knew immediately that it was one of the Japanese fishing floats she had sworn to find before going home.

"Great," he called. "Now can we have lunch?"

If she heard him she gave no sign—she was totally engrossed in examining the float, as if looking for the flaw that ought to be there; to find a perfect one was almost too much good luck. But it *was* perfect. Elaine looked happily up at her husband as he settled next to her on the log.

"It's not even chipped," she said softly. She held it up to the light and watched the dancing refraction of the sun through the blue glass. "It's an omen," she declared.

"An omen?"

She grinned impishly. "Of course. It means we're going to find the right place today."

"We'd better," Brad said gloomily. "If we don't, we're in trouble. There aren't many more places left to look."

Elaine stood up decisively. "Come on," she said. "Back to the car with you. I'm going to look at the map, and I'll bet the first place I pick will be exactly what we've been looking for."

In the car Elaine carefully packed the sparkling blue globe in her purse, then picked up the map.

"Clark's Harbor," she announced.

"Clark's Harbor?" Brad repeated. "Where is it?"

"About twenty miles south."

Brad shrugged. "It'll do for lunch." He started the engine, put the car in gear, then pressed the accelerator. Beside him, Elaine settled confidently in her seat.

"You seem awfully sure," Brad said. "And you're thinking about more than a place for lunch."

"I am."

"Mind telling me why?"

"I told you—the float is an omen. Besides, it sounds right. 'I'm in Clark's Harbor writing a book.' It sounds very professional. And of course you're going to write a very professional book."

"I wonder," Brad mused with a sudden sense of misgiving. "Am I making a big mistake? I mean, taking a whole year off just to write a book that might not even sell—"

"Of course it will sell," Elaine declared. "Millions of people will gobble it up."

"A book on bio-rhythms?"

"All right," she said, unconcerned. "So it'll only be hundreds of thousands."

"Tens of tens, more likely," Brad said darkly.

Elaine laughed and patted his knee. "Even if it doesn't sell at all, who cares? We can afford the year off, and I can't imagine a better place to spend the time than out here. So even if the book is only an excuse to spend a few months at the beach—which it isn't, of course—" she added quickly, "it's still worth it."

"And what about my patients?"

"What about them?" Elaine said airily. "Their neuroses will keep, with Bill Carpenter looking out for them. He may not be the psychiatrist you are, but he's not going to kill your patients."

Brad lapsed into silence. Elaine was right. It was a comfortable silence, the kind of silence that comes only between people who love and understand each other, a silence born, not from lack of anything to say, but rather from a lack of necessity to say anything at all.

They had been combing the peninsula for two weeks, looking for the right town in which to spend the year Brad estimated it would take him to complete his book. But there had been something wrong with every town they had seen—too commercial or too shabby, too self-consciously quaint or too self-satisfied. Today, Brad knew, they would either find the right town or give up the search, for if they continued on, they would be into the unrelieved dullness of Aberdeen and Hoquiam, having made a complete circuit of the peninsula. Maybe Elaine's right, Brad thought. Maybe Clark's Harbor is the right place. He rolled the name of the town around in his mind. Clark's Harbor. Clark's Harbor. It had a nice lilt to it, like an old New England fishing village.

"It's right up ahead," Elaine said softly, breaking the silence.

Brad realized he hadn't been paying much attention to the road, driving more by habit than by concentration. Now he saw they were in the outskirts of a town.

It didn't seem to be a large town, which was fine, and it seemed to be well tended, which was even better. The houses were scattered along the road, frame houses, some neatly painted, others weathered to a silver patina by the sea wind. But even the older structures stood firmly upright, solidly built to withstand the elements.

They drove down a slight incline into the heart of Clark's Harbor. It was little more than a village. There was a side street running perpendicular to the highway, and Brad made a right turn onto it. The incline steepened and they dropped quickly into the center of the village. The street ended at a wharf. Brad brought the car to a stop and he and Elaine looked curiously around.

"It looks like something out of New England," Elaine said softly, echoing Brad's thought. "I love it."

And it did look like a picture-postcard New England town. The buildings that clustered along the waterfront were all of a type: neat clapboards, brightly painted, with manicured gardens flowering gaily in the spring air. Set apart, grandly aloof from the rest, was an old Victorian building, its lawn and garden neatly bounded by a white picket fence. A hand-lettered sign proclaimed it the Harbor Inn.

There were several people on the streets, enough so the town seemed busy but not frantic. One or two glanced at the Randalls' car, but with no particular interest. No one stopped to stare; no one gestured or commented. Brad frowned slightly, feeling a strange lack of curiosity in the people who had glanced at them so disinterestedly. Always sensitive to her husband, Elaine looked quickly at him, concern clouding her face.

"Is something wrong?" she asked.

"I don't know," Brad said. Then he grinned at her. "What do you say we get something to eat?"

Rebecca Palmer had noticed the strange car passing by as she was about to go into Blake's Dry Goods, but she was preoccupied with other things. Right now she was more concerned with her shopping than with who might have arrived in Clark's Harbor. The dark green Volvo had seemed somehow familiar, though. Wishful thinking; she pushed it out of her mind.

She pulled a cart from the row that stood waiting just inside the front door and began wheeling it slowly through the aisles, stopping to look at a display of china that struck her as being in particularly bad taste, even for dime-store dinnerware. Shaking her head sadly at the garish pink and blue pansies that paraded helplessly around the perimeter of the plates, she moved on, picking up an item here and there and depositing it in the basket of the cart.

The crash came as she was pausing in front of a rack of inexpensive dresses. She whirled around and saw George Blake hurrying toward the china display. Satisfied that the accident had had nothing to do with her, Rebecca turned back to the rack and continued her search for a dress that would set off her almost ethereal prettiness. Rebecca had a fragile look to her, and it was difficult for her to find clothing that didn't overwhelm her. She was about to give up her search when she heard Mr. Blake behind her.

"You're going to have to pay for that stuff." His voice was gruff, as if he was expecting to be contradicted. Rebecca turned and looked shyly at him.

"I beg your pardon?"

"The china," Blake said accusingly. "You're going to have to pay for the things you broke."

"But I didn't have anything to do with that," Rebecca explained. "I was standing right here, looking at the dresses."

"I saw you looking at the china," Blake said evenly.

Rebecca frowned unhappily. "But that was five or ten minutes ago. And I didn't even touch it."

Blake's face darkened, and Rebecca almost recoiled from the man's unconcealed hostility.

"Don't lie to me, Mrs. Palmer. You must have knocked the stack over. There isn't anybody here but you and me."

Rebecca glanced quickly around and saw that he was right. Except for her and the proprietor, the store was empty.

"But I didn't have anything to do with it," she insisted helplessly. "I told you, I wasn't anywhere near that table."

Blake just stared at her.

"Don't know why you want to say something like that," he said finally. "Ever since you and your family got here, we've all known there was something funny about you. Now I guess I know what it is—you're a liar."

"I am not!" Rebecca flared. "If I'd done it, I'd admit it, and pay for the damage. But I didn't do anything."

"All right," Blake replied. "I'll take your word for it. But if you don't mind, I'll just put all that stuff in your basket back on the shelves."

"You'll do *what?*"

"I don't want you shopping here anymore," Blake said. "I suppose you have a right to be in Clark's Harbor, but that doesn't mean I have to sell to you. From now on take your business somewhere else."

Rebecca Palmer bit her lip and forced herself not to burst into tears. What is it, she asked herself. What is it about this town? But she knew there was no point in asking Blake, less point in arguing with him.

Silently, Rebecca left the dry goods store, wondering how she would explain the incident to her husband and how he would react to it. Not well, she was sure. Glen Palmer controlled his artist's temperament well, but sometimes he blew. This, she was sure, would make him blow.

"There's a café," Elaine Randall said, pointing. The restaurant was on the second floor of a two-story building, above a tavern. The Randalls had to pass through the tavern to go upstairs, and Brad glanced around when his eyes had adjusted to the gloom. The bar was nearly empty—only a couple of old men sitting at a scarred oak table, a checkerboard and a pitcher of beer between them. He grinned his approval to Elaine and followed her upstairs.

The café, in contrast to the bar, was nearly full. There was one empty table by the window, and the Randalls headed for it. Brad scanned the menu, deciding on a crab salad without really considering the options, then put the menu aside in favor of his favorite hobby: people watching.

A few minutes later a waitress appeared and took their order. When she was done, Elaine placed the menu back in its holder behind the napkins and folded her hands.

"Well?"

"Well, what?"

"Tell me who's here."

"Not much to tell, really," Brad said. "It looks to me like mostly fishermen—"

"Very astute of you," Elaine broke in, "considering there's a wharf right outside the window."

"Also some housewives and shopkeepers," Brad continued, ignoring the gibe. "And one person I can't figure out."

"Where?" Elaine asked, glancing around. "Never mind—it has to be that man sitting by himself over there. I see what you mean."

"Really? What do I mean?"

"He's different from the rest of them," Elaine said. "He looks like he doesn't quite fit in, and knows it."

Brad nodded and glanced once more at the man they were talking about. It was his clothes, Brad decided, and something about his face. Like a number of the men they'd seen, this one wore jeans and a faded work shirt, but somehow he wore them differently. It was the fit of them. They fit too well. And the face. What was it about the face? Then it hit Brad: the man had recently shaved off a beard, leaving a pallor where the lower part of his face had been protected from the sun. And something else hit Brad: a sense of recognition. He was almost sure he knew the man.

Before he could ask Elaine about it their food arrived and the Randalls began eating, though every now and then Brad's glance moved curiously to the man whose clothes fit and who had just cut off his beard. The man kept his eyes on his plate and ate steadily, not rushing, but wasting no time. Once he signaled for more coffee. The waitress poured it willingly but didn't stop to chat for a few seconds as she did with everyone else in the café. When the man finished his meal, he dug into his pocket, dropped some money on the table, and started to leave. But as he moved toward the stairs his eyes suddenly met Brad's, and he stopped short. A grin lit his face and he moved quickly across the room, his hand extended in greeting.

"Dr. Randall? Is it really you?"

Brad recognized him then and stood up. "Glen Palmer! For Christ's sake! I've been sitting here all along, sure I recognized you, but I couldn't place you."

"It's the beard," Glen Palmer answered. "I shaved it off when we moved out here."

"Sit down. This is my wife, Elaine. Honey, this is Glen Palmer, the father of Robby Palmer."

Elaine's brow furrowed with puzzlement, then cleared as she extended a hand in greeting. "Of course," she said, smiling. "How is he? Brad tells me there was some kind of miracle."

"That's the only word to describe it," Palmer agreed as he sat down. Brad looked at him expectantly, wanting to bombard Palmer with questions but reluctant to embarrass the man.

Robby Palmer, Glen's nine-year-old son, had been under Brad Randall's care for nearly three years, a victim of hyperkinesis. It had been a particularly severe case. The first time he had seen the child, Robby was six years old, and unable to sit still for more than a second or two, talking constantly, compulsively, his hands and feet always moving, sometimes only nervously, but more often destructively. Brad had quickly learned to remove all breakable things from his office when Robby Palmer was coming. A small boy with an angel's face and a "devil" within. There was something inside him, some malfunction in his nervous system, that kept him moving, relentlessly, exhaustingly, sometimes frighteningly. The child had been subject to sudden fits of senseless rage, and it had been during these fits that his violence would surface, his small hands darting out to seize the closest objects—any objects—and hurl them at the nearest window, wall, or person. Brad had a memory, one he would not soon forget, of two pieces of Steuben crystal, his two favorites, bought when he could ill afford them, that had been smashed irreparably one afternoon by a mildly upset Robby Palmer, who had then stared at the splinters of glass, puzzled, as if he wondered what had happened to them. There had been no evidence of remorse in the child, no fear of punishment. Only a second's detached coldness, as if the shattered figurines had nothing to do with himself, before the compulsive nervous motion took hold again.

One day, a few months ago, Robby Palmer had stopped coming to see Brad Randall, and Brad had never understood why. When he had tried to talk to the Palmers about it they had only said there was a miracle and left it at that. Silently, Brad Randall wondered if Clark's Harbor had anything to do with that miracle. Now Glen told him.

"You won't believe it," he was saying. "The change in Robby is absolutely incredible. Ever since we brought him out here. He's calm, Dr. Randall. He's still active, but it isn't like it used to be. Now he's like other children."

"But what caused it?" Brad asked.

Glen Palmer shrugged. "I haven't any idea. We came out here on a camping trip and stopped just north of town, at a place called Sod Beach. And Robby calmed down. Just like that," he said, snapping his fingers. "And he stayed calm as long as we were on the beach. So we moved out here."

"It doesn't make any sense," Brad mused.

"Maybe not," Palmer agreed. "But we don't question it. Whatever demons were in him, they're gone now. Gone forever."

Brad's fingers drummed softly on the table top as he turned Glen's statement over in his mind, trying to figure out what could have cured Robby's disorder. It had been a problem case too long, and Brad was always skeptical of "miracles." "I wonder if I could see him?" he asked.

"Why not?" Glen agreed amiably. "He always liked you."

"Tell that to my receptionist," Brad chuckled. The receptionist had lived in terror of Robby's visits to the office, and often made up reasons not to be there when the child arrived.

Glen glanced up at the clock on the wall. "Tell you what," he said, "why don't you come out to our place this evening or tomorrow morning? Are you staying in town?"

"I guess we might as well," Elaine said uncertainly, knowing Brad would want to. "Is there a decent place?"

"The Harbor Inn, down on the waterfront," Glen said. "It's the only place." He stood up. "Look, I've got a lot to do this afternoon. See you later, okay?"

"Sure," Brad said. Before he could say anything else Glen Palmer hurried away from their table and disappeared through the door.

33

"That was sudden," Elaine commented.

"It was, wasn't it?" Brad agreed. Then he noticed that as soon as Palmer left a buzz of conversation had started among the remaining patrons of the café.

"Well," a woman at the next table said a bit too loudly to her lunch partner. "At least he's shaved off that awful beard."

"Not that it matters," the other woman replied. "He still doesn't fit in around here."

"You'd think he'd get the message," the first woman said. "Everybody else like them has caught on right away and left us in peace."

"My Joe offered to buy that building of theirs just yesterday," the second woman said. "And do you know what Glen Palmer told him? He told him it wasn't for sale. Joe told him he'd better sell while he could, before he ruined it completely, but Palmer told him he wasn't ruining it—he was remodeling it."

"Into an art gallery," the first woman sniffed. "What makes him think he can make a living with an art gallery in Clark's Harbor? And that wife of his—makes pottery that looks like mud pies and thinks people will actually buy it!"

The conversation continued to buzz around them. From the few words Brad could catch, he knew they were all talking about the same person—Glen Palmer. Everyone, apparently, talked *about* him. No one had talked *to* him.

"Maybe I was wrong," Brad heard Elaine say. She also was listening to the comments from the other tables.

" 'New England,' you said." Brad gave her a wry

smile. "Sounds to me like you were right on target. These people don't seem to like strangers any more than villagers do anywhere else."

"It's kind of scary, isn't it?" Elaine asked.

Brad shrugged. "I don't know. I think it's more or less to be expected. We'll probably get the same treatment no matter where we go. But it's just a matter of time. People have to get used to you, particularly in places like this. I'll bet a lot of people in this town rarely see someone they don't know. When they do they get suspicious."

Elaine fell silent and continued eating her lunch. The psychiatrist in Brad was enjoying himself, finding the hostile attitudes of the locals "interesting," and she wasn't sure she approved. But, she quickly reminded herself, you knew when you married him that he was a psychiatrist; you have nothing to complain about. She concentrated on looking out the window and did her best to ignore the chatter going on around her.

It wasn't until they were finishing their coffee that Brad spoke again.

"I think we should look around."

"I'm not so sure . . ." Elaine began.

Brad tried to reassure her. "Honey, any small town is going to be the same, and if we're going to live in a place like this for a year, we're going to have to tolerate some hostility and suspicion at first. It goes with the territory: if you want to be in a small town, you have to put up with small town attitudes."

He paid the check and they left the café. Downstairs, in the tavern, Brad saw that the checker game seemed not to have progressed at all. One of the old men stared intently at the board, the other out the window. If either of them noticed the Randalls neither gave a sign.

"Let's look around the wharf," Brad suggested, as they came out into the sunlight.

Most of the slips were empty, but five or six fishing boats were still tied up, with men working on them, repairing nets, tinkering with engines, inspecting equipment. They walked the length of the wharf, pausing to inspect each boat as they passed it. No one spoke to them, and once, when Brad offered a tentative "hello," there was no response.

"They don't talk much, do they?" Elaine observed as they neared the end of the pier.

"Odd, isn't it?" Brad replied. "Apparently the image of the happy fisherman hasn't reached Clark's Harbor yet." He glanced around as if unsure what to do next. "Shall we go for a ride?"

Before Elaine could answer him there was a blast of a siren and a police car pulled up to the wharf. From the driver's side a barrel-chested man of about sixty emerged, then circled the car to open the door for a heavyset woman. She got out of the car, one hand clutching the police officer's arm, the other holding onto a crumpled handkerchief.

All activity on the wharf came to a halt as the men on the boats stared at the new arrivals.

"Something wrong, Chief?" a voice called.

"Something's always wrong when Harney Whalen comes to the wharf," another voice shouted.

Police Chief Harney Whalen didn't acknowledge the second voice, but chose instead to answer the first.

"Don't know," he called out. "Miriam Shelling here

can't seem to find Pete. Any of you guys seen him?"

There were negative murmurings among the fishermen, and they began leaving their boats to gather around the chief. Miriam Shelling still clung to Whalen and dabbed at her eyes with her handkerchief.

"He went out last night," she said, looking from one of the men to another, then another, her eyes never resting for long on any single face. "He said he'd be back about four o'clock this morning, but he never came in."

One of the fishermen nodded in agreement. "Yeah, he was right behind me when I went out last night, but he didn't come back in when I did. He's probably found a school and wants to get all he can."

Miriam Shelling shook her head. "He wouldn't do that," she insisted. "He'd know I'd be worried. He'd at least have called me on the radio."

The men exchanged glances among themselves. Harney Whalen looked uncomfortable, as if he was wondering what to do next, when the silence was broken by the blast of an air horn. Everyone turned toward the harbor, where a small launch was speeding toward the wharf. Miriam Shelling's fingers tightened on the police chief's arm.

The launch pulled up into one of the empty slips and a line was tossed out, caught, and tied to a cleat. A man leaped from the small boat, his face pale. He looked quickly around, his eyes coming to rest on Harney Whalen.

"Are you a policeman?"

"I'm the chief," Whalen said. "Something the matter?"

The man nodded. "I found a boat drifting out there.

When I hailed it there wasn't any response, so I went aboard. The boat was deserted."

"Where is it?" Whalen asked.

"It's anchored about a mile north, maybe three hundred yards out," the man said. "It's called the *Sea Spray*."

"That's Pete's boat," Miriam Shelling cried. The man stared at her for a moment, then pulled Whalen a few feet away. When he spoke again his voice dropped low.

"Its nets were out," he said softly. "I decided to pull them in. And they weren't empty."

Whalen glanced quickly at Miriam, then back to the stranger.

"A body?"

The man nodded. "I brought it back with me."

Whalen moved to the launch and stepped down into it. The fishermen crowded around as Whalen pulled back the tarpaulin that lay bundled in the stern. Pete Shelling's vacant eyes stared up at them.

Ten yards away the Randalls watched as the fishermen reacted to the death. They stared mutely down into the boat, then one by one began drifting away, as if somehow embarrassed to be in the presence of death. They passed Miriam Shelling silently, offering her neither a word nor a gesture of comfort. When they were gone and only Harney Whalen and the owner of the launch remained, Miriam finally stepped forward and peered down at her husband. She froze for a moment, then wailed his name and threw herself into Harney Whalen's arms. He held her for a moment, then spoke quietly to the man who had brought Pete Shelling home. Finally he led Miriam

Shelling from the wharf, helped her back into the police car, and drove her away.

"My God," Elaine breathed softly. "How awful."

Brad nodded, his eyes still fixed on the wharf. Elaine grasped his arm.

"Let's get out of here," she said. "Please?"

Brad seemed not to hear her. "Did you notice?" he asked. "It was almost as if nothing had happened. They didn't speak to her, they didn't speak to each other, they didn't ask any questions, they didn't even seem surprised. It was almost as if they were expecting it."

"What?" Elaine asked blankly.

"The fishermen. They didn't react to that man's death at all. It was almost as if they were expecting it, or it didn't have anything to do with them—or something. But what happened to him could happen to any of them."

Elaine looked carefully at her husband. She knew what was coming. She tried to head it off.

"Let's leave, Brad," she said. "Please? I don't like Clark's Harbor." But it was too late, and she knew it.

"It's fascinating," Brad went on. "Those men didn't react like normal people at all. Not at all." He took Elaine's hand and squeezed it.

"Come on," he said, "let's find that inn."

"We're staying?" Elaine asked.

"Of course." Brad grinned. "What else?"

Elaine felt a twist of fear deep in her stomach and forced it away, telling herself it was unreasonable. But deep inside, the fear remained, unreasonable or not.

Far out on the horizon, a storm was gathering.

3

The Harbor Inn, its Victorian façade painted a fresh white with sky-blue trim, perched almost defiantly in the center of a neatly tended lawn. It gazed suspiciously out over the water, as if it expected the sea to snatch it away at any second. From a room on the second floor Elaine Randall stared at the sea in unconscious imitation of the inn. She listened to the wind whistle under the eaves of the old building and marveled that the fishing boats, secured against the growing storm, rode so easily in the choppy water of the bay. As rain began to splash against the window she turned to her husband.

"I suppose it will do for one night," she said doubtfully, glancing around the room. Brad grinned at her.

"You love it and you know you love it," he chuckled. "If it hadn't been for that drowning, you'd be happy as a clam."

Elaine sat down heavily in the slipcovered wing chair that filled one corner of the small room and tried to analyze her feelings. She knew Brad was right: if they hadn't been on the wharf when that man's body had been brought in, she would now be raving about the room, raving about the town, and excitedly planning to spend a year here. But the fisherman's death had drained her enthusiasm, and now she looked bleakly at the antique furnishings of the equally antique inn and found herself unable to muster any positive thoughts at all.

"It's run-down," she said sourly.

"It isn't at all," Brad countered. "All things considered, it's remarkably well kept up."

"If you like this sort of thing."

"Which you do," Brad said emphatically. "Look at that washstand. Not a chip in the marble anywhere, and if that oak isn't hand rubbed, I'll eat it for dinner."

Elaine examined the washstand closely and had to admit that Brad was right—it was a genuine antique and it was flawless. Forcing her negative feelings aside, she made herself look at the room once again. She had to concede that it was charming. There was no trace of standard hotel furnishings, nothing to indicate it was anything but the cozy bedroom of a private home. The double bed sported what was obviously a handmade quilt, and all the furniture was good sturdy oak. Not fancy, but warm and functional.

"All right," Elaine gave in. "It *is* nice, and it's exactly the sort of thing I love. I just wish it weren't in Clark's Harbor."

"But if it weren't in Clark's Harbor it wouldn't exist, would it?" Brad reasoned.

"You're not going to trap me into *that* old argument. Besides, you know perfectly well what I'm talking about. You're just trying to be ornery."

"Me?" Brad said with exaggerated innocence. "Would I do a thing like that?"

"Yes, you would," Elaine replied, trying to keep her

41

voice severe. "But I won't fall for it. If I did, in another minute you'd have me all turned around and I'd be begging you to let us stay here at least for a few days. But I don't want to stay. I want to go back to Seattle, and I want to go in the morning."

"Yes, ma'am," her husband said, clicking his heels and saluting. He smiled at his wife and wondered how serious she was—and how much arguing he was going to have to do to convince her to stay in Clark's Harbor for a while. He decided to approach the problem obliquely. He began untying his shoes.

"I've been thinking about Robby Palmer," he said neutrally.

Elaine caught on immediately. "The book," she said. "You've decided to write your book about him, haven't you?"

"I don't know," Brad countered. "I'd like to find out what happened to him, though. The kind of disorder he has doesn't just clear up as Glen said it did. It just doesn't happen."

"But if it did?" Elaine asked.

"Then it's worth knowing about. My God, if there's something out here, something about the area, that affects children like Robby, and helps them, then the world should know about it."

"What would you call the book? *Paradise Found?*"

"Well, a book about Robby Palmer might have a wider appeal than a book about bio-rhythms," Brad said defensively.

"Why don't you write about both?" Elaine offered. "Get both audiences?" She began laughing at her own joke, but stopped when she saw the look on Brad's face. "Did I say something?" she asked warily.

"I don't know," Brad said. He kicked his shoes off, then tossed his socks after them. He stretched out on the bed and opened his arms invitingly. Elaine moved from the chair to the bed and snuggled close to him. His arms pressed her against his chest; one hand stroked the back of her neck softly. The patter of rain against the window became a steady drumming. And he knew he was about to win: they would not be going home in the morning.

"Do you really hate it here all that much?" he asked after a moment.

Elaine wriggled sensuously and nuzzled Brad's neck, then once more tried to sort out her feelings.

"I suppose it was mostly that body," she said finally, shuddering slightly at the memory. "I keep telling myself that the same thing could happen anywhere— I mean, fishermen drown all the time, don't they?— but I keep seeing that face, all blue and bloated, and I'm afraid that I'll always associate that memory with Clark's Harbor." She paused and felt Brad stir. "You want to stay here, don't you?"

"Well, it's certainly the prettiest place we've seen so far, and it seems perfect for what we want. It's isolated and it's small and there isn't much chance that we'll get so caught up in the social whirl that I won't get any writing done."

"Social whirl, indeed," Elaine chuckled. "I'll bet that boils down to an ice-cream social at the church once a month. But I don't know, Brad. I keep telling myself to forget about that man, but even when I do, there's something about this place. Something that just doesn't seem right. I suppose it's partly the way Glen Palmer was treated in the café this afternoon."

"We've already been through that," Brad pointed out.

"I know and I agree with you. There's bound to be some of that sort of thing anywhere we go. But I just have a bad feeling about the whole place. Maybe it's this storm." As if on cue, a flash of lightning illuminated the room and the drumming of the rain was momentarily drowned out by a crash of thunder. Elaine, who usually liked storms, winced.

"Or maybe it's your woman's intuition?"

"If you want to call it that."

"Well, I like it here," Brad said decisively. "I think the whole place is fascinating. The people intrigue me. I suppose they interest me professionally. They seem sort of detached, if you know what I mean, as if they live together but they don't really care about each other. It's an interesting phenomenon, almost a contradiction in terms. A small, close-knit village, probably inbred as hell, yet no one seems to have any emotional involvement with anyone else. At least not on the surface. They probably cover a lot."

"Maybe it's just that nobody liked the poor man who drowned," Elaine suggested.

"Maybe so," Brad agreed. "But I think it's something else, something deeper." He broke off and the two of them nestled together on the bed listening to the storm. Outside, the wind was building, and the inn was beginning to creak softly.

"I even love the weather," Brad said softly. "It makes me want to make love."

Elaine pulled away from her husband and stood up. A moment later her skirt dropped to the floor, followed by her blouse. She stood naked in front of Brad and arched her back, her breasts jutting forward. She smiled softly down at him.

"One nice thing about a storm," she whispered, "is that you can never hear what's going on in the next room."

Then she slipped into bed.

Two miles out of Clark's Harbor, at the north end of a crescent of sand that was called Sod Beach, a single soft light glowed in the darkness from inside a tiny cabin. Too weak to illuminate even the corners of the room, it barely penetrated the dense black woods that nearly surrounded the structure. Rebecca Palmer, peering at the dishes she was washing in the dimness of the lantern light, cursed quietly to herself—nearly whispering so that her words would not be audible. But her son's ears were sharper than she thought.

"Daddy!" Robby Palmer cried out with all the puritanical fervor of his nine-and-a-half years, "Mommy said a bad word!"

Glen glanced up from the game he was playing with his daughter and regarded his son seriously. "Well, I suppose we'll have to do something about that, won't we?" he observed mildly. Robby bobbed his head in agreement, but before he could say anything more his little sister's voice interrupted.

"Which one?" she demanded. "The one that means poop?"

Robby looked at her scornfully. "Not that one, Missy. Everyone says that one. She said the one that means screw."

Missy turned to her father, her seven-year-old face

alive with curiosity. "I don't know that one. Which one is that?"

"Never mind," Glen said gently, then turned his attention to his wife. "What's wrong, honey?"

Rebecca bit her lip, stilling her sudden urge to cry. "Oh, nothing, I suppose. I just wish we had electricity out here. I can't even see if these dishes are clean."

"What's to worry about?" Glen said lightly. "If you can't tell if they're clean, we certainly won't be able to tell if they're dirty, will we?" Then, sensing that his attempt at humor was a mistake, he got to his feet and moved closer to Rebecca. Robby took his sister by the hand and led her into the tiny room that served as their bedroom. With the children gone, Glen drew his wife into his arms and held her close.

"It's rough, isn't it?" he said. Her face pressed against his chest, Rebecca nodded. For a moment she thought she was going to lose control and let her tears flow, but she decided to curse instead.

"Fuck it all," she said softly. "Fuck it all." Then, feeling a little better, she pulled away from Glen and grinned uncertainly. "I'm sorry," she said. "I'll be fine —really I will. I seem to be able to handle the big things—it's always some dumb *little* thing that sets me off, like kerosene lanterns that don't give off as much light as a forty watt bulb. Not that we'd have any electricity tonight even if we had electricity," she added as a flash of lightning illuminated the room and the immediate clap of thunder flushed the children from the bedroom. Missy climbed into her father's arms, while Robby stood in the doorway, his arms clasped tightly around a wriggling black-and-white spaniel. Glen felt a surge of relief at the appearance of the children, the relief that comes when a moment of tension is suddenly broken. He knew the break was only temporary, that the pressures that were building in both of them would have to be defused. But he had no idea how.

The Palmers had been in Clark's Harbor only five months, but the months had not been easy. At first Glen and Rebecca had told each other that the coldness they felt from the town was only natural, that things would warm up for them. But Clark's Harbor remained cold, unwelcoming, and many times they had thought of leaving.

If it hadn't been for Robby they probably would have left.

Robby had never been an easy child. From the time he was a year old, Glen and Rebecca had realized that he was "different." But only in the last three years had they truly begun to understand that Robby was not just "different," not just precocious as they had assumed. He was, in fact, ill, and the older he got, the worse his illness became. Slowly, insidiously, Robby's hyperkinesis had begun destroying all of them. Glen found himself increasingly unable to work, unable to concentrate, unable to create. And nearly all Rebecca's time was taken up by what she had come to think of as "tending" Robby. She could hardly call it raising him, not even call it supervising him. It was cleaning up after him, trying to anticipate him, struggling to stay ahead of him. Each year Rebecca had become more tired, more irritable, more desperate.

Only Missy had been unaffected.

Missy, two years younger than her brother, had always remained calm, had learned early to take care of herself, knowing somehow that her brother had special needs that she did not have.

Then they had come to Clark's Harbor.

When Glen had first suggested that a vacation might help them all, Rebecca had resisted, certain it would be no vacation at all, but only more of the same—Robby constantly talking, constantly moving, poking at his sister, demanding things, becoming suddenly violent. But Glen had prevailed. They had left Seattle and driven out to the peninsula, camping on the beaches. Finally they had come to the crescent of beach just north of Clark's Harbor and pitched their tent.

There, the miracle had happened.

Neither one of them had noticed it at first. It was Missy who brought it to their attention. "Something's wrong with Robby," she said one afternoon.

Rebecca dropped the pair of jeans she was scrubbing, and ran out to the beach. She saw Robby playing near the surf line, building a sand castle, patiently building up the walls and parapets, digging the moats, and constructing drainage systems against the incoming tide. Rebecca watched, stunned, for a minute, then called to Glen.

"Look," she said when he appeared on the beach.

Glen looked. "So?" he asked. "What's so special about a kid building a sand castle?"

"It's Robby," Rebecca said softly. "And he hasn't torn it down."

It was true. Something had dispelled Robby's frenetic restlessness. He sat quietly in the sand building his castle. They waited for the moment when he would suddenly jump to his feet, kick the structure all over the beach, and begin screaming and crying, venting his frustrations on whatever—whoever—was closest. But it didn't happen. He continued working on the castle until it was built to his satisfaction, then looked up and, seeing his parents, waved to them.

"Look what I built," he called. Glen and Rebecca, with Missy trailing behind, solemnly inspected Robby's work. At first they didn't know what to make of it, so used were they to his habit of starting something, then wrecking it and moving immediately on to something else. And yet there it was, a maze of walls and moats, stretching almost fifteen feet along the beach.

"He's been working on it all morning," Missy said proudly.

"The tide will wash it all away," Glen pointed out, more to soften the inevitable blow than to disparage the work.

"That's okay," Robby said. "I can build another one further up." He took his sister by the hand and started down the beach, walking slowly so that his stride matched Missy's shorter steps. Glen and Rebecca watched them go, wondering what had happened, and waited for the terror to surface again.

But it didn't, not once in the five days they spent on the beach, which they found out was called Sod Beach. It didn't appear until they left Sod Beach and started back to Seattle. It started in the car the morning after they began the trip south. Robby became his familiar nervous self, fidgeting, teasing his sister, needing constant stimulation, interested in nothing.

Back in Seattle they told Brad Randall what had happened on Sod Beach, but he had no explanation. A fluke, he said, a coincidence. But Glen and Rebecca couldn't accept that. All they knew was that on Sod Beach their son had been a normal nine-year-old boy. And so, during one long night of talk, they decided to leave Seattle. They would take the few thousand dollars Rebecca had inherited from her grandmother and move to Clark's Harbor. There they would open a small art gallery, and with a little luck they would be able to make a living.

But the luck hadn't come. They had quickly discovered that Clark's Harbor was not the least bit interested in them or their plans. They had succeeded in buying the cabin on Sod Beach and making a down payment on a building which they were in the process of converting into a gallery. But the conversion was slow. Materials Glen needed never seemed to be in stock; deliveries seemed to take forever. Twice Glen had hired local men to help him with the work, but he had quickly discovered that the locals, either through inexperience or malice, were more a hindrance than a help.

Robby, though, was flourishing. The hyperkinesis that had plagued him throughout his short life had vanished as soon as they moved into the cabin on Sod Beach and showed no signs of recurring. Glen glanced at his son. He was sitting cross-legged on the floor, playing quietly with his dog while Missy watched. If it hadn't been for Robby, Glen and Rebecca would have left Clark's Harbor. But for him they stayed.

"Did something happen today?" Glen suddenly asked Rebecca.

She nodded. "I wasn't going to tell you about it, but I suppose I might as well. It was weird."

She told him about the incident at Blake's Dry Goods, while Glen listened to the strange story in silence. When she was finished, he shrugged.

"So we don't shop at Blake's anymore," he said. "All things considered, I don't suppose it'll make much difference."

"It'll be a damned nuisance," Rebecca snapped. Seeing Glen flinch, she was immediately sorry. "Well, I suppose worse things could have happened. And I suppose they will."

Glen was about to reply when Robby suddenly came into the room. Sensing that the boy was about to ask a question about what had happened to his mother that day, and not wanting to have to explain, Glen decided to divert him.

"Guess who I saw today?"

Robby looked at him curiously. "Who?"

"Dr. Randall."

"Who?" Robby asked blankly.

Rebecca's response was more positive. "Dr. Randall? Why didn't you tell me? Where was he? Is he still in town?"

"One at a time," Glen protested. "He and his wife are on vacation and they happened to be at the café when I went in for lunch. They're staying at the inn, and I told them to stop by tonight or tomorrow."

"Company . . ." Rebecca breathed, then glanced quickly around the tiny room, wondering what the Randalls would think of it. Robby was still gazing at his father.

51

"Who's Dr. Randall?" he asked again.

Behind him Missy's voice piped up. "Oh, Robby, he was your doctor. Don't you remember?"

"No."

"You never remember *anything*," Missy taunted him.

"You'll remember him in the morning," Glen said, putting a quick end to the budding argument. "I think it's time you two were in bed."

"It's too early," Robby objected automatically.

"You don't know what time it is," Rebecca said.

"Well, whatever time it is, it's too early," Robby insisted. "We always stay up later than this."

"Not tonight, you don't," Glen said. "Come on, both of you."

He picked his daughter up and took his son by the hand. A moment later they were all in the tiny bedroom the two children shared. Glen helped them into their pajamas, then tucked them into the bunk beds, Robby on top and Missy below. He had started to kiss them good-night when Missy spoke.

"Daddy, can we have a light on in here?"

"A light? Since when do you need a light?"

"Just for tonight," Missy begged. "I don't like the storm."

"It's only wind and thunder and lightning, darling. It won't hurt you."

"Then what about Snooker?" Robby put in. "Can't he sleep with us tonight?"

Snooker, the small black-and-white spaniel, stood in the doorway, his tail wagging hopefully, his soulful brown eyes pleading. Glen almost gave in, then changed his mind.

"No," he said firmly. "He can't. You know very well that dogs belong outside, not inside."

"But he'll get all wet," Missy argued.

"He'll survive. He sleeps under the house anyway."

Before the children could argue any more, Glen kissed them both and picked up the lantern. "See you both in the morning," he said, then pulled the door closed behind him.

He put a protesting Snooker outside, then sat down next to Rebecca, slipping an arm around her.

"Don't let it get to you," he said softly. "By tomorrow old Blake will have forgotten all about his damned dishes."

"Hmm? Oh, I wasn't worried about that. It's Robby."

"Robby?"

"How could he have forgotten Dr. Randall?"

"Children do that."

"But, my God, Glen, he spent two or three hours a week with Randall for almost three years."

"Then he's blocked it." Glen shrugged. "What's so mysterious about that?"

"I didn't say it was mysterious," Rebecca said. "It just seems . . . odd, I guess."

They fell silent then and sat quietly in front of the fire, listening to the wind and the pounding of the surf.

"I do love it here," Rebecca said after a while. "Even when I think I can't make it through another day, all I have to do is listen to that surf and I know everything's going to be all right." She snuggled closer. "It is, isn't it?"

"Of course it is," Glen said. "It just takes a little time."

A few moments later, as Glen and Rebecca were about to go to bed, a small voice summoned them to the bedroom. Missy sat bolt upright in the lower bunk while Robby peered dolefully down at her from the upper.

"I told her not to call you," Robby said importantly.

"I heard something outside," Missy declared, ignoring her brother.

"What did you hear, darling?" Rebecca asked gently.

"I'm not sure, but it was something."

"Sort of a rustling sound?"

The little girl's head bobbed eagerly.

"It was probably just a branch rubbing against the house," Glen said reassuringly.

"Or old Snooker looking for something," Robby added.

"It was something else," Missy insisted. "Something's out there."

Glen went to the small window and pulled the makeshift drapery aside. Beyond the glass the darkness was almost palpable, but he made a great show of looking first in one direction, then another. At last he dropped the curtain back into place, and turned to his daughter, who was watching him anxiously from the bunk. "Nothing there."

Missy looked unconvinced. "Can I sleep with you and Mommy tonight?"

"Oh, don't be such a baby," Robby said scornfully. Missy cowered under the quilt at her brother's reproach. But Rebecca leaned over the tiny face, and kissed it gently.

"It's all right, sweetheart," she murmured. "There's nothing outside, and Mommy and Daddy will be right in the next room. If you get frightened, you just call us and we'll be right here."

She straightened, winked at her son, and left the room. After kissing each of his children once more, Glen followed his wife.

"Are you asleep?" Robby whispered.

"No." Missy's voice seemed to echo in the darkness.

A flash of lightning lit the room, followed immediately by a thunderclap.

"I wish it would stop," Missy complained.

"I like it," Robby replied. "It makes me feel good." There was a silence, then the little boy spoke again. "Let's go outside and find Snooker."

Missy crept out of bed and went to the window, straining to see in the blackness. "It's raining. We'll get soaked."

"We can put on our slickers."

"I don't think Snooker's out there," Missy said doubtfully.

"Yes he is. Daddy says he sleeps under the house."

Robby climbed down from the top bunk and crouched next to his sister. "It'll be fun," he said. "It'll be an adventure."

"I don't like adventures."

"Fraidy cat."

"I'm not either!"

"Then come outside with me." Robby was pulling on his clothes. After watching him for a few seconds, Missy, too, began dressing.

"What if Mommy and Daddy hear us?" she asked as Robby opened the window.

"They won't," Robby replied with the assurance of

his nine-and-one-half years. He began climbing over the sill. A moment later the children were outside, huddled against the cabin wall, trying to shelter themselves from the rain and wind.

"Snooker?" Robby called softly. "Come here, Snooker."

They waited, expecting the spaniel to come bounding out of the darkness, wagging his tail and lapping their faces.

He didn't come.

The two children looked at each other, unsure what to do next. Robby made the decision.

"We'd better go find him."

"It's too dark," Missy complained.

"No it isn't. Come on." Robby started through the trees toward the beach. Hesitantly, Missy followed him.

As soon as he was clear of the woods, the force of the wind and rain hit Robby full in the face, filling him with a strange sense of exhilaration. He began running through the storm, listening to the roaring surf, calling out into the night. Behind him, her small feet pounding the packed sand, Missy ran as hard as she could to keep up with her brother. Though she could barely see him, she could follow the sound of his voice as he called out for the recalcitrant dog.

"Snooker! Snooooooooker!!"

Suddenly Robby stopped running and Missy caught up with him. "Did you find him?"

"Shh!"

Missy lapsed into silence, and stared at her brother. "What's wrong?" she whispered.

"Listen!"

She listened as hard as she could, but at first all she heard was the wind and the surf. Then there was something else.

A crackling sound, like twigs breaking.

"Someone's here," she whispered.

A dark figure, indistinct in the blackness, moved out of the woods and began coming across the beach toward them.

"Daddy?" Missy piped in a tiny voice, then fell silent as she realized that it was not her father. She moved closer to Robby, taking his hand in hers and squeezing it tight. "What'll we do?"

"I don't know," Robby whispered. He was frightened, but he was determined not to let his sister know it. "Who's there?" he said in his bravest voice.

The shadowy figure stopped moving toward them, then a voice, old and unsteady, came across the sand.

"Who's that yourself, standing out in the rain?"

"Robby Palmer," Robby said automatically.

"Well, don't just stand there! Come over here where I can see you."

Robby, pulling Missy with him, started toward the man, his fear vanishing. "Who are you?"

"Mac Riley." The old man was in front of them now, his leathery features more distinct. "What are you doing out here?"

"Looking for our dog," Robby replied. "He's supposed to sleep under the house, but he isn't there."

"Well, if he's smart he isn't on the beach either," Riley said. "This isn't a good beach to be on. Not on a night like this."

"Then why are you here?" Missy asked.

"Just keeping an eye on things," Riley said mysteriously. The rain suddenly stopped and Riley looked up toward the sky. "Well, I'll be damned," he said softly. "They must be working overtime tonight."

"Who?"

Riley reached out and rumpled Robby's wet hair.

"The ghosts. This beach is full of them."

The two children drew closer together and glanced around warily.

"There's no such thing as ghosts," Missy said.

"Spirits, then," Riley corrected himself. "And don't say there's no such thing. Just because you haven't seen something, don't believe it doesn't exist."

"Have you ever seen them?" Robby asked.

"Many times," Riley said. "And always on nights like this, when the tide's high, and the wind's blowing. That's when they come out here and do what they have to do."

"What do they do?" Robby demanded.

The old man gazed at the two children, then lifted his eyes and stared out at the angry sea.

"They kill," he said softly. "They kill the unwary stranger."

Robby and Missy looked at each other, spoke no words, but simultaneously bolted and began racing for home, the wind clutching at them, the surf pounding in their ears.

Mac Riley, standing still on the beach, watched them until they disappeared into the night, then turned and started back into the woods.

Behind him, on the beach, something moved.

Something indistinct, something almost formless in the blackness.

4

Elaine Randall woke early the following morning, momentarily disoriented. She lay quietly in bed next to her husband, staring at the ceiling, waiting for the confusion to pass. The blast of an airhorn jolted her into reality and she remembered where she was. Next to her Brad stirred in his sleep, turned over, and resumed his light snoring. Elaine, fully awake now, left the bed and went to the window.

The storm had passed on to the east and in the sparkling clear morning light Clark's Harbor seemed to beckon to her. She watched a small trawler chug slowly away from the wharf, then, remembering the storm of the previous night, decided to do some early morning beachcombing. She dressed quickly, resisting her impulse to wake Brad, and slipped from the room. As she passed the desk the same little man who had checked them in the afternoon before smiled brightly at her and bobbed his head in greeting. Elaine returned the smile, then walked briskly through the front door into the fresh salt air. She shivered, and drew her sweater more closely around her.

The street was deserted. Elaine hurried across it, then walked along the sea wall to the pier. For a moment she was tempted to explore the wharf, but the memory of the dead fisherman flooded back to her and she chose instead to clamber down the short flight of stairs that would put her on the beach. It wasn't until she had walked a hundred yards along the sand that she realized she was in the wrong place for beachcombing: the harbor was too well protected for much to have washed up. She strode purposefully toward the north point of the bay, enjoying the soft lapping sound of the water and the increasing warmth of the morning sun. Above her a cloudless sky matched the blue of the ocean, and the breeze barely frosted the surface of the water with foam.

She rounded the point and found herself on a rocky beach mounded with driftwood. She picked her way slowly over the uneven ground, stopping now and then to poke at a likely looking chunk of wood, each time half-expecting to find one of the incredibly blue glass balls. Each time she was disappointed—but only briefly: the search was half the fun.

Forty minutes later she came to another point. Beyond it, to the north, the rocky landscape changed radically. Warmed by her discovery, Elaine stood looking out over a magnificent unspoiled beach. It was a long, wide crescent of sand, broken in two places by creeks wandering across the beach on their way to the sea. At the far end of the crescent, almost hidden in the woods, she could barely distinguish a tiny cabin tucked neatly away among the trees. Much closer, and in stark contrast to the distant cabin, a ramshackle old house stood on the sand, its wood siding silvered by the wind and salt. It had the lonely empty look of abandonment, and Elaine had an urge to explore. Only her city dweller's sense of impropriety kept her from acting on her curiosity. She made a mental note to tell Brad about the old house. His sense of what was proper, and what was not, allowed him to do things she would never do. Perhaps if she hinted broadly enough he would insist on coming back to do a little snooping.

She began walking along the beach, poking into the mounds of kelp that had been washed up by the tide. Every now and then she stooped, picked up a rock or a shell, examined it, then dropped it back to the sand. Finally she gave up the search of the surf line, and made her way to the omnipresent mound of driftwood that lay above the high tide line, forming a barrier between the beach and the woods beyond. She clambered carefully over the logs, her eyes darting from nook to cranny, hoping to discover hidden treasure, but finding instead only rusted beer cans, old tires, and pieces of fishnet.

When she was halfway up the beach she sat down on a log to watch the sea. The morning surf had a soft look to it and she was able to count seven separate ranks of breakers, testifying to the gentle slope that extended from the beach far out toward the horizon. She watched the surf for a long time, listened to its rhythmic throbbing, and realized that her trepidation of the night before had all but vanished. The silent serenity of the deserted beach enveloped her, and she found herself fantasizing about what it would be like to live here, spending her days wandering the beach while Brad wrote. She began to picture herself trying her hand at watercolors, then laughed out loud at her sudden desire to take up painting seascapes. The sound of the breakers swallowed up her solitary laughter. That pleased her too. She could talk to herself for hours on end out here and never have to worry about being overheard. She experimented with it for a couple of minutes, then lapsed back into silence and continued her lazy examination of the beach.

At first she wasn't sure she was seeing anything at all, but the more she stared, the more certain she was that there was something buried in the sand. It was no more than a slight rise in the flatness of the beach that she dismissed as a natural contour caused by the surf. But the more she stared at it, the more conscious she became that except for that single spot the beach was pancake flat. She found a stick and began walking toward the slight hump in the sand.

It was about midway between the driftwood barrier and the surf line, and as she approached it, it almost disappeared. Had the sun been any higher, the bright light would have effectively flattened the bulge—a small mound two or three feet across—and she never would have seen it. She stared down at it for a moment, hesitating, then jabbed at it with her stick.

The stick went easily into the sand for an inch or two, then stopped. She pushed, and the stick sunk in a little deeper, then sprang back when she released the pressure. Whatever it was, it wasn't hard.

She began scraping the sand away, first with the stick, then with her hands. Her fingers touched something. Something soft, like fur. A seal, she told herself, I've found a dead seal. She picked up the stick again, and began digging in earnest.

It wasn't until the tail emerged that Elaine knew what she had found. A dog, not a seal. Her first impulse was to leave it alone. If it had been a seal, she probably would have. Her curiosity would have been satisfied and she would have been content to leave it where it lay, for nature to take its course. But a dog was something else. A dog was someone's pet. Somewhere, someone was going to miss this animal. Perhaps, she told herself, it isn't quite dead. She continued digging.

Minutes later the corpse was exposed. Elaine stared down at it, afraid she was going to be sick. It looked so pitiful, lying limply in the sand, its coat matted with slime. She knew immediately that it had been dead for several hours, but still she felt impelled to make sure. With the stick, she prodded at the dead animal. The body moved, but the head did not. She prodded at the head, then, and it moved around at an unnatural angle. With a shudder Elaine realized that its neck was broken. She dropped the stick and glanced wildly around, looking for help. The beach was still deserted. She looked back to the dog, and wished she hadn't. Its eyes were open, and the dead eyes stared up at her as if pleading for her to do something. But all she could do was rebury it. Using the stick, she did the job as quickly as she could. Then she began running blindly back down the beach, hoping that the image of the dead creature would leave her as she left the place where she had found it.

Brad was standing at the desk chatting with the manager when Elaine burst through the door of the Harbor Inn. His smile disappeared when he saw his wife's strained look. He followed her up the stairs to their room.

"What happened?" he asked. "You look like you've seen a ghost."

"I found something on the beach," Elaine said tightly. "I think I'm going to be sick." She sat heavily on the bed and her hands moved instinctively to her stomach, as if trying to stop the heaving there. Looking at her ashen face, Brad felt his own stomach tighten. He sat down beside her, slipping his arm around her.

"What was it?" he asked softly.

"A dog," Elaine said, choking. "A poor little dog. It was buried in the sand."

Brad's brow knotted in puzzlement. "Buried? What do you mean?"

Elaine leaped to her feet and stared furiously down at her husband. "Buried! I mean it was dead and it was buried! Its neck was broken and whoever did it buried the poor thing in the sand! Brad, let's get out of here. I hate this place. I want to go home."

Brad took her hand and pulled her back down on the bed beside him. "Now calm down," he said, "and tell me what happened. And don't dramatize it. Just tell me what you found."

Elaine breathed deeply, composing herself, then told him what had happened. When she was finished, Brad shrugged. "That doesn't sound so horrible," he commented.

"Well, it *was* horrible. You weren't there. You didn't see it."

"No, I wasn't," Brad said reasonably. "But how can you be so sure that someone killed it, then buried it in the sand?"

"What else could have happened?" Elaine demanded.

"There was a storm last night, right?"

Elaine nodded mutely.

"Well, didn't it occur to you that the dog could have been playing on the beach and been hit by a chunk of driftwood? That could certainly break its neck. And then the surf does the rest, burying it in the sand. It seems to me that if someone maliciously killed a dog the beach is the last place he would have buried it. The surf could easily have exposed it. If you're going to bury a dog you bury it where it will stay buried, don't you?"

Suddenly Elaine felt foolish. She smiled sheepishly at Brad. "Why did you marry me?" she asked. "Don't you get sick of me overreacting to everything?"

"Not really. It makes a nice balance, since I tend to underreact." He smiled mischievously. "Maybe that's what makes me a good shrink. I hear the most incredible tales from my patients and never react to them at all. Want to hear some?"

"I certainly don't," Elaine said, blushing deeply. "Didn't you ever hear about the confidentiality between doctors and patients?"

"That's for courts, not for wives," Brad said easily. "Come on, let's go get some breakfast."

A few minutes later, as they passed through the lobby, the manager asked them if they'd be checking out that morning. Elaine started to tell him that they would, but Brad squeezed her hand.

"We'll be here a few more days," he said. He avoided Elaine's eyes as she stared at him accusingly. "I want to take a look at Robby Palmer," he muttered. But Elaine was sure it was more than that.

An hour later, after she had eaten, Elaine began to feel better. The sun still shone brightly and Clark's Harbor, basking in the brilliance, once more seemed as charming as it had when they had discovered it the day before. The images of the dead fisherman and the broken corpse of the dog faded from her mind, and Elaine began to wonder if it might not be fun to spend a year here. After all, she told herself, fishermen do drown, but they don't drown every day. It was just a coincidence.

Rebecca Palmer parked the battered minibus in front of the building her husband was remodeling and hurried inside. For a second she thought the place was deserted, but then a pounding from the back room told her that Glen was there, and working. She called out to him.

"I'm back here." His voice suggested that he wasn't going to come out, so she moved quickly around the half-finished display case, and stepped into an alcove that would eventually be an office.

"This son-of-a-bitch doesn't want to fit," Glen said with a grin. He struck the offending shelf once more, then tossed the hammer aside.

"If you'd measure before you cut, it might help," Rebecca pointed out. She picked up the hammer, knocked the shelf loose, measured first the board, and then the space it was supposed to fit in, then the board once more. She set the board on a pair of sawhorses, picked up a skillsaw, and neatly removed an eighth of an inch from one end of the plank. Seconds later it sat securely and steadily in place. Glen gazed at his wife admiringly.

"I didn't know you could do that."

"You never asked. Maybe from now on you should take care of the house and I'll do the remodeling."

"That would give Clark's Harbor something to talk about, wouldn't it? Want some coffee?" Without waiting for a reply, Glen poured them each a cup, then winked at Rebecca. "Perked with genuine electricity," he teased. "By the way, your latest batch of pottery came out without a single crack. One of these days, with a little luck, I'll get this place in shape to start selling some of it."

"You'd better. I have a whole new batch in the van. Give me a hand with it, will you?"

They transferred the unfired pottery to the shelves around the kiln, then put the finished pieces from the night before carefully aside.

"Now all I have to do is collect Snooker and I can get back home to work," Rebecca said when they were done.

"Snooker?"

"Didn't you bring him in with you this morning?" Rebecca asked.

"I didn't see him at all this morning," Glen replied.

"That's funny. When he didn't show up for his breakfast I assumed you'd brought him with you."

"Did you try calling him?"

"Of course. Not that it ever does any good. Well, I suppose he'll show up when he's good and ready. But I hope he's ready by this afternoon or the kids are going to be upset. I told them you had him." Rebecca shrugged. "It was either that or let them search the beach instead of going to school."

"Searching the beach might have been more educational," Glen said.

"Oh, come on, the school isn't that bad. Maybe it isn't as good as the one in Seattle, but at least both kids can go to the same school."

"And get hassled by the same kids."

Rebecca looked exasperated, and Glen was immediately sorry he had started in on the school. "I guess I'm the one who's paranoid today, huh?"

Rebecca smiled, relieved that there wasn't going to be an argument. "I wonder what will happen if Clark's Harbor ever gets to both of us on the same day?"

"We'll get over it," Glen said. "After all, it may be rough here, but it's not as rough as it was when Robby was sick. Whatever this place deals out to us, it's worth it, just to see Robby turning into a normal boy."

"It is, isn't it?" Rebecca smiled. "And it's beautiful here on days like today. I'm not sorry we came, Glen, really I'm not. And things are going to be fine as soon as this place is finished and open for business. But the first five hundred in profits goes to put electricity into the cabin, right?"

"Right. That should take about five years, the way I figure it."

Before Rebecca could respond, they heard the door of the gallery open and close, then a voice called out tentatively.

"Hello?"

Rebecca and Glen exchanged a look as they moved to the front room. Visitors to the gallery were rare. This one was totally unexpected.

Miriam Shelling stood just inside the front door, her hands behind her, clutching at the knob. Her hair hung limply around her face and there was a wildness in her eyes that almost frightened Rebecca.

"Mrs. Shelling," she said quickly. "How nice to see you. I'm so sorry about—"

Before she could complete the sentence, Miriam Shelling interrupted her.

"I came to warn you," she said harshly. "They're going to get you, just like they got Pete. It may take them awhile, but in the end they'll get you. You mark my words!" She glanced rapidly from Rebecca to Glen and back again. Then she lifted one arm and pointed a finger at them.

"Mark my words!" she repeated. A moment later she was gone.

"Jesus," Glen breathed. "What was that all about?"

Rebecca's eyes were still on the doorway where the distraught woman had stood. It was a few seconds before she answered.

"And we think we have it bad," she said at last. "We should count our blessings, Glen. We don't have any electricity and we feel a bit lonely, but we have each other. Mrs. Shelling doesn't have anything now."

"She looked a little crazy," Glen said.

"Why wouldn't she?" Rebecca flared. "What's the poor woman going to do with her husband gone?"

Glen chose not to answer the question. "What do you suppose she meant—'they got him'? Does she think someone killed Pete? And they'll get us too? She must be crazy."

"She's probably just upset," Rebecca said with compassion. "People say funny things when something like that happens to them. And it must have been horrible for her, being right there on the wharf when they brought him in."

"But why would she come here?" Glen wondered. "Why would she come and tell us something like that?"

"Who knows?" Rebecca shrugged. But she wished she did know.

Miriam Shelling walked purposefully along the sidewalk, muttering to herself, seeing nothing. The few people who saw her coming stepped aside, but it would have been difficult to tell if it was out of fear or respect for her grief. She didn't pause until she reached the tiny town hall that housed the police department. She marched up the steps and into the building, coming to a halt only when she was in front of Harney Whalen's desk.

"What are you going to do?" she demanded.

Harney Whalen stood up and stepped around the desk, holding out a hand to Miriam. She ignored it and stood rooted to the floor.

"Miriam," Whalen said. He saw the wildness in her eyes. He glanced quickly around, but he was alone with the upset woman. "Let me get you a chair," he offered.

She seemed not to hear him. "What are you going to do?" she demanded once more.

Whalen decided the best course was to act as if everything was all right. He retreated behind his desk again and sat down. Then he looked up at Miriam Shelling. "I'm not sure what you mean," he said quietly.

"Pete. I mean Pete. What are you going to do about finding the people who killed him?"

A memory stirred in Harney Whalen and a tiny shiver crept up his spine, settling in the back of his neck. There had been another woman, long ago, who had said these same words. *Who killed him?* Then, a few days later. . . He forced the memory away.

"No one killed Pete, Miriam," he said firmly. "It was an accident. He fell overboard and got caught in his nets."

"He was killed."

Harney shook his head sorrowfully, partly for the woman in front of him, and partly for the difficulty she was going to cause him. "There isn't any evidence of that, Miriam. I went over his boat myself yesterday afternoon. Chip Connor and I spent almost two hours on the *Sea Spray*. If there had been anything there we would have found it."

"What about the man who brought him in?"

"He's a lawyer from Aberdeen. Last night, when Pete drowned, he was home in bed. Believe me, we checked that out first thing."

When Miriam showed no signs of moving, Harney decided to try to explain what must have happened to her husband.

"Miriam, you've lived here for fifteen years," he began. "You know what it's like out there. Fishermen drown all the time. We've been damned lucky more of ours haven't been lost, but our boys tend to be careful. All of them but Pete grew up here, and they know better than to go out alone. The storms come up fast and they're mean. Pete knew that too. He should never have gone out by himself. It was an accident, Miriam, and that's all there is to it."

"That's all you have to say?" Miriam said dully. "You're not going to do anything?"

"I don't know what else I can do, Miriam. Pete was by himself out there and nobody saw what happened."

"Somebody saw it," Miriam said quietly. "Somebody was out there when it happened."

"Who?" Whalen inquired mildly.

"It's your job to find out."

"I've done what I can, Miriam. I've talked to everybody in the fleet and they all say the same thing. They went out together and they came back together. All of them except Pete. He stayed out alone when the fleet came in. The storm was already brewing and he should have come in with the rest of them. But he didn't. That's all there is to it. It's over."

"It's not over," Miriam said, her voice rising dangerously. "I know it's not over." For a moment Harney Whalen was afraid she was going to go to pieces. But she merely turned and left his office. He watched her go. He was still watching when his deputy, Chip Connor, came in.

"What was that all about?" Chip asked.

"I'm not sure," Harney replied. "Miriam seems to think what happened to Pete wasn't an accident."

Chip frowned. "What does she expect us to do?"

"Search me." Whalen shrugged. "We did everything we could yesterday." Then he scratched his head. "Say, Chip, when I was down on the wharf yesterday there were a couple of strangers down there. Looked like city people."

"So?"

"So I don't know," Whalen said testily. "But do me a favor, will you? Go over to the inn and ask Merle if they're still here, and if they are, how long they're planning to stay."

Chip looked puzzled. "What business is it of ours?"

Harney Whalen glared at his deputy. "Someone died here, Chip, and there's strangers in town. Don't you think we ought to find out why they're here?"

Chip Connor started to argue with his chief, but one glance at Whalen's expression changed his mind. When Harn Whalen set his jaw like that, there was no arguing.

Feeling somewhat foolish, he set off to talk to the proprietor of the Harbor Inn.

5

"Morning, Merle."

He recognized Chip Connor's voice immediately, but Merle Glind still jumped slightly, nearly knocking his thick-lensed glasses from their precarious perch on his tiny nose. One hand flew up to smooth what was left of his hair, and he tried to cover his embarrassment at his own nervousness with a broad smile. The effect, unfortunately, was ruined by his inability to complete the smile. His lips twitched spasmodically for a second, and Chip waited patiently for the odd little man to compose himself.

"Is something wrong?" Merle asked. His rabbity eyes flicked around the hotel lobby as if he expected to find a crime being committed under his very nose.

"Nothing like that," Chip said easily, wishing he could put Merle at his ease. But as long as Chip could remember, Merle Glind had remained unchanged, fussing around the inn day and night, inspecting each seldom-used room as if it were the Presidential suite of a major hotel, going over and over the receipts as if hoping to find evidence of embezzlement, and constantly poking his head into the door of the bar—his major source of income—to count the customers. When

Chip was a boy, Merle had always been glad to see him, but ever since he had become Harn Whalen's deputy three years ago, Merle had begun to show signs of acute nervousness whenever Chip appeared at the Harbor Inn. Chip supposed it was simply a natural wariness of the police, amplified by Merle's natural nervousness and not modified in the least by the fact the innkeeper had known Chip Connor since the day he was born.

"Well, there's nothing going on here," Merle hastened to assure him. "Nothing at all. Nothing ever goes on here. Sometimes I wonder why I even keep the place open. Gives me something to do, I suppose. Thirty-five years I've had this place, and I'll have it till I die." He glanced around the spotless lobby with unconcealed pride and Chip felt called upon to make a reassuring comment.

"Place looks nice," he said. "Who polishes the spittoons?"

"I do," Merle said promptly, holding up a can of Brasso he mysteriously produced from somewhere behind the counter. "Can't trust anybody else—they'd scratch the brass. Nothing as bad for a hotel's reputation as scratched brass. That and dirty linen. And I don't mind saying that in thirty-five years I've never yet rented a room with dirty linen. Old, maybe, but not dirty," he finished with a weak attempt at humor. Chip laughed appreciatively.

"What's the occupancy?"

"Twenty percent," Merle responded proudly. Then, honesty prodding him, he added, "One room occupied, four empty."

"Who's the customer?" Chip said casually.

"Harney want to know?" Merle's eyes narrowed immediately.

"You know Harn," Chip replied. "Keeps an eye on everything. But this time he has a reason. Something about Pete Shelling."

Merle clucked sympathetically, then realized the import of what Chip had just said.

"Harney doesn't think—" he began, then broke off, not wanting even to voice the awful thought. Visions of the hotel's ruined reputation danced in his head.

"Harney doesn't think anything," Chip said, reading the little man's mind. "It's just that Miriam Shelling was in this morning claiming that Pete was murdered. Harney's just doing his job, checking out everything."

Relieved, Merle Glind pushed the register across the counter, turning it so that it faced Chip. It wasn't anything unusual, he told himself. Whenever there were guests at the hotel either Chip or Harn stopped by to check them out. No reason to be nervous, no reason at all. Still, he felt anxious, and peered at Chip as the deputy examined the latest entry in the register.

"Randall," Chip read the entry out loud, "Dr. and Mrs. Bradford, from Seattle." He looked up at Merle. "Vacationing?"

"I don't ask questions like that," Merle said pompously, though Chip knew that he did. Then, lowering his voice: "I did notice they had quite a bit of luggage though, so I suppose they're on some kind of trip."

"Staying long?"

"A couple of days. He told me this morning."

"Says he's a doctor. I wonder what kind of doctor?"

"Well, I'm sure I don't know," Merle said. "But I

suppose I could find out. Do you think it's important?" he added eagerly.

"I doubt it," Chip gave a short laugh. "But you know Harney. Doesn't matter if it's worth knowing or not, Harn wants to know it. Think you could find out a couple of things for me?"

"I can try, that's all I can do."

"Well, if you can find out what kind of doctor Randall is and why they chose Clark's Harbor, let us know, okay?" He winked at Glind, pushed the register back across the counter, and left the inn.

Chip drove slowly through Clark's Harbor, looking for nothing in particular, since nothing was likely to happen. Eventually he found himself approaching the tiny schoolhouse that had served the town for three generations.

He pulled the car to a stop and sat watching the children playing in the small yard next to the building. He recognized all of them and knew most of them very well. He, himself, had gone to school with their parents.

His eyes fell on two children who stood apart from the rest, a little boy and his younger sister. He knew who they were—the newcomers, the Palmer children. And he knew why they were standing apart—they had not yet been accepted by the rest of the children of Clark's Harbor.

Chip wondered how long it would take before Robby and Missy Palmer would be part of the crowd. The rest of the year? Part of next year? Longer?

The children, he knew, were no different from their parents. If anything, they were worse.

If their parents didn't like strangers the children would hate them.

If their parents made remarks about the Palmers, the children would taunt the Palmers' children.

There was nothing Chip could do about it. Indeed, Chip didn't even worry about it. He started the engine and drove away.

In the schoolyard Robby Palmer watched the police car disappear into the distance and wondered why it had stopped. He knew Missy, too, had been watching, but before he could make any comment, he heard his name being called.

"Robby! Little baby Robby!" The voice was taunting, hurting. Before Robby even turned around he knew who it was.

Jimmy Phipps. Jimmy was bigger than Robby, a year older, but Robby and he were in the same grade. Jimmy had made it clear from Robby's first day at school that he thought the younger boy should be in a lower grade—and that he would make Robby's life miserable. Now, when Robby turned, he saw Jimmy Phipps standing a few feet away, glowering at him.

"You want to fight?" Jimmy challenged him.

Robby shook his head, saying nothing.

"You're chicken," Jimmy said.

"He is not!" Missy snapped, leaping to her brother's defense.

"Don't say anything, Missy," Robby told his sister. "Just act like he isn't there."

Jimmy Phipps reddened. "Your daddy's a queer," he shouted.

Robby wasn't sure what the word meant but felt called upon to deny the charge.

"My daddy's an artist!" he declared.

"And my dad says all artists are queers," Jimmy replied. "My dad says your parents are commies and bums and you should go back where you came from."

Robby glared at the bigger boy, his eyes blazing with anger. He knew he shouldn't swing at him—his parents wouldn't approve. But how else could he defend himself from Jimmy Phipps's taunts? He took a step forward and saw three other boys line themselves up behind Jimmy.

"Get him, Jimmy," Joe Taylor urged. "Rub his face in the dirt."

"I don't want to fight," Robby said in a final effort to avoid a fracas.

"That's 'cause you're chicken!" Jimmy cried. His friends urging him on, he leaped on Robby, his fists pummeling the smaller boy.

Robby fought back and managed, somehow, to get on top of Jimmy, but then the other boys crowded in, grabbing Robby and holding him while Jimmy Phipps recovered himself.

"Let go of him!" Missy screamed. "You let go of my brother!"

She aimed a kick at one of the boys, but Robby stopped her, telling her to stay out of it. Then he jerked suddenly, struggled free, and threw a punch at Joe Taylor. Joe's nose started to bleed immediately and he ran off toward the schoolhouse, howling in pain and clutching his injured face. The other boys looked on in surprise. Jimmy Phipps, about to leap on

Robby again, stopped and stared, suddenly unsure of himself. Robby, though small, apparently packed a wallop.

"You leave me alone," Robby said. "And you take back what you said."

"All right," Jimmy Phipps said. "You're not chicken. But your daddy's still a commie queer. My dad says so."

Robby jumped on the bigger boy, but the fight was suddenly stopped when their teacher appeared, grabbing each of the boys by the shoulder and separating them by pure force.

"That will be enough," she said. "What's this all about?"

"It's Robby's fault, Miss Peters! He gave Joe Taylor a bloody nose and jumped on Jimmy Phipps!"

Miss Peters had been teaching at the Clark's Harbor school for thirty years. She was sure there was more to the story than that, but she had learned long ago that getting the whole truth out of half a dozen ten-year-olds is harder than undoing the Gordian Knot. The most effective way to deal with a situation like this was to listen to no one at all.

"I don't care what happened," she said. "Robby, your clothes are filthy and it looks like you're going to have a black eye. Go home for the rest of the day." Jimmy Phipps grinned maliciously but Miss Peters put a quick end to his triumph.

"As for you, James, you can spend this afternoon cleaning the school, and the rest of you can help him!" She took Missy by the hand and started back inside.

Robby stood glowering at his tormentors for a moment, then started toward the schoolyard gate. Behind him, Jimmy Phipps couldn't resist a parting shot.

"We'll get you for this!" he shouted. "You'll wish you never came to Clark's Harbor!"

Robby Palmer, his eye beginning to swell, burst into tears and began running home.

Rebecca gave the pottery wheel a final kick, gently molded the clay between the fingers of her right hand and the palm of the left, then wiped the dampness from her hands while the wheel coasted to a stop. She surveyed her work with a critical eye. The rim of the vase should be a little thinner, perhaps a shade more fluted. Then, with a sigh, she decided to leave well enough alone. Heavy, chunky pottery was her style—the fact that it was easier for her to execute was a bonus—and why take a risk she didn't have to take? She brushed a strand of long dark hair away from one eye, then carefully removed the nearly finished vase from the wheel.

She left the old tool shed that had been converted into a makeshift pottery and walked slowly toward the cabin to check on her bread dough. To her right the beach arched invitingly away to the south, white sands glistening, and for a moment she was tempted to go off beachcombing, looking for items that could eventually be sold in the gallery. But somehow it didn't seem fair to abandon herself to the beach while Glen was cooped up in the gallery, struggling with two-by-fours that refused to bend themselves to his desires. Which was strange, she reflected, considering that he could do anything at all with wood-carving tools. In fact, Rebecca considered Glen to be a better wood sculptor than painter, but she would never tell him so. Yet when it came to a simple thing like measuring and cutting a shelf, he was a dead loss. She smiled to herself as she pictured the finished gallery, its shelves all slightly lopsided. No, she decided, Glen's sense of artistry would make the gallery look right, no matter how ill-fitting everything might be.

With one last longing look at the beach, she made herself continue on into the cabin. She surveyed the bread dough dolefully. In fairness to Glen, there were things she wasn't very good at either, bread making among them. The dough, which should have risen by now, sat stolidly where she had left it. It seemed, if anything, to have shrunk. She poked at it, hoping to set off some small, magical trigger inside, that would start it swelling up to what it should be. Instead, it resisted the pressure of her finger and looked as if it resented the intrusion. Rebecca contemplated alternate uses for the whitish mass, since it was obvious that it was never going to burst forth from the oven, a mouthwatering, golden-brown, prize-winning loaf. Finally, since she could think of nothing better, she simply dumped the mass of dough onto a cookie sheet, shoved it into the oven, and threw another piece of wood into the ancient stove, hoping for the best.

She was about to move on to another of her endless tasks when she heard Robby's voice. She wasn't sure it was his at first, but as it grew louder she had a sudden feeling of panic.

"Mommy, Mommy!" The child's voice came through the woods. And again: "Mommy! Mommy!"

Dear God, Rebecca thought, it's starting up again.

He's done something awful at school and they don't want him back, and now what are we going to do? With a shock she realized how near the surface the old fears, the fears she had lived with for so many years, were. She thought she had buried them. Since they had come here Robby had been so well, she believed she'd put them aside forever. Now, as Robby's cries drew closer, Rebecca struggled to control herself. She had never been good at dealing with her son's violent outbursts. She could feel the terror rising inside her. Dear God! Why wasn't Glen here?

"Mommy!"

Rebecca dashed out of the cabin just in time to see Robby emerge from the woods. Fear clutching at her, she saw that his nose was bleeding and his clothes were a mess. Then he was upon her, his arms wrapped around her, his head buried in her stomach. He was crying.

"It's all right," she said. "It's all right. Mommy's here, and everything's going to be fine." God, she prayed silently, please let everything be fine. Please . . .

Still sobbing, Robby let himself be led into the cabin. Rebecca braced herself for trouble as she began cleaning him up, but Robby sat quietly while she washed his face. Most of her fear left her: it wasn't the hyperkinesis then. It was something else. But what? He should be at school, not home, bloody and crying.

"What happened, Robby?" she said when the bleeding had stopped and most of the smudges had been removed from his face.

"I had a fight," Robby said sullenly.

"A fight?"

Robby nodded.

"What was it about?"

"You and Daddy."

"Me and Daddy? What about us?"

"They were calling you names and saying we shouldn't have come here." He looked beseechingly at his mother. "Why didn't we stay in Seattle?"

"You were sick there."

"I was? I don't remember."

Rebecca smiled at her son and hugged him. "It's just as well you don't remember," she said. "You weren't very happy when you were sick, and neither were Daddy or Missy or I."

Robby frowned. "But we're not very happy here, are we?"

"We're happier here than anyplace else," Rebecca whispered. "And things will get better. Just don't listen to them when they say things about you."

"But they weren't saying anything about *me*," Robby said. "They were saying things about you and Daddy."

"Well, it's the same thing. Now I want you to promise me you won't fight anymore."

"But what if they beat up on me again?"

"If you won't fight back they won't do much to you. It won't be any fun for them and they'll leave you alone."

"But they'll think I'm chicken and they won't play with me."

Rebecca suddenly found herself wondering if she was getting old, for she had no answer for Robby's statement. What he had said was true, but in her adulthood she had forgotten the level on which children think. She decided to drop the entire subject and let Glen deal with it when he got home.

"I don't suppose there's any point in my suggesting you go back to school this afternoon, is there?" she said.

"I won't go," Robby said flatly. He decided not to mention that he'd been sent home.

She surveyed the bruises on his face critically, then relented. "Do you feel up to helping me out or would you rather play on the beach?"

"I'd rather play on the beach," came Robby's prompt reply.

"Somehow I thought you would." Rebecca grinned. "But here's the rules."

"Aw, Mom!"

"No, 'aw, Moms,' thank you very much. Either listen to the rules and obey them, or stay here and help me." Robby's expression told her he'd listen to the rules. "Stay within a hundred feet of the house. And just so you can't claim you don't know what a hundred feet is, see that big tree?" She pointed to an immense cedar that dominated the strip of forest beyond the beach. Robby nodded solemnly. "That's a hundred feet away. Don't go past that tree. Also, stay out of the driftwood. You could slip and break your leg."

"Aw, Mom . . ." But the protest faded at Rebecca's upraised finger. "And stay out of the water. Okay?"

"Okay."

"And make sure you come if I call you."

She stood in the doorway and watched her son scamper out onto the beach. Once more Rebecca marveled at the fact that she could let him play alone now without having to worry constantly about what he might be up to.

Happily, Rebecca returned to her chores.

* * *

Brad Randall parked in front of the inn, turned off the engine, then slapped his forehead as he remembered.

"Damn," he said. "We forgot all about it!"

"All about what?" Elaine asked. They had spent the entire day poking around Clark's Harbor and she couldn't imagine what they might have missed.

"The Palmers. We said we'd drop in on them."

"Well, it's too late now," Elaine replied, glancing at the sinking sun. "Besides, he was probably just being polite. I mean, it's not as if they're old friends. We hardly know them."

"But I do want to see Robby again," Brad said. "If there's really been a miraculous cure, I want to see it for myself."

"Maybe you can see him tomorrow," Elaine suggested. "Right now I'm bushed."

"I did sort of run you ragged, didn't I?" Brad chuckled. "But what do you think? I mean, what do you really think?"

"I don't know." Elaine was pensive. "It's beautiful, it really is, and if it hadn't been for that poor man yesterday and that dog this morning, I'd be all for it. But I just don't know."

"It was coincidence, honey," Brad argued. "The same thing could have happened anywhere."

"But they happened here," Elaine said stubbornly, "and I'm sorry, but I can't get them out of my mind." Then she relented a little. Clark's Harbor *was* beautiful, and she knew Brad had fallen in love with it. "Let's sleep on it, shall we?"

They got out of the car and walked to the hotel gate. Elaine paused, staring up at the building. "I still say it's on the wrong coast," she said. "And not just the hotel. The whole town. It's so neat and so tidy and so settled looking. Not like most of the towns on the peninsula that sort of fade in, sprawl, then fade out again. This place seems to have cut a niche for itself in the forest and huddled there. As though it knows its bounds and isn't about to step over them."

Brad smiled. "Maybe that's what appeals to me," he said, "I guess it strikes a chord in me somewhere. I like it."

They strolled across the lawn arm-in-arm and went into the hotel. Behind his counter, Merle Glind bobbed his head at them.

"Have a nice day?"

"Fine," Brad answered. "Pretty town you have here. Beautiful."

"We like it," Glind responded. There was a pause, and Brad started toward the stairs.

"You folks on vacation?" Merle suddenly asked.

Brad turned. "In a way. Actually we're looking for someplace to live for a while."

"We already got a doctor," Merle said hastily. "Doc Phelps. Been here for years."

"Well, I wouldn't be any threat to him. I'm not that kind of doctor and I wasn't planning to practice anyway. Frankly, I doubt there'd be much call for my kind of doctoring out here."

"Well, if you're not going to work, what are you going to do?" Merle Glind didn't try to disguise the suspicion in his voice. As far as he was concerned anyone under seventy-five who didn't do an honest day's work was a shirker.

"I thought I'd try to write a book," Brad said easily.

Merle's frown deepened. "A book? What kind of a book?"

Brad started to explain but before he could get a word in Elaine had cut him off. "A technical book," she said. "The kind nobody reads, except maybe a few other psychiatrists."

If he'd known his wife any less well Brad would have been hurt. Instead, he gave her an admiring wink. Elaine had just rescued him from a long explanation of the subject of his book and the inevitable, endless questions about bio-rhythms. "It seemed to me this might be the perfect place to write it," he said now. "Lots of peace and quiet."

"I don't know," Merle said pensively. "Seems to me you'd be better off up in Pacific Beach or Moclips or one of those places. That's where the artists hang out."

"Right." Brad grinned. "And party and drink and do all the things they shouldn't do if they want to get any work done. But Clark's Harbor doesn't look like that kind of town."

"It's not," Glind said emphatically. "We're working folk here and we mind our business, most of us. It's a quiet town and we like to keep it that way."

Elaine sighed to herself. With every word the odd little man spoke Brad's resolve to move to Clark's Harbor would strengthen. His next words proved her right.

"I've been looking around today. Not too many houses on the market, are there?"

"Nope," Merle said. "Not a one, and not likely to be. Most of the houses here get passed on from one generation to the next. The Harbor isn't like so many little towns. Our children stay right here, most of them."

"What about renting? Are there any houses for rent?"

Merle appeared to think for a minute, and Brad wasn't sure whether he was running his mind over the town or trying to decide how to evade the question.

Merle, for his part, decided to duck the issue entirely. "Only one that I know of belongs to the police chief, Harney Whalen. Don't know if it's for rent, though. You'd have to talk to Harn about that."

"Does anybody live in it now?" Brad pressed.

"Not so far as I know. If he's got people out there Harn hasn't told me. But then, it wouldn't be any of my business, would it?"

Realizing he was unlikely to get any information out of the old man, Brad dropped the subject. "Got any recommendations for dinner?" he asked. Merle smiled eagerly.

"Right through the door. Best food and drink in town. Drinks sixty cents a shot and the freshest seafood you can get. Cook gets it right off the boats every day." When he saw Elaine peering into the empty dining room and bar, he added: "Won't be anyone in there yet, of course, but just wait till later. Place'll be packed. Absolutely packed."

"Maybe we'd better make reservations," Elaine wondered aloud.

"Oh, no need for that," Merle said. "No need at all. I'll make sure there's a table for you. What time do you want to eat?"

"Seven? Seven thirty?"

Merle Glind wrote himself a hasty note and smiled

up at the Randalls. "There you are. All taken care of, see? No need for reservations at all—just leave it to me."

Two minutes later, in their room, Elaine threw herself onto the bed and burst into laughter. "I don't believe it," she cried. "He's too perfect. Do you know, Brad, I think he actually didn't realize he was taking a reservation? It's incredible!"

Brad lay down on the bed beside his wife and kissed her gently. "Now what do you think?" he asked.

"I think we have enough time before dinner," Elaine replied. She began unbuttoning Brad's shirt. . . .

Merle Glind sat nervously at his desk and his eyes kept flicking to the stairway as he dialed the phone. It rang twice, then was answered. Briefly, he filled Harney Whalen in on what he'd found out about the Randalls. When he was done there was a silence before the police chief spoke.

"So they're planning to stay awhile, are they? Well, maybe they will, and then again, maybe they won't. Thanks Merle, you've been a big help."

Merle Glind, feeling pleased with himself, put the receiver back on the cradle, then went into the dining room, where he put a small sign on one of the tables. "Reserved," the sign said.

6

Harney Whalen glanced at the clock, drummed his fingers nervously on the worn oak surface of his desk, then rose and paced to the window, where he stood staring down the street, as if his stares could hurry the arrival of Chip Connor. His deputy was late, and that was unusual. Anything unusual worried Harn Whalen, and too many unusual things were happening in Clark's Harbor the last couple of days. First Pete Shelling (nothing more than an unfortunate accident, of course), and now these Randall people, acting like they wanted to move to the Harbor. Now *that* was upsetting.

Harney moved away from the window and unconsciously flexed his still-solid body, patting his firm belly with the palm of his right hand. Then he reseated himself at his desk, pulled the meager file on Pete Shelling to a spot in front of him, and read it once more. He was still reading it, scowling, when Chip Connor finally appeared.

"Thought you'd decided to take the evening off," Harney observed as he glanced at Chip.

"Just having a little dinner," Chip replied mildly. "Anything doing?"

"Not really, except I had a call from Merle Glind a few minutes ago." Chip's brow arched curiously as he waited for the chief to continue. "Seems they think they'd like to settle down here for a while," Harney said.

"They?"

"That guy Randall and his wife at the inn."

Chip frowned. That spelled trouble. As long as he'd known Harn Whalen, which was all of his life, Harn had had an aversion to strangers, a distrust that sometimes seemed to go beyond the natural feelings of most of the Harborites. Chip supposed it was not really so strange. Harn knew everyone in town—he was related to half of them, including Chip—and his knowledge of them made his job much easier. He knew them all inside out—who were the troublemakers, who were the drunks, and what was the best way to handle everybody. But strangers were an unknown quantity, and Harn Whalen didn't like unknown quantities. Strangers upset the balance of the town. For a while no one reacted the way he was supposed to react, and that made Harn Whalen's life more difficult. And then there were the outsiders themselves to deal with. For Harn, that was the hardest part. Among his own people he was fine, but introduce him to a stranger and he'd clam right up. He'd watch them warily, from a distance, as if he half-expected them to do something to him. It had been that way with the Shellings for a long time after Pete and Miriam arrived in Clark's Harbor. It had taken Harney nearly five years just to offer them a nod of greeting. Chip supposed he understood though. He felt much the same way himself. By the time he was as old as Harney, and as set in his ways, he'd probably have all the same reactions as the chief. But Harn was up to something now; that was for sure.

"What do they want here?" Chip said finally.

"Merle says the guy's planning to write some kind of book and thinks this is a good place to do it."

"Well," Chip mused, "you've got to admit it's quiet here."

"And that's the way I like it," Harney said. "Won't stay quiet, though, if the place fills up with city folk. They always bring their noise with them. Like Palmer and his wife."

"They haven't been much trouble," Chip suggested.

"Pounding all day?" Whalen countered.

"Well, you can't remodel a building without some pounding."

Whalen grunted in reluctant assent. It was true, but that didn't mean he had to like it. He decided to shift gears. "Don't know what he thinks he'll accomplish by opening an art gallery here," he grumbled. "Nobody's going to buy his junk."

"Then he won't be here long, will he?" Chip grinned. "I'd think you'd be down there every day helping out. After all, the sooner he gets the place open, the sooner he'll go broke, right?"

Harney looked sourly at his deputy but couldn't help smiling.

"You're too sharp for me, Chip. Too sharp by a long shot. So tell me, what'll we do about the Randalls? I'm just not sure I can stomach another set of strangers right now. They upset me. And don't give me any lectures about how I can't keep the town the same forever—maybe I can't, but as long as I'm chief of police, I'll damn well try."

"What are they going to do about a place to live?"

"Merle told them to come and talk to me."

"Then it's easy," Chip suggested. "Just tell them the old house isn't for rent."

"I told that to the Palmers but it didn't stop them. They just talked old Mrs. Pruitt into selling them that crummy cabin at the other end of the beach. If she'd have talked to me first, I'd have bought the cabin myself, but she didn't. No, I think the best thing to do is just try to talk them out of the whole idea. If that doesn't work, I'll rent the old Baron place to them. A month on Sod Beach in that wreck ought to change their minds for them."

"You're a devious old man, Harn," Chip said with a smile.

"Not devious at all," Whalen said. "I just don't like strangers. Now, why don't you get to work on Pete Shelling? The file's right here."

"What's to work on?"

"Search me." Harney shrugged. "As far as I'm concerned it was just an accident, but I figure if Miriam Shelling should come walking in here again, it wouldn't hurt at all to be 'working on the case,' if you know what I mean."

Chip laughed out loud. "*Now* tell me you aren't devious."

"The old dog knows some old tricks, that's all," Harney said with a wink. A moment later he was gone and Chip Connor was alone in the tiny police station.

*　*　*

Glen Palmer watched the police chief drive past the gallery and started to wave, as he did every day. But suddenly he changed his mind and his hand dropped back to his side, the gesture uncompleted. What was the point? Whalen never returned the greeting, never even so much as glanced his way. Glen wasn't sure if it was conscious rudeness or if the man was merely preoccupied, but he knew he resented it. The chief's coldness seemed symbolic of the attitude of the whole town. Glen had come to believe that if he could only win the chief's approval, his acceptance in Clark's Harbor would begin. But so far he had been unable to make a single dent in Whalen's shield of hostility. All in good time, he told himself for the hundredth time, all in good time.

That was also the attitude he was trying to take about the gallery itself, but it was more difficult every day. He glanced around at the front room. Tomorrow he would begin spending all his time on the display area. The office could wait, but the display area could not. If he could finish it in the next couple of weeks they could open for business by Memorial Day—and the hell with what the office looked like.

It would be a pretty gallery, Glen was sure. The rough-hewn plank paneling would show off his primitive painting style to its best advantage, and his sculptures, finely finished and glowing with their hand-rubbed patina, would provide a nice contrast. Reluctantly, he decided to swallow his pride and ask Rebecca to pitch in. With a wry chuckle he admitted to himself that her help would speed the work fivefold at least. He should have done it weeks ago but his ego had prevented it. And now another afternoon was gone with not enough done. Time to call it a day. He put his tools away, locked up the building, and climbed into the ancient Chevy that served as the Palmers' second car. It refused to start.

"Damn," he said aloud. He twisted the key again and listened to the angry grinding of the starter. Three tries later he got out of the car and raised the hood to stare at the engine. But he knew even less about motors than he did about carpentry. He slammed the hood down again and, with the blind faith characteristic of people who know nothing about cars, got in and tried the starter once more. Again the grinding noise, but weaker this time. Glen decided to give it up before he ruined the battery as well.

He searched his mind. Pruitt's gas station would be closed by now. He considered searching out Bill Pruitt and talking him into taking a look at the car. No good. Pruitt had never been particularly friendly, less so after his mother had sold the Palmers their cabin— no doubt against Bill's advice. Glen was sure that even if the owner of the town's sole service station could be persuaded to do something with the car, the bill would be padded because of the late hour. He'd leave the Chevy where it was and walk home. He could take care of it in the morning.

He walked along the road at first, thinking of trying his luck at hitchhiking, but soon put that idea aside: he was enjoying the walk and the exercise was relaxing, so he left the road and cut through the forest to the ocean, emerging from the woods at the south end of Sod Beach, near the old house he and Rebecca had originally tried to rent. Now he was glad Harney

Whalen had refused to rent to him: though the house was larger than the Palmers' cabin, it stood exposed on the beach, unprotected by the sheltering forest that nearly surrounded the tiny home he and his family occupied. And it had that awful look of abandonment, a look he hadn't recognized the first time he had seen the place. Then it had seemed picturesque; now he found it forbidding.

He skirted the house quickly and made his way down to the surf line, where the sand was packed hard and walking was easy. In the distance he was pleased to see the faint glow of the lantern in his window, just beginning to contrast with the fading light of the evening. Smoke curled from both chimneys of the cabin and he wondered what Rebecca was fixing for dinner.

He almost passed Miriam Shelling without seeing her, and probably would have if she hadn't waved to him. At her movement he veered away from the lapping water to angle across the beach.

"Hello," he said as he approached her, smiling tentatively.

Miriam stared at him for a long time, not speaking. Glen was about to turn away from her when she raised her hand again and made a vague gesture.

"You didn't believe me, did you?"

It was an accusation. Glen hedged, studying her. "I'm not sure what you mean," he said. The odd glaze was gone from her eyes; now she seemed to be nothing more than a tired middle-aged woman.

"Today," she said, "when I came into your—what do you call it?"

97

"The gallery?"

Miriam nodded. "The gallery," she repeated dully. "You should have believed me."

Glen watched the woman carefully, trying to fathom what might be going on in her mind. She seemed much more in control of herself now than she had earlier. But you never knew with people like her.

"What are you doing out here?" he asked.

"Waiting."

"Waiting? For me?"

"Maybe. I don't know. I'm just waiting. Something's going to happen, and I'm waiting for it."

"But why here?" Glen pressed.

"I don't know," Miriam said slowly. "It just seemed like a good place to wait." Suddenly her eyes were filled with anxiety as she looked up at Glen. "It's all right, isn't it? You don't mind if I wait here?"

"No, of course I don't mind. I don't own the beach. But it will be getting cold soon."

"A storm's coming," Miriam Shelling said softly. "A big one. Well, it doesn't matter anymore. It can't hurt Pete now."

"But what about you?" Glen asked gently. He wondered if he ought to invite Mrs. Shelling home with him, then thought of the children. He didn't want them hearing any of this ominous nonsense she kept muttering.

"I'll go home soon," she said. "I guess I can wait there just as well as here. You go on now—I'll be all right."

Glen started away but turned back when he heard Miriam Shelling calling to him.

"Young man? You be careful, you hear? It's going to be a big storm."

Glen smiled at her and waved. "I'll be all right," he called. He walked on and didn't look back again till he was near the cabin. When he did finally turn, Miriam Shelling was gone. Glen felt an odd sense of relief, as if a momentary threat had passed. He went into the cabin as the last of the sunlight faded from the beach.

"I didn't hear you drive up," Rebecca said as Glen came in.

"I didn't drive—I walked."

Rebecca felt a sinking sensation as the meager balance in their checking account flashed in front of her eyes. "What happened to the car?" she asked.

"I wish I knew. It wouldn't start, and you know how I am with cars. I thought about walking over to see if I could find Bill Pruitt but he charges double after six."

Rebecca was about to press him for details when the children came tumbling out of their tiny bedroom, Missy demanding to be picked up and Robby saying, "Look at me! Look at me!"

Glen swung his daughter off the floor, then looked at his son. He set Missy back down and knelt next to Robby.

"What happened to you?" He asked the question of Robby but his eyes went immediately to Rebecca.

"He was defending our honor," Rebecca began, but Robby cut in.

"I had a fight," he said in a rush. "Four guys ganged up on me and I got a black eye, but I won. Did you bring Snooker home?"

Glen glanced at Rebecca but she shrugged help-lessly. "No, I didn't," he said. "He must be off on a hunting expedition."

"He's never stayed away all day," Robby said accus-ingly.

"Well, he must be getting adventurous, just like his master," Glen replied. "But he'll be back, you'll see. Just wait until morning."

"He's not coming back," Missy said softly. She looked ready to cry. "He's not ever coming back."

"He is too," Robby shot back.

"Of course he's coming back, Missy," Rebecca said. "Why wouldn't he?"

"I don't know," Missy said, her eyes brimming with tears. "But he's not coming back, and I miss him." The tears overflowed and she fled to the bedroom, where she flung herself on her bunk. Rebecca looked help-lessly at Glen, then went after her daughter. Robby stared at his father.

"He is coming back, isn't he?" he asked plaintively.

"Of course he is, son; of course he is," Glen said. But he suddenly had the sinking feeling that the dog was not going to return.

After dinner they put the children to bed, then Glen threw another log on the fire. Rebecca watched him but didn't speak until he had finished poking at the blaze and sat down again.

"Glen, what's wrong?"

"I don't know. Little things, I guess. The car and the gallery and now Snooker. I think Missy's right. I don't think he's coming back."

"Don't be silly. What could have happened to him? Of course he'll be back."

"There's something else too."

Rebecca suddenly stiffened. Whatever he was about to say, it was going to be important. She could tell by the look in his eyes.

"I saw Miriam Shelling tonight."

Rebecca relaxed. "Did she come back to the gallery?"

"She was on the beach when I came home. Sitting on a piece of driftwood, staring out at the sea."

"Lots of people do that," Rebecca said. She rummaged through her sewing box, searching for a button. "I do that myself and so do you. It's one of the joys of living out here."

"She said she was waiting for something. It was weird."

"Waiting for what?"

"I don't know. I'm not sure she knew herself. But she said a big storm was coming and told me to be careful."

"That makes sense," Rebecca said. "Did she say anything else?"

"No." There was a long pause, then: "Maybe we ought to give it up."

Rebecca put down her sewing and stared at Glen. "Now you are sounding like I did yesterday. But you'll get over it, just like I did." Then she chuckled softly. "You know what? While you were busily getting yourself into a funk today, I was getting out of mine. I decided I really love this place. I love living near the water and the forest, I love the peace and quiet, and I love what's happening to my children, especially Robby. So you might as well get yourself into a better frame of mind, my love, because I've decided that no

101

matter what happens, I'm going to see things through right here. And so are you."

Glen Palmer looked at his wife with loving eyes and thanked God for her strength. As long as I have her, he thought, I'll be fine. As long as I have her.

And then a premonition struck him, and he knew that he wouldn't always have Rebecca, wouldn't have her nearly long enough. He rose from his chair, crossed the small room, and knelt by his wife. He put his arms around her and held her tightly and tried to keep from crying. Rebecca, unaware of the emotions that were surging through her husband, continued sewing.

Harney Whalen stretched, snapped the television set on, then wandered over to the window before he sat down to watch the nine o'clock movie. His house, the house he had been born in and had grown up in and would undoubtedly die in, sat on a knoll that commanded a beautiful view of Clark's Harbor and the ocean beyond. He watched the lights of the town as they twinkled on around the bay, then looked up at the starless night sky. A layer of clouds had closed in and the feel of the air told him that another storm was brewing. Harney hated the storms and sometimes wondered why he stayed on the peninsula. But it was home, and even though he'd never appreciated the weather, he'd learned to live with it. Still, he began his usual round of the house, checking that all the windows were tightly closed against whatever might be coming in from the sea.

His grandfather had built the house, and he'd built it well. It had stood against the Northeasters for more than a century, and its joints were as snug as ever, its foundation maintaining a perfect level. Only the roof ever demanded Harney's attention, and that only rarely. He wandered from room to room, not really seeing the furnishings that filled them but feeling their comforting presence, and wondering idly what it would be like to be one of those people who spent their lives like gypsies, wandering from one residence to another, never really putting down roots anywhere. Well, it wasn't for him. He liked knowing that his past was always around him. Even though he lived by himself in the house now, he wasn't really alone—his family was all around him and he never felt lonesome here.

He made a sandwich, then opened a can of beer to wash it down with. By the time he returned to the living room, the movie had begun, and he sat down to munch his sandwich contentedly and enjoy the film.

Sometime during a barrage of commercials he felt the uneasiness begin, and he glanced around the room as if half-expecting someone to be there. He noticed then that the wind had come up and left his chair to go again to the window. It had begun raining and the water on the glass made the lights of Clark's Harbor appear streaked and blurred. Harney Whalen shook his head and returned to his chair in front of the television set.

He tried to concentrate on the movie, but more and more he found himself listening to the wind as it grasped at the house. Each time he realized he didn't know what was happening on the television screen, he snapped himself alert and forced his attention back to it.

The storm grew.

Just before the end of the movie Harney Whalen felt a nerve in his cheek begin to twitch and wondered if he was going to have one of what he called his "spells." A moment later, as he was about to put the last bite of his sandwich into his mouth, his face suddenly contorted into an ugly grimace and his hands began twitching spasmodically. The scrap of sandwich fell to the floor beside his chair, and Harney Whalen stood up.

Robby and Missy lay awake in their bunks, listening to the rain splash against the window.

"You want to go look for him, don't you?" Missy suddenly whispered in the darkness, a note almost of reproach coloring her voice.

"Who?" Robby asked.

"Snooker."

"He's out there, isn't he?"

"Could we find him?"

"Sure," Robby said with an assurance he didn't feel.

"But what about the ghosts?"

"There isn't any such thing." Robby climbed down from the top bunk and sat on his sister's bed. "You didn't believe that old man, did you?"

Missy squirmed and avoided looking at her brother. "Why would he lie?"

"Grown-ups lie to children all the time, to make us do what they want us to."

Missy looked fearfully at her brother. She wished he wouldn't say things like that. "Let's go to sleep."

Robby ignored her and started dressing. Missy watched him for a moment, then she, too, began pulling her clothes on, all the time wishing she were still in bed. But when Robby opened the window and crept out, Missy followed him.

As soon as they were on the beach Missy thought she saw something, but it was too dark to be sure. It was a shape, large and dark against the heaving ocean, that seemed to be moving near the surf line, dancing almost, but without a pattern. She clutched Robby's hand.

"Look," she whispered.

Robby peered into the darkness. "What is it? I don't see anything."

"Over there," Missy hissed. "Right near the water." She pushed up against Robby, squeezing his hand so hard it hurt.

"Let go," Robby commanded, but the pressure remained.

"Let's go into the woods," Missy begged. "It'll be safer there."

Robby hesitated, then decided to go along with his sister; if Snooker was anywhere around, he was likely to be in the woods. They were creeping over the barrier of driftwood when Missy suddenly yanked on Robby's arm.

"Something's happening," she whispered. "Let's hide!"

Robby stiffened, then made himself look around, but there was nothing. Only the blackness of the night and the noise of the wind and surf, building on each other into a steady roar. Still, when Missy tugged on his arm again, he let himself be pulled down into the shelter of a log.

* * *

A few yards away Miriam Shelling stirred slightly, a strange sensation forcing itself into her consciousness. Her fingers were tingling and her hair seemed to stand on end, as if charged with static electricity. She stared blankly into the night, her confused mind trying to match the eerie feeling with the terrifying images she saw on the beach. Strangers, strangers with odd, dead-looking eyes, their faces frozen in silent agony, their arms raised, their hands reaching, clutching at something Miriam couldn't see.

She rose and began walking across the beach, drawn to the eerie tableau by a force beyond her control.

Missy peered fearfully over the top of the log, her eyes wide and unblinking.

There were several shapes on the beach now, but they were all indistinct—all except one, which moved outward toward the ocean slowly, steadily. Missy wanted to call out into the darkness, to disturb the strange scene that seemed to be unfolding silently in the maelstrom of noise that filled the night. But she couldn't find her voice, couldn't bring herself to cry out. Instead, transfixed, she watched as the strange forms, the forms that seemed to glow against the dark backdrop of sea and sky, circled slowly around the other shape, the distinct shape, the shape she knew was human.

They closed on the human figure, circling ever more tightly, until Missy could no longer tell one from another. When the single figure finally disappeared, Missy came to life, fear overwhelming her. She reached out to clutch Robby's hand.

Robby was gone.

Panicked, Missy forced herself to look back out at the beach once more.

The beach was empty.

Where only a moment before the night had been filled with activity, with frightening shapes moving about in the dimness, now there were only blackness and scudding clouds.

Terrified, Missy ran for home.

When she got there Robby was in his bunk, sleeping peacefully.

On Sod Beach, the rising tide washed the sand from the corpse of the dog, and moments later a wave, whipped abnormally large by the wind, swept Snooker's remains out to sea.

By then the children were both in bed, though Missy was not asleep, and Miriam Shelling had disappeared from the beach.

7

Merle Glind glanced nervously at Brad and Elaine Randall as they came down the stairs the next morning and busied himself with the previous day's receipts. It was the fifth time he had checked them through. As soon as they passed his desk, his eyes left the ledgers and followed the Randalls out the front door.

"Did you get the feeling Mr. Glind wasn't too pleased to see us?" Elaine asked Brad as they descended from the porch.

"Maybe he had a bad night," Brad suggested.

"I don't think he approves of us," Elaine said, squeezing Brad's arm. "And I suspect he won't be the only one. I mean, after all, planning to spend a whole year just writing a book? It *is* scandalous." She sighed dramatically, sucked in the fresh morning air, and looked around. "Shall we go to the café? I'm hungry."

"I vote for the police station," Brad replied. "If there really is a house for rent we might as well get started— from what Glind had to say yesterday it might take all day just to talk what's his name into renting it to us."

"His name is Whalen, darling, and if I were you I'd

remember it. He looks like a real red-neck to me, a small town dictator, and you won't win any points with him by not being able to remember his name."

They walked along the waterfront, then turned up the hill on Harbor Road. A few minutes later they had found the tiny police station.

"You'd be the Randalls?" the police chief said without standing up. Brad and Elaine exchanged a quick glance, then advanced into the room. Harney Whalen looked as if he'd been expecting them.

"Brad Randall, and this is my wife, Elaine." Brad was careful not to preface his name with his title. But it was soon apparent that there were few secrets in Clark's Harbor.

"Dr. Randall, isn't it?" Harney said mildly. "They tell me you're a psychiatrist." He neither invited the Randalls to sit down nor told them who "they" might be.

Brad immediately decided there was more to Whalen than a mere "small town dictator." He clearly knew something about manipulating people and putting himself in a position of strength. Well, two could play that game. "You don't mind if we sit down, do you?" he asked mildly, seating himself before Whalen had a chance to reply. Elaine, taking his cue, took a chair close to Brad.

Whalen surveyed them for a minute, feeling somehow slighted. He wasn't sure exactly what had happened, but he suspected he had lost the upper hand. The feeling annoyed him. "What can I do for you folks this morning?" he asked, though he knew perfectly well why they were there.

"They told us you have a house for rent," Brad said.

He took a certain malicious pleasure in using the same vague "they" that the police chief had used on him, but Elaine shot him a look that told him to stop being cute and get on with it.

"That depends," Whalen said. "I might, and I might not. I think maybe I'd like to talk to you a little bit first."

"That's why we're here," Brad said with a smile. "We like the town."

"Can't say I blame you," Whalen replied. "I like Clark's Harbor myself. I was born here. So were my parents. My grandparents helped found the Harbor, back when it was a lumbering town. Still a little lumbering going on, but the big company closed years ago. Now it's mostly fishing. You fish?" Brad shook his head. "Too bad," the chief went on. "If you don't fish there isn't much else to do. You live in Seattle?" he suddenly asked, shifting the subject abruptly.

"Seward Park," Elaine answered. When the chief looked blank, she explained. "It's on the lake, at the south end."

"Sounds nice," Whalen commented neutrally. Then, eyes narrowed: "Why do you want to leave?"

"We don't, not permanently. I've been kicking around an idea for a book for quite a while, though, and in Seattle I just never seem to get to it. You know how it is—if it's not one thing it's another. I finally decided that if I'm ever going to get the damned thing written, I'd have to get out of town for awhile."

"Why Clark's Harbor?" the chief probed. "Seems to me there's a lot of better places for you than this. Pacific Beach or Moclips, or up to Port Townsend maybe."

Elaine smiled at the chief cordially, but she was growing annoyed by all his questions. If he has a house to rent why doesn't he just say so, she thought. Why the cross-examination? It's as though he doesn't want us here, the same as Mr. Glind. Being unwanted was a new experience for Elaine. Suddenly she was determined—almost as determined as Brad—to settle in Clark's Harbor and *make* these people accept her. Carefully keeping her annoyance concealed, she spoke warmly.

"But those are exactly the sorts of places we *don't* want to be," she said. "What we need is someplace quiet where Brad can concentrate. I don't know about Pacific Beach, but Port Townsend has entirely too many people who spend all their time having parties and talking about the books they're *going* to write. Brad wants to avoid all that and get the book written."

"Well, you people seem to know what you want," Harney said when she was finished. He smiled thinly. "Ever been on the peninsula during the winter?"

The Randalls shook their heads.

"It's cold," Whalen said simply. "Not a nice kind of cold like you get inland. It's a damp cold and it cuts right through you. And it rains all the time—practically every day. Not much to do during the winter, either— you can walk on the beach, but not for very long. Too cold. There's no golf course and no movies and only one television channel. And I might as well tell you, we Harborites aren't very friendly. Always been that way, likely always will be. We stick close together— most of us are related one way or another—and we don't take kindly to strangers. As far as we're concerned, if you weren't born here you're a stranger."

111

"Are you telling us not to come to Clark's Harbor?" Elaine asked.

"Nope. Only telling you what the town's like. You can make your own decision about whether you want to come. But I don't want you coming to me six months down the road and saying I didn't tell you this or I should have told you that. I believe in playing fair, and I believe people should know what they're getting into."

"Then you do have a house for rent?" Brad asked.

"If you can call it a house," Harney said, shrugging his shoulders.

"Tell us about it."

"It's out on Sod Beach. Been empty for quite a while." He smiled tightly at Elaine. "Ever cooked on a wood stove?"

She hadn't, but wasn't about to admit it to Whalen. "I can manage," she said softly, and prayed that Brad wouldn't laugh out loud. He didn't.

"You'll have to," Whalen said flatly. "The place has no gas or electricity."

"Running water?" Brad inquired.

"That it has, but only cold. Hot water you'd have to boil on the stove. As for heat, there's a big fireplace in the living room and a smaller one in the master bedroom. Nothing in the upstairs, but it doesn't get too bad since the stairs act like a chimney."

"You don't make it sound very inviting," Elaine admitted. In her mind's eye she pictured the old house she'd seen on the beach the day before, almost sure that was the one the police chief was describing. "How long has it been since anybody's lived there?"

"Nearly a year," Whalen replied. "As a matter of fact, most of their stuff's still there."

"Still there?" Brad repeated. "What do you mean?"

"They skipped out," Whalen said. "They got behind on the rent and one day I went out to tell them to pay up or go elsewhere, but they'd already gone. Took their clothes and their car but left everything else and never came back. So there's some furniture there. If you want the place I suppose you could use it. Don't think you'll want it though."

"Really?" Elaine said, trying to keep the sarcasm out of her voice but not entirely succeeding. "Why? Is it haunted?"

"Some people think so. It's the beach, I imagine."

"What about the beach?"

"It didn't used to be called Sod Beach. That just sort of came into being by accident. Used to be called the Sands of Death years ago. Then the maps shortened it to S.O.D., and that eventually got turned into Sod Beach."

"The Sands of Death," Brad said softly. "I'll bet there's a story about that."

Whalen nodded. "It was the old Klickashaw name for the beach. Can't remember what the Indian words were, if I ever knew. It don't matter anyhow. What matters is why they called the beach the Sands of Death. The Klickashaws had a wonderful custom— makes a hell of a good story for scaring kids with. It seems they had a cult—they called themselves Storm Dancers—that used to use the beach for executions."

"Executions?" Elaine echoed the word hollowly, not sure she really wanted to hear the tale.

113

"The story goes that the Klickashaws didn't like strangers any more than we do now. But they dealt with them a little bit different than we do. We at least tolerate 'em if we don't exactly make 'em welcome. The Indians didn't."

"You mean they took them out on the beach and killed them?" Brad asked.

"Not exactly. They took them out to the beach and let the sea kill them."

"I'm not sure I understand," Elaine said softly.

"They buried them in the sand," Harney Whalen said. His voice had become almost toneless, as though he was repeating the tale by rote. "They'd wait till low tide, then put their victims in a pit, and cover them with sand until only their heads were left showing. Then they'd wait for the tide to come in."

"My God," Elaine breathed. She could picture it in her mind—the terrified victims waiting for death, watching the surf's relentless advance, feeling the salt water lap at them, then slowly begin to wash over them; she could almost hear them gasping for air during the increasingly short intervals between the waves, and finally, inexorably . . . She forced the horrifying image from her mind and shuddered. "It's horrible," she said.

But Brad didn't appear to hear her. His eyes were fixed on the iron-haired police chief. "I don't see what that has to do with people not staying in your house on the beach," he said.

Whalen's smile was grim. "The legend has it, those people are still buried in the sand out there and that their ghosts sometimes wander the beach at night. To warn strangers about the beach," he added, leaning back in his chair to stare at the ceiling for a while before he spoke again. "Don't know if there's any truth to it, but I do know nobody ever stays in that house for long."

"Which might have something to do with the lack of amenities, right?" Brad said.

"Might," Whalen agreed.

"When can we see the house?" Brad asked. There was little point in further discussion. They would look at the house; either it would be suitable or it wouldn't.

"If you really want to look at it I suppose we could go out there right now. Frankly, I don't think you'll like it."

"Why don't you let us decide that?" Elaine said, forcing her voice to be cheerful. "We might like it a lot more than you think."

Before Whalen could respond to this the telephone rang. He plucked the receiver up.

"Chief Whalen," he said. Then he listened for a moment. Both Brad and Elaine were sure that his face turned slightly pale. "Oh, Jesus," he said softly. "Where is she?" There was another silence, then Whalen spoke again. "Okay, I'll get out there as fast as I can." He dropped the phone back on the hook and stood up. "It'll have to wait," he said. "Something's come up."

"Something serious?" Brad asked.

Whalen frowned, started to say something, then seemed to change his mind. "Nothing that concerns you," he said, almost curtly. Brad and Elaine got to their feet.

"Maybe later this afternoon—?" Brad began.

But Whalen was already on his way out the door.

The Randalls followed him to his car. For a second
Brad thought he had forgotten them, but as he started
the motor Whalen suddenly stuck his head out the
window. "Tell you what," he said. "Meet me out at
the house, about three. Merle Glind at the inn can tell
you how to get there." He gunned the engine, flipped
the siren on, and took off with a resentful screech from
the tires. The Randalls stood alone on the sidewalk,
watching the car speed away.

"Well," Brad said when Whalen was out of sight.
"What do you think about that?"

"He burned me up," Elaine said, glancing over her
shoulder to make sure no one but Brad was close
enough to hear. "My God, Brad, he acted like the
whole town is some kind of private preserve. Like nobody has a right to live here unless his great-grand-
parents were born here."

"Kind of got your hackles up, did it?" Brad grinned.

"Damn right it did. I'll cook on that damned wood
stove of his for the rest of my life if I have to, just to
let him know he can't always have things the way he
wants them."

"You might hate the house," Brad cautioned her.

She smiled at him almost maliciously. "Do you want
me to describe it to you, or would you rather be surprised?"

"What are you talking about?"

"The house. I've seen it. I'm sure it's on the beach I
was on yesterday, where I found the dead dog."

"You're kidding."

"No, I'm not. I walked right by it. It has to be the
one. It was the only house on the beach and it looked
as though no one had lived in it for years."

"What's it like?"

"I think a realtor would describe it as 'a picturesque beach charmer, perfect for the handyman, needs work, easy terms.' "

"Doesn't sound too promising."

"Mr. Whalen certainly didn't lie to us, I'll say that much."

They walked back to the inn. They would have a leisurely lunch, then walk up the beach to meet Harney Whalen at the old house. But when they reached the hotel they found Merle Glind in a state of extreme excitement.

"Isn't it terrible?" he asked them. When they looked totally blank, he plunged on. "Of course you haven't heard. It wouldn't mean anything to you anyway, would it?"

"What wouldn't?" Brad asked. "What happened?"

It was as if a door had slammed shut. The moment Brad asked the question, Merle Glind went rigid. His eyes narrowed and his mouth closed in a tight, thin-lipped line. Finally, he spoke. "It's none of your business," he said. "You take my advice, you go back where you belong."

Then, unable to resist, he told them.

Rebecca Palmer finished cleaning up the mess from breakfast and took the pan of dirty water outside to empty it onto the tiny cedar tree she had planted near the pottery shed. She examined the fragile-looking plant carefully, pleased to see that the makeshift fence she had rigged up around it seemed to be working—the little cedar showed no new signs of having served as dessert for the neighborhood deer. She was about to go back into the cabin when she heard the first faint sounds of the siren. At first she wasn't sure what it was, but as it grew louder she frowned a little. A fire truck? An ambulance? It was louder now, headed in her direction—but there was nothing out here except their own cabin. Deciding it must be Harney Whalen after a speeding car that hadn't had the sense to slow down as it passed through the Clark's Harbor speed zone, she went on into the cabin. But when the siren stopped abruptly a few seconds later and she thought she heard sounds of shouting, she went back outside.

There *were* voices coming from the woods now. She thought she could hear someone calling out, "Over this way," but she wasn't sure.

Rebecca took off her apron, tossed it onto a chair just inside the door, and strode out onto the beach. When she thought she was close to the place where the shouting had been going on, she picked her way carefully over the driftwood barrier and headed into the woods. A minute later she wished she'd followed the road.

The ground was nearly covered with ferns and salal, and everywhere she stepped there seemed to be an ancient, crumbling log buried in the undergrowth. She stopped after a while and strained her ears, trying to pick up the sounds of the voices that had drifted so plainly over the beach. Finally she called out.

"Hello? Is anybody out here?"

"Over here," a voice came back. "Who's that?"

"Rebecca Palmer."

"Stay away," the voice called. "Go back to the house

and stay there. Someone will come over in a little while."

Rebecca paused, debating what she should do. It didn't take her long to make up her mind. She plunged onward toward the anonymous voice, annoyed at being told what to do on what she was almost sure was her own property.

After a few seconds she thought she could make out a flash of movement off to the left. Whatever was happening, it was definitely happening on the Palmers' land.

"Who's there?" she called.

"It's me, Mrs. Palmer," the voice came back, "Chief Whalen. Just go back home and I'll send someone down as soon as I can."

The hell I will, Rebecca thought. If something's going on, I have a right to know what it is. She'd be damned if Harney Whalen was going to tell her what to do. She pressed on through the tangle of undergrowth and suddenly broke through into a small clearing. Harney Whalen and Chip Connor and a man Rebecca didn't recognize stood in the clearing, looking upward. Automatically, Rebecca's eyes followed theirs. Suddenly she wished she had done what Whalen had told her to.

Rebecca began screaming.

"Oh, God," Whalen muttered under his breath. Then, aloud, he said, "Take care of her, will you Chip? Get her out of here." He pulled his eyes away from Rebecca, and looked once more up into the trees. . . .

8

Miriam Shelling's body hung limply ten feet above the ground. Her eyes bulged grotesquely from her blackened face, and her tongue hung loosely from her mouth. The rancid smell of human excrement drifted on the breeze—Miriam had evacuated her bowels at the moment her neck had snapped.

A small group of people stared uncomprehendingly up at her, their stupor unbroken by Rebecca Palmer's screams. At the order from the chief, Chip Connor separated himself from the group and went to Rebecca, leading her away by the same route as she had come.

"Oh, God," Rebecca repeated over and over again. "What happened to her? What happened to her? Last night—" she broke off suddenly, but Chip prompted her.

"What about last night?" he asked. They emerged from the forest and Chip helped her over the pile of driftwood, then gently guided her toward the cabin.

"Nothing," Rebecca said. For some reason she didn't want to tell the deputy that her husband had seen, even talked with, Miriam Shelling on the beach the evening before. She remained silent as they walked.

"Will you be all right?" Chip asked when they were inside the cabin.

"I'll be fine," Rebecca replied weakly. "Well, not fine exactly, but you go ahead and do what you have to do. I'll take care of myself."

Chip looked at Rebecca carefully, wondering if what she had seen could have put her into a state of shock; then, realizing that he probably wouldn't recognize shock if he saw it, he decided to go back to the clearing. When Doc Phelps arrived, Chip would have him come over and check on Mrs. Palmer. Patting her gently on the hand and assuring her that everything would be all right, Chip started back to the small clearing.

Rebecca watched him go, strangling back a sob. As soon as he disappeared from sight she wished she'd told him that she wasn't all right. She shivered a little, and put on a sweater even though the day was bright and warm, then built up the banked fire until it blazed hotly.

She said she was waiting for something, Glen had said last night. She was sitting on a piece of driftwood, and she was waiting for something. Suddenly Rebecca had a vision of Miriam Shelling sitting quietly, watching the beach, waiting for Death to come and take her to her husband. But why the beach, Rebecca wondered. Why out here?

In the clearing, Harney Whalen was wondering the same thing. He was remembering the previous day, too, when Miriam Shelling had appeared in his office demanding that he do something. She had been upset—

121

very upset. He searched his mind, trying to remember every detail of what she had said, trying to find something—anything—that should have warned him that she was about to do something drastic. But there was nothing. She had only been demanding that he find whoever had killed her husband. And then, a sudden hunch coming into his mind, he left the clearing and beat his way through the woods to the beach. He looked out across the expanse of sand, then glanced north and south, taking a quick bearing. His hunch was right—Miriam had chosen a spot almost directly onshore from the place Pete Shelling had gotten caught in his own nets. Wondering if it meant anything or was merely a coincidence, he retreated back to the clearing. Doctor Phelps was waiting for him.

"Why hasn't she been taken down?" the old doctor demanded. He stared accusingly at Whalen over the rims of his glasses.

"I wanted to wait for you," Whalen said, trying not to feel defensive. But the doctor, eighty-six years old and still going strong, had treated Harney Whalen when the police chief was a child and never let him forget that as far as he was concerned, Whalen was a child still.

"Well, it's pretty obvious she's dead, isn't it?" Phelps said sourly. "Am I supposed to climb up there myself to see what happened?"

Whalen was about to begin climbing the tree himself when Chip Connor reappeared.

"Chip? Think you can get her down?"

Chip forced himself to stare up into the tree once more, though his stomach rebelled every time his eyes fell on Miriam's face. He examined the branches carefully.

"No problem," he said out loud. Privately he wondered how he was going to be able to lower the body to the ground without—he broke off the thought without completing it and started up the tree. The climb was easy—the branches almost formed a ladder. A minute later he was level with the branch from which Miriam hung. Though it was invisible from below, a neat coil of rope lay in the fork of the tree. Carefully, Chip examined the knot from which Miriam was suspended, though a glance had told him how to get her down. All that held Miriam to the tree was a double slip knot, the kind children make in a string when they first discover how to knit it into a rope. He picked up the coil of rope and dropped it down. Then he made his way back to the ground.

"Give me a hand, will you, Harn?" he asked. He took hold of the rope that now dangled from the tree and yanked on it. He felt a double jerk as the knot gave way. Then, with the chief helping him, he gently lowered the corpse out of the tree.

Doctor Phelps examined her slowly, first cutting the rope away from Miriam Shelling's neck, then going over the body carefully, adjusting his glasses every few seconds as they slid down his nose. Finally he stood up, shrugged, and shook his head sadly.

"Why do they do it?" he muttered, almost under his breath.

"Suicide." Harney Whalen made the question a statement.

"Looks like it," Phelps agreed. "But damned strange if you ask me."

123

"Strange? What do you mean?"

"Not sure," the doctor said. "Seems like I remember something like this before. A fisherman dying and his wife hanging herself a few days later. It's these damned storms."

Whalen looked at the old doctor and Phelps smiled self-consciously. "Didn't know the weather affects people?" he said. Without waiting for a reply, he went on: "Well, it does. There's winds some places—down south, and in Switzerland and a couple of other places. They make people do funny things." He paused significantly. "And we've got these damned storms. Whip up out of nowhere, blow like hell, then they're gone. Vanished. They don't show up inland, they don't show up north or south. Just here. Makes you wonder, doesn't it?"

"No," Whalen said flatly. "It doesn't. What makes me wonder, is why she chose Glen Palmer's property to kill herself on. If she did."

"She did, Harn, she did," Phelps assured him. "Can't put this one on anybody. Not Palmer, not anybody."

"Maybe not," Whalen growled. "But I can try."

The old doctor stared at Whalen in puzzlement, then started toward his car. There was nothing further he could do. Behind him he heard Whalen begin giving orders for photographs to be taken and the body removed. But he was sure Whalen was not thinking about the orders he was giving. He was thinking about something else. Phelps wished he knew what it was.

They had barely spoken during lunch. As he finished his coffee and poured the last of a bottle of wine into his glass, Brad decided to face the issue.

"It's bothering you, isn't it?" he asked abruptly, sure that Elaine would know what he was talking about.

"Shouldn't it?" Elaine snapped. "We've been here two days and two people and a dog have died."

"You don't know how long the dog had been dead," Brad said.

"Then let's stick to the people."

"All right. How many people do you think die in Seattle every day? Or didn't you know that Seattle has the second highest suicide rate on the coast?"

"I know," Elaine said darkly, resenting her husband's logic.

"Then I should think you'd be wanting to pick up and move out. I'll bet the rate here is considerably lower than it is in Seattle. And frankly, I'm not terribly surprised by what happened."

Elaine looked sharply at Brad. "You aren't?"

"Think what it must have been like for her. Her husband was a fisherman—probably no insurance, and certainly no retirement fund with widow's benefits. He probably didn't even have any Social Security. Now, what is there for a woman in her position? Welfare? Small town people are very prideful about things like that."

"She could have sold the boat," Elaine said doggedly. "My God, Brad, women are widowed every day, but they don't kill themselves over it." She drained her wineglass, then set it down and sighed. "Oh, come on," she said tiredly. "Doesn't it all seem just a little strange to you?"

"Of course it does. But you have to be reasonable. It would have happened whether we'd been here or not.

125

Two days earlier or two days later, and we never would have known about it. You're acting as though it's some kind of—I don't know—omen or something. And that's nonsense."

"Is it?" Elaine said softly. "Is it, really? I wish I could believe that, but there's something about this place that gives me the willies." She stood up suddenly. "Let's get out of here. Maybe the sunshine will help."

Brad paid the check and they made their way out of the café and down the stairs. In the tavern the same elderly men were playing checkers, as they had been the day before yesterday. Neither of them looked up at the Randalls.

"Let's walk up the beach," Elaine said. "Maybe by the time we get to the house Whalen will be there. If he isn't, I suspect we can get in by ourselves—it didn't look capable of being locked."

They retraced the path Elaine had taken the previous morning, but to Elaine it all looked different now. The sun had warmed the afternoon air, and the crackle of the morning freshness had long since gone. As they made their way across the point that separated the harbor from the beaches, Brad inhaled the scent of salt water mixed with pine. "Not like Seattle," he commented.

"There's nothing wrong with the air in Seattle," Elaine said defensively.

"I didn't say there was," Brad grinned at her. "All I said was that this isn't like the air in Seattle, and it isn't. Is it?"

Elaine, sorry she'd snapped at him, took his hand. "No," she said, "it isn't, and I'm being a ninny again. I'll stop it, I promise." She felt Brad squeeze her hand

and returned the slight pressure. Then she saw a flash of movement and pointed. "Brad, look!" she cried. "What is it?"

A small creature, about the size of a weasel, sat perfectly still, one foot on a rock, staring at them, its tiny nose twitching with curiosity.

"It's an otter," Brad said.

"A sea otter? This far north?"

"I don't know. It's some type of otter though. Look, there's another!"

The Randalls sat down on a piece of driftwood, and the two small animals looked them over carefully. After what seemed to Elaine like an eternity, first one, then the other returned to its business of scraping at the pebbles on the beach, searching for food. As soon as the pair began its search, four smaller ones suddenly appeared as if they had received a message from their parents that all was well.

"Aren't they darling!" Elaine exclaimed. At the sudden sound the four pups disappeared and the parents once again turned their attention to the two humans. Then they, too, disappeared.

"Moral:" Brad said, "never talk in the presence of otters."

"But I couldn't help it," Elaine protested. "They're wonderful. Do you suppose they live here?"

"They probably have a Winnebago parked on the road and just stopped for lunch," Brad said dryly. Elaine swung at him playfully.

"Oh, stop it! Come on, let's see if we can find them."

Her vague feeling of unease—what she called the willies—was gone as she set off after the otters, picking her way carefully over the rocky beach. She knew it was no use, but she kept going, hoping for one more glimpse of the enchanting creatures before they disappeared into the forest. It was too late; the otters might as well have been plucked from the face of the earth. She stopped and waited for Brad.

"They're gone," she sighed.

"You'll see them again," Brad assured her. "If they're not on this beach they're probably on Sod Beach. It's the next one, isn't it?"

Elaine nodded and pointed. "Just beyond that point. If you want we can cut through the woods."

"Let's stick to the beach," Brad said. "That way I can get a view of the whole thing all at once."

"Sort of a general overview?" Elaine asked, but she was smiling.

"If you want to put it that way," Brad said with a grin.

They rounded the point and Brad stopped so suddenly Elaine almost bumped into him. "My God, it's beautiful, isn't it?" She came abreast of him and they stood together surveying the crescent that was Sod Beach. The sky was cloudless and the deep blue water and the intensely green forest were separated by a strip of sand that glistened in the brilliant sunlight, highlighted by the silvery stripe of driftwood sparkling next to the woods. The breakers, eight ranks of them, washed gently in, as if caressing the beach. Brad slipped his arm around Elaine's shoulders and pulled her close to him. With his free arm, he pointed.

"And that, I take it, is the house?"

Elaine's head moved almost imperceptibly in assent. For one brief moment she wished she could deny it, and instead say something that would take them forever away from Clark's Harbor and this beautiful beach with its bizarre past. For an instant she thought she could see the victims of the Sands of Death buried to the neck, their pitiful wailings lost in the sea wind and the roar of the surf that would soon claim them as its own. Then the vision was gone. Only the weathered house remained on the beach and, far off at the opposite end, the tiny cabin.

"Well, we won't have many neighbors, will we?" Brad said finally, and Elaine had a sinking sensation in her stomach. Brad had already made up his mind. She pulled free of his encircling arm and started moving up the beach.

"Come on," she said. "We might as well see what it's like." Brad trotted silently after her, ignoring the negative tone in her voice.

They had walked once around the house when Harney Whalen arrived, appearing suddenly out of the woods.

"Didn't think you folks were here yet," he called to them. "There wasn't any car out on the road."

"We walked along the beach," Brad replied, extending his hand to the approaching police chief. Whalen ignored the gesture, instead mounting the steps to the porch and fishing in his pocket for keys.

"It's not in very good shape. I haven't even had it cleaned since the last people . . . left."

Brad and Elaine exchanged a look at his slight hesitation, but neither one of them commented on it.

"The place seems to be sound enough," Brad remarked as Harney opened the front door.

"All the old houses are sound," Whalen responded. "We knew how to build them back then."

"How old is it?"

"Must be about fifty or sixty. If you want I suppose I could figure it out exactly. Don't see any point in it, though." His tone said clearly to Brad, Don't bother me with foolish questions.

But Elaine plunged in. "Did your family build it?" she asked. Whalen looked at her sharply, then his face cleared.

"Might say we did; might say we didn't. We sold the land the house is on and my grandfather helped build the house, then we bought it back when the Barons . . . left." Again there was the slight hesitation, and again the Randalls exchanged a look. Brad wondered how much more there was to the story and why the chief didn't want to tell them all of it. Then he looked around and realized that Whalen hadn't been kidding when he said the place hadn't been cleaned.

If it hadn't been for the layer of dust covering everything, Brad would have sworn the house was inhabited. Magazines and newspapers lay open on the chairs and floor, and the remains of a candle, burned to the bottom, sat bleakly on a table. There wasn't much furniture—only a sofa and two chairs—and what there was had obviously been obtained secondhand.

"They left in a hurry, didn't they?" Brad asked.

"Like I told you, skipped right out on me," Whalen said. Then, before Brad could comment further, he began telling them about the house.

"That's a double fireplace over there. The other side opens in the kitchen, and between the two of them the downstairs stays pretty warm. There's a bedroom through that door that I suppose you'd want to use, unless you've got kids. If you do, I'd put them in there, just in case of fire. It's a lot easier to get out of the first floor than the second."

"We don't have children," Elaine said, and stuck her head in the bedroom. It was a large room, facing the beach, and one wall was partly brick. She heard Whalen behind her explaining.

"The brick's part of the fireplace. The whole house is built around the fireplaces. You'd be surprised how much heat comes through those bricks, especially if you keep fires going in both rooms. Don't know why they don't build houses like that anymore—with all the talk about energy, you'd think they'd want to. But no, they build them with the fireplaces on an outside wall, and you can kiss the heat good-bye.

"If you go through there," he went on, "there's the bathroom—that opens into the kitchen as well. It's not so convenient for guests, but for whoever's living here it works just fine."

Elaine followed his directions and found herself in a small and incredibly grimy bathroom. She went through it and into the kitchen, where she stared at the forbiddingly large and ungainly wood stove. It seemed to challenge her, and she glared at it, silently telling the stove that come what may, she would learn to make it behave. But she wasn't too sure.

The kitchen was as filthy as the bathroom. The pots and pans used for the preparation of what had apparently been the last tenants' final meal were still stacked unwashed in the sink. Elaine swallowed hard, wondering if she would be expected to clean up the mess in the event they rented the place, and pushed on into the dining room.

The table was set, and at each place there was the remains of a half-eaten meal. The food had long since decayed, but from the looks of things it was an abandoned dinner. In the center of the table an ancient glass kerosene lamp stood, and Elaine could see that it was empty: whoever had lived here must have gotten up in the middle of dinner and left without even putting the lamp out. The lamp—God knew how much later—had simply burned itself out.

She was about to ask Whalen what had happened— why his tenants had "skipped out" in the middle of dinner—when she became aware that Brad was already talking to the police chief.

"How much would you want if you were to sell the place?" he was asking. Elaine felt her stomach sink again, and was relieved to hear Whalen's reply.

"It's not for sale," he said in a tone that left no room for argument. "It was a mistake when my grandfather sold the land in the first place. I won't repeat that mistake."

"You're going to pass it on to your children?"

"I never married," Harney replied. "Got lots of family, though. Most of the town is related to me one way or another. I wouldn't be surprised if my deputy wound up with this place—he's some kind of nephew."

"Well, let's talk about a lease, then," Brad said.

"Why don't we look at the upstairs?" Elaine interrupted.

Whalen shrugged and pointed the way toward the staircase that separated the living room from the dining room. He stayed downstairs as Brad followed Elaine to the second floor.

As soon as they were alone Elaine turned to her

husband. "My God, Brad, it's a mess," she began.

Brad laughed. "Of course it's a mess, and I'll bet we can get it cheap. But picture it cleaned up. It's sound as a dollar and the location is perfect. Peace, quiet, and an unbeatable view. All it needs is a coat of paint on the inside and it'll be wonderful."

"But there's no electricity," Elaine protested.

"Well, you've always said you longed for the simple life," Brad teased.

Elaine wasn't amused. "Not this simple," she said, frowning. Then, at the look of deep disappointment on her husband's face, she relented. "Brad, it'll be so much work, you won't get anything done on your book for weeks!"

"I can think while I paint," Brad said. "It won't be like Seattle, where I have to keep my mind on my work every minute. And chopping wood is good exercise. I could stand to lose a few pounds." He patted his flat firm stomach with the confidence of a man who hadn't gained an ounce in ten years.

"If I have to cook on that stove, you'll lose more than a few pounds."

"You can learn," Brad said, and there was a pleading tone to his voice that Elaine had rarely heard in the twelve years of their marriage.

"You really want it, don't you?" she asked quietly, looking deep into his eyes.

He nodded. "I love it," he said. "I don't know exactly why, but I have a feeling about it. It's as though the whole place is calling out to me. Elaine, if I'm going to be able to write that book at all, I'm going to do it here."

She gave in, as she always did. If Brad wanted it

that badly, she would learn to live with it. "All right," she said, smiling with a confidence she didn't feel. "We might as well have a look around up here and see how bad it is."

"You mean it?" Brad asked eagerly. And seeing the look on his face, Elaine realized that she did mean it. Her smile turned genuine.

"Come on, Randall, let's see how much work it's going to take to make this place livable."

Harney Whalen was not waiting for them downstairs.

They found him on the beach in front of the house, his eyes fixed on the horizon. When they followed his gaze Brad and Elaine saw nothing but the sea and the sky, meeting darkly in a low bank of fog that seemed to be hanging barely within their vision.

"Mr. Whalen?" Brad said softly. There was no response from the police chief. "Mr. Whalen?" Brad repeated, louder this time. Whalen swung slowly around to look at them, his hands clenched into fists, the knuckles white with apparent strain.

"Are you all right?" Elaine asked. Whalen nodded curtly.

"We want the house," Brad said.

"No, you don't. And it doesn't matter anyhow, 'cause I won't sell it."

There was an intensity in his voice that Elaine found disturbing. But Brad ignored it. "We want to lease it," he said.

Whalen seemed to turn the matter over in his mind, then slowly unclenched his fist and put a hand inside his jacket.

"This is the lease. Take it or leave it."

Brad glanced at the lease, noting the rent—two hundred dollars a month—and ignoring most of the body of the agreement. It was a standard form, already filled out. Elaine handed him a pen and he quickly signed both copies, returning one to Whalen, keeping the other. Whalen took the signed lease disinterestedly, replaced it in his inner pocket, then suddenly pointed north. "See that cabin up there? Almost hidden in the trees? Those are your nearest neighbors. The Palmers." He stared at the distant cabin for a long time, then turned back to the Randalls. "The Palmers are strangers here too," he said darkly. Then he stalked off toward the woods.

Brad and Elaine watched him go, then started back south toward the Harbor and the inn.

"You know something?" Brad said after a long silence. "I'm not sure he even knows we leased the place. It was like he was in some kind of a trance."

Elaine nodded thoughtfully. "That was the impression I got too. Well, it's too late now. He signed it. The place is ours."

She turned back for a final look at the old house. For an instant she thought she saw something at the window—a face, but not really a face. More like a shadow.

She decided she was imagining things.

9

The dining room of the Harbor Inn was quiet that evening; Brad and Elaine Randall dined in isolation. The same small card sat on their table that had been there the previous evening, but there seemed to be no reason for its presence—only one other table was filled. The rest, set and waiting, remained deserted. A few people sat at the bar, but their conversation was minimal, and what there was, was whispered in low tones impossible to overhear.

"If you stretch your ear any further, you'll fall off your chair," Elaine finally said. Neither of them had spoken for minutes. It was as though the Randalls had almost unconsciously matched the silence that shrouded the room. Now her words seemed to bounce off the walls, and Elaine glanced around to see if anyone had overheard her. Apparently no one had—the other table of diners appeared to be engrossed in their steamed crab, the drinkers continued to stare morosely into their glasses.

"I can't figure it out," Brad said as he surveyed the quiet room. "I'd have expected the place to be full tonight, alive with people gossiping about—what was her name?"

"Miriam Shelling," Elaine supplied.

"Mrs. Shelling, yes. But from what little I've been able to hear, no one seems the least bit interested in her or what happened to her."

Just then Merle Glind bustled up to them, recommending the blueberry pie for dessert. Brad declined, but while Elaine struggled with herself, torn between her weight and her desires, he decided to pump the little hotel proprietor.

"Kind of quiet in here tonight, isn't it?"

Glind's head moved spasmodically and he took a quick inventory of the room, his expression testifying to a sudden fear that something must have gone wrong. When nothing looked amiss he turned back to Brad.

"About the same as usual," he said nervously. "About the same as usual."

"I'd have thought you'd have a good crowd tonight, all things considered," Brad ventured carefully.

"All things considered?" the little man repeated. "All what things?"

"Well, it just seems to me that people would be wanting to talk tonight."

"What about?" Glind asked blankly.

"Mrs. Shelling?" Brad suggested. "I mean, isn't it a little unusual to have a woman commit suicide here?"

"Why, I don't know," Glind said vaguely, appearing to turn the matter over in his mind. "But now that you mention it, I suppose it is." There was a long pause, then Glind spoke again. "Not that it's any of our concern, of course."

Elaine frowned slightly and gazed at the strange man. "I should think it would be everyone's concern," she said softly. "I always thought that in towns like this everyone looked after everyone else."

"We do," Glind replied. "But the Shellings weren't really part of the town."

"I thought they lived here." Brad's voice was flat, as if he were merely prompting a statement he knew was inevitable.

"Oh, they lived here, but they were newcomers. They didn't really belong."

"Newcomers? How long had they lived here?"

Glind shrugged as if it was of no consequence. "Fifteen, twenty years. Not long." The Randalls gazed at each other across the table, silently exchanging a thought. *How long does it take? How long, before you're a part of Clark's Harbor?* Their unspoken exchange was broken by Merle Glind's forced cheer.

"What about that pie? I guarantee it myself!"

Elaine jumped a little, as if she had been lost somewhere, and without thinking she accepted Glind's offer. He scurried away. When they were alone Brad and Elaine smiled weakly at each other.

"Fifteen or twenty years," Elaine said wryly. "Somehow I'd been thinking in terms of a couple of lonely months and then the Welcome Wagon suddenly appearing."

"Look at it this way: what would you have in common with most of these people anyway? We've always been pretty self-sufficient—"

"Pretty self-sufficient is one thing," Elaine interrupted. "Being pariahs is absolutely another."

"I wouldn't worry too much about it," Brad reassured her as the pie arrived. "Somewhere in Clark's Harbor there's got to be someone who'll welcome us. It's just a matter of finding them."

Elaine bit into the pie and was pleased to find that it met her expectations. Then a thought hit her. "The Palmers!" she exclaimed.

Brad understood at once. "Of course," he said, smiling. Then he dropped his voice a little in a surprisingly good imitation of Harney Whalen's morbid bass tones. "They're strangers here, you know!"

Elaine laughed and eagerly finished her pie.

"It doesn't concern us!" Glen Palmer said for the fourth time. He tried to smile, but the hollow, sunken look in his wife's eyes frightened him.

"How can you say that?" Rebecca shot back. "She was found on our land, Glen." When he didn't respond she pressed harder. "That clearing *is* on our property, isn't it?"

"Yes, I suppose it is," Glen admitted reluctantly. "But it still doesn't concern us."

"What about the children? Suppose they'd been the ones to find her, Glen. Just suppose that on their way to school Robby and Missy had decided to cut through the woods and found her?"

She could see that her point was being lost on her husband and she searched desperately for a way to make him understand.

"You can't imagine what it was like," she went on limply. "You just can't imagine it." She was about to describe the grisly scene for him once more when she heard the children coming in.

"What *what* was like?" Robby demanded. Rebecca

139

stretched her arms out to her son but Robby backed away and moved to his father's side. His child's mind knew something was wrong between his parents, and he was instinctively drawn to his father. "You mean Mrs. Shelling?" he guessed.

"How did you know about her?" Rebecca gasped.

Robby's face broke into a grin. "Jimmy Phipps went home for lunch and his mother told him all about it. Did you really see her?"

For a split second Rebecca considered denying it. But she and Glen had always been truthful with their children. Now, though it might cause her pain—indeed, it was sure to—she felt she had to discuss what had happened with Robby. "Yes," she said slowly, "I did."

Robby's eyes widened. "Did she really crap her pants?" he demanded. Rebecca winced, but Glen had to suppress a grin.

"It's something that happens to people when they die, dear," Rebecca said gently.

"What did she look like? Jimmy Phipps said her face was all blue and her tongue was hanging out."

Rebecca, remembering, had to fight to control a contracting stomach. "It doesn't matter what she looked like, Robby," she said almost desperately.

Robby's mind worked at the problem, trying to decipher why the appearance of the body didn't matter. It had certainly mattered to Jimmy Phipps. He turned to his father, as if the problem was one only a man could solve.

"What happened to her?" he asked gravely.

"She was very unhappy, Robby, and she just decided

she didn't want to live anymore. Can you understand that?"

Robby nodded gravely. "I feel like that sometimes, but then the storms come and I feel better."

"Oh, Robby," Rebecca cried. She knelt by her son and drew him closer to her. "You mustn't ever feel that way. Not ever! Why, what would we do without you?"

A small frown knit Robby's brow and he disentangled himself from his mother. "It hardly ever happens," he said impatiently. "And anyway, it isn't such a bad feeling. In a way it's kind of exciting." Then, before his parents could pursue the subject any further, he posed another question. "Did Mrs. Shelling do a bad thing? I mean, if she didn't want to live anymore, why should she have to?"

Rebecca and Glen exchanged a glance, and Glen knew it was going to be left up to him to answer his son's question.

"It just isn't the best thing to do," he said carefully. "If you have a problem, it's much better to try to find a way to solve it. Dying doesn't do any good at all, for anyone."

The answer seemed to satisfy the boy. He shrugged, then gazed up at his father. "Can I go look for Snooker?"

"No!" Rebecca snapped without thinking. Suddenly the idea of her son out on the beach, the beach on which Miriam Shelling had spent her last hours, terrified her. "It's too late," she said hurriedly, trying to take the sting out of her words as Robby recoiled. "You should both be in bed."

"I'll go out in a little while and have a look," Glen

141

promised his son. But for the first time since they had come in Missy spoke.

"You won't find him," she said. "He's gone and we aren't ever going to see him again."

"You keep saying that," Robby said. "But you don't know."

"I do too know," Missy shot back, her voice rising.

Rebecca almost intervened, but suddenly a quarrel between her children seemed a welcome respite from the strain she had been feeling all day. "Why don't you two take your fight into the bedroom?" she suggested.

The children stared at their mother, shocked into silence by her failure to try to mediate between them. A moment later, warming to their argument, they tumbled off to the tiny bedroom.

As soon as they were gone Rebecca turned to Glen. "And I don't want you going out there either," she said.

"I don't see that there's much choice now," Glen said with a shrug. "I already promised Robby and I can't really back out of it. Besides, we've been walking on the beach at night for months. You know as well as I do that it's perfectly safe."

"That was before last night," Rebecca said, shuddering. "It's all different now."

"It is not different, Rebecca," Glen said, placing his hands on her shoulders and forcing her to look at him. "Miriam Shelling's problems had nothing to do with us, and it has nothing to do with us that she killed herself out here." He laughed, but there was no mirth in the sound. "Well, at least now we know what she was waiting for." He began putting on his coat.

"Please?" Rebecca pleaded. "At least wait until I've calmed down." Glen tossed his coat aside, sat down on the couch next to his wife, and drew her near him. In the bedroom, the argument subsided. For a while, the tiny cabin was quiet.

"Let's go for a walk," Brad suggested as he and Elaine stepped out of the dining room. "It's gorgeous tonight—no storm and a full moon." He grinned suggestively. "And we haven't been romantic on a beach in years."

Elaine started to protest but changed her mind before an expression of doubt even clouded her face. She had been silly enough for a while; it was time to start acting like an adult. "Best idea you've come up with since we got here," she said with a wink. "I'll go up and get our coats."

A few minutes later they were on the beach, and as she watched the moonlight glisten on the water, Elaine was glad she'd put aside her trepidations. The steady rhythm of the surf, soft tonight in the stillness, soothed her. She took Brad's hand.

"Let's walk up to the house," she said. "I'll bet it's beautiful in the moonlight."

They walked slowly, enjoying the night-quiet. When they came to the rocky stretch just before Sod Beach, they moved with particular care, hoping for a glimpse of the otter family. But there was nothing except a sudden clattering sound from somewhere overhead. They looked up in time to see the silhouette of an owl as it left the branch of a tree, swooping low, then beating its way up to cruise over the beach.

"We won't see the otters tonight," Brad commented. "They'll have packed the pups off somewhere."

"He's so big," Elaine said as the owl disappeared. "His wingspan must be six feet."

"Gives him lots of glide. That way his prey doesn't have any warning before he dives."

They rounded the point and Sod Beach suddenly lay before them, its vibrant colors flattened by the darkness to dramatic shades of black and white. The sand seemed to gleam with a fluorescence of its own in the silvered light, and the bank of driftwood lining the length of the beach glowed whitely. In the midst of the pale expanse of sand, the old house stood, dark-shadowed, aloof from the eerie moonlight that bathed its surroundings.

"It's like a fantasy," Elaine whispered. "I've never seen anything so beautiful."

Brad said nothing but pulled his wife close to him. They stood for a long time, trying to comprehend the almost unearthly beauty of the place and listening to the soft music of the gentle surf. Finally they walked out onto the beach, leaving a double row of footprints neatly embedded in the otherwise unmarred smooth damp sand.

They circled the house, but widely, as if unwilling to come close enough to discover the flaws in the ancient structure. Neither of them suggested going in, certain that the tired remains of the last tenancy would pull them away from the magic of the night. Instead, after completing their survey of their new home, they continued walking up the beach until, by mutual but unspoken consent, they settled themselves on the sand, leaning against one of the massive driftwood stumps.

"I take it all back," Elaine said. "This place is paradise."

Brad reached in his coat pocket and pulled a pipe and some tobacco from its depths. He stuffed the pipe, lit it, put the tobacco back in his pocket, and stared out to sea.

"I've been thinking," he said. "I'm going to change the thrust of the book."

Elaine stirred against him, then settled in closer. "What made you think of that?"

"Lots of things. This place. Robby Palmer."

"Robby Palmer?" Elaine sat up, looking sharply at her husband. "That's a hell of a change, from bio-rhythms to Robby Palmer!"

"Not necessarily. There's something about this place, something that affects everybody here one way or another. Who knows? It might have something to do with bio-rhythms. And if I can find out, it would make a great book. Particularly if I can use Robby Palmer to tie it all together. Think of it: a place—this place— where something seems to screw people up. People like Miriam Shelling, and maybe Harney Whalen. But for Robby, who was already screwed up, whatever it is that's here straightens him out."

"How lucky for you that Robby just happens to live up the beach," Elaine said sarcastically.

Brad ignored the gibe. "It could be a very valuable book," he said. "In more ways than one."

"You mean a best seller?"

"Not *just* a best seller. Something worthwhile too. And if I could make a lot of money from a book . . ." His voice trailed off and he left the thought hanging.

"Well, I still don't like the idea, but do what you

want." Elaine's arms slipped around Brad and she hugged him tightly. "You always do."

"That doesn't make me sound very nice," Brad said softly.

Elaine smiled in the darkness, knowing Brad would feel the smile even if he didn't see it. "I didn't mean it that way. I just meant that in the end you usually do what you want to do. It's usually the right thing to do and I don't have any objections to it, but it's still true."

"You know what you are?"

"What?" Elaine asked.

"A hopelessly unliberated woman."

"You found me out," Elaine replied. "But don't tell anybody about it—it's not very fashionable."

"Fashionable enough for me," Brad whispered. His hand slid inside her coat and began caressing her breast. "Everything about you is fashionable enough for me." He nuzzled her, then whispered in her ear. "When was the last time we made love on a beach?"

"We never did," Elaine whispered back. "But there's a first time for everything." Her fingers began fumbling with his belt, and she felt the hardness in his trousers. She wriggled in the sand, and pulled him over on top of her. . . .

"I think we ought to go look for him again," Robby Palmer whispered to his sister.

"He isn't out there," Missy whispered back. "He's gone and we're never going to see him again." She turned over in the lower bunk and buried her head in the pillow.

"He isn't either," Robby insisted. "He's probably

caught in a trap in the woods or something." He slid down from the upper bunk and poked at Missy. "Are you asleep?"

"Stop that," Missy complained, wriggling down under the covers. "I'll call Mother."

"If you do I won't take you with me."

Missy sat up and peered at her brother. "I won't go out there again," she whispered. Robby shrugged. "It's too dark," Missy said, glancing at the curtained window.

"It is not," Robby countered. "The moon's out and it's shining on the water. Look."

Reluctantly, Missy left her bed and peeked out the window. A deep shadow hung just outside the cabin, but through the trees she could see the silvery light playing on the water.

"We should stay in bed," she decided.

"Well, you can stay in bed if you want," Robby said, pulling his jeans on. "I'm going out to find Snooker."

Missy crept back into bed and pulled the covers up under her chin. She watched with wide eyes as Robby finished dressing. Then he carefully opened the window and climbed out. As soon as he was gone Missy jumped out of bed and ran to the window. Her brother was nowhere in sight. She wished he hadn't gone out. Not after last night. She stayed at the window for a minute, then made up her mind.

Rebecca looked up from her knitting as her daughter appeared in the doorway of the tiny bedroom.

"Can't sleep, darling?" she asked.

"Robby's gone," Missy said. "He went out to look for Snooker. I told him not to, but he went anyway."

Rebecca felt a stab of fear in her heart and turned

147

to Glen. He was already on his feet, pulling his windbreaker on.

"When did he leave?"

"Just now," Missy said, her eyes bright as she watched her father dash to the front door. "He's all right, Daddy," she called, but Glen was gone. Rebecca put her knitting aside and gathered Missy into her arms.

"Of course he is," she said softly, "of course he is." But inside, she wasn't sure.

Robby dashed around the corner of the house and into the woods. As soon as he was gone his sister would tell on him. Girls were like that, he thought, wishing he had a brother instead of a sister. Then he forgot about Missy and concentrated on making his way through the woods. He followed the path that would lead him out to the main road but turned off to the right before he got to the highway. He knew this path would take him through the woods, but he wasn't sure where it would come out. And it all looked different at night, even with the moonlight. There were shadows everywhere—shadows that completely blotted out the path and made the trees seem bigger and more forbidding than they were in the daytime.

When he heard his father's voice calling him a few minutes later, he almost went back, then changed his mind. Missy would laugh at him. He hurried along the path, trying to see, but stumbling every few steps as his toe caught on roots that lay hidden in the darkness. Then he came to a clearing and stopped.

Something inside him told him that this was the spot where Mrs. Shelling had hanged herself. He stared around, searching the trees, trying to determine which branch she might have used. A sudden sound startled him, then an enormous shadow swept across the clearing. A bird, Robby told himself. It's just a bird. But he left the clearing and continued along the path. Behind him he thought he could hear his father's footsteps, following him. He walked faster. Then he began running.

Brad and Elaine Randall lay in each other's arms, enjoying the closeness they always felt after making love.

"That was nice," Elaine murmured. "Am I wicked for thinking sex is always better outdoors?"

"Not wicked," Brad replied. "Just sensuous."

Elaine poked him and he poked her back. They began tickling each other, rolling in the sand and giggling, until Elaine suddenly stopped and lay still.

"Did you hear something?"

"Just the surf."

"No, something else. A shout."

Brad listened for a moment but could hear nothing but the crashing of the surf. Suddenly a shadow fell over them and Brad looked up. A cloud had covered the face of the moon and the night grew darker.

"I don't hear anything," he began, but Elaine cut him off.

"Shh." She listened intently, then spoke again. "There's something there," she whispered. "I hear something in the woods." She pulled her coat tight around her and stood up.

"Don't be silly," Brad said. "It's nothing, just some animal." But his eyes went to the forest, peering into

149

its blackness. Then he heard it: the crackling of twigs. He got to his feet, pulling Elaine up next to him, an arm protectively around her shoulders. He heard a shout from far up the beach and the crackling sound again. Closer. It seemed to be in the woods directly in front of him.

"Who's there?" he called.

Silence.

"Who is it?" Brad called again. The sounds began again, louder now, and heading right toward them. He moved Elaine behind him, so that whoever—whatever—was coming out of the woods would face him first.

The cloud that had covered the moon drifted on, and the beach was once more bathed in an eerie glow. Looking at him from the other side of the pile of driftwood was a small and very worried face.

"It's all right," Brad said softly. "Come on over here."

Robby Palmer, his terror easing, began scrambling through the driftwood. Whoever these people were, he would be safer with them. He had not felt safe in the woods. Not safe at all.

10

Robby hesitated at the top of the mound of drift-wood, suddenly unsure of himself. For a second he was tempted to take off, not back into the woods, but up the beach toward the soft glow that emanated from the window of the cabin. When Elaine suddenly stepped out from behind Brad, Robby made up his mind.

"I'm looking for my dog," he said shyly.

"Isn't it a little late for that?" Brad asked. "Most nine-year-olds are home in bed."

Robby cocked his head inquisitively. "How did you know how old I am?"

"Now how could I forget something like that?" Brad said. Then his brow furrowed. "Don't you recognize me?"

Robby shook his head.

"I'm Dr. Randall, from Seattle. You really don't remember me?"

"Are you the doctor I went to when I was sick?"

"That's right."

"I don't really remember being sick either."

Before Brad could pursue the subject, Elaine went to Robby and knelt beside him.

JOHN SAUL

"Do your parents know where you are?"

"I think so," Robby replied. "I think I heard my father calling me a little while ago."

"Did you answer him?"

Robby shook his head. "It might not have been my father," he said. "It might have been somebody else."

"Who?" Brad asked.

"I—I'm not sure," Robby stammered.

"Well, I think we'd better get you home. I'll bet your parents are worried sick about you."

"But I have to find my dog," Robby protested. "He's been gone two nights now and Daddy won't go look for him." Robby looked to be on the verge of tears and Elaine put her arms around him. She was suddenly sure that the dog she had found on the beach had been his. "There, there," she soothed him. "Don't you worry about anything. He's probably wandered off somewhere, but he'll come home."

"Missy says he won't," Robby said flatly. "She wouldn't help me look for Snooker either, because she says he's gone."

Before either of the Randalls could determine the meaning of this odd statement, they heard a call from the forest.

"Robby? Robby!"

"Over here!" Brad shouted. "On the beach!"

A moment later Glen Palmer broke out of the forest at almost the same spot where Robby had appeared a few minutes earlier.

"Dr. Randall! What are you doing out here? You haven't seen Robby around—" He broke off as he saw his son and climbed swiftly over onto the beach. "Robby! I've been looking for you!"

152

"I was trying to find Snooker," Robby wailed. "You said you were going to look for him but you weren't, so I—" He ran to his father and buried his face against him. Glen held him for a moment, looking helplessly at the Randalls, then disentangled himself from his son. He knelt down and met the boy's tear-filled eyes.

"I was going to come out and look for him but your mother needed me," he explained. "We were talking, and as soon as we finished, I'd have come out looking."

Robby peered doubtfully at his father, wanting to believe him, and Glen shifted his own gaze to Brad Randall.

"You haven't seen a dog out here, have you?" he asked doubtfully. Elaine's eyes darted to the child, and she bit her lip.

"We've only been here a few minutes ourselves," she said, evading the question entirely. She'd tell Palmer the bad news when the boy was out of hearing. "We wanted to see what the place looked like at night."

Glen looked puzzled. "Sod Beach?"

"The house," Elaine explained. "We rented the old house today." She gestured in the direction of the dilapidated structure, but Glen's puzzlement only seemed to deepen.

"Whalen rented it to you?" he asked. He shook his head. "Well, I'll be damned."

"He didn't seem too eager but he gave in," Brad said with a chuckle. The chuckle faded as he remembered the police chief's odd behavior just before the lease was signed, but he didn't mention it to Glen.

"He wouldn't rent it to me at all," Glen said almost bitterly. Then he brightened. "Say, why don't you walk up the beach with me? Rebecca's waiting for me—all upset about Robby—and I'd better get back. Besides, you promised to stop by yesterday and then you didn't. Rebecca hasn't said anything but I think she's disappointed. Frankly, she doesn't have many people to talk to out here."

"Of course," Elaine said immediately. "We should have stopped today but we've just been so busy. I mean, coming to a decision like the one we just made takes all your concentration. But it was rude of us, wasn't it?" She took Glen's arm and started up the beach, leaving Brad to walk with Robby. Brad, sensing immediately that his wife was going to tell Glen about the dog, kept Robby occupied. And while he kept the boy busy, he observed him.

The change in Robby was as dramatic as Glen had described it. Not a trace remained of the frenetic, anguished child Brad Randall remembered so vividly. Instead, he found himself walking along the beach with a remarkably normal nine-year-old boy, a child who was obviously active, but not overactive; who talked easily, readily, but not with the frenzied pace he had constantly displayed only months before. As they walked Brad found his puzzlement at the change deepening, found himself wondering exactly what could have happened to Robby Palmer, or what might still be happening to him. The boy was almost *too* normal. Brad found it vaguely disturbing. . . .

When she was sure they were out of earshot of her husband and Glen Palmer's son, Elaine suddenly turned to Glen. "Was your dog black-and-white, sort of a spaniel?"

"You've seen him?" Glen asked eagerly.

"I think so," Elaine replied, her voice somber. "Yesterday morning I took a walk on the beach. I found a dead dog, buried in the sand. It was medium-sized, black with whitish patches."

"That sounds like Snooker," Glen said. "He was a mutt, but there was a lot of springer spaniel in him." He paused for a moment, then: "You say he was buried in the sand?"

"Not very deep. The sea might have done it, I suppose, but I'm not sure. His neck was broken."

Glen stopped and turned to face Elaine. "Broken? What do you mean?"

"I'm not sure," Elaine said unhappily. "He didn't seem to have any other injuries, but his neck was broken. Brad said he could have been hit by a piece of driftwood that was coming in on the surf the night before. . . ." She trailed off, thinking the story sounded hollow. As if he read her mind, Glen shook his head.

"Doesn't sound very plausible, does it?"

"I didn't think so," Elaine said. "I suppose I should have told you before, but I didn't want to, not in front of Robby."

"Of course not," Glen agreed. "I'll wait a day or so—maybe try to find the kids a new puppy—then tell them. Or maybe I won't tell them at all. I'll just find them another dog and that'll take their minds off Snooker."

Robby and Brad caught up with them in the trees in front of the Palmers' cabin, and as they approached, Glen called to his wife.

"Rebecca? Come on out here—we've got company!"

Rebecca appeared at the door and, seeing her son,

immediately swept him into her arms. Robby wriggled, protesting that he was fine, and finally Rebecca let him go, straightened up, and looked with surprise at Brad and Elaine.

"You remember Dr. Randall, of course," Glen said. "This is his wife, Elaine. I found them on the beach near the old Baron house. They've leased it and we're going to be neighbors, so I brought them home for a glass of wine."

"Come in," Rebecca urged them. "It's not nearly as big as the house you got, but there's room for everyone." She led Brad and Elaine into the small main room and pressed them to take the two chairs usually reserved for her and Glen. "Let me get Robby settled in bed. Glen, why don't you open the wine?" She disappeared into the tiny bedroom, and while Glen poured four glasses of wine Elaine and Brad inspected the cabin, Brad curiously, and Elaine carefully. By the time Rebecca reappeared Elaine was ready.

"Can you really cook on that stove?" she asked, making the question almost a challenge.

Rebecca looked blank for a second, then burst into laughter.

"It isn't nearly as difficult as it looks," she said. "Come here and I'll show you what happens." She bent over the stove with Elaine, demonstrating how the various vents worked and how to control the fire so that the burners would operate at various levels of heat.

"The main trick is to keep the fire fairly small so that you can move it around and control it. Otherwise the thing gets so hot you can't even get close to it. But if your husband is anything like mine," she finished, "you won't have any problem—there won't ever be enough wood to build a really big fire."

Elaine shook her head doubtfully. "I don't know," she said. "Something tells me we're going to be eating out a lot."

"We can't," Rebecca said. "And even if we could, we wouldn't. Much as I hate to admit it, I've gotten to the point where I actually enjoy cooking on this thing. The worst part of living on the beach is bathing."

"My God," Elaine breathed, closing her eyes as if to shut out a hideous vision. "I hadn't even thought about that!"

"You'll learn to *dream* about it," Rebecca laughed.

Elaine turned to her husband. "Did you hear that, Brad?"

"I heard." Brad looked unconcerned. "And I know perfectly well that I'm capable of getting myself spotless in one small pan of hot water. And after I've bathed in it, I can shave in it."

Elaine gaped at him. "You? You're the one who loves to use up all the hot water with twenty-minute showers."

"If it's available, why not?" Brad countered. "But loving to do it and having to do it are two different things. Just give me a couple of quarts of hot water— I'll be fine."

"Good," Elaine said sarcastically. "Then you can boil a gallon at a time and I'll use what's left."

"Before we get too involved in the glories of primitive living," Glen interrupted, "I have a question. How on earth did you get Harney Whalen to rent you the old Baron house? We tried, and he absolutely refused."

"Maybe he didn't want to rent to someone with children," Elaine suggested.

"That old house?" Rebecca said. "I don't mean to sound negative—God knows it's a lot better than this —but still, it isn't a place children can do much damage to."

"It was something else," Glen said. "I'm still not sure exactly what it was. I thought it had something to do with us personally at first, but then I changed my mind. I figured he just didn't want to rent the house at all, especially to strangers. I guess I was wrong."

"I'm not so sure," Brad said pensively. "He wasn't eager to rent to us either. When he finally did he was acting strange, almost as though he was thinking about something else entirely."

"That *is* strange," Rebecca commented.

"This whole place is strange," Brad offered. "I think I'll write a book about it."

"A book?" Glen looked at Brad critically, then shook his head. "Nope. You don't look like a writer."

"I'm not," Brad said. "But I've been kicking around an idea for a book for a long time. Now seems like a good time to do it, and Sod Beach seems like a good place. So here we are."

"Just like that?" Rebecca asked.

"Well, not quite," Elaine replied. "We have to go back to Seattle and close up our house. But I should think we'll be moving out here in a couple of weeks."

"Two weeks," Rebecca said, almost under her breath. "I can make it that long." She hadn't intended to speak out loud, but everyone in the room heard her.

Glen looked embarrassed, but Brad decided to probe.

"I'm not sure what that means," he said with a tentative smile that he hoped would put Rebecca at her ease.

Rebecca flushed a deep red and tried to recover herself. "Nothing, really," she began. Then she changed her mind. "Yes, I do mean something by it," she said. "It's damned lonely out here and sometimes I'm frightened. You have no idea how glad I am that you're going to be living just down the beach. I know it may sound strange since I barely know you, but sometimes this place gets to me. Now I won't be the only one."

"The only one?" Elaine repeated Rebecca's last words.

"The only stranger here," Rebecca said. Then she looked from Brad to Elaine, her expression almost panicky. "You *are* strangers here, aren't you? You don't have relatives in Clark's Harbor?"

"I see," Elaine said, leaning back and relaxing. She smiled at Rebecca. "No, we don't know a soul here except you, and we're not related to anybody, and," she added in a rush, "I know exactly what you're talking about. It's not easy to be a stranger in Clark's Harbor, is it?"

"It's terrible," Rebecca said softly. "Sometimes I've wanted to just pick up and leave."

"Why haven't you?" Elaine asked.

"Lots of reasons," Rebecca said vaguely. "We've got most of our money tied up here—not that there's very much of it. If we were to leave now we wouldn't have anything left."

"And, of course, there's Robby," Glen added quietly.

159

Rebecca looked almost embarrassed but Brad picked the subject of Robby up with apparent eagerness. "The change in him is almost unbelievable. In fact, if I hadn't seen him myself, I wouldn't have believed you. And you don't have any idea what caused it?"

"Not the slightest." Glen shrugged. "But we aren't about to question it either. As long as Robby stays the way he is now, we'll stay in Clark's Harbor, come what may."

"How bad has it been?" Elaine asked. "Or am I prying?"

"You're not prying at all," Rebecca said emphatically. "In fact, maybe it would be good for us to talk about it, just to hear what someone else thinks. Sometimes we think we're paranoid about Clark's Harbor. But frankly, I hate to subject you to it—it's so depressing." She picked up the bottle of wine and refilled everyone's glass.

"Oh, come on," Elaine said. "If nothing else at least it'll let us know what we're in for."

Softly, almost as if she were ashamed, Rebecca explained how they had come to feel that the whole town was somehow united against them. "But there's never anything you can put your finger on," Glen finished. "Every time something goes wrong there's always a reasonable explanation. Except that I always have the unreasonable feeling that if I weren't a stranger here none of it would ever have gone wrong at all. And then, of course, there was this morning."

"This morning?" Elaine thought a moment. "Oh, you mean Mrs. Shelling?"

Glen nodded and Rebecca's face tightened.

"Did you know her?" Brad probed.

"Not really," Glen said. "I ran into her last night on the beach. Apparently just before she did it."

"Just before she did it?" Elaine echoed. "You don't mean—?"

"It happened on our property," Glen said. "Our land goes back into the woods to the road, then parallels the road for a hundred feet or so. Miriam Shelling hanged herself from one of our trees."

"Oh, God," Elaine said softly. "I'm so sorry. Rebecca —it must have been terrible for you."

"I keep seeing her," Rebecca whispered. "Every time I close my eyes I keep seeing her. And the kids— what if one of them had seen her?"

"But it wasn't anything to do with you," Brad said.

"Wasn't it?" Rebecca's face was bleak. "I keep wondering. We talked to Miriam yesterday. She came to the gallery and started ranting at us. We thought she was just upset—"

"Obviously she was," Brad pointed out.

"She kept saying 'they' got her husband and 'they' were going to get us too. And then last night—" Rebecca broke off her sentence and fought to keep from bursting into tears. While she struggled to hold herself together, her husband spoke.

"So you can see, it hasn't been easy." He laughed self-consciously. "Some welcome we're giving you, huh? Really makes you want to settle down here, doesn't it?"

"Actually, yes, it does," Brad said. The Palmers stared at him. "You mentioned paranoia, and I'm not sure you were so far off base. You two have been living in pretty much of a vacuum out here as far as I can tell. Odd things happen in vacuums. Things get blown all out of proportion. Things that would seem small in ordinary circumstances suddenly seem terribly important. And the longer it goes on, the worse it all seems to get. But the key word is 'seems.' How bad are things, really? Are you going to be able to open the gallery before you run out of money?"

"It looks like it, but I'm not sure how we've managed."

"You want me to tell you? By working steadily along, dealing with whatever has happened. Actually, everything has gone pretty much according to plan, hasn't it?"

"Well, I'd hoped to have the gallery open by now—"

"Hoped," Brad pounced. "But what had you *planned* on?"

Glen grinned sheepishly. "Actually, if you get right down to it, I'm a little bit ahead of schedule. I allowed a lot of time for clumsiness."

"So what's really gotten to you is the attitude you've run into, or more accurately, what you *think* you've run into."

"Oh, come on, Brad, be fair," Elaine cried. "You know damned well what Clark's Harbor is like for strangers. You can read it all over the place. And you heard as well as I did what those people were saying about Glen the first day we were in town."

"They were talking?" Glen said, unable to keep the bitterness out of his voice. Elaine looked away, wishing she hadn't spoken so quickly.

"Well, that's something new," he went on. "When I'm around it's like everyone's been struck dumb. What were they saying?"

"Oh, just the typical small town stuff about artists," Elaine said, forcing a lightness she didn't feel into her voice. But Rebecca would not let the subject drop.

"It must have been more than that," she said gently. "Otherwise you wouldn't have remembered it."

"Well, the gist of the conversation—if you can call it that, since it was mostly just backbiting—was that no one in town seems to be glad you're here," Elaine told them. "But *I'm* glad you're here," she went on, "for the same reasons you're glad we're coming. Maybe we can take the curse off the place for each other." Elaine caught herself and glanced from one face to the other. "Sorry about that. I'm beginning to sound like Miriam Shelling, aren't I?"

"Don't worry about it," Rebecca said. "Suddenly, with some people around and a couple of glasses of wine, I think I'm beginning to see some reason again. But an hour ago I wasn't. Is there any more wine in that bottle?"

Glen poured them each another round, then went out to find another log for the fireplace.

"I really am glad you're going to be here," Rebecca said while he was gone. "I had no idea how dependent I'd become on people till we moved up here and all of a sudden there wasn't anyone to talk to. Sometimes I've thought I was going out of my mind, and I think Glen's felt the same way. We've been holding on for so long now, telling each other it's going to get better. But until tonight I didn't believe it. Now I do." She grinned suddenly. "I hope I don't get to be a nuisance—I suspect I'll be running up and down the beach every five minutes at first, just making sure you're really there."

"You'd better be," Elaine replied. "If you're not I'll have to do all the running, just to find out how to survive without electricity."

"Why don't you talk to Whalen about putting some in?" Glen said, returning in time to hear the last. "It shouldn't cost much from where you are—the main line runs out almost as far as your house."

"Not worth it," Brad said. "And even if it were I doubt Whalen would go for it. For some reason he seems to be rooted in the past. He made a big deal out of telling us the old Indian story about the Sands of Death."

"That's not so funny, considering what happened last night," Elaine pointed out.

"Except that Mrs. Shelling killed herself," Brad said. "No one else was involved, and she certainly wasn't buried on the beach in the style of the story Whalen told us."

No, but the dog was, Elaine thought suddenly. She said nothing, standing up instead: sending Brad a signal that it was time for them to leave.

A few minutes later they started the long walk back down the beach.

Glen and Rebecca watched them go until they were only shadows in the moonlight. Then they closed the cabin door and put their arms around each other.

"Things are going to get better now, aren't they?" Rebecca whispered.

"Yes, honey, I think they are," Glen said softly. He didn't tell Rebecca about the strange feeling he had gotten while he was out getting the log: *the strange feeling of being watched. . . .*

11

"Well, that's that," Elaine said as she closed the last suitcase and snapped the latches into place. She began her final inspection of the room, pulling each of the drawers open, then moved on into the bathroom. "Damn," Brad heard her say.

"The hair dryer?" he called.

"What else?" Elaine replied, returning to the room with the offending object in her hand. She stared glumly at the suitcase on the bed, mentally rearranging it so that the cumbersome dryer would fit. "Maybe I'll just throw it on the back seat," she speculated. She tossed the hair dryer onto the bed and dropped heavily into one of the chairs, glancing around the room as if she expected some other item she had overlooked to appear suddenly from her new vantage point.

"You were right," she said suddenly. "This *is* a nice room. In a way I hate to leave it."

"We'll be back."

"Yes, but not here." She sighed and got to her feet, reaching for the coat Brad was holding. "Do I need this today?" She looked doubtfully out the window;

the sun was shining brightly and the harbor lay softly blue below her.

"It's a bit snappy out," Brad said. He picked up the dryer. "What about it? The back seat?"

Elaine scowled at him playfully and reopened the suitcase.

"As if you didn't know." She quickly reorganized the suitcase, mostly a matter of stuffing several of Brad's shirts further into a corner, and crammed the dryer in. It was a struggle but the suitcase closed.

"How come the dryer always winds up ruining *my* clothes?"

"Yours are cheaper, and besides, you don't care how you look," Elaine teased. "Come on, let's get it over with."

Each of them picked up two suitcases and they left the room, its door standing open, to make their way down stairs. Merle Glind looked up when he saw them coming but didn't offer to help them with the luggage.

"Checking out?" he inquired.

"No, actually we're just moving our luggage around," Brad replied, but the sarcasm was lost on the little innkeeper. He set the luggage down and tossed the key onto the desk. Glind picked it up and examined it carefully, then pulled their bill from a bin on his desk, matched the room number to the number on the bill, and began adding it up. Brad suppressed a smile as he noted that their bill had been the only one in the bin, and wondered what Glind would have done if the numbers had failed to match. He handed Glind a credit card, which was inspected minutely, then signed the voucher when it was presented to him. He wasn't surprised when Glind carefully compared the signature on the voucher with the one on the back of the card. Finally Glind returned the plastic card and smiled brightly.

"Hear you folks rented the old Baron house," he said.

"That's right," Brad said neutrally as he slipped his credit card back into his wallet.

"Not much of a house," Merle remarked. "No electricity. I wouldn't be surprised if the roof leaks."

"Well, we'll be living mostly on the first floor anyway, so I don't expect a few leaks will bother us."

Merle stared hard at Brad, then decided he was being kidded. He chuckled self-consciously. "I suppose you folks know what you're doing," he said, "but if I were you, I'd think twice, then think twice again before I moved out there."

"You mean the legend?"

Glind shrugged. "Who knows? But Harney Whalen believes in the legend, and he's part Indian."

"The police chief?" Elaine asked unbelievingly. "He certainly doesn't look it!"

"Take another look," Merle replied. "If you know, it shows up right away. Anyway, he thinks there's something to the legend. That's why he doesn't like to rent the house out there. Fact is, I'm surprised he rented it to you."

"Well, he didn't seem too eager," Brad said.

"Don't imagine he was. And if I were you I'd have let him discourage me. That's a bad place out there— no mistaking it."

Elaine suddenly felt angry, and her eyes narrowed.

"Exactly what do you mean?" she demanded.

Her tone seemed to frighten the nervous little man

and he retreated a step back from the counter. "N-nothing, really," he stammered. "It's just the stories. You must have heard the stories."

"We've heard them," Brad said levelly, "and frankly, we don't put any stock in them."

Glind's eyes suddenly clouded over and he almost glared at them. "Well, that's up to you," he said stiffly. "For your sake I hope you're right." But his tone told them that his hope was faint. Brad and Elaine picked up their suitcases and left the Harbor Inn.

"That really burns me up," Elaine grumbled as they carefully fit the suitcases into the car. "It's almost as though he was trying to scare us off."

"That's exactly what he was trying to do," Brad said, slamming the trunk closed. He heard something crack inside and ignored it. "But it won't work, will it?" He smiled confidently at his wife, knowing her instinctive reaction to Glind's tactics would be to prove the odd little man wrong.

"No, it won't," Elaine said defiantly as she got into the car. She waited until Brad was behind the wheel before she spoke again. "The way I feel now, I wish you'd been able to talk Whalen into selling the place to us!"

"That's my girl!" Brad said happily, reaching over to pat her on the leg. Suddenly Elaine stared suspiciously at him, her eyes narrowing and a tiny smile playing around her mouth. "Did you put him up to that? Just to bring me around?"

"Absolutely not," Brad said sincerely, staring straight ahead through the windshield. Then he turned and grinned at her. "But if I'd thought of it I would have!"

"Bastard!" Elaine said, laughing suddenly. Then: "Hey, let's stop and see Glen Palmer before we leave, just to say good-bye."

"I'd already planned on it," Brad said easily. He turned the corner and headed up Harbor Road toward the main road. A few minutes later they pulled up in front of the gallery.

Brad and Elaine were standing in front of the gallery, trying to picture what it might look like when it was finished, when Rebecca Palmer appeared at the front door.

"I was hoping you two would show up," she said happily. "That's why I came in this morning. A little bird told me you might stop on your way back to Seattle. Come on in—I've got coffee going."

She led them into the gallery. A moment later Glen appeared from the back room.

"Rebecca's little bird was right, I see. Well, what do you think?" The Randalls looked around as Glen led them through the room, explaining what would eventually be where, trying to build a visual image for them with his words. He was only half-successful, but Brad and Elaine admired the work anyway. Glen looked just a little crestfallen.

"You can't see it, can you?"

"Just because I can't see it doesn't mean it isn't there," Elaine protested. "Let me see it again when it's finished. Did you say there's some coffee?"

"Some beer too," Glen offered. "Come on back and see what I got this morning."

In the back room, standing on its hind legs and

whimpering plaintively, a tiny puppy peered at them from the confines of a small carton.

"Oh, he's adorable!" Elaine cried, sweeping the puppy into her arms and cuddling it. "Where did you find him?"

"I didn't," Glen said. "He found us. He was sitting out front this morning when we arrived."

"But he can't be more than eight weeks old," Elaine protested. "What would a puppy that young be doing wandering around at night?"

"Search me," Glen said. "I asked a couple of people about him this morning but no one seems to know where he might have come from. Bill Pruitt down at the gas station said sometimes people from Aberdeen or Hoquiam come up here and dump puppies instead of having them put to sleep. I figure if nobody comes looking for him today, he's ours."

Elaine carefully put the puppy back in its box. Immediately it began trying to scramble out again, its tiny tail wagging furiously.

"Was Snooker's neck really broken?" Rebecca suddenly asked. Elaine looked at her sharply and bit her lip.

"Glen told you?"

Rebecca nodded mutely.

"Well, then there isn't any use lying about it, is there?" She smiled weakly. "I'm sorry. When I found him I had no idea he was your dog."

"What did you do with him?"

"I left him where he was," Elaine said gently. "I didn't know what else to do."

"Well, there isn't anything to be done now, is there?"

"There wasn't anything to be done when I found him, Rebecca. He'd been dead for hours, I'm sure."

"I know," Rebecca replied. "But it just seems too coincidental, Snooker getting his neck broken and then Mrs. Shelling—" She let the sentence hang, then pulled herself together and tried to smile. "I'm sorry," she said. "These things have just gotten to me. I'll be so glad when you're back, Elaine. All of a sudden I just don't like the idea of being out at Sod Beach all by myself."

"That's nonsense," Elaine said with a certainty she didn't feel. "It's a beautiful beach and you've been very happy there. It's absolutely silly to let this get to you."

"I know," Rebecca said. "And if it were just one thing—even if the one thing was Miriam Shelling—I think I'd be all right. But two things? It just seems spooky."

"Another minute and you're going to start sounding like Merle Glind," Brad said.

"Merle?" Glen said the name sharply and Brad's attention was drawn away from Rebecca. "What did he have to say?"

"Not much, really," Brad answered. "Some nonsense about what a mistake we're making moving out to the beach. Without really saying it, he managed to imply that there's something to that legend of Whalen's. Say, did you know that Whalen's part Indian?"

"Not me," Rebecca said. "But now that you mention it, I suppose he does have that look."

Outside, a car pulled up and the group suddenly fell silent, waiting for the door to open. When it didn't

Rebecca got up and went to look out. "Well, speak of the devil," she said. Frowning slightly, Glen joined his wife. Outside, Harney Whalen was standing next to the Randalls' car, one foot on the bumper, writing in what appeared to be a citation book. "What the hell is he up to?" Glen muttered. He started for the front door but was stopped by Brad's voice.

"I'll take care of it, Glen. It's my car he's got his foot on." He went to the door and stepped outside. "Good morning," he said cheerfully. The police chief didn't respond.

"Something wrong?" Brad asked. Whalen glanced up at him, then finished writing and tore a page from the book. He handed it to Brad.

"Parking ticket," he said evenly, his eyes boring into Brad's.

Brad grinned crookedly. "A parking ticket?" he repeated vacantly. "What are you talking about?"

"Car's parked illegally," Whalen stated. Brad glanced around, looking for a sign that would tell him he had broken the law. There was none.

"It isn't posted," he said.

"It's not illegal to park here, Randall," the chief said. "It's the way you parked. Rear end of the car is over the pavement."

Brad walked around the car. The edge of the pavement, indistinct in the dust, appeared to be no more than an inch or two under the side of the Volvo. Suddenly he knew what was going on. "I'm sorry," he said easily. "Very careless of me. How much is this going to cost?"

"Ten dollars," Whalen said. His face wore what appeared to be an insolent smile, as if he were waiting for Brad to protest the citation. Instead, Brad simply reached for his wallet, pulled out a ten-dollar bill, and handed it to the chief together with the citation.

"I assume I can pay you?" he asked politely.

"No problem," the chief said, pocketing both the citation and the money.

"I'll need a receipt for that," Brad said.

The police chief glared at him for a second, then moved to his patrol car. He sat behind the wheel and scribbled a receipt, then returned to the spot where Brad waited for him.

"Be more careful next time," he said, handing the receipt to Brad. He turned and started back to the black-and-white.

"Chief Whalen?" Brad called. The policeman turned and stared at him. "If you think you can scare me off with a phony parking ticket, you're wrong," Brad said quietly. "It's going to take a lot more than that to keep me out of Clark's Harbor."

Harney Whalen pulled at his lower lip and seemed to turn something over in his mind. When he finally spoke his voice was just as quiet as Brad Randall's had been.

"Dr. Randall, I don't give phony tickets. Your car is parked illegally, so I cited it. If I wanted to keep you out of Clark's Harbor, believe me, I could. I tried to tell you what things are like here. Now, you want to come out here or you want to stay away, that's your business. But don't come to me looking for trouble—you're likely to get it. Do I make myself clear?"

Brad suddenly felt foolish. Perhaps he'd been mistaken and the ticket hadn't been the harassment he'd assumed it was. And yet it had to be—the violation, if indeed it was a violation, was so trivial. He decided to drop the matter, at least for the moment.

"Perfectly clear," he said. "If I was out of order I apologize."

The chief nodded curtly and wordlessly, got into his car, and drove away. Brad watched him go, then went back into the Palmers' gallery.

"What was that all about?" Elaine asked. "Was he giving us a ticket?"

"He gave us one and I paid it," Brad said pensively.

"What for?" It was Rebecca, a look of concern on her face.

"Apparently I parked illegally. It seems the right rear corner of the car is an inch or two over the pavement."

"And he cited you for that?" Glen was outraged. "That's ridiculous!"

"I thought so too, but I didn't push it. No sense getting off on the wrong foot."

"Sometimes I don't think there's a right foot," Glen said bitterly. There was a silence, and Rebecca moved to him and took his hand.

Elaine looked down at her watch. "It's time to get going," she said softly. "It'll take us at least three hours to get home."

Rebecca suddenly put her arms around Elaine and hugged her. "Don't change your mind," she whispered.

"Not a chance," Elaine assured her. "This town's got my dander up now." She pulled away from Rebecca. "Give us a week, more or less, and we'll be back. Okay?"

Rebecca nodded. "I feel silly," she said. "But all

of a sudden things seem like they're going to be fine. Hurry back."

"We will," Brad said. "And I expect to find this place finished by then. If it's not I'll have to pitch in and do it myself."

"I'll hold you to that," Glen promised him. He and Rebecca walked with the Randalls to their car, then watched them drive away.

"I hate to see them go," Rebecca said. "What if they change their minds and don't come back?"

"They'll be back," Glen told her. "Now come on in and forget about them for a while. There's lots of work to be done and a puppy to be taken care of."

Together, the Palmers went back into the gallery.

"What are you thinking about?" Brad asked as they drove away from the gallery.

"Nothing much," Elaine said, not sure she wanted to share her thoughts with Brad. She was afraid she was being silly. She didn't fool her husband.

"Worried again?" he guessed.

"I suppose so. Maybe we jumped in too fast. I mean, a house at the beach is one thing, but without electricity and in a town that doesn't seem to want us?"

"It isn't the whole town," Brad pointed out. "It's only Harney Whalen and Merle Glind. There are also Glen and Rebecca, who want us very much."

Elaine lapsed back into silence. Resolutely, she put her thoughts aside. But as they drove further and further away from Clark's Harbor, the thoughts kept coming back: *And they're strangers,* she thought. *Strangers, just like us. And just like the Shellings.*

* * *

Harney Whalen waited until the Randalls' car was completely out of sight before he pulled out from behind the billboard and headed back into town. As he made the turn onto Harbor Road he glanced at the Palmers' gallery with annoyance and wished once more that they had taken him up on his offer to buy them out. Then, with the offending gallery behind him, he looked out over the town. *His* town. He had a proprietary feeling about Clark's Harbor, a feeling he nurtured. Now it lay before him, peaceful and serene in the morning sun.

He pulled up in front of the tiny town hall and ambled into his office. Chip Connor was already there, enjoying a steaming cup of coffee. When Harney came in Chip immediately poured a cup for his boss.

"Well, they're gone," Harney said.

"Gone? Who?"

"The Randalls. Left just now."

"But they'll be back," Chip pointed out.

"Maybe," Harney drawled. "Maybe not." He sat down and put his feet up on his desk. "Beautiful day, isn't it, Chip?"

"For now," the deputy commented. "But a storm's coming. A big one."

"I know," Whalen replied. "I can feel it in my bones."

Harney Whalen smiled and savored his cup of coffee and waited for the storm.

BOOK TWO

Night Waves

12

The Reverend Lucas Pembroke peered over the tops
of his half-glasses at the sparse crowd that had gathered in the tiny Methodist church and tried to blame
the poor attendance on the weather. It had been raining almost steadily for the last five days—ever since
Miriam and Pete Shelling had been buried—and the
Reverend Pembroke wanted to believe that it was the
weather that was keeping people away. Only a few,
the bored and the curious, had showed up at the
burial. Lucas had hoped that more would turn out
for this service. It seemed almost useless for him to
have driven all the way up from Hoquiam just to hold
a service for two people he hardly knew in front of
an audience of less than ten. Perhaps, he reflected, if
the bodies were here . . . He let the thought die and
chastised himself for its uncharitability.

No, it was something else, something he had been
acutely aware of ever since he had added Clark's
Harbor to his circuit. He had felt it from the first: a
standoffishness among his congregation that he had
never completely overcome. It was as if they felt that
though they ought to have a pastor for their church,
still, an outsider was an outsider and not to be com-

pletely accepted. Lucas Pembroke had thought he had come to grips with the situation in Clark's Harbor, but the deaths of Pete and Miriam Shelling had hit him hard. Of all his congregation they had been the only ones who had ever really let him know they appreciated his weekly trips to the Harbor, perhaps because they, too, had never felt particularly welcome here. He missed the Shellings, so he had decided to hold a service to say farewell to them. Apparently not many people in Clark's Harbor shared his feelings.

Merle Glind was there, of course, but Lucas was sure that Glind's presence was due more to his innate snoopiness than to any feelings for Pete and Miriam. Glind sat in the fourth pew, about halfway between the door and the chancel, and his small, nearly bald head kept swiveling around as he noted who was there and who wasn't.

Other than Glind, only three fishermen and Harney Whalen represented the town at the service. But in the front pew, off to one side, Rebecca and Glen Palmer sat with their children, strangely out of place. They had never been in the church before, and Lucas wondered what had brought them here today. He glanced at the clock he had placed above the door of the church to remind him of the time when his tendency to ramble on too long got the best of him, and decided he had delayed long enough.

He began the service.

An hour later the small assemblage filed out of the church. Harney Whalen was the first to leave, and Pembroke noticed that the police chief seemed to be in a hurry. He hadn't stopped to chat, even for a minute or two. Merle Glind paused briefly to pump Lucas's hand, then, mumbling that he had to get back to the inn, bustled off. As soon as he was gone, Rebecca Palmer stepped up to him.

"It was a very nice service, Mr. Pembroke," she said shyly.

"I'm glad you came." Pembroke's response was warm. "So few did, and it always hurts me when people stay away from a funeral. I suppose I can understand it but it always makes me feel lonely. I didn't know you knew the Shellings," he added, making it almost a question.

"We didn't, really," Glen answered. "Actually, I don't think I ever spoke to Mr. Shelling. But I talked to Mrs. Shelling the night she died, and we just felt that we should come."

Lucas Pembroke shook his head sympathetically. "It must have been very difficult for you," he said to Rebecca. "If there's anything I can do . . ."

"I'm fine now," Rebecca assured him. "Really I am. Your service helped. I know it sounds strange, but I thought if we came it might help me stop thinking about it. And I think it will."

"Come back again," Lucas urged. "I mean for the regular services, of course. We don't have a large congregation and I hate to preach to an empty church. Makes me feel unimportant, I suppose," he joked.

The Palmers assured him that they would, but the minister was sure they wouldn't. He couldn't really say he blamed them. They were undoubtedly feeling the same chill he had felt when he first came to the Harbor, and he suspected they would continue to keep pretty much to themselves. He watched them leave

181

the church, then turned his attention to the three fishermen.

The youngest of them, Tad Corey, was one of Pembroke's regular parishioners. "Tad," Lucas said warmly. "It was good of you to come. Although I must say I'm surprised."

"It wasn't my idea, Reverend," Tad Corey said genially. "I told Mac Riley here, that there were better things to do than spend the day in church, but he wouldn't listen." There was no malice in Corey's voice, and he winked at the pastor as he said it. Lucas Pembroke chuckled appreciatively and turned his attention to the oldest of the three fishermen.

"I don't see you very often, Mr. Riley," he observed.

The old man, his eyes almost lost in the wrinkles of his weathered face, didn't seem to hear Pembroke. Instead, his attention was centered on Missy and Robby Palmer, who stood a few feet away staring curiously at the fisherman. Pembroke sensed a silent interchange taking place between the ancient fisherman and the two children, a shared experience that they were now remembering, and keeping to themselves.

Riley broke the moment and smiled at the minister.

"Not likely to see me here often either," he rasped. "After seventy years of fishing these waters I know too much of too many things. There are things going on here. Things you don't know anything about."

"Well, I'm glad to see you made it today," Lucas Pembroke said uneasily, wondering what Riley was trying to tell him.

"Pete Shelling was a good fisherman," the old man continued, and Pembroke was grateful to be back on familiar ground. "Never knew his wife very well but I knew Pete. It's a shame, that's what it is. A crying shame."

"Well, accidents do happen," Lucas said consolingly.

"Yes," Riley agreed tartly. "But not often." He turned away from the pastor and started to leave the church. When he was a few paces away he called, without turning around: "You boys planning to waste the whole day?"

Tad Corey and the third fisherman, Clem Ledbetter, exchanged a quick glance, bade the pastor good-bye, and hurried after Riley. Lucas Pembroke watched them go, then went back into the church. He began tidying up the few hymnals that had been used during the service and wondered what to do with the flowers he had brought with him for the occasion. He considered using them again on Sunday, then quickly, almost spitefully, rejected the idea—he didn't think the people of Clark's Harbor would appreciate the gesture. But if he took them home to Hoquiam, his landlady would be thrilled. She might even fix a decent dinner.

Harney Whalen walked into his office and settled into the chair behind his desk. He shuffled through some papers, but Chip Connor wasn't fooled. Something was on Harn's mind.

"Kind of quiet, aren't you?" Whalen finally asked.

"Nothing to say. All quiet." He paused a moment, then decided to goad his chief. "Quiet as a funeral," he added.

Harney looked up at him then, and leaned back in the chair. "Is that supposed to be a hint?"

"I guess so," Chip said mildly. "How was it?"

"A funeral's a funeral," Whalen said. "First time I've ever been to a double one with no bodies, though."

"Lots of people?"

"Not really. Old Man Riley."

"Granddad? That doesn't surprise me." Chip grinned. "Sometimes I think he has a fixation about funerals. Like if he skips one the next one will be his. I suppose Tad and Clem were with him?"

"Yup. Those three and me, and four other people. Bet you can't guess who the other four were."

Chip turned it over in his mind. From the way Whalen had said it, it must not have been anyone he was likely to think of. Then it came to him.

"Not the Palmers?" he asked.

"Right on the money," Harney said. "Now you tell me. Why would the Palmers be at that funeral? Hell, hardly anybody was there and everybody in town knew the Shellings better than the Palmers did. So why'd they turn up?"

"How should I know?" Chip asked. "Why did they?"

"Good question," Whalen said sarcastically. "Guess who's going to find out the answer?"

"I see," Chip said heavily, standing up. "You want me to go on over there and have a little talk with Palmer?"

"Right," Whalen replied. "No rush, though. Anytime before tomorrow will be fine."

He watched his deputy leave and wondered how Chip would handle the situation; wondered, indeed, why he even wanted Glen Palmer questioned. Doc Phelps had said Miriam Shelling killed herself. But Harney Whalen didn't believe it. There was something more—something else happening, and Harney was sure that it involved the Palmers. It was just a hunch, but Harney Whalen trusted his hunches.

The Palmers walked the few blocks to the service station, paid an inflated repair bill without comment, and drove back to Sod Beach in silence. The silence was respected even by the children, who seemed to know that for the moment they should be quiet. Glen turned the Chevy off the main road and they bumped over the last hundred yards into the clearing where their cabin stood.

"Can we go out on the beach now?" Robby begged as he and Missy scrambled out of the back seat.

"Don't you think you ought to go to school?" Rebecca suggested.

"Aw, it's after lunchtime already." Robby's face crumbled and Rebecca softened immediately.

"Well, I don't suppose one day will hurt you," she said. "Why don't you let Scooter out before he ruins the house completely?" Before she had finished the words Missy and Robby were racing to the door of the cabin. A moment later the tiny puppy tumbled happily out to chase the children. Glen and Rebecca watched the scene until the trio disappeared around a corner toward the beach, then went inside.

"Damn that dog," Rebecca said as she saw the pile in the middle of the rug. They had given up trying to confine the puppy to a box after the first day, when he had earned his name by chewing a hole through every box they had put him in, then scooting under the nearest piece of furniture, waiting for someone to chase him. Also, the name was close enough to that of the disappeared Snooker that the puppy would re-

185

spond even when the children slipped and called him by their previous pet's name. All in all, the puppy had worked out very well, and the Palmers had been spared the task of telling the children what had happened to the spaniel: since Scooter's arrival, they both seemed to have forgotten the black-and-white mutt. The only problem was Scooter's recalcitrance at learning the basics of being housebroken. Rebecca found a scrap of newspaper and gingerly picked up the pile, took it outside, and dumped it into the garbage can.

"Want to go out on the beach?" she asked Glen when she came back in. "The sun's about to break through and you know how I feel about the children being out there by themselves."

Glen looked at his wife speculatively. This was the first time she had let them play on the beach at all since the day Miriam Shelling had died. He decided to approach the subject obliquely.

"Are you glad we went to the service?" he asked.

Rebecca seemed surprised by the question. "Well, of course I'm glad we went. I was the one who insisted we go, remember?" Then she suddenly realized what he was getting at. Instinctively, she started for the door, then stopped herself.

"It really is over, isn't it?" she said.

"It was over as soon as it happened, darling," Glen said gently. "But you needed that service just to tell you so."

"I know," Rebecca replied. "And I don't mind telling you that I feel pretty silly about it now, but it really shook me up."

"Well, at least the kids have the beach again. I don't

know about you, but I was beginning to go a little crazy with them and that puppy underfoot all the time." He opened the ice box. "Tell you what. Let's make some sandwiches and have a picnic on the beach. I'll forget about going back to the gallery and you forget about whatever you were going to do this afternoon, and we'll have a little wake for the Shellings, just the four of us."

"We're not Irish," Rebecca protested.

"We can pretend." Glen grinned. "Besides, you know as well as I do that those kids are going to have a million questions. So we might as well make a party out of answering them."

For the first time in days Rebecca's depression suddenly lifted and she realized she was once again happy to be at the beach. She hugged Glen and kissed him firmly.

"What's that about?" he said after he returned the kiss.

"Nothing in particular. Just to let you know that I appreciate having such a wonderful husband." She looked out the window just in time to see the clouds break and the sun pour through. The leaden-gray sea suddenly turned a deep blue, and the green of the forest sprang to life. "The storm's over," she said. "I can hardly believe it."

"I wouldn't believe it if I were you," Glen said. "According to the old-timers I've heard talking around town, the last few days have just been a prelude. The real storm's been sitting out there waiting to come in."

Rebecca made a face at her husband. "Well, aren't you just the prophet of doom?"

"Only repeating what I heard."

"And do you believe everything you hear?" Rebecca teased. "Come on, let's make hay while the sun shines!"

Clem Ledbetter set aside the net he was working on and shook a cigarette from a crumpled package he fished from his pants pocket.

"What do you think?" he said to no one in particular as he lit the cigarette and took a deep drag on it.

"You gonna work or smoke?" Tad Corey asked. "I know you can't do both."

"I was thinking about Miriam Shelling," Clem said, ignoring Tad. "It just don't make any sense to me."

"Lots of things don't make sense." Mac Riley set aside his work and pulled out his pipe. As he carefully packed it from an ancient sealskin tobacco pouch, he peered at Clem. "What is it in particular?"

"Miriam Shelling. It just don't make sense, her killing herself. She just wasn't the kind of woman to do something like that."

"What makes you such an expert?" Corey asked. "You and her closer than you let on?"

"Shit, no. It's just that she didn't seem like the type, that's all. Me and Alice knew Pete and Miriam as well as anybody around here and if you ask me, the whole thing doesn't make any sense."

"Pete Shelling was a fool," Tad Corey said vehemently. "Anybody who stays out alone like that is a fool."

"That may be," Clem said. "But Pete was a good fisherman and you know it. He ran a good boat—I never once saw *Sea Spray* but what everything wasn't in order. Not like some people I could name whose boats look like pigsties."

Tad refused to rise to the bait. "Kept his boat too neat if you ask me," he said.

"Maybe so," Clem said doggedly. "But someone who kept his boat as neat as Pete Shelling did just isn't likely to let himself get caught in his own nets. And Miriam—well, she knew what she was getting into when she married Pete. Any woman who marries a fisherman knows. So when something like that happens they don't go out and kill themselves."

"Well, what's done is over with," Tad replied. "I don't know why we're wasting time talking about it. Pete Shelling never did fit in around here, and I for one don't give a damn about it one way or another. As for Miriam, well, Harn Whalen says she killed herself, and that's that."

"Is it?" Mac Riley's quavering voice inquired. "I wonder."

He'd set his pipe down as he listened to the two younger men talk, but now he picked it up and relit it. He puffed on it for a few minutes. Clem and Tad had begun to suspect that the old man had drifted off in his own mind when he suddenly started speaking again.

"I remember something that happened a long time ago, not so very long after you two were born. There were a couple of people here, a man and his wife. Don't know where they came from—fact is, I might never have known—but anyway, he was a fisherman. And one day I found his boat drifting off Sod Beach, just about where that feller found Pete Shelling's boat. He was caught in his nets, just like Pete Shelling."

"So?" Tad Corey asked. "I don't see what's so strange about that. The currents off that beach get pretty wild

189

sometimes, and it isn't that hard to lose control of your nets if you don't know what you're doing. So two people die there the same way in forty years. I don't see how that means anything. If it were two people in a month, say, or maybe even a year, that'd be one thing. But forty years? Shit, Riley, the only thing that surprises me is that there haven't been more."

"You didn't let me finish my story," the old man said patiently. "A couple of days after I found that man his wife died."

"Died?" Tad asked. "What happened to her?"

"Hanged herself," Riley said quietly. "I ain't going to say it was from the same tree as Miriam Shelling used, but you can believe me when I tell you it wasn't far from it."

The two younger men stared at the old man, and there was a long silence. Finally Clem spoke.

"Were they sure it was suicide?"

"Nobody had any reason to doubt it," Riley said. "But if you ask me, what happened to them and what happened to the Shellings is a little bit too close for comfort."

"But it doesn't make any sense," Clem Ledbetter said softly.

"Doesn't it?" Riley mused. "I wonder. I just wonder."

Tad and Clem exchanged a worried glance, but Riley caught it.

"You think I'm a senile old man, don't you?" he asked them. "Well, I may be, and then again, I may not be. But I can tell you one thing. That sea out there, she's like a living thing, she is. And she has a personality all her own. The Indians knew that and they respected her. The Indians believed that a spirit lives in the sea and that she has to be appeased."

"That's bullshit," Corey said.

"You think so? Well, maybe you're right. But what the Indians said makes a lot of sense when you think about it. We get a lot from the sea, but what do we ever put back? Not much of anything. It's not that way with, say, farming. Farmers take a lot out of the soil, but they put a lot back in too. Well, the Indians thought the same thing was true of the sea. You had to offer it something in return for all it gave you. And they did. Out there on what they used to call the Sands of Death."

"I've heard the stories," Clem said.

"About what they used to do to strangers out there? Sure, everyone's heard those stories. But there are other stories, stories that aren't talked about so much."

"For instance?" Clem asked.

"When I was a little boy, I remember my father telling me the old Klickashaw customs. One of 'em had to do with fishermen that died at sea. The Indians didn't believe in accidents. Not a'tall. If somebody died there was always a reason, likely an offended spirit. The story was that if a fisherman died, it meant the spirit of the sea was angry."

"What did they do?"

"They made a sacrifice," Riley said quietly. "They took the wife of the fisherman out to the Sands of Death and offered her to the sea. Usually they hanged her in the woods out there, but sometimes they just strangled her or broke her neck and left her on the beach."

"Jesus," Clem breathed softly.

The old man smoked his pipe for a while and stared out at the calm sea. "Makes you wonder, doesn't it?" he said finally. "I hadn't thought about that story for years, not until Miriam Shelling died. But I wonder. I just wonder if maybe the Indians didn't know some things we don't know. We live off the sea here, and what do we do in return? Dump our garbage in. I suppose we can't blame the sea if she wants something more every now and then."

"You mean you believe those old Indian stories?" Tad gasped.

Riley looked sharply at the younger man. "Got no reason not to," he said. "And a lot of reasons to believe them. I've been living with the sea for most of a century now and one thing I've learned. Never underestimate her. You may think you've got her by the tail but you haven't. Any time she wants to, that ocean can pick herself up and smash you down.

"At night, usually," he went on, more softly now. "You have to be particularly careful of her at night. She can be smooth as glass, and you almost fall asleep. But that's what she wants. She wants you to relax. Then all it takes is one good wave and it's over. She's got you. Just like she got Pete Shelling, and that other fisherman so long ago."

"And their wives too?" Tad scoffed.

"That's the beach," Riley replied. "And it's just as dangerous as the ocean, particularly at night when the tide's high and the wind's blowing. The Indians used to call them the night waves. It was when the night waves were coming in that they made their sacrifices. . . ."

He trailed off and there was a long silence while

Corey and Ledbetter digested what Riley had told him.

"Do you really believe all that?" Ledbetter finally asked.

"I do," Riley said. "And if you live long enough, you'll believe in it too." As if to signal an end to the conversation, Riley tamped out his pipe, put it back in his pocket, and stood up. "What do you say we call it a day?"

Clem and Tad stowed the nets and the three men left the wharf, heading for the tavern for an afternoon drink. When they had gotten their glasses and settled at a table, Tad Corey suddenly spotted Harney Whalen.

"Hey, Harn," he called. "Come over here a minute."

The chief approached their table and pulled up a chair.

"You're part Indian, aren't you?" Tad asked him. Whalen nodded.

"Well, Riley here has just been telling us some old Indian legends."

Whalen studied the old man and seemed to consider his words carefully. "What were you telling them about?" he asked.

"The night waves," Riley replied. "And how dangerous they are."

Harney Whalen fell silent and appeared to be thinking. Then he smiled at Corey and Ledbetter.

"I know about the night waves," he said. "And you can relax. The night waves are only dangerous to strangers. And we're not strangers, are we?"

13

Chip Connor was up early the next morning after a night of fitful sleep disturbed by dreams in which he saw the faces of the Shellings staring at him, their dead eyes accusing him. The dreams made no sense. Each time they woke him he had lain in bed breathing hard, watching the shadows play on the ceiling until he drifted off into another nightmare. Finally, as the sun came up he had left his bed and put on a pot of coffee, then sat by the window sipping his coffee and trying to figure out what his dreams had meant. But he came to no answers—they were simply dreams.

At nine, he decided it was time to start the day. He dressed slowly, almost reluctantly. He put on his uniform, knotting the necktie carefully, and surveyed himself in the mirror. He grinned self-consciously as he realized that his dark, almost brooding good looks combined perfectly with the uniform to make him look almost a caricature of a recruitment-poster cop.

He drove more slowly than usual as he made his way toward the village, but it wasn't until he neared the Harbor Road turnoff and saw the Palmers' gallery that he realized why he had been feeling strange all morning. He pulled off the highway and sat in his car for a few minutes thinking.

He had been relieved yesterday afternoon when he found the gallery locked and Glen Palmer apparently gone for the day. He had considered driving out to Sod Beach but had quickly dismissed the idea, telling himself that he had tried to follow Whalen's orders but had been unable to locate Palmer. He had known, of course, the real reason he hadn't driven on out to the beach. He wasn't looking forward to questioning Palmer. In fact, he was dreading it. But now, seeing the door to the gallery standing open and an array of paintings propped neatly against the front of the building, he knew he could not put it off. Harn would be on him first thing this morning, wanting to know what Glen Palmer had had to say, and Chip wasn't about to report that he had been unable to locate Palmer.

He got out of the car, slammed the door moodily, and started toward the gallery. Suddenly a picture caught his eye and he paused to look at it. It was an oil painting of the old Baron house out on Sod Beach, and at first Chip was unable to figure out exactly what it was that had caught his attention. Then he realized it was something about the house itself. A shadow behind one of the windows, a shadow that came from within the house, as if someone were standing just out of sight but the artist had somehow captured the essence of his presence. For a second Chip was almost sure that he could make out the figure, and felt a shudder of recognition, but when he looked more closely, it was just a shadow.

He examined the rest of the paintings. They were good. Unconsciously he loosened his tie as he went into the gallery.

Glen Palmer glanced up from the display case he was staining and felt a wave of hostility pass through him as he recognized Chip Connor. He stood up and tried to smile.

"Don't tell me I've broken the law now," he said.

"Not as far as I know," Chip replied. "I was just looking at the pictures. Are they yours?"

"Every single one of them, unless you'd like to buy one. In that case it would be yours."

"I meant did you paint them?" Chip said self-consciously.

"Yes, I did."

"That one of the old Baron house . . ." Chip began. He wasn't sure how to put his question, so he let it drop.

"It's two hundred dollars," Glen said. "Including the frame."

"Too much for me," Chip said ruefully. "But there's something about it. This might sound dumb, but who's in the house?"

Glen suddenly smiled and felt some of his initial hostility drain away. "You noticed that? You've got a sharp eye."

Chip ignored the compliment and repeated the question. "When I first glanced at the picture I thought I recognized the person in it, but when I looked more closely, there isn't anybody. Only a shadow. I was just wondering who you had in mind when you put the shadow in."

Glen looked appraisingly at Chip and wondered

what had prompted the question. He remembered painting the picture several weeks earlier, remembered thinking it was almost finished when suddenly he had, almost without thinking, put the shadow in the window. After he'd done it he'd realized that it belonged there. He still wasn't sure why.

"What makes you ask?" he countered.

Chip shrugged uncomfortably. He was making a fool of himself. "I don't know. It's just that I thought— well, for a second I thought it was Harn. Harney Whalen."

Glen frowned slightly, then his expression cleared. "Well, that seems natural enough. It's his house, isn't it? But I didn't have anyone in mind. I guess it's whoever you want it to be."

Chip shifted his weight and wondered how to come to the point of his visit—the point that Harney Whalen had ordered. He decided to stall for a while.

"Are you selling much?"

"Nothing so far. But this is the first day I've displayed anything and it's still early. I should think hordes of customers will be stampeding in any minute now."

"Not much traffic this time of year," Chip commented. "And most people don't stop here anyway."

"It should pick up next month. I just thought I'd put some things out in case someone drove by. And it worked," he said, brightening. "You stopped."

Chip nodded and again shifted his weight. Glen was suddenly very sure that Chip had not stopped because of the pictures—there was something else. He decided to wait it out and let Chip make the first move.

"Well, if there's nothing else I can do for you I'll

get back to work." He turned his back on the deputy and picked up his brush, acutely aware that Chip didn't move.

"Mr. Palmer," Chip said, "I have to ask you some questions."

Glen put his brush down again. "About what?"

"You were at the service for the Shellings yesterday," Chip said.

"So?"

"I didn't know you were that close to them."

"I don't think that makes any difference. Is it against the law to go to a funeral?"

"No, of course not," Chip said hastily. "I just . . . Oh, shit!"

Glen Palmer's eyes narrowed, and Chip could feel the hostility coming from them almost as if it were a physical force. "Look, Mr. Palmer, I'm only following orders. Harn asked me to come over here and talk to you, so here I am. But I'm not even sure what I should be asking you."

"Maybe you should tell Whalen that if he wants to talk to me he should do it himself."

"Now wait a minute," Connor said. "If Harney Whalen wants some questions answered, it doesn't matter if he asks them or if I ask them." Suddenly he was angry at Palmer. "So why don't you just tell me why you and your family were at that funeral, and we can get this over with."

Glen felt his own anger swell. "Because there's no reason on earth why I should," he said. "As long as my family and I obey the law, what we do and where we go is none of your affair, none of Harney Whalen's affair, none of Clark's Harbor's affair, understand?"

"I understand, Mr. Palmer," Chip said levelly, controlling his rage. "But there are a few things *you* should understand. You moved here. We didn't come to you. You don't fit in here, and I think everyone in town, you included, knows it. Now if you want to cooperate with us, I'm sure we'll cooperate with you. But it seems like you've got a bad attitude. All I did was come in to ask a few questions and you're acting like you're on trial or something!"

"How do I know I'm not?" Glen shot back. "You want to know how I feel? I feel like ever since my family and I got here we've been on trial for something. No, that's wrong. We've been found guilty and there hasn't even been any trial. I didn't come here with a chip on my shoulder, Connor, but I'm sure getting one. I don't appreciate having my wife accused of breaking up the merchandise down at Blake's, or having my son ganged up on at school. I don't appreciate the fact that every time I order something at the lumberyard it takes weeks to get it, and when I do get it it's usually damaged. And I sure don't appreciate having the police come to see me simply because I attended a memorial service for a woman who killed herself on my property! Now maybe if this town had been taking a different attitude toward me over the last few months, I might feel a little different. But frankly, Connor, unless you can give me a damned good reason why I should answer your questions, you can take your damn questions and shove them up Harney Whalen's ass."

Chip Connor turned a deep scarlet. His hand began clenching into a fist. Glen thought for a moment that the deputy was going to hit him, and he prepared himself to fight back. But then Connor's hand relaxed and the blood began draining from his face. He was breathing hard, though his moment of fury had passed.

"I'm only trying to do my job," he said softly. "If Harn asks me to do something, I do it."

"Did he ask you to talk to everybody who was at the Shellings' funeral?"

"No, of course not," Chip said. "Only you."

"Why? What am I suspected of? My God, Connor, he died in a fishing accident and she killed herself! I just can't see why Whalen's so interested in my motives."

"It's just Harney," Connor said patiently. "You have to understand. He takes everything that happens in this town very personally. He wants to know why things happen, and the only way he can know that is by knowing everybody."

"Then he should come and talk to me himself," Glen insisted.

Chip Connor shook his head and wondered why Glen Palmer couldn't seem to grasp what he was saying. He decided to try one more time. "Look, Harney doesn't like strangers—he doesn't like to talk to them, he doesn't like to deal with them, he doesn't even want to be around them. So he sent me. All he wants to know is why you were at the Shellings' funeral. Is it really so much to ask?" He held up his hand against Glen's imminent protest and kept talking. "And don't start in about what right I have to ask you the questions. I'm sure I don't have a legal leg to stand on. But please, try to remember where you are and who I am. I'm just the deputy in a small town, and I really don't want to make any trouble for you or anybody else. Is it such a big secret, anyway?"

Glen Palmer was quiet for a minute. Finally, he decided that Chip Connor was right. He didn't have anything to hide, and he was beginning to sound paranoid. He grinned sheepishly.

"Well, if you really want to know, it wasn't even my idea. It was my wife's—Rebecca's. Ever since she saw Mrs. Shelling—you know—"

"I know," Chip said. "I took her home, remember?"

"Yes, of course." Glen threw him a small smile, then went on. "Well, anyway, Rebecca was very upset. She couldn't seem to get it out of her mind. And she thought if we went to the funeral it might put an end to the whole thing for her, if you know what I mean."

"I think so," Chip said, nodding. "That's it?"

"That's it," Glen said. He chuckled softly. "I sure kicked up a hell of a fuss over nothing, didn't I?"

"Seems like it," Chip agreed. The two men remained silent for a while, then Chip spoke again. "Mind if I ask a question?"

"Do I have to answer it?"

"Not if you don't want to."

"Shoot."

"Would you mind telling me why you kicked up such a fuss? Why don't you try giving *us* a chance?"

"It seems to me the town could give us a chance too."

"I think we are," Connor said. "We aren't the friendliest people in the world, but we're not so bad either. It's sort of a trade-off. We get used to you and you get used to us." He turned to go. "I'd better get on down

201

and report to Harn. But he's never going to believe that I spent nearly an hour here and all I have to report is that you went to the service because your wife wanted to."

"Tell him you beat the information out of me with a rubber hose," Glen said. "Or wouldn't he believe that either?"

"Not a chance. He always says that when they passed out the meanness in the family I was standing behind the door."

"The family?" Glen asked. "Are you and Whalen related?"

"Sure. He's sort of an uncle. His mother was my grandmother's sister on my father's side. That's where we get our Indian blood. The sisters were half-breeds. Of course nobody would call them that now, but that's what they were always called around here."

"They must have had it rough," Glen commented.

"I imagine they did," Chip mused. "For that matter, I guess it wasn't always easy for Harney, either. You see? You and your family aren't the only ones who have it rough around here."

They walked to the front of the gallery together. Outside, Chip paused once more to look at the painting.

"I like the picture, but I sure wouldn't want to live in that house," he said.

"Don't tell me it's haunted," Glen laughed.

"No, it's broken-down," Chip replied. "Are those people really going to live out there?"

"The Randalls? They sure are. He's going to write a book, and we're looking forward to having some neighbors. We won't be the only strangers in town for a change."

Chip got into his car, slammed the door, and rolled the window down. He stuck his hand out the open window.

"Well, good luck. Frankly, I don't think you're ever going to make a nickel on your gallery, but I hope I'm wrong. I think you made a big mistake in choosing Clark's Harbor to try something like this."

"Well, we didn't really have much choice in the matter," Glen said, taking Chip's hand and shaking it firmly. "Sorry I gave you such a rough time."

"If it's the worst time we ever have we're both in good shape," Chip replied. Then he started the engine and a moment later pulled onto the highway, made a neat U-turn, and headed for town. Glen watched until he'd disappeared, then went back into the gallery.

As he continued staining the display case he'd been working on, he thought over the conversation with Connor and decided that maybe he'd been wrong. Maybe he *was* paranoid and the town wasn't really out to get him. But then Miriam Shelling's words came back to him, ringing in his ears.

*"They're going to get you! Just like they got Pete.
. . . They'll get you too!"*

14

The folder on the deaths of Pete and Miriam Shelling lay open on the desk in front of him, but Harney Whalen wasn't reading. By now he knew the contents of the folder—could repeat them verbatim, if necessary. Still, none of it made sense. Despite Miriam's insistence to the contrary, Whalen was still sure Pete's death had been an accident. But Miriam Shelling's was something else.

Somebody strangled her.

The words crawled up from the depths of Whalen's mind, tormenting his sense of order. Suicide fit for Miriam Shelling; murder didn't. Even so, those three words kept coming to him. *Somebody strangled her.* But Whalen could find no reasonable motive for someone to want to kill Miriam Shelling. So he went back once more, as he had periodically over the last several days, to considering unreasonable motives. And, as always, the name Glen Palmer popped into his head.

He glanced at the clock, then at his watch, annoyed that Chip Connor had not yet come in this morning. He was about to phone him when Chip suddenly appeared in the doorway.

"You keep banking hours?" Harney growled.

"Sorry," Chip said quickly. Something was eating at Whalen this morning. "Talking to Palmer took longer than I expected."

Whalen's brows rose skeptically. "I thought you were going to take care of that yesterday."

"I tried," Chip explained. "But the gallery was closed, and when I drove out to the Palmers' nobody was home." Chip excused himself for the small lie: after all, there was a good possibility the Palmers hadn't been home the previous afternoon. Whalen seemed satisfied. He looked at Chip expectantly.

"You want to tell me what you found out?"

"Not much of anything. His wife wanted to go to the funeral, so they went. That's all there was to it."

Whalen stared at Chip. "How long did you talk to him?"

"An hour, maybe a little longer," Chip said uncomfortably.

"And all you found out was that his wife wanted to go to the funeral, so they went?" Whalen's voice dripped sarcasm and Chip winced.

"I found out some other things, too, but they don't have anything to do with the funeral." He decided to try to shift the conversation a little. "Frankly, Harn, I don't see what's so important about that funeral. Why are you so concerned about who was there?"

"Because I don't think Miriam Shelling committed suicide," Whalen said flatly. Chip gaped at him, and Whalen grinned, pleased that he had disturbed his deputy's normal calm.

"I don't understand—" Chip began, then fell silent as Whalen made an impatient gesture.

"There's nothing to understand," the chief snapped. "It's nothing but a hunch. But over the years I've learned to pay attention to my hunches, and right now my hunch tells me that there's more to Miriam Shelling's death than a simple suicide."

"And you think Glen Palmer had something to do with it?"

Whalen leaned back in his chair and swiveled it around to gaze out the window as he talked. "When you live in a town all your life you get so you know the people. You know what they'll do and what they won't do. As far as I know, nobody in town would kill Miriam Shelling. So it has to be a stranger. Palmer's a stranger."

Chip felt baffled: it didn't make sense—none of it made sense. As if he had heard Chip's unspoken thought, Whalen began explaining:

"He was the last person to talk to her. She was saying strange things. Probably acting crazy, like she was when she came in here the day before, and she scared him. Hell, maybe she even attacked him. How the hell do I know? But it happened on his property, and he was the last person to talk to her, and I can't see that anybody else in town would do something like that."

"But that certainly doesn't mean Glen Palmer did it," Chip protested. "It doesn't even mean that *anybody* did it!" Now he spoke his earlier thought out loud. "It doesn't make any sense."

"No, and if you'll notice, I haven't charged him with anything, have I? I didn't say it makes sense, Chip. Hell, I didn't even say he did it. All I said is that if Miriam was murdered, a stranger did it. Palmer's a stranger, and he could have done it."

"So what are you going to do?" Chip asked, confused by Whalen's logic, but curious.

"Same thing you're going to do. Keep my ears open, my mouth shut, and my eye on Glen Palmer."

"I don't know," Chip said, shaking his head doubtfully. "I just don't think Palmer could have done it. He just doesn't seem to me like the type who would do a thing like that."

"But you don't *know*," Whalen replied. "And until we do know I think Palmer's a damned good suspect."

Chip wanted to protest that there was no need for any suspect at all, but Whalen was too caught up in his "hunch" to be dissuaded now. So instead of protesting he tried to defend Glen Palmer.

"I think we ought to be a little bit careful of him," Chip said reluctantly.

"Careful? What do you mean?"

"He's pretty upset right now. In fact, he almost refused to answer my questions. Claimed I didn't have any right to ask them."

Harney Whalen's face paled and his hands twitched slightly. "Did he now?" he growled. "And what did you have to say to that?"

"I told him I didn't have any right to question him but that I thought he ought to cooperate with me. With us," he corrected himself. Then his face twisted into a wry grimace. "That's when he suggested maybe the town could cooperate with him. His gallery hasn't been going very well."

"Nobody ever thought it would. He's mad because nobody's buying his junk?"

"No," Chip said mildly. "He just thinks that everybody in town's been trying to make it difficult for him. Thinks people are holding up on deliveries and delivering bad goods—that sort of thing."

"Tough," Whalen replied. "Everything takes time out here, and everybody gets damaged goods now and then. What makes him think he's special?"

"He doesn't think he's special," Chip said. He could feel his patience wearing thin and wondered why Harn was so hostile toward Palmer. "Anyway, he's almost got the place finished. In fact, he's displaying some of his stuff outside the building this morning. You ought to go take a look. Some of it isn't half-bad. In fact, there's a picture of the old Baron place that I bet you'd like."

But Harney Whalen was no longer listening. He was glaring at Chip. "Did I say something wrong?" Chip asked.

"He's displaying his merchandise outside?" Whalen said.

"Yeah," Chip replied, wondering what could be wrong. "He's got maybe fifteen or twenty canvases lined up against the building so you can see them as you drive by."

"And you didn't cite him?" Whalen demanded.

"Cite him?" Chip was totally baffled now. "For what, for Christ's sake?"

"Peddling," Whalen snapped. "We have an ordinance here against peddling without a license. If he's displaying stuff outside he's peddling."

"Oh, come on," Chip said. "That's ridiculous. Even if there is such an ordinance, when did we ever enforce it?"

"That's not the point," Whalen said stubbornly.

"Well, it seems to me that if you're going to enforce it against Glen Palmer, you'd better be ready to enforce it against anybody in town who violates it, because I'll bet Palmer will start watching."

"Yeah, I'll bet he just would at that," Whalen agreed. Then a slow smile came over his face. "So I won't cite him. But I'll get those pictures off the highway, just the same."

Chip frowned and stared suspiciously at the chief. "What are you going to do?"

"Come along and find out."

Something inside Chip told him that whatever Whalen was planning, it wasn't something he wanted any part of. He shook his head. "No thanks. I'll hang around here."

"Suit yourself," Whalen said. "But if you change your mind, drive on up to the highway in about ten minutes. Just pull off the road and wait." He put on his hat, glanced at himself in the mirror on the inside of the door, and left. A moment later Chip saw him leave the building and get into the police car.

Chip picked up the file on Whalen's desk, glanced at it, then closed it and put it in the file cabinet, locking the drawer after he slid it shut. He wandered around the office for several minutes, looking for something to do.

"Ah, shit," he muttered to himself finally. He put his own hat on, closed the office door behind him, and went to his car. A few seconds later he was on his way up Harbor Road. When he got to the intersection with the highway, he pulled off the road, parked where he would have a good view of the Palmers' gallery, and waited.

He didn't have to wait long. In the distance behind him, Chip heard the faint wailing of the siren on Harn Whalen's car. As it grew louder he began to think that Whalen must be pursuing a speeder. The car would be coming into sight any minute.

But no speeding car appeared. Instead, the wail only increased, and suddenly Chip saw the police car roar around the bend, lights flashing, siren screaming. As the car charged into the stretch of straight roadway, it seemed to accelerate, and Chip tore his eyes away from it to look ahead, almost expecting to see Whalen's prey disappear around the next curve. But all he saw was Glen Palmer coming out of the gallery, a puzzled look on his face.

Chip realized then what was about to happen. He leaned on his own horn, hoping to warn Glen, but it was too late. Whalen, in the speeding black-and-white, roared by him, and the sound of Chip's horn was drowned in the shriek of the siren. Then, just as he was about to pass the gallery, Whalen swerved to the right, slightly off the pavement.

Glen Palmer jumped back before he realized that the car had not been aimed at him. Indeed, he wasn't even sure that it had been aimed at all, the swerve had been so slight and so quick. But the right tires of the police car hit a long, narrow puddle, and the muddy water cascaded over Glen, soaking him to the skin. Almost before he realized what had happened he thought of the pictures.

They lay in the mud, most of them knocked over by the force of the cascading water. Without even looking at them, Glen was sure they were ruined. He stared at them, rooted to the spot, seeing weeks of work destroyed in an instant.

He was still standing there when Chip Connor raced by him and began grabbing the paintings, snatching them out of the mud, taking them inside the gallery, then coming back for more.

"Well, for Christ's sake, don't just stand there," Chip cried. "Help me get these things inside."

* * *

Harney Whalen glanced in the rearview mirror just in time to see the last of the cascading water pour over the pictures, then put his eyes back on the road. He moved his foot from the accelerator to the brake, slowing the speeding squad car enough to keep it on the road as he went into the curve that would cut the gallery off from his view. He left the siren on for a moment, enjoying the wailing sound that poured from the roof of the car, then reached up to snap it off: Palmer had gotten the message. Not, Whalen reflected, that he really cared—if he hadn't, Whalen could always repeat the performance.

Close to Sod Beach, he decided to stop and have a look at the Baron house. He turned the police car into the nearly invisible lane that cut through the woods toward the beach and parked it when he could drive no farther.

From outside the house looked no different than it had ever looked, and Whalen didn't bother to inspect the porch that ran almost all the way around it. Instead he let himself in through the kitchen door, closing the door behind him.

He made a mental note to hire a couple of the local

kids to clean the place up. It wouldn't cost much to have the rotting garbage removed and the dishes washed and put away. If the sink wasn't scoured, the ancient wood stove not cleaned, and the floor still badly stained, it wouldn't matter—nobody was living there, and Whalen had no intention of having anybody live there.

A faint memory stirred at the back of his mind. Something about the Randalls. They had wanted to rent the place but he had refused.

Again the faint stirring. Whalen shook his head, trying to catch the elusive memory, then dismissed it. He *had* refused to rent the house to them. He was sure of it.

He wandered through the lower floor and picked up a stray sweater that lay haphazardly on one of the worn-looking chairs. Then he saw a fire neatly laid in the fireplace and felt vaguely annoyed. Before he could define his annoyance a chill suddenly came over him and he impulsively lit the fire. The chill stayed with him. He pulled one of the old chairs close to the hearth and sat in it, huddling his bulk far back in the chair. As the fire blazed into life and began to spread its warmth through the room, a light rain began to fall, streaking the windows of the old house and blurring the view of the ocean.

Harney Whalen sat alone, watching the flames and listening to the rain. He could feel a storm building.

Glen Palmer stood up, tossed the muddy rag into a corner, and surveyed the painting carefully.

"Well, it isn't ruined anyway," he said. The seventeen canvases were scattered over the floor of the gallery, and Chip Connor knelt by one—the one of the Baron house on Sod Beach—carefully wiping away the flecks of mud that clung to its frame. There were streaks of brown across the surface where he had clumsily tried to blot up the muddy water. "Let me do that," Glen said. "It isn't nearly as fragile as it looks."

"Sorry," Chip mumbled. "I was only trying to help . . ."

"You already helped," Glen said. "If you hadn't been there I probably would have stood there like a dummy all day." He glanced up at Chip and thought he saw a flash of embarrassment on the young deputy's face. He concentrated his attention on the picture in front of him then, and tried to keep his voice level. "What the hell was that all about, Connor?"

"I guess Harney must have lost control of the car for a second," Chip offered. He knew it wasn't true, knew he should tell Palmer what had happened: that Harney Whalen had deliberately tried to destroy the paintings. And yet, he knew he wouldn't. Harney Whalen was his boss and his uncle. He'd grown up with Whalen, and trusted him. He didn't understand why Harn had done what he'd done, but Chip knew he wouldn't tell Palmer the truth about it. Yet even as he told Glen Palmer the lie he was sure that Palmer knew. He wondered what would happen if the artist pushed him.

For his own part, Glen Palmer forced himself to keep working steadily on the canvas. Connor was lying. He had an urge to turn on the deputy and force the truth out of him, but he had, that morning, established some kind of truce with Connor and he didn't want to disturb it. So he concentrated on cleaning away the ugly stains on the painting, and forced himself to calm down. When he was sure he could face Chip Connor with a steady expression he stood up, turned, and offered his hand.

"Well, I guess it doesn't matter exactly what happened, does it? It's over and there isn't much either one of us can do now."

Chip felt a knot of tension in his stomach suddenly relax, a knot he hadn't even realized was there. He had a sudden urge to tell Palmer the truth and opened his mouth. But he couldn't say the words. Instead his mouth worked a moment, then closed again. He took Palmer's extended hand and shook it.

"Are they all ruined?" he asked.

Glen forced a smile and tried to reassure the deputy with a lie of his own. "I don't think it's so bad. Oil paints are pretty waterproof. The damage would have been a lot worse if I'd had the pictures facing the wall. The water would have hit the bare canvas, and it would have been a hell of a mess." He glanced at his watch. "Jesus, did you know we've been working for almost an hour? What do you say we have some lunch?"

"Lunch?" Chip repeated the word tonelessly, as if it had no meaning.

"Yes, lunch. You know, a sandwich and a beer? I have some in the back if you're hungry."

"I don't think—" Chip began, but Glen cut him off.

"Look, it's the least I can do. Unless there's something you have to do."

Chip chuckled. "Most of my job is just sitting around the station keeping Harn company. Except on week-ends, when we usually have to break up a fight or two. Otherwise, not much ever happens around here."

"So you might as well have a sandwich and a beer," Glen urged. Then: "If you don't stay I'll just spend the rest of the day getting pissed off at your boss."

"Well, I guess I couldn't blame you," Chip said, his smile fading into an expression of concern. "I know it was an accident, but still—"

"So do Whalen a favor and keep a citizen from getting mad at him. Besides, I could use the company."

Chip started to refuse, then changed his mind. There was a quality to Glen's voice that reached inside him, and he realized that it was the same quality he'd heard in Harn Whalen's voice now and then—not often, but on nights when Whalen seemed to be lonely and wanted Chip to hang around late, not because he had anything on his mind, but because he needed company.

"Let me pull the car up," he said. "So I'll be able to hear the radio if Harn calls me."

Chip spent most of the afternoon at the gallery. He and Glen split the lunch that Rebecca had packed and polished off the best part of a six-pack.

As he ate, Chip wandered around the gallery asking questions about the remodeling.

"Deciding what to do was easy," Glen said. They were standing under a large window that Glen was cutting. It was an odd shape, but it appeared to fit into the space Glen had allocated for it. "For instance, that window. It was just a matter of extending the line from that beam over there, carrying the ledge over the door on across, and then duplicating the pitch of the roof. Bingo—an interesting window that seems to have been part of the original design." He grinned ruefully. "The only problem is, I can't figure out how I'm going to keep the roof up. I cut a support post out to make the window."

"No problem," Chip said. "Cut another foot off the support, then build a lintel between the posts to support the one you cut. That way you have plenty of support for the roof and it doesn't ruin the shape of the window."

Glen studied the wall for a minute, then shook his head. "You'd better show me," he said finally. "I can see what I want as an artist, but as a carpenter I'm pretty much of a loss."

Chip found a ladder, dragged it over, and climbed up, explaining as he did so. Then, seeing the baffled look still on Glen's face, he climbed down and stripped off the jacket of his uniform.

"Got a saw? It won't take me more than an hour to put it in for you."

For a while Glen tried to help, but soon realized the deputy didn't need any help. He went back to the soiled pictures and began the tedious work of cleaning the stains from them. He moved slowly and methodically, using tiny brushes, picks, pieces of straw, anything he could find to lift off the bits of mud without disturbing the colors beneath. The cleaning went better than he had hoped; only a few of the canvases would even need a touch-up. By the time he had repaired the worst of the damage Chip had finished the lintel and was in the process of pulling down the shelves Glen had worked so hard to put up.

"What are you doing?" Glen cried. "Those things took me almost a week to build."

Chip nonchalantly continued to pry the shelves loose from the wall. "Were you planning to use these shelves?"

"They're display shelves for my wife's pottery."

"Didn't you ever hear of a toggle bolt? These nails will hold the shelves up, but the shelves won't hold anything. Look."

He grabbed one of them with his left hand and pulled it off the wall. "What's your wife going to say when all her pottery falls on the floor? Have you got any toggle bolts?"

"I don't think so."

"I'll run down to Blake's and pick some up. Do you have an account there?"

Glen gaped at the deputy. "An account? Are you serious? Didn't I tell you this morning what happened to my wife down there?"

Chip suddenly looked embarrassed, and Glen wished he'd kept his mouth shut. He dug into his pocket and pulled out his wallet.

"Will this be enough?" he asked, handing Chip a five-dollar bill.

"That'll be plenty," Chip said. "Why don't you finish pulling those shelves down while I'm gone." He picked up his coat and started for the door, but Glen stopped him.

"Chip?"

The deputy stopped at the door and turned around.

217

"I don't know exactly why you're doing all this for me, but thanks."

Again Chip looked embarrassed, but then he grinned. "Well, if we're going to have an art gallery in town we might as well have one that won't fall down the first week." His face reddened slightly. "Besides, I guess I sort of owe it to you." Before Glen could reply Chip pulled the door open and stepped out into the rain.

Neither Glen nor Chip noticed that all afternoon the police radio in Chip's car had remained silent.

The light rain that had been falling all afternoon grew heavier as the storm moved relentlessly toward the coast; the wind picked up, and the tide turned. Sod Beach took on a foreboding gloom, and Robby and Missy, their slickers already dripping wet, started toward the forest.

"We should go home," Missy complained. "It's cold and the rain's starting to come down my neck."

"We're going home," Robby explained. "We're going to take the path through the woods, so we won't get soaked."

"I'd rather go along the beach," Missy sulked. "I don't like the woods. Or we could go into the old house and wait for the rain to stop."

"The rain isn't going to stop." Robby grabbed his sister by the hand and began leading her toward the woods. "Besides, we aren't supposed to go anywhere near that house. Mommy says empty houses can be dangerous."

"It isn't empty," Missy replied. "There's someone there. There's been someone there all afternoon."

Robby stopped and turned to the little girl. "That's dumb," he said. "Nobody lives there. Besides, how would you know if someone was there?"

"I just know," Missy insisted.

Robby glanced at the old house, bleak and forbidding in the failing light, then pulled at Missy once more.

"Come on. If we aren't home pretty soon, Daddy will come looking for us." He started picking his way over the driftwood, looking back every few seconds to make sure Missy was behind him. Missy, more afraid of being left behind than of the woods, scrambled after him.

15

Max Horton glanced at the threatening sky, then adjusted the helm a few degrees starboard, compensating for the drift of the wind that buffeted the trawler.

"Jeff!" He waited a few seconds, then called again, louder. "Jeff, get your ass up here!"

His brother's head appeared from below. "What's up?"

"This storm's going to be a real son-of-a-bitch. Take over up here while I figure out where's the best place to put in."

Jeff took over the helm and Max went below to pore over a chart. He switched on the Loran unit he'd installed a month earlier, then pinpointed their exact location on the chart that was permanently mounted on the bulkhead. They could probably make it to Grays Harbor, but it would be tricky. If the storm built at the rate it had been going for the last hour there was a good chance they'd be trying to batter their way into port through a full gale. He looked for something closer and found it. A minute later he was back at the wheel.

"Ever heard of Clark's Harbor?" he asked Jeff.

Jeff thought a minute, then nodded. "It's a little

place—just a village. They've got a wharf though."

"Well, I think we'd better head there. We could probably make it on down to Grays Harbor, but I don't like the feel of things." He pulled *Osprey* around to port and felt the roll change into a pitch as the boat responded to the rudder. The pitch was long and slow with both the wind and the sea at their stern, and Max chewed his lip tensely as he tried to gauge how much time he had before he'd have to bring the boat around, throw out a sea anchor, and ride it out.

"I told you we shouldn't have come this far south," Jeff muttered.

"Huh?"

"I said, I told you we should have stayed up north. We've heard the stories about the freak storms down here. This isn't any big surprise!"

"It isn't any big disaster either," Max replied. "We've got the wind and the tide working for us, and we can make Clark's Harbor in thirty minutes. Is there any coffee down there?" He jerked one thumb toward the galley, then quickly replaced his hand on the wheel as *Osprey* began drifting off course. Jeff disappeared and returned with a steaming mug, which he placed in a gimbaled holder near Max's right hand. Then he lit two cigarettes and handed one to his brother. Max took the cigarette and grinned.

"Scared, kid?"

Jeff grinned back at Max, feeling no resentment at being called "kid." Max had always called him that, but he had always used the term fondly, not patronizingly, and Jeff had never objected, even though both of them were now nearing thirty.

The trawler, a commercial fisherman, was their joint

property, but Jeff always thought of it as Max's boat. Max was the captain—always had been and always would be—and Jeff was a contented mate.

There was a two-year difference in their ages, but they had always been more like friends than brothers, even when they were children. Wherever Max had gone he had taken Jeff with him, not because their parents made him do it, but because he liked Jeff. If Max's friends objected to the "kid" tagging along, they were no longer his friends.

They had bought *Osprey* four years ago, when Max was twenty-five and Jeff twenty-three. Jeff had been very worried the first year, sure that the immense loan would sink them even if the sea didn't. But the sea had been kind to them, and it looked as though the loan would be paid off by the end of the current season—all they really needed was four or five more really good catches, and Max seemed to have a nose for fish.

It was Max's nose that had brought them here today. The rest of the fleet that worked out of Port Angeles had stayed safely in the Strait, but Max had gotten up that morning and announced that he "smelled" a school of tuna to the south. They would go after it and spend the night in Grays Harbor before heading back north the following day.

He had been right. The hold was filled with tuna, and all had gone according to plan. Except for the storm. It had come upon them suddenly, as if from nowhere, giving them no time to complete the run south.

Now they were moving steadily if sluggishly through the heaving sea. A constant stream of rain mixed with salt spray battered against the windows of the wheelhouse, but Max held his course by compass, only occasionally glancing out into the gathering darkness. After some twenty minutes had passed in silence, he spoke.

"I'm going to have to send you outside."

Jeff checked the buttons on his slicker and put on his rain hat.

"What am I looking for?"

"Chart shows some rocks in the mouth of the harbor. They should be well off the port bow, but keep a lookout. No sense piling this thing up when it's almost paid for."

Jeff left the wheelhouse and felt the wind buffet him. He clung to the lifelines strung along the length of the boat and made his way slowly forward until he was in the bow pulpit. He strained to see through the fading afternoon light, and his stomach knotted as he thought of what might happen if he failed to see the rocks.

And then they were there, sticking jaggedly above the surface, fingers of granite reaching up to grasp the unwary. Jeff waved frantically, but even before he made the gesture, he felt *Osprey* swinging slightly to starboard: Max must have seen the rocks at almost the same instant he had. He watched the water swirling and eddying around the reef as they swept past; then, when the danger had disappeared beyond the stern, he returned to the wheelhouse.

Max was finishing his coffee, one hand relaxing on the wheel, grinning cheerfully.

"You could have given them a little more room," Jeff commented.

223

"A miss is as good as a mile," Max replied. "Want to take her in?"

"You're doing fine. I'll get ready to tie up."

A few minutes later, as the trawler crept into a vacant slip, Jeff jumped from the deck to the wharf and began securing the lines. On board, Max cut the engines.

Jeff had just finished tying the boat up when he became conscious of someone standing nearby watching him. He straightened up and nodded a greeting. "Some storm," he offered.

"You planning to spend the night here?" Mac Riley said.

"On board," Jeff replied.

"Storm's going to get a lot worse before it gets better," Riley said dourly. "Don't think you can do it."

"Do it? Do what?"

"Spend the night on that boat. We got a regulation against that here. Too dangerous."

Max came out of the wheelhouse in time to hear the last, and jumped from the deck to join Jeff on the wharf.

"What do you mean, too dangerous?" he challenged. "You've got a good harbor here."

"Didn't say you don't," Riley responded, unperturbed. "But in a storm like this anything can happen. So you won't sleep on your boat."

Max stared at the old man, annoyed. "I could take her out in the middle of the harbor and drop anchor."

"You could just scuttle her right here too, but I don't think you will."

Max looked over his shoulder and saw the wind-whipped whitecaps that covered the small bay. All around him, securely moored though they were, the other boats rocked and groaned restlessly, complaining at their captivity.

"You got any suggestions?"

"The inn's right up there," Riley said, jerking a thumb shoreward.

Jeff and Max exchanged a look and nodded in unspoken agreement. While Max prepared the boat for the night, battening her down against the storm, Jeff and Riley started toward shore, the wind and spray whipping at their backs. As they hurried toward the Harbor Inn, a bolt of lightning flashed out of the sky and the roar of thunder rolled in from the angry sea.

The lobby of the inn was deserted, but when Jeff banged impatiently on the bell that sat on the counter Merle Glind appeared at the dining-room door. He blinked rapidly and stared at Jeff over the rims of his glasses.

"Something I can do for you?" he piped anxiously.

"A room," Jeff said. "I need a room for the night."

Merle bobbed his head, and scuttled around the end of the counter, flipped open the reservation book, and studied it intently. Then he peered up at the young man and frowned.

"I've got a room," he announced victoriously, as if he had had to search for a highly unlikely cancellation. "Just one night?"

"Depends on how long the storm lasts," Jeff explained. "My brother and I were heading for Grays Harbor, but it got so bad we put in here. If it blows over tonight we'll head out tomorrow."

Merle Glind pushed the register toward him, collected his money, and handed him a key.

"No baggage?"

"We're not on vacation," Jeff said. "All we need is a place to sleep."

Glind nodded amiably and watched the fisherman go up the stairs. Then he returned to the dining room and climbed onto the barstool he had been occupying when the bell had interrupted him.

"Guests?" Chip Connor asked.

"Couple of fishermen coming in out of the rain," Merle said. He peered out the window, seeing nothing but the reflected lights of the dining room wavering in the rivulets of water that ran down the glass. "Can't say I blame them. Not fit for man nor beast out there tonight." He frowned slightly. "One of them's still out there."

Chip slid off his own stool, and dropped two dollars onto the bar. "Order me another, will you? I'd better give Harn a call. You know how he is."

"Use the phone behind the bar," Glind said. "Save yourself a dime."

Chip suppressed a grin and didn't tell Merle that he had never intended to use any other phone. He went to the end of the bar and fished the phone off the shelf below it. First he dialed the police station. When there was no answer there, he called Harney Whalen at home. He let the phone ring ten times, then dropped it back on the hook.

"Well, I tried," he said, picking up the fresh drink that waited for him. "At least I tried." Then, remembering what Harn had had to say to him that morning when he reported not having gotten much information out of Glen Palmer, Chip made a mental note to try to reach the chief later.

"So that's what happened," Glen Palmer said. He had just finished telling Rebecca about the strange sequence of events that day—first Chip Connor's questioning and the near fight, then Whalen's deliberate attempt to ruin the paintings, and finally Chip's help at the gallery all afternoon.

"First I thought he was just trying to cover Whalen's ass," he mused. "He wouldn't admit Whalen did it on purpose, and I figured he hung around for a while just to calm me down, but now I don't know. If I hadn't called a halt I think he'd still be there, tearing apart everything I've done and doing it all over again." He grinned, remembering. "You should have seen him. It was like what I'd done was a personal affront, but he never said a word. Just kept fixing things. I have a feeling I haven't seen the last of him. Oh, and we now have a charge account at Blake's."

When Rebecca made no reply Glen came out of his reverie and studied his wife. Her brow was knitted into a frown. She seemed to be listening to something, but Glen was sure it wasn't him.

"Rebecca?"

She jumped a little and smiled at him self-consciously. "I'm sorry," she said. "I wasn't listening." Then, with an apologetic smile, she murmured, "It's the storm, I guess. I'm still a little nervous. It seems like whenever there's a storm out here something terrible happens."

"Now that isn't true and you know it," Glen protested. He was feeling very good and wasn't about to let his wife spoil it.

"I know," Rebecca agreed ruefully. "I suppose I'll get over it. But there's something else too."

"Something else?" Glen's voice took on an anxious tone, and he wondered what she hadn't told him.

"It's Missy. She says there was someone in the old house this afternoon. The Randalls' house."

"How did she know?"

"Search me," Rebecca said, shrugging helplessly. "Robby says they weren't anywhere near the place, but Missy insists that someone was inside the house."

Glen frowned, then called the children. They came out of their bedroom, Robby carrying Scooter. The puppy squirmed in his arms, and when Robby finally set him down he hurled himself at Glen, scrambling clumsily into his lap and licking his face.

"What's this I hear about someone being in the Randalls' house?" Glen asked as he struggled to contain the puppy.

"I didn't say anyone was there," Robby said self-righteously. "Missy said someone was there, but she was wrong."

"I wasn't either," Missy said hotly. Her tiny face screwed up and she looked as though she was about to cry. "I said Snooker wasn't coming back too, and he didn't, did he?" she demanded, as if it would provide proof of her honesty.

"No, he didn't," Glen said patiently. "And I'm not saying no one was in the Randalls' house today. I only want to know how you knew someone was there."

Missy, mollified by what her father had said, turned

the matter over in her mind. When she finally spoke her face looked perplexed. "I don't know how I know," she said. "I just know."

"You don't know," Robby said scornfully.

"Now, Robby, don't say that," Glen objected. "She might have seen something, or heard something, and has just forgotten about it."

"Smoke," Missy said suddenly. "I saw smoke coming out of the chimney."

"You didn't either," Robby argued. "Smoke's the same color as clouds, and you wouldn't have seen it even if there was any."

Missy started to argue but Rebecca cut them both off.

"That's enough. Now take Scooter back into your room and get ready for bed."

"Can he stay inside again tonight?" Robby demanded. It was a request he had made every night since the arrival of the puppy, and it had always been granted, partly because of what had happened to Snooker, and partly because Scooter was so tiny and appealing that neither Rebecca nor Glen had had the heart to make him stay outside. Now Rebecca nodded her head in resignation.

"Just make sure he stays in his box. I don't want him messing up the blankets."

"He's almost housebroken," Robby said eagerly, hoping he could gain a little ground in his campaign to make the dog a bedmate. Unfortunately Scooter chose that moment to squat in the middle of the floor and form a puddle under his belly. Neither Glen nor Rebecca could contain the urge to giggle, and Robby, realizing he and Scooter had lost the argument, snatched the puppy up and scolded it severely. Scooter lapped wetly at Robby's face.

"Get him out of here," Rebecca cried. Laughing, she shooed her children and their pet back to their room and wiped the mess off the floor. As she finished she realized Glen was putting on his raincoat.

"Where are you going?"

"I think I'll take a walk down the beach and have a look at the Randalls' place. If there *is* someone there, I'll report it to Chip Connor."

"In this rain?" Rebecca protested. "Honey, you'll be soaked to the skin—it's pouring out there, and the wind's nearly tearing the roof off."

"Does that mean you don't want to come with me?" Glen asked innocently. Rebecca glared at him.

"That means I don't want you to go at all."

Glen gave her a quick hug and kissed her on the nose. "Well, I'm going and that's that. If we're ever away, I hope the Randalls will keep an eye on this place. It seems to me that the least I can do is keep an eye on theirs. And if Missy thinks she saw someone—"

"She didn't say she saw anyone."

"Well, she saw smoke."

"She said that tonight," Rebecca argued. "She didn't say anything about it this afternoon. I think she was just trying to convince us that someone was there. I probably put the idea into her head myself when I said she might have seen something."

"But she might have seen smoke," Glen countered, "and if she did I want to know what's going on."

Rebecca sighed, knowing further argument was useless. "All right, but be careful. Please?"

"Nothing to worry about," Glen reassured her. "I'll be back in half an hour, probably sooner."

A moment later he was gone. Rebecca strained to see him from the window as he went out into the night. But the storm swallowed him up, and she was left to wait alone and worry.

16

Max Horton surveyed the cabin of the trawler, making a final inspection before going ashore. He'd been working steadily for half an hour, though he could have finished the job of putting the boat to rights in ten minutes. He'd been dawdling, making the work last, enjoying his solitude, enjoying the boat. But now the job was done and he could no longer delay joining his brother at the inn. A slight smile crossed his face as he anticipated the warm glow that a hot brandy and water would bring.

Then he heard a sound. It was faint, nearly drowned out by the storm raging in from the sea, and indistinct. But it sounded like a hatch cover being dropped into place.

A sense of impending danger made Max's spine tingle, and he moved quickly to the hatchway.

He was only seconds too late.

Osprey was adrift.

It was already too far from the wharf for Max to attempt a jump, and even if it had been closer, the water was too rough. Then, as a bolt of lightning lashed out of the sky, Max saw the figure on the wharf. It stood perfectly still, hands on hips, head thrown back as if in laughter. The screaming wind drowned out any sounds and the effect of the silent, maniacal laughter chilled Max.

The brilliance of the lightning faded away as the crash of thunder shook the pitching trawler. Max ducked back into the wheelhouse, fumbling in his pocket for his keys. He jammed the ignition key in its lock, twisted it violently, and pressed the starter of the port engine.

Nothing happened.

He pressed the other starter. Again nothing.

He glanced out the window in time to see the wharf disappear into the darkness, and realized the boat was riding the turning tide. He was being drawn toward the mouth of the harbor—and the waiting rocks.

He jabbed at the recalcitrant starter buttons once more, then threw the switch that would drop the main anchor. When it too failed to respond, he left the wheelhouse and moved as swiftly as he could to the stern. He kicked open the anchor locker on the deck and hurled the anchor over the side.

Then he watched as ten feet of line played out and the frayed end of the line disappeared into the blackness of the water.

Something had done its job well.

Max yanked open the hatch cover over the engine compartment and dropped nimbly into the space between the two big Chrysler engines. At first glance everything seemed to be normal, but as he flashed his light over the immense machines he noticed something.

The wiring.

The new wiring that he and Jeff had installed only

a week ago had changed. The insulation was gone,
burned off as if it had been hugely overloaded, or
struck by lightning. The copper wiring, pitted and
looking worn, gleamed dully in the glow of his flashlight.

He scrambled out of the engine compartment and
replaced the hatch cover. He returned to the wheelhouse and tried to assess the situation. Only then did
he realize he was trembling with frustration and rage.
He groped in his pockets, pulled a crumpled pack of
cigarettes out, and lit one. He sat quietly at the helm
and dragged deeply on his cigarette, forcing himself
to calm down, analyze the situation, then do whatever
had to be done to save the ship. Once more an image
of the fingers of rock looming out of the mouth of the
harbor came into his mind. . . .

Glen Palmer approached the old Baron house
cautiously. He had intended to walk along the beach
and arrive at the house from the seaward side, but the
storm had quickly driven him into the comparative
shelter of the woods. He had walked quickly, though
the sodden ground had sucked at his shoes. The wind
screaming in the treetops above him had chilled his
spirit as the rain, funneling through the dense foliage,
had chilled his body.

Finally he had found the path that would take him
back to the beach—the same path his children had
used that afternoon—and he had broken out of the
woods only forty feet from the house. The house itself blended almost perfectly with the blackness of
the night, and only occasional flashes of lightning
revealed that it still stood, a silent sentinel on the

beach, testimony to the long-disappeared people who had built it. No light seeped from its dark windows, no clue as to what might lie within escaped its walls. As he made his way around it, Glen shivered, less from the cold than from the deathly stillness that seemed to emanate from the house.

He paused when he found the kitchen door unlocked, sure that something was wrong. Then he entered the kitchen, flashing his light from one corner to another, illuminating first a wall, then the sink, next the icebox, and finally the door to the dining room. He didn't call out, not out of a fear of alerting anyone who might be inside, but because of deep certainty that the house was empty.

He went confidently into the dining room, again flashed the light briefly around, then moved on to the living room. It was then he knew that someone had been there.

It was at least ten degrees warmer here, and the air was drier—the mustiness of the house had been dispelled in the living room, and the slightly sweet, yet acrid smell of a wood fire lingered. He went to the fireplace and snapped the flashlight off. In the sudden blackness the dull red of a banked fire glowed dimly. Glen put out a foot and kicked the remains of the fire. The thin layer of dead ash fell away and the fire leaped into life. Glen frowned at it and shook his head, wondering whether Missy really had seen the smoke that must have been curling from the chimney only a couple of hours ago. Or had it only been a lucky guess?

He moved slowly through the rest of the house, examining everything more carefully. There was no sign of vandalism, no sign that anything had been disturbed at all. Whoever had been here had apparently borne the house no ill will; even the fire seemed to have been tended to.

Glen returned to the living room. The fire had built itself up to a steady blaze. He looked around for a poker, intending to break it down again, but found nothing. He sank into the chair facing the hearth and wondered if it would be safe to leave. But as he listened to the raging storm, he decided to wait awhile, at least until the fire burned down. It would give the storm time to spend itself, and himself time to dry out and warm up. He got up and went to the window that faced north, flashed his light steadily five times, then returned to the chair in front of the fire. If Rebecca was watching she would know he was all right.

On the fishing trawler, Max Horton returned to the engine compartment for a more thorough investigation. There was an off chance that what damage had been done could be repaired and Max could get at least one of the engines going. A close examination dashed his hopes, and he returned to the deck. He cast the beam of the flashlight ahead and immediately realized that the boat had drifted around and was now proceeding stern first. He grabbed a large bucket and ran to the bow, where he tied the bucket to one of the mooring lines. He threw the primitive sea anchor overboard, hoping the current would catch it with enough strength to pull the trawler around. Then he began to consider the advisability of abandoning the boat.

The wind seemed not to be slackening at all—if

anything, its intensity was increasing, and it was an onshore wind. If he could rig a sail on the dinghy he just might make it back to safety. But if the sail failed to work the ebbing tide would carry him out to sea. It was this possibility that made up his mind for him.

If he stayed on the trawler and the sea anchor held, there was a good chance he could ride out the storm, providing he missed the rocks at the mouth of the harbor. But in the dinghy he would have no chance. True, the wind might carry him shoreward, but the combination of wind and tide would surely capsize him. If that happened he would be unconscious in ten minutes, dead in twenty. In daylight he might have risked it, counting on someone to come to his rescue. But at night, in the storm, he would be on his own. He decided to stay with the boat.

As he came to his decision another flash of lightning rent the sky and he tried to get his bearings. The sea anchor had worked, and the trawler was now riding with the tide, her bow into the wind. Far ahead, Max thought he could barely make out the jagged points of the reef, and he told himself that with a little luck he would clear them on the starboard side. He returned to the wheelhouse and lit another cigarette. All he could do was wait.

Harney Whalen parked his car in front of his house and hurried up the steps to the front door, pushing it open, then closing it behind him before he turned on the lights. His uniform was soaking wet; he felt cold clear through to his bones. And his heart was pounding.

He stripped off his dripping clothes and put on a

robe, then turned up the heat, lit a fire in the fireplace, and mixed himself a strong brandy and water. He slugged the drink down, mixed another, then went to the bathroom. As the hot water streamed over him and the chill slowly dissipated, his pulse slowed, and by the time he stepped out of the shower, dried himself, and settled down in front of the fire to sip his second drink he felt much better. But he still wasn't entirely sure what had happened.

He remembered being out at Sod Beach, sitting in front of the fire, enjoying the rain and the solitude. He had listened to the storm bear down on the coast, even gotten up once to watch the thunderheads gather before moving in to lash out at Clark's Harbor. He had built up the fire then and settled back into the chair, and begun to daydream. But he must have fallen asleep, or had one of his "spells," for the next thing he remembered he was in his car, driving home. And try as he would, he couldn't account for his uniform being soaked through: the car had been parked only ten or twenty yards from the Baron house. Surely his clothes wouldn't have gotten that wet even if he had crawled the distance.

An image flickered in his mind for a split second, then disappeared: he thought he saw himself on the beach, walking in the storm, staring out to sea. And there was something else, something just beyond his vision. Shapes, familiar shapes, and they were calling to him. But everything was confused, and Whalen couldn't decide whether he'd had a flash of an old memory or whether it was simply his imagination.

He mixed a third drink, weaker this time, and pondered the advisability of discussing the "spells" with

Doc Phelps. But Phelps would insist on giving him a complete examination, and Harn wasn't sure he wanted to go through that. You never knew what the doctors might find, and Harn was only a couple of years from retirement. No sense rocking the boat . . .

The ringing of the telephone broke his train of thought.

"Whalen," he said automatically as he picked up the receiver.

"Harn? Where've you been?" Chip Connor's voice sounded almost accusatory, and Whalen scowled.

"Out," he said flatly. There was a slight pause, and Harney felt better as Chip's sudden discomfort projected itself over the telephone line.

"I've been trying to get you all evening," Chip said, his voice conciliatory now. "Thought you'd want to know a couple of fishermen checked into the inn."

"Fishermen?" Whalen repeated.

"Couple guys from up to Port Angeles. Merle says they were heading to Grays Harbor but the storm drove them in here."

Whalen shrugged indifferently. "They have any trouble?" he asked.

"Trouble? No, not that I know of. I just thought you'd want to know they were here."

"Okay," Harn said. "Thanks for calling." He was about to hang up when he suddenly thought of something else. "Chip?"

"Yeah?"

"Anything happen today?"

"Nothing at all," Chip told him. "Quiet as a tomb."

"How'd you like what I did to Palmer?"

There was a silence, and for a moment Harn wasn't

sure Chip had heard him. He was about to repeat his question when his deputy spoke.

"I'm trying to act like it was an accident, Harn," Chip said hesitantly.

"It wasn't," Harn growled.

"No, I guess it wasn't." There was another silence, longer than the previous one, as each man waited for the other to speak. Chip weakened first. "I told Palmer it was an accident, Chief."

"I wish you hadn't," Whalen said. "I wish you'd just let him worry."

Chip decided to let the matter drop. "Well, I'll see you in the morning," he said.

"Yeah," Whalen said shortly. "See you in the morning." He dropped the receiver back on its cradle, picked up his drink, and went to the window. He stared out at the storm, not quite seeing it, and his brow furrowed into a deep scowl. All in all, he decided, it had been a rotten day. And the worst of it was, there were parts of it he couldn't even remember. Then he chuckled hollowly to himself, thinking that it didn't much matter—the parts he couldn't remember probably weren't worth remembering anyway.

Jeff Horton glanced at his watch, then went to the window of his hotel room. He tried to make out the wharf a hundred yards away, but the storm was impenetrable. He looked once more at his watch. He had been in the room for nearly forty-five minutes; Max shouldn't have taken more than ten to batten down the boat.

He turned from the window, pulled on his slicker,

and left the room. He stopped downstairs and glanced at the bar, but Max wasn't there. Only Merle Glind, perched on a stool, chattering amiably to a young policeman next to him. Jeff went out into the storm.

Even on the wharf the fury of the storm blinded him, and he moved slowly, peering up at each boat as he came abreast of it. Then he came to the empty slip.

The storm forgotten, Jeff stared at the gap which he was sure had been occupied by *Osprey*. He told himself he was wrong, that they had moored the trawler farther out. He broke into a run, struggling against the gale, and made his way to the end of the wharf. There were no other empty slips, and no sign of *Osprey*. He was about to turn back and walk the wharf once more when the night again came alive with lightning, a blue-white sheet that illuminated the whole horizon. The flash pulled his eyes seaward. Far out in the harbor, nearing its mouth, was the silhouette of a boat.

There was no question in Jeff's mind. The boat was *Osprey*, and she was headed directly for the rocks. The white light faded back into blackness, but Jeff stayed rooted to the dock, his eyes straining to pierce the darkness, his mind crying out for another flash of lightning to let him see that the boat had swept past the beckoning fingers of stone. The seconds crept by.

Max Horton was staring numbly out the windshield of the wheelhouse when the sheet of lightning tore the curtain of darkness from his eyes and he realized instantly that the boat was going on the rocks. They

241

loomed dead ahead, only yards away, the sea swirling around them, churning itself into foam as it battered at the ancient barrier.

The imminent peril jerked him out of the lethargy he had sunk into during the past thirty minutes, and he grabbed a life jacket, securing it around his waist. Then he left the wheelhouse and began preparing the dinghy for launching. He pulled its cover free and released the lines that secured it to the davits, then began lowering it into the turbulent sea as it swung free.

He was too late.

The tiny dinghy hit the water and was immediately caught in the eddying currents around the reef. It swamped, then settled into the water, only its gunwales still above the surface.

Finally *Osprey* too became entangled in the furious currents, and her stern swung around. Broadside, she hurled herself onto the rocks, shuddering as her planking split amidships. She settled in the water, groaning and complaining, as the sea pressed in upon her, grinding her against the rocks, tearing her to pieces.

Beneath the surface one of the fuel tanks collapsed under the pressure, and suddenly the hull filled with fumes.

Seconds later, *Osprey* exploded.

Max Horton was blown overboard by the force of the explosion, briefly stunned by the icy water, but began swimming as soon as he came to the surface. It was only a gesture—the tide took him, pulled him away from the flaming wreckage, pulled him away from what might have been the security of the rocks. As soon as he realized what was happening he stopped swimming and rolled over on his back, to watch his trawler go up in flames. He felt the cold begin to grip him, felt the lethargy sink in.

And then the wreck began to fade from his vision. At first he thought it was because he was drifting out on the tide, but then he knew it was something else. Silently, he apologized to Jeff for what had happened, then gave in to the sea. His eyes closed and the storm suddenly was no longer threatening. Now it was lulling him, rocking him gently to sleep. He looked forward to the sleep, though he knew he would never wake up. . . .

The ball of fire rising from the sea didn't register on Jeff immediately. It wasn't until the roar of the explosion hit him seconds later that he realized what had happened. By then the flames had become a fiery beacon in the mouth of the harbor, an inferno of glowing red intertwined with veins of oily black smoke. Then the other fuel tank blew and a second ball of fire rose into the night sky. Jeff Horton, his mind numb with shock, began crying softly, his tears mixing with the rain and salt spray.

Glen Palmer didn't see the first explosion, but when the shock wave hit the old house on the beach he leaped to his feet and ran to a window. He saw the red glow immediately and was staring at it when the second explosion ripped through the night. He grabbed his flashlight and charged out of the house, running along the beach toward the wharf. It wasn't until he'd reached the small point that separated Sod Beach from the short stretch of rocky coast that he realized the explosion had not been at the wharf. It was out in the harbor, far out. And then he knew. A boat had gone on the rocks.

He dashed across the long sand spit that formed the northern arm of the bay and arrived at the wharf just as Merle Glind and Chip Connor stepped out onto the porch of the inn. He started toward them, but as he glanced out the length of the wharf to the fire far beyond, he realized someone was there.

Framed against the inferno, the black silhouette of a man stood quietly, almost sadly, staring out to sea. Glen Palmer changed his mind. Instead of going to the inn, he hurried out onto the wharf.

From his window Harney Whalen gazed out on the fire burning brightly in the harbor.

"Son-of-a-bitch," he said softly to himself. "Somebody's sure got themselves in a peck of trouble tonight."

He went to his bedroom, shed his robe, and began dressing in a clean uniform. He didn't hurry—he'd lived in Clark's Harbor long enough to know that no matter what had happened out there, there wasn't much he could do about it tonight. Not tonight, and not tomorrow.

Not until the storm broke.

Sometimes it seemed to Harney Whalen that in Clark's Harbor the storms never broke.

He was about to leave the house when the telephone rang. He didn't bother to go back. He already knew why it was ringing.

17

Glen Palmer reached out and touched Jeff Horton on the shoulder. Jeff turned, and Glen recoiled slightly from the vacant look in the young man's eyes and the dazed expression that had wiped all traces of emotion from his face.

"What happened?" he asked gently.

Jeff blinked twice and his mouth worked spasmodically. "My brother—" he said. "Max—the boat . . ." The reality of it seemed to hit him then like a physical force, and he sank slowly to his knees and buried his face in his hands. His shoulders shook with the sobs that wracked his body.

Glen bit his lip nervously, uncertain what to do. He thought he probably should go to the inn and ask Merle Glind to report what had happened, but he didn't want to leave the grieving young man alone. Then he heard the sound of running feet pounding on the wharf. There was no need to go to the inn.

He knelt next to Jeff and squeezed his shoulder.

"Is it your boat out there?"

Jeff nodded, unable to speak.

"And your brother . . . ?"

Jeff looked up then, and the slackness in his face

had been replaced by a grimace of confusion and pain.

"He was only going to batten down and grab a couple of charts—" Jeff tried to explain. "He said he'd be right back. But he didn't come back—" Sobs overtook him and he leaned heavily against Glen, his body heaving.

"Glen?" The voice was tentative, and Glen looked up to see Chip Connor standing over him. "I thought it was you. What the hell's going on?"

Glen shook his head. "I don't know. I just got here myself."

"I told Merle to call Harn Whalen," Chip said. Then he too knelt beside Jeff Horton. "That your boat out there, buddy?"

Jeff nodded miserably. Chip gazed out into the night. The fire was dying down; the driving rain and wind would put it out in a matter of minutes. "Let's get over to the inn," he said softly. "No point in staying here."

Supporting Jeff Horton between them, Chip and Glen started back along the wharf. After a few steps Jeff seemed to come to his senses a little and was able to walk unaided. Every few steps he would stop, turn, and gaze out at the blaze for a few seconds. Then, finally, he turned to look and saw only the blackness of the night. The fire was out; *Osprey* had disappeared. Jeff didn't look back again.

Merle Glind bustled up to the trio as they entered the inn. "I called Harney," he chirped breathlessly. "There wasn't any answer."

"Don't worry about it," Chip told him. "He probably saw the fire from up on the hill and left by the time you called. Why don't you give this guy a slug of brandy—he looks like he could use it."

Jeff was slumped in a chair. The bright light of the inn revealed an ashen face, the stubble of a day-old beard, and red-rimmed eyes that made him seem old and broken. The vacant stare Glen had noticed when he first found Jeff had returned, and once more his face had gone slack.

"I think we'd better call a doctor," Glen said. "I think he's in shock."

"Call Phelps," Chip said.

Glen quickly made the call and was returning to the lobby when Harney Whalen lumbered through the door. Whalen glanced around, sizing up the situation, then approached his deputy.

"What the hell's going on?" he asked, echoing Chip's question of only a few minutes ago. "Is everybody all right?"

"We don't know yet," Chip replied. "I was in the bar with Merle, having a couple drinks, when we heard the explosion. I thought it was thunder but then we saw the fire. Merle called you and I went down to the wharf. Glen Palmer was there with this guy." He nodded toward Jeff Horton, who sat staring at the floor, his hands clutching the glass of brandy Merle Glind had brought from the bar. If he was aware of the conversation between the chief and his deputy, he gave no sign. Whalen's eyes narrowed slightly as he looked Jeff over, then he approached the young man.

"You want to tell me what happened?" he asked. His voice held neither hostility nor concern; it was his professional voice, the voice he habitually used before he had made up his mind.

"I don't know what happened," Jeff said absently. He still stared at the floor.

"My deputy tells me you were out on the wharf when that boat blew up."

Jeff nodded and sipped his drink.

"Mind telling me what you were doing out there?"

Jeff frowned a little, as if trying to remember. "I was looking for my brother . . . I was looking for Max . . ." he trailed off, then suddenly took a long swallow of brandy, and set the empty glass down. Whalen sat down next to him.

"Why don't you start at the beginning?"

"There isn't anything to tell," Jeff said slowly, making an effort to keep himself under control. "I was up in our room waiting for Max. He was going to secure the boat for the night—he shouldn't have been more than ten minutes. After forty-five minutes I looked for him in the bar over there, then went down to the wharf. The boat was gone. I didn't believe it at first, but then there was a bolt of sheet lightning and the whole harbor lit up. And I saw *Osprey*. She was heading out of the harbor, right toward the rocks—" He broke off, seeing the explosion once more, hearing the dull booming sound, watching the trawler burn. He struggled with himself and regained the composure that had nearly collapsed. "I have to go out there," he said dully. "I have to go out and look for Max."

"You aren't going anywhere tonight, son, and neither is anyone else," Whalen said emphatically. "No sense having two boats piled up on those rocks."

Doc Phelps arrived then, and immediately began examining Jeff Horton. While he bent over the young man, Whalen turned his attention to Merle Glind.

"Who is he?" he asked Glind quietly.

"His name's Jeff Horton," Glind said. "He checked in about five thirty, six o'clock. He's from Port Angeles." Glind frowned, as if remembering something. "Didn't Chip call you? I was sure he did."

"He called me," Whalen said patiently. "But that didn't mean this was one of the same guys he told me about. Did you hear what Horton just told me?"

Glind bobbed his head. "Not that I was eavesdropping, mind you. You know me, Harney—I'd never try to listen in on something that's none of my business. But he is a guest in my hotel and I figured—" Before he could continue, Whalen cut him off.

"Merle, it's all right. All I want to know is if you can verify any of his story."

Glind thought hard and finally nodded. "I can verify the time he went out. I was sitting with Chip and I was facing the door. I saw him stick his head in and look around. Then he went out and about five minutes later, maybe less, the explosion happened. He couldn't have had anything to do with it, Harn. There wasn't enough time. It'd take any boat a lot longer than that to get from the wharf to the rocks."

"You don't say," Whalen said, scowling at the little man. Merle flushed and his glance darted toward the bar.

"I'd better be getting back to business," Glind said anxiously. "Likely to be a lot of customers in here tonight. Not every night we have excitement like this." Rubbing his hands together in anticipation of the cash he expected to see flowing over the bar this evening, he hurried away. Whalen watched him go and shook his head sadly, pitying the fussy little fellow who tried so hard to fit in—and failed so miserably. But Whalen forgave him his shortcomings: he and Merle Glind had grown up together.

He was about to ask Dr. Phelps about Jeff Horton's condition when Chip Connor waved to him. He and Glen Palmer had been talking near the registration counter. Whalen looked inquiringly at Chip.

"Do you need me for anything?" Chip asked him. "If you don't, I thought I'd run Glen home. He's afraid his wife will be worrying about him."

"Well, she's just going to have to worry awhile longer, I'm afraid," Whalen said, his voice hard, uncompromising. "I have a few questions to ask you, Palmer."

Glen started to argue, then changed his mind. An argument would only make Whalen determined to keep him even longer. Instead, he turned to Chip.

"I know it's a hell of a thing to ask, but do you think you could run out there anyway, just to let her know I'm all right?"

"No problem," Chip said. "Unless Harn has something pressing he wants me to take care of." He turned to the chief, and Whalen chewed his lip, thinking. Finally he nodded curtly.

"All right, but don't be gone all night. I'm going to need you later."

"I'll be back in half an hour," he promised. He went to the bar, and returned a minute later with his raincoat. "Anything special you want me to tell her?" he asked Glen. Glen shook his head.

"Just tell her what's happened and not to worry. Tell her I'll be home when I get there."

Chip nodded and went out into the storm. Glen

waited until he was gone, then went over to Whalen, who was talking to Dr. Phelps.

"Shall we get started?" he asked as amiably as he could. "I'd just as soon not be here all night. It's been a long day."

"I'll bet it has," Whalen replied. "It's likely to be a lot longer before it's over. Why don't you have a seat. I'll get to you when I get to you."

"Is it all right if I wait in the bar?" Glen asked.

"Suit yourself. Just don't try to leave the hotel."

Glen chose to ignore the veiled threat, and nodded briefly. He ordered a beer and prepared to drink it slowly. He was going to have a long wait.

Rebecca Palmer sat by the fireplace and tried to concentrate on her knitting, but she was unable to complete more than a stitch or two before she set her work aside and went to the window once more, straining to see beyond the wet blackness of the rain and the wind.

It had been almost an hour and a half since Glen had left the cabin, and he should have been back at least an hour ago. She had stayed by the window after he left, and fifteen minutes later had seen his flashlight, dim but distinct, going steadily on and off. She had relaxed then and waited for him to return, sure she had read his signal correctly. But then—she wasn't sure how much later—she had heard the explosion and run to the window to see the ball of fire far beyond the beach. There had been a second explosion, a second fireball, and a blaze out at sea.

Since then, nothing.

Innumerable trips to the window.

Impulses to go out on the beach and search for Glen.
Attempts to concentrate on her knitting.

And a continually growing fear.

Something had happened. She didn't know why, but she was sure the explosions at sea had something to do with Glen's protracted absence. But what?

It was the not knowing that was the worst. If only they had a telephone. If only the storm weren't so bad. If only the children were old enough to stay by themselves. But there was no phone, the storm showed no signs of abating, and the children could not be left alone. Even the puppy was too young to serve as a guardian.

She was about to go to the window again when she thought she heard a car door slam. She froze where she was, listening intently. Then came the knock at the door.

Rebecca felt her heart begin to pound as she went to the door, but before she reached out to pull it open, something in her mind rang a warning bell.

"Who is it?" she called softly, not wanting to wake the children.

"Chip Connor," came the reply. Rebecca threw open the door and stared up at the deputy, her fear growing.

"What is it?" she cried. "What's happened?"

"Nothing's happened, Mrs. Palmer. Well, nothing's happened to Glen, anyway. May I come in?"

Rebecca felt the tension she had been under suddenly release; her knees felt weak. "Of course," she said, stepping back to make room for the deputy. She closed the door after him, then went to the fire. She poked it, then turned to Chip.

"What's happened? Where's Glen?"

"He's fine, Mrs. Palmer. He asked me to come out here and tell you he's all right. He'll be back as soon as he can." He saw the look of bewilderment on Rebecca's face and decided he'd better explain things. Fast. "There was an accident. We still don't know exactly what happened," he began, but Rebecca cut him off.

"An accident?" she said dazedly. "What kind of accident? Was it that fire? I saw a fire out in the water. Was that it?"

Chip nodded. "That's it. A boat that was tied up in the harbor for the night wound up on the rocks in the mouth of the harbor. It blew up."

"My God," Rebecca breathed. "Was anyone hurt?"

"Someone may have been on the boat. We don't know for sure yet. Anyway, when I got to the wharf Glen was already there. He saw as much of what happened as anybody. So Whalen asked him to stick around for a while." Chip saw no point in telling Rebecca that her husband had been ordered to stay at the scene, not invited.

"Thank God," Rebecca sighed. "You don't have any idea of how worried I was. He should have been back, and then I saw those awful explosions, and—" she stopped talking when she saw the expression on Chip's face.

"You mean he wasn't here when the explosions happened?" he asked.

"No, of course not," Rebecca said. "Didn't he tell you?"

"He didn't tell me much of anything," Chip replied. "Where was he?"

"He'd gone down the beach to check on the old house—the one the Randalls are going to move into. Missy—our daughter—thought there was someone in the house this afternoon, so Glen went down to check on it. He must have seen the explosions from there and gone to the wharf."

"How long was he gone? Before the explosions, I mean?"

"I'm not sure," Rebecca began. Then she realized what Chip was getting at. "My God, you don't think Glen had anything to do with those explosions, do you?"

"Of course not," Chip said immediately. "But I want you to tell me exactly what happened." He got out a notebook and a pencil, then saw the look of fear in Rebecca's eyes, the same fear he had seen in Glen's eyes earlier. He smiled at her reassuringly. "Mrs. Palmer, you don't have to answer any of my questions if you don't want to. But I hope you will. I want to put down in this notebook, right now, everything you can remember about what you and Glen talked about, why he went out, what time he went out—everything. I'm absolutely sure that everything you tell me will match up exactly with what Glen tells Harn Whalen. And then I'll be able to back him up, because I'll have the same story from you before you and Glen could possibly have talked to each other."

Rebecca turned it over in her mind and tried to figure out what Glen would want her to do. She remembered Glen talking about this man, telling her he'd spent most of the day helping him—helping *them*. Now here he was, volunteering to help them again.

Or was he? She gazed into his eyes, trying to read his motives.

His eyes were clear.

"My name's Rebecca," she said softly. "Glen told me about what you did today. I want to thank you."

Chip flushed and kept his eyes on the pad. "It's okay," he said. "I had a good time doing it." Then he looked up at her. "What about the questions? Will you answer them?"

"Of course," Rebecca said. "Where shall we start?"

The third beer was sitting untouched in front of Glen when Harney Whalen stepped through the door to the bar and called him.

"Palmer, you want to come in here now?"

Glen slid off his stool, and went into the lobby. Dr. Phelps had left, after concluding that Jeff Horton was suffering from a mild case of shock that would pass before morning. The doctor had assured Whalen that there was nothing about the young fisherman's condition that would make it inadvisable for Harn to question him, and Whalen was in the final stages of doing just that. As Glen appeared in the lobby he looked up.

"I want you and Horton here to come down to the station. We might just as well fill out the official reports tonight, while everything's still fresh in your memories."

Glen grinned wryly, and said, "I'm not sure anything's still fresh in my memory. I've been drinking beer for almost an hour." Then he glanced around the room and his grin faded. "Where's Connor?"

"He hasn't come back yet," Whalen informed him. "You ready?"

Glen shrugged, as if to imply that he had no choice, then followed Jeff Horton and Harn Whalen to Whalen's black-and-white. Minutes later they were in the police station.

"Okay, Palmer," Whalen said without preamble, "let's have it."

"Have what?" Glen asked. "I'm afraid you've kept me around all night for nothing. I don't have any idea what happened."

"Maybe you'd like to tell me about how you happened to be on the wharf?"

"I saw the explosions and ran to the harbor. Then I saw this fellow at the end of the dock. I went out to see if he needed any help. That's all there was to it."

Whalen studied him through narrowed eyes for a few seconds. "You sure must run fast. The wharf's a long way from your house."

"I wasn't at home," Glen said, offering no more information.

"Why don't you tell me just where you were?" Whalen growled.

"Actually I was in your house, at the other end of Sod Beach from mine. From there it isn't very far to the wharf. Just around the point, across the rocky beach and the sandbar."

Whalen's fingers drummed on the desk. He seemed to be turning something over in his mind.

"How did you happen to be the only one who went out on the wharf? Merle and Chip were both outside, but they didn't go out on the dock."

"They probably didn't see any reason to go. From

where they were standing they wouldn't have been able to see Jeff. I only saw him because he happened to be between me and the fire. If I hadn't, I would have gone to the inn. But I saw him, so I went out on the wharf."

"What the hell were you doing in my house?" Whalen said suddenly, changing the subject of the conversation so violently that for a second Glen drew a blank. Then he recovered himself.

"You might say I was doing you a favor," he said, controlling his anger. Who the hell did Whalen think he was? "My daughter thought someone was in the house this afternoon, and I thought I ought to check up. Or don't you care who goes in and out of your own property?"

"What I care about or don't care about is my own damned business, mister. Understand? Next time you think someone might have been in that house you tell me about it. Don't go snooping around on your own."

Glen felt his fury almost choking him but he held it back. "Fine," he said tightly. "But in case you're interested, which apparently you're not, someone was in that house today. And he hadn't been gone long when I arrived. There was a fire still burning in the fireplace. It had been banked, but not for long."

"You're right," Whalen said easily. "I was in the house this afternoon." Then he jerked a thumb at Jeff Horton. "You ever see him before tonight?"

"No."

"What about you, Horton? You ever see this guy before?"

"I already told you, Chief, I've never seen anybody around here before tonight. Not you, not him, not anybody. Now, for God's sake, aren't you going to do anything about my brother?"

"And I've already told you," Whalen mimicked him, "there's nothing we can do about your brother. If he was on that boat he died when it blew. If he went overboard he didn't last more than twenty minutes in the water. In ten minutes a man passes out, out there. In ten more minutes he's dead. So you'd better hope that your brother was never on that boat. And that seems pretty unlikely, since you claim the boat was headed directly for the rocks."

"What the hell are you saying?" Jeff cried.

"I'm saying that unless one of you two is lying, it looks to me like your brother got on that boat and deliberately piled himself up."

"That's a fucking lie!" Jeff yelled. "He was securing the boat for the night. Max would never do anything like that. Never!"

A slow smile came over Whalen's face. "What are you saying then? That someone killed him? Cut the boat loose? Steered it out onto that reef?"

"Something like that," Jeff replied. "I don't know why, and I don't know who, but it was something like that. But we won't know anything about it until we go out there, will we?"

"No," Whalen agreed, "we won't. Meantime, Horton, I think maybe you'd better plan on sticking around to answer some more questions. You too, Palmer."

Glen's fury finally exploded. "Are you out of your mind?" he yelled at the police chief. "You tell me right now, Whalen, am I under arrest or not?"

"You're not," Whalen said mildly, almost enjoying the other man's rage. "Not yet."

"And I damned well won't be," Palmer declared. "I had no motive, I wasn't there. Hell, I don't even know what kind of a boat it was. Dammit, Whalen, all I did was try to help out." He stalked out of the police station, half-expecting Whalen to stop him. But he didn't.

Instead, when they were alone, Whalen turned to Jeff Horton.

"I don't like what happened here tonight," he said softly, almost menacingly. "I don't like it at all. I intend to find out what happened though, and I intend to see to it that it never happens again. And once I've found out I'll expect you to get out of Clark's Harbor. I don't like strangers. They bring trouble. You've brought trouble, and your friend Palmer's brought trouble. So hang around only as long as I tell you to. Then get out. Understand?"

Jeff Horton, still numbed from the shock of what had happened, nodded mutely and told himself he wasn't hearing what he thought he had just heard. As he walked slowly back to the hotel, Jeff cursed the storm that had brought him to Clark's Harbor, cursed Clark's Harbor, and cursed Harney Whalen.

His impulse was to leave. He had no baggage, nothing. He could simply check out of the inn, walk up to the main highway, and thumb a ride north. But he knew he couldn't.

He had to stay in Clark's Harbor.

He had to find Max.

As the storm slashed rain in his face, Jeff tried to

tell himself that he would find his brother, that Max would be all right.

His guts told him he was wrong. His guts told him Max was not all right; nothing would ever be all right again.

Glen Palmer was still almost shaking with rage when he left the police station. He began walking toward the harbor before he stopped to think it out. He wondered if Rebecca might drive in to pick him up, but decided she wouldn't—she didn't like leaving the children by themselves. Then he remembered Chip Connor. The deputy still hadn't returned, but if Glen followed the road Chip might pass him and give him a lift. He turned around and began walking up Harbor Road. He had just reached the intersection with the main highway when a pair of headlights appeared from the north. Glen stepped out into the road and waved. The car pulled up beside him.

"Climb in," Chip called. "I'm so late now a few more minutes won't matter. Is Harn mad at me?"

Gratefully Glen got into the car, and as Chip made the U-turn that would take them back north, he asked the deputy for a cigarette.

"I quit a couple of years ago," he said as he lit it. "But after what just happened, I think I'm going to start again."

Chip glanced at him, then his eyes went back to the road.

"If you want to cuss Whalen out," he said, "could you wait until you're home and I'm gone?"

"What does that mean?" Glen asked.

"Ah, shit, I don't know," Chip said. Then he grinned

crookedly at Glen. "You know, it would have been a lot easier for you tonight if you hadn't gone out playing good citizen."

"Rebecca told you where I was?"

"I asked her. And don't worry, I told her she didn't have to answer any questions."

"But why did you even ask any?"

"Just in case," Chip said. He turned off the highway into the narrow drive that led to the Palmers' cabin. He pulled up as close to the little house as he could but didn't turn off the engine. "I'm not coming in. I'd better get back to town and see what Harn's got." He paused. Glen had started to get out of the car when Chip spoke again. "Glen?" Glen turned back to the deputy. "I'm not sure how to say this, but I like you and I like your wife. That's why I didn't want to hear you cuss Harney out. I know what must have happened down there, and I have a feeling it isn't over yet." He paused, suddenly unsure of himself, then plunged on. "That's why I wanted to get Rebecca's story before you talked to her. Look, try to keep cool, okay? Harney can be hard to deal with, particularly if he doesn't know you. But he's fair. I know you don't think so, but he is. Or anyway, he tries to be," Chip added, remembering the spattered paintings that morning.

Glen took a deep breath, then let it out in an even deeper sigh. "I don't know," he said finally. Then he chuckled hollowly. "But I guess I have no choice." He extended his hand to the deputy. "I'll sit tight and we'll see what happens. Thanks for the ride. And everything else too."

The two men shook hands and Glen got out of the

car. The rain had let up a little, and Glen waited until Chip had disappeared into the night before he went in.

Rebecca was waiting for him. She threw her arms around him, and hugged him tightly.

"What's happening? Dear God, Glen, what's happening here?"

"I don't know," Glen whispered gently. "But whatever it is, it doesn't have anything to do with us. Nothing at all."

He wished he was as certain of that as he had tried to sound. But something was happening, and he could feel himself and his family getting caught up in it. Without telling Rebecca, he decided to call Brad Randall in the morning.

In the tiny bedroom adjoining the main room of the cabin, Missy and Robby lay in their bunks, neither of them asleep. Robby's eyes were closed, but Missy was wide-eyed, staring at the bed above her. When she spoke her voice sounded hollow in the darkness.

"Are you all right?" she whispered.

There was a moment's silence, then Robby's voice drifted back to her. "I think so. But I've been feeling funny for a long time."

"I know," Missy said. "I had a dream." Her voice faltered, then went on. "It was scary. And I don't think I was asleep."

Robby crept down from the upper bunk and crouched by his sister. "What was it?"

"I'm not sure," the little girl said shyly. "I thought you were in it, but you seemed big. Real big. And not like you."

Robby frowned and waited for Missy to continue. When she remained silent he asked a question.

"Was I . . . all right? Or was I sick again?"

"You were . . ." Missy began, but broke off when she couldn't find the right words. She started again. "You were making things happen. You made a boat sink and you laughed. At least I think it was you. Maybe it wasn't," she added hopefully.

Robby shook his head in the darkness. "I don't remember anything," he said vaguely. "I couldn't sleep and I wanted to go outside."

"Why didn't you?" Missy asked.

"You would have told Mom and Dad," Robby said matter-of-factly. He climbed back up into the top bunk.

Again there was a silence, and the two children listened to the storm howling outside.

"I wish it would stop," Missy said quietly.

"I do too," Robby agreed.

Suddenly, without any warning, the rain stopped and the wind died.

Silence fell over Sod Beach.

BOOK THREE

Storm Dancers

18

Elaine Randall was staring disconsolately at the dishes stacked on the kitchen counter. There seemed to be so many of them, now that they had been taken out of the cupboard, that she couldn't decide whether to pack them in a box to be taken to Clark's Harbor or to haul them down to the large storeroom in the basement where most of their personal effects were going to be stored while they were gone. Finally she evaded the issue entirely by turning her attention to the pots and pans. Those were easy—the old, battered ones went with them, the good ones stayed behind. She was about to begin packing what seemed to her like the ninety-fifth box when the telephone rang. Gratefully, she straightened up and reached for the phone.

"I'll get it," Brad called from the living room, where he was filling cartons with books.

"Some people get all the breaks," Elaine muttered loudly enough so she was sure Brad heard her.

"Hello?" Brad said automatically as he picked up the receiver.

"Brad? Is that you? It's Glen Palmer."

"Hi!" Brad exclaimed warmly. "What's up?"

There was a slight hesitation, then Glen's voice came over the line once more, but almost haltingly.

"Look, are you people still planning to move out here?"

"Imminently," Brad replied. "I'm packing books and Elaine's working on the kitchen. Sort of a last vestige of sexism, you might say." When the joke elicited no response, not even the faintest chuckle, Brad frowned slightly. "Is something wrong out there?"

"I don't know," Glen replied slowly. "A boat cracked up on the rocks out here last night."

"Last night? But it was calm and clear last night."

"Not in Clark's Harbor, it wasn't. We had a hell of a storm."

Brad's brows rose in puzzlement, but then he shrugged. "Well, anybody who goes out in 'a hell of a storm' deserves to go on the rocks," he said complacently.

"Except that nobody knows how the boat got there. Your landlord seems to think I had something to do with it."

"You? What gave him that idea?"

"I don't know. I don't know anything anymore." There was a silence, then Glen's voice went on, hesitantly, almost apologetically. "That's why I called you. Everything seems crazy out here and I didn't have anyone else to talk to. How long before you'll be coming out?"

"Not long," Brad said. "Today, in fact."

"Today?" There was an eagerness in Glen's voice that Brad found disturbing.

"We're packing up the last of our stuff. The truck should be here around noon. I'd say we should be there somewhere around four, maybe five o'clock."

"Well, I guess I won't crack up by then," Glen said, but his voice shook slightly. "I hate to tell you this, Brad, but something horrible is going on out here."

"You make it sound like some kind of conspiracy," Brad said, his curiosity whetted. "You sure you're not letting your imagination get the best of you?"

"I don't know," Glen said. "How many times have I said that? Look, do me a favor, will you? Come see me this afternoon or this evening? If I'm not at the gallery I'll be at home."

"I'd planned on it anyway," Brad assured him. "And look, don't get yourself too upset. Whatever's happening, I'm sure there's a reasonable explanation."

"Well, I'm glad you're sure. All right, no sense running this call up any higher. See you later."

As Brad said good-bye he realized Elaine was standing in the archway that separated the living room from the dining room, a curious expression on her face.

"What's going on? Who was that?"

"Glen Palmer."

"What did he want?"

"I'm not really sure," Brad mused. "He's all upset about something. A boat went on the rocks last night and Glen seems to think Harney Whalen wants to blame it on him."

"I didn't know Glen even had a boat."

"It wasn't his boat apparently." He shrugged, and began packing books again. "I told him we'd be out there this afternoon, so he didn't go into the details. But he sure sounded upset."

Elaine stayed where she was and watched Brad work. Then she moved to the living-room window and stared out at Seward Park and the lake beyond. "I wonder if we're making a mistake," she said, not turning around.

"A mistake?" Brad's voice sounded concerned. Elaine faced him, letting him see the worry on her face.

"It just seems to me that maybe we shouldn't go out there. I mean, there really isn't any reason why you can't write here, is there? Certainly our view is as good as the view from the beach, and you don't have to be bothered with interruptions. A lot of people manage to live like hermits in the middle of the city. Why can't we?"

"I suppose we could," Brad replied. "But I don't want to. Besides, maybe something *is* going on out there."

"If there is I don't want any part of it," Elaine said with a shudder.

"Well, I do. Who knows? Maybe I'll get a best seller out of this whole deal."

"Or maybe you'll just get a lot of trouble," Elaine said. But she realized that there was going to be no argument. Brad's mind was made up, and that was that. So she winked at him, tried to put her trepidations out of her mind, and went back to her packing.

She finished in the kitchen at the same time Brad sealed the last carton of books. As if on cue the truck that would move them to Clark's Harbor pulled into the driveway.

Jeff Horton stayed in bed as long as he could that morning, but by ten o'clock he decided it was futile and got up. It had been a night of fitful sleep disturbed by visions of the fire, and through most of the small hours he had lain awake, trying to accept what had happened, trying to find an explanation. But there was none.

Max had been securing the boat. That was all.

He wouldn't have taken her out. Not alone, and certainly not in a storm.

But he must have been on the boat or he would have come to the inn.

If he was on the boat, why did it go on the rocks? Why didn't he start the engines?

There was only one logical answer to that: the engines had been tampered with. But by whom? And why? They were strangers here; they knew no one. So no one here would have any reason to sabotage the boat.

None of it made any sense, but it had cost Jeff dearly. His brother was gone, his boat was gone, and he felt helpless.

Several times during the night he had gone to the window and tried to peer through the darkness, tried to make himself see *Osprey* still tied up at the wharf, floating peacefully in the now-calm harbor. But when morning came Jeff avoided the window, postponing the moment when he would have to face the bleak truth of the empty slip at the dock.

Merle Glind peered at him dolefully when he went downstairs, as if he were an unwelcome reminder of something better forgotten, and Jeff hurried out of the inn without speaking to the little man. He paused on the porch and forced himself to look out over the harbor.

Far in the distance the mass of rocks protruded from the calm surface of the sea, looking harmless in the morning sunlight.

There was no sign of the fishing trawler that had gutted itself on them only hours ago.

Seeing the naked rocks, Jeff felt a surge of hope. Then his eyes went to the wharf, and there was the empty slip, silent testimony to the disappearance of *Osprey*. Jeff walked slowly down to the pier, to the spot where the trawler should have been moored. He stood there for a long time, as if trying by the force of his will alone to make the trawler reappear. Then he heard a voice behind him.

"She's gone, son," Mac Riley said softly. Jeff turned around and faced the old man.

"I warned you," Riley said, his voice gentle and without a trace of malice. "It's not safe, not when the storms are up."

"It wasn't the storm," Jeff said. "I don't care how bad that storm was, those lines didn't give way. Someone threw them."

Riley didn't argue. Instead, his eyes drifted away from Jeff, out to the mouth of the harbor. "Sort of seems like the wreck should still be there, doesn't it?" he mused. Before Jeff could make any reply, the old man continued, "That's the way she is, the sea. Sometimes she throws ships up on the rocks, then leaves them there for years, almost like she's trying to warn you. But not here. Here she takes things, and she keeps them. Reckon that'll be the way with your boat. Wouldn't be surprised if nothing ever turns up."

"There's always wreckage," Jeff said. "It'll turn up somewhere."

"If I were you I'd just go away and forget all about it," Riley said. "Ain't nothing you can do about it, son. Clark's Harbor ain't like other places. Things work different here."

"That's just what the police chief said last night," Jeff said angrily. "What do you mean, things work different here?"

"Just that. It's the sea, and the beach. The Indians knew all about it, and they thought this was a holy place. I suppose we do too. Strangers have to be careful here. If you don't know what you're doing, bad things happen. Well, I guess you know about that, don't you?"

"All I know," Jeff said doggedly, "is that my boat's wrecked and my brother's missing."

"He's dead, son. If he was on that boat he's dead." There was no malice in Riley's voice; it was simply a statement of fact.

"If his body turns up then he's dead," Jeff replied. "As long as there's no body he isn't dead."

"Suit yourself," Riley said. "But if I were you I'd just head on back to wherever you came from and start over again. And stay away from Clark's Harbor."

He reached out and patted Jeff on the shoulder, but Jeff drew angrily away.

"I'm going to find out what happened," he said.

"Maybe you will, son," Riley said placidly. "But I wouldn't count on that. Best thing to do is learn to live with it, like all the rest of us."

"I can't," Jeff said almost inaudibly. "I have to know what happened to my brother."

"Sometimes it's better not to know," Riley replied. "But I guess you can't understand that, can you?"

"No, I can't."

"You will, son. Someday, maybe not very far down the road, you'll understand."

The old man patted him on the shoulder once more and started back toward shore. Then he turned, and Jeff thought he was going to say something else, but he seemed to change his mind. Wordlessly, he continued on his way.

Jeff stayed on the wharf awhile longer, then began walking south along the narrow strip of beach that bordered the harbor. Somewhere, parts of *Osprey* must have been washed ashore. If he was lucky, one of those parts might offer some clue.

The storm of the night before had left a layer of silt on the beach, washed down from the forest above. Wet and thick, it clung to Jeff's boots as he trod slowly out to the end of the southern arm of the harbor. Nowhere did he find even a trace of wreckage. He hadn't really expected to. If there was going to be anything it would probably be north, taken out by the ebbing tide, then carried up the coast on the current. But from the end of the point he would have a good view of the rocks. Perhaps something would be visible from there that couldn't be seen from the wharf.

There was nothing, only the black and glistening crags of granite, clearly visible and unthreatening in the calm sea. Nowhere was there a sign of the damage they had wreaked the night before, nowhere a scrap of the boat that had broken up on them.

Jeff lingered on the point for a while, almost as if his proximity to the scene of the disaster would somehow help him to determine what had happened. But the reef merely mocked him, taunting him with its look of innocence.

After thirty minutes he turned away and started back along the beach.

He didn't go out to the end of the sand spit at the north end of the harbor. Instead he followed the worn path that cut across it to the rock-strewn cove beyond. Jeff explored the small beach carefully, inspecting pieces of driftwood that appeared to have been brought to shore the night before, his eyes carefully searching for any familiar object, any broken piece of flotsam that might be part of the vanished trawler. Again there was nothing.

Finally he rounded the point and stood at the southernmost tip of Sod Beach. For the first time his eyes stopped searching the shore at his feet and took in the beauty of the spot. It seemed incongruous to him that something as magnificent as this could be here, in the middle of such deadly surroundings. The beach lay bathed in sunlight, and the surf, free to wash the shore here, had cleaned away the silt that covered the harbor sands. Only a haphazard scattering of driftwood gave evidence of the storm that had battered the coast the night before, and even that, strewn evenly over the beach, only enhanced the beauty and peace of the place.

Jeff began walking the beach, no longer really looking for wreckage from *Osprey*. The splendor of the white sands had overcome him, and for the moment he forgot about the previous night and let its serenity wash over him. He picked up a small stone and threw it expertly at one of the logs that lay along the tide line, then laughed out loud as the tiny brown shape of a baby otter sprang out from behind it, peered vacantly at him for a moment, and began scurrying toward the woods.

He began running, and the running felt good, felt free. He could feel the tension he had been under releasing itself as he ran and pushed himself harder. When he felt his breath grow short and his heart begin to pound, he slowed to a trot, then gave it up entirely and sat panting on a log, facing the surf.

He had been staring at the object floating in the water for several seconds before he even realized he was watching it. It was about thirty yards out and nearly submerged; all that showed above the surface was a grayish mass, gleaming wetly in the sunlight. At first Jeff thought it was a piece of driftwood, but as the surf carried it slowly shoreward he realized it was something else. It looked like canvas. Jeff stood and advanced toward the water, straining for a better view of it, sure that it was from *Osprey*.

The object washed back and forth, but finally a large breaker rolled in, caught it up, and threw it forward. Jeff dashed into the surf, his outstretched hands reaching to grasp it.

He had a firm grip on it before he realized it was Max.

The body, limp and grayish, was suspended under the sodden life preserver. Without thinking, Jeff grasped his brother under the arms and pulled him up onto the beach, far beyond the reach of the surf, and lay him gently on his back.

He wrestled with the straps of the life jacket, tugging at swollen strips of material, forcing them loose.

Then he cast the preserver aside and pressed violently on Max's chest. A stream of water gushed from between the lips of the corpse, and there was a faint gurgling sound as the water was replaced by air when Jeff released the pressure.

Feverishly, he worked over his brother's body. He knew Max was dead, yet his mind refused to accept the fact. Over and over he applied pressure to the torso, but after the first efforts no more water appeared. Max lay limp and unresponding on the sand.

Jeff gave it up finally and crouched on his haunches next to his brother, staring down into the open, unseeing eyes. When he could stand it no longer he gently closed the eyelids. For the rest of his life he would live with the memory of Max's eyes, staring up at him from the sand, almost reproachful.

Jeff began to cry, his sobs shaking him, his tears flowing freely. And then, a few minutes later, it was over.

Jeff Horton picked up his brother's body, cradling it in his arms, and began to walk back down Sod Beach, back toward Clark's Harbor.

A few minutes later the beach was empty once more, except for the gulls wheeling overhead and the baby otter playing in the driftwood. All was peaceful.

But far out to sea, beyond the horizon, the clouds began to gather and the wind began to blow. Another storm was coming to life.

19

"How much farther?" Elaine asked.

"Five miles? Ten? Something like that," Brad answered. "Please note that it isn't raining."

"Noted," Elaine said. By rights they should have run into the storm that had battered Clark's Harbor the night before, and Elaine had made a bet with Brad that they would make the entire drive out to Clark's Harbor in a downpour. But as they swung around Olympia and started west, they encountered nothing but clear skies, and for the last two hours they had been enjoying the warmth of a spring sun. A ground layer of mist lay in the valleys, intertwined with the ferns and salal that blanketed the area in a spectrum of greens, broken by the brown trunks of the giant cedars and the silvery whiteness of budding aspens. Here and there a rhododendron was bursting with color, the sunlight flashing in the raindrops caught in its petals.

"You want to pay off now or wait till we get there?"

"I'll wait," Elaine said complacently. "You never know when it might cloud up. If there's even a drop of rain while we're unloading, I win."

Brad glanced up at the clear blue sky, and grinned.

"I can't lose." He glanced in the rearview mirror, as he had every few minutes for the last three and a half hours, checking to make sure the truck was still following behind them. "I can't believe how much stuff they jam in those trucks," he commented.

"I can't believe how much stuff we're dragging with us," Elaine replied archly. "The house out here *is* furnished as I recall."

Brad shrugged indifferently but couldn't keep himself from flushing slightly. As the movers had begun loading Brad had begun adding things to the load. His desk and chair had been first, followed by an ancient leather-upholstered club chair that Elaine had claimed would fit in perfectly since it was nearly as dilapidated as the furniture already in the house on Sod Beach.

When he had started to add the television and stereo console, Elaine had drawn the line, reminding him that there was no electricity in their new home.

Finally they had been ready to go; the truck was almost full and the storage room in the basement almost empty. But, as Brad kept insisting, at least they were getting their money's worth out of the truck.

They swung around a bend in the road. They were almost in Clark's Harbor. Ahead of them they could see the intersection with Harbor Road and, just beyond, Glen Palmer's gallery.

"Are we stopping at the gallery?" Elaine asked as Brad began slowing the car.

"I thought I'd stop off at the police station first and pick up the key," Brad replied. "Then you can ride on out to the house in the truck and supervise the unloading while I talk to Glen."

"The hell you will," Elaine protested. "If you think I'm going to try to get all that junk into the house by myself, you're crazy! Besides, I want to see Glen too!"

"All right, all right," Brad said. He completed the turn and they started down the gentle incline into the village. "Well, whatever's going on, it certainly looks peaceful enough."

Elaine couldn't disagree; Clark's Harbor, basking in the sunlight, lay clustered peacefully around the harbor, its brightly painted buildings sparkling against the backdrop of blue sky and water. Once again Elaine was reminded of a New England fishing village, an image enhanced by the small fleet that was neatly moored at the wharf.

They pulled up in front of the police station and Brad told the truck driver to find someplace to park the truck for a few minutes without blocking traffic. Then he and Elaine went inside.

They found Harney Whalen in his office talking on the telephone. He looked up, stared at them in apparent surprise, then returned to his telephone call. Elaine lit a cigarette and occupied herself by peering uncomfortably out the window. But Brad made no attempt to conceal the fact that he was listening to Whalen's end of the conversation.

"I'm telling you," Whalen was saying, "there isn't any point in your coming up here. It was an accident, nothing more. There's nothing to investigate. Not even a trace of wreckage has washed up. Only the body."

He listened then, his eyes on the ceiling, almost closed, as if whatever he was hearing was hardly worth listening to.

"Listen," he said finally, apparently interrupting

whoever was on the other end of the line. "I looked the body over, and Doc Phelps looked the body over. Now, I'm no expert, but Phelps is. And we both agree the guy drowned. Looks like the guy went overboard when the boat cracked up. Hell, nobody can last long in the water this time of year."

He seemed about to say more but fell silent again, and Brad assumed that whoever he was talking to was objecting to something Whalen had said.

"Well, anyway, I'm gonna ship the body up to Port Angeles tomorrow. The guy's brother's hanging around getting on everyone's nerves, and I've just about had it with the whole thing. So if you want to do anything—look at the body or something—you'd better do it today."

Just then the door to the police station opened and a young man Brad didn't recognize came in. Whoever he was, he was not a native of Clark's Harbor. He seemed very upset—his face was flushed and his eyes flashed with anger. He glanced at Brad and Elaine, then turned his attention to the police chief, who was still on the phone. As he listened, Harney Whalen watched the young man pace the small room impatiently. In his mind Brad put it all together and decided this was the brother of the dead man, and that he had stumbled into the "something horrible" Glen Palmer had been talking about on the phone that morning.

"All right, all right," Whalen said at last. "I'll wait till you get here." He slammed the receiver down and stared balefully at the young man.

"What is it now, Horton?" he said levelly.

Jeff Horton stopped pacing and stood squarely in

front of Whalen's desk, glaring at the police chief.

"Who the hell do you think you are?" he demanded.

"I think I'm the police chief here," Whalen said easily, enjoying the young man's discomfiture. "What of it?"

"That gives you the right to decide what's to be done with my brother's body?"

"You heard?"

"I heard. And I'd like to know why you didn't tell me you were releasing it. I can get it home myself."

"Fine," Whalen replied, getting to his feet. "I just thought I'd save you the trouble."

"Save me the trouble!" Jeff exclaimed. His face turned scarlet and his fists began working spasmodically. "I don't need anybody to save me any trouble. I need someone to help me find out what happened to Max." Then, as suddenly as his face had turned scarlet, it drained of color and became an ashen gray. Brad stood up and moved to the young man's side.

"Sit down," he said gently but firmly. When Jeff started to resist, Brad took his arm. "If you don't sit down, you're going to pass out," he said. He pushed Jeff into the chair he had just vacated and made him put his head between his knees. "If you start feeling like you're going to be sick, lie down on the floor. You'll feel foolish but it's better than throwing up. Now breathe deeply."

Brad turned his attention to Whalen. "What's going on?" he asked.

"It's between him and me," Whalen declared. "It doesn't have anything to do with you."

"I'm a doctor and this fellow's not in the best shape. I'm just wondering why."

"And I'm telling you it's none of your concern," Whalen snapped.

"Whose concern should it be?" Jeff said, sitting up again. He looked at Brad. "Who are you?"

"Brad Randall," Brad said, extending his right hand. "I'm a doctor from Seattle. I take it it's your brother who died?"

Jeff nodded. "This guy keeps claiming it was an accident but I don't believe it. And now he's made plans to ship Max home and he didn't even tell me about it."

"Max, I assume, is your brother. Mind telling me your name?"

"Jeff. Jeff Horton."

"Fine, Jeff. Now, what happened?"

But before Jeff could tell him, Harney Whalen interrupted. "This your office all of a sudden, Dr. Randall?" he said unpleasantly. " 'Cause you're sure acting like it is."

Brad bit his lip. "Sorry," he said. "It isn't any of my business, of course. But Jeff seems pretty upset, and dealing with people who are upset happens to be my specialty." When Jeff looked at him quizzically, Brad winked. "I'm a psychiatrist."

Elaine stood up suddenly, and the movement caught Brad's attention, exactly as she had intended.

"Why don't I take Jeff out for a cup of coffee while you settle our business with the chief?" she suggested. "All right?"

Brad knew immediately his wife was trying to defuse the situation. He smiled at her gratefully. "If you don't mind," he said, knowing she didn't; knowing, in fact, that she had taken the situation in hand.

"Of course I don't mind." She turned to Whalen and smiled at him. "Is there anything I'll need to know about the house right away?"

Whalen shook his head slowly, glancing from one of the Randalls to the other and back again. But before he could speak Elaine plunged on.

"Fine. Then we'll see you in a few minutes," she told Brad. She took Jeff Horton by the arm and pulled him to his feet. Jeff, looking baffled, offered no resistance as she led him from the office.

"Do you have the keys?" she heard Brad asking Whalen as she walked down the corridor. She silently congratulated herself. Maybe the wrong member of their family was the psychiatrist.

"It hasn't been easy for you, has it?" Elaine asked Jeff. They were sitting in the café, drinking their second cup of coffee, and Jeff had told Elaine what had happened.

"That's putting it mildly," Jeff said bitterly. "The worst of it is, I'm not going to be able to hang around here any longer, and the minute I leave that police chief is going to drop the whole thing. Hell, he almost has already."

"It might really have been an accident," Elaine offered.

"If it were anyone but Max, I'd agree. But Max was one of those people who just doesn't have accidents. He was always methodical, always careful. He always said there's no such thing as an accident. Like the other night, when the storm caught up with us? Anyone else would have tried to make it down to Grays Harbor, and if they hadn't made it, it would have been called an accident. But Max would have called it damned foolishness and blamed it on the skipper."

"And he would have been right," Elaine agreed.

"For all the good it did him. Anyway, *Osprey* couldn't have slipped her moorings by accident. Somebody cast her lines off the dock, but I can't get that police chief to do anything about it. It's like he just doesn't care."

"I don't think he does," Elaine said softly. Before Jeff could ask what she meant she changed the subject. "What are you going to do now?"

"Go back up north, I guess, and start over. But without Max it isn't going to be easy."

"Can't you stay here awhile?"

"I'm broke. I can pay for one more night at the hotel and that's it. But I want to stay and find out what happened to Max." He looked deeply into Elaine's eyes and his voice took on an intensity that almost frightened her.

"Somebody killed Max, Mrs. Randall. I don't know who, but somebody killed him. I have to find out why."

Elaine studied the young man opposite her and tried to weigh what he had said. Still in shock, she thought, and badly shaken up. Yet what he had said made sense. If his brother had been as careful as Jeff claimed —and she had no reason to doubt it—then it seemed unlikely that the trawler's getting loose had been an accident. And if it wasn't an accident . . .

"Look," she said suddenly. "If it's that important for you to stay around here for a while, you can stay with us. It's primitive, but it's free."

"With you?" Jeff seemed totally bewildered. "But you don't even know me."

Elaine smiled warmly at him. "If you hadn't said that I might have been worried. Anyway, that makes us even: you don't know us, either. Believe me, after a couple of days we'll know each other very, very well. The house we rented isn't big and it doesn't have any electricity. I'm told the plumbing works but I'll believe it when I see it. There's a couple of bedrooms upstairs, guest rooms, and you might as well be the first guest." Before Jeff could reply Elaine glanced at her watch and stood up. "Come on, we've been here long enough. If Brad isn't through with Mr. Whalen yet, something's gone wrong. And the movers must think we've died."

"Movers?"

"I told you we were just moving in. That was a sort of a lie, really. We haven't moved in yet. As a matter of fact, we just got to town half an hour ago."

Taking Jeff by the arm, she led him out the door.

They almost bumped into Brad as they turned the corner onto Main Street, and Elaine knew by the look on his face that something was wrong. "What's happened?" she asked.

Brad stared at her blankly for a moment, then chuckled hollowly. "You won't believe it," he said. "Whalen didn't remember renting the house to us."

"Didn't remember? Are you serious?"

Brad nodded. "That's why he looked so surprised when we walked into his office. He thought we were gone for good. I had to show him the lease before he'd give me the keys to the house. I guess we were right when we thought he was in some kind of trance the day he showed us the place." He saw Elaine turn slightly pale and decided now was not the time to pursue the subject. Instead, he made himself smile genially at Jeff Horton. "I assume Elaine invited you to stay with us?"

"If it's all right with you, Dr. Randall."

"My name's Brad, and of course it's all right with me. If she hadn't invited you I would have. We'd better get going though, or the movers are going to dump our stuff in the street. Whalen'll lead us out there, just to make sure the place is all right."

As if on cue, Harney Whalen emerged from the police station and stared balefully at the three of them. When he spoke his words were obviously directed at Jeff.

"I thought you'd be on your way by now."

"I'm not going anywhere," Jeff said softly. "Not till I find out what happened to my brother."

Whalen's tongue worked at his left cheek as he thought it over. "Still staying at the hotel?" he asked finally.

"He'll be staying with us," Elaine said flatly, as if to end the discussion.

"That so?" Whalen said. "Well, I guess it's none of my business, is it. You want to follow me?"

"Sure," Brad replied. He turned and signaled the movers, who were lounging against the fender of their truck half a block away. They ground their cigarettes out and climbed into the cab. "We'll be right behind you," Brad called to Whalen, who was already in his police car. Whalen's hand, black-gloved, waved an acknowledgment, but he didn't speak. Instead he simply started his engine and pulled away from the curb, his face expressionless as he passed them. The Randalls, with Jeff Horton, followed. Behind them, the moving truck closed the gap.

Harney Whalen drove the black-and-white slowly and kept his eyes steadily on the road. But he was driving automatically, guiding the car almost by instinct. His mind was in turmoil.

Jeff Horton wasn't going to go home.

Instead he was going to stay in Clark's Harbor, stirring up trouble.

And the Randalls. Where had they come from? He searched his mind, trying to remember having signed a lease.

His mind was blank. He remembered showing them the house, but as for a lease—nothing. Absolutely nothing.

More trouble.

Harney Whalen didn't like trouble. He wondered what he should do about it.

And he wondered why strangers kept coming to Clark's Harbor. It had never been a good place for strangers.

Never had been, and never would be.

20

The procession made an odd spectacle as it moved out of Clark's Harbor, the black-and-white police car leading the way with Harney Whalen at the wheel, his eyes fixed firmly on the road in front of him, an odd look on his face: a look that would have told anyone who happened to see it that Whalen's mind was far away. Behind him were the Randalls, with Jeff Horton in the back seat. Elaine made sporadic attempts at conversation, but all three of them were preoccupied with their own thoughts, and they soon fell silent. The small moving truck brought up the rear.

It's almost like some bizarre funeral cortege, Elaine was thinking. She glanced out the side window of the car and saw several people standing on the sidewalk, having left whatever they had been doing to watch the newcomers make their arrival. Their faces seemed to Elaine to be impassive, as if the arrival of the Randalls would have no effect on them whatsoever—something to be observed that would not change their lives. And yet, as she absorbed their strange impassivity, Elaine began to feel as if there was something else, some fear that they were trying to cover up. She glanced quickly at Brad, but he was concentrating on the road, unaware of the watching faces on the sidewalks. Then they turned up Harbor Road, leaving the village behind.

The procession headed north on the highway, passed Glen Palmer's gallery, and quickly disappeared around the bend that would take them close to the coastline. Harney Whalen increased his speed, and the car and truck behind him accelerated. They were cruising at the speed limit when Whalen suddenly noticed the two children in the road ahead. For a few seconds he kept up his speed, bearing down on Robby and Missy Palmer, the car hurtling forward straight toward them. Whalen felt himself freeze at the wheel, unable to move. Then, as the gap between himself and the children quickly closed, he forced his right foot off the accelerator, hit the brake, swerved, and leaned on the horn.

Missy scrambled off the pavement into the ditch almost before the sound of the horn split the air. But Robby remained in the road, turning slowly to stare at the oncoming car as if he didn't recognize that he was in danger.

"Robby!" Missy screamed. And then the horn was followed by the shrieking of tires being ripped loose from their grip on the pavement as the police car began to fishtail. Finally Robby moved.

It was a lazy movement, slow and methodical.

He stepped casually out of the path of the speeding police car, then watched idly as it skidded in a full circle, left the pavement, and came to rest on the opposite side of the street. As soon as it stopped Harney Whalen leaped from the driver's seat and started toward Robby.

Brad Randall was already bringing his car to a halt almost on the spot where the children had been. He hadn't seen anything until Whalen's brake lights had flashed on, the sound of the horn had hit him, and the police car had gone into its skid. Only at the last instant had he seen Missy leap off the road, then Robby moved slowly away from the path of the car.

"My God," he said as he brought his own car to a stop. "He damn near ran them down. Didn't he see them?"

"He must have," Elaine said. She paused a second and a strange note crept into her voice. "Those are the Palmers' children! Are they all right?"

Before Brad could answer, Elaine had scrambled out of the car and knelt beside Missy. The little girl was sobbing, and Elaine gathered her into her arms.

"It's all right. Everything's okay. Nobody's hurt."

"He did it on purpose," Missy sobbed. "He tried to run over us."

"No," Elaine purred soothingly. "Nobody did that. Nobody would want to run over you."

Then Harney Whalen was there, standing over her, his face pale, his hands shaking. "What the hell were you kids doing?" he demanded.

Elaine pulled the sobbing Missy closer to her and stared up at Whalen, her brows knitted into a scowl of anger.

"Didn't you see them?" she demanded. "They must have been right in front of you." She looked quickly around, searching for Brad, needing his support. Then she saw him crouched down next to Robby, checking the boy over. "Is he all right?" she called.

"He's fine," Brad replied. "Not a scratch on him. Just scared."

"I'm not scared," Robby replied.

"If you aren't you should be," Brad said, tousling the boy's hair. "Didn't anybody ever tell you not to walk in the street?" Then he turned to Whalen.

"Didn't you see them?" he asked, echoing Elaine's question.

"It happened so fast," Whalen said. "All of a sudden there they were."

"You must have seen them in plenty of time," Brad protested.

Whalen stiffened and glared at Brad. "Well, I didn't," he said. "But I saw them soon enough. Nobody got hurt; nobody except me even got shaken up. So that's that, isn't it?"

"Is your car okay?" Brad asked.

"It's fine," Whalen assured him. "The shoulder's almost level on that side." He started moving toward the car, but Brad stopped him.

"Don't you think we should offer the kids a ride home?"

Whalen glanced from Missy to Robby, then back to Missy.

"How about it? You two want a ride in the police car?"

Robby's face brightened immediately but Missy frowned.

"No," she said with finality.

"We can take you home," Elaine offered.

"That's all right," Missy said. "We can walk."

"Are you sure?" Elaine looked anxiously at the little girl, almost as if she thought the child should be unable to walk. Missy unconsciously pulled away from her. "We're not supposed to ride with strangers," she said carefully.

"We're not strangers," Elaine countered. Missy looked at her thoughtfully, then shook her head.

"We don't want to," she said. Her lip began to quiver, as if she were about to begin crying again.

Elaine stood up, shrugged, and sighed. "Well, if you're sure you're all right . . ." she began. She looked helplessly at Brad, but he was staying out of the situation, faintly amused by his wife's efforts with the children. Whalen, accepting Missy's decision as final, returned to his car and began maneuvering the vehicle back onto the road.

Reluctantly, Elaine followed Brad back to their car, where Jeff Horton was still sitting in the back seat. Twice she looked back at the children, but they didn't move. Robby was watching the police car, but Missy seemed not to be watching anything. It was almost as if she were waiting for something, but Elaine hadn't a clue as to what it might be. She got into the passenger seat next to Brad just as Harney Whalen finished turning the police car around. A minute later the procession was once more under way.

"He wanted to run over us," Missy said to Robby as the two cars and the truck disappeared from view.

"He didn't either," Robby replied. He glared at his sister, wishing she weren't so stubborn. "How come you didn't let us ride in the police car?"

"I don't like that man. He wants to hurt us."

"That's dumb. Why would he want to hurt us?"

"I don't know," Missy said petulantly. "But he does."

293

Robby decided not to argue the point. "Well, we could have ridden with the Randalls."

"Mommy and Daddy don't want us to ride with strangers."

"They aren't strangers. He used to be my doctor, and they're moving into the house on the beach."

"Well, I don't know them," Missy insisted. "So they're strangers." Then she looked at her brother quizzically. "How come you stayed in the street?"

"I didn't," Robby replied.

"Yes, you did. I yelled at you, and you just stood there."

Robby scratched his head thoughtfully. "I don't really remember it," he said. "It happened too fast. Anyway, I got out of the way, didn't I? I didn't just jump like a scared rabbit like *some* people did. Let's cut through the woods and go home by the beach," he suggested.

"I don't want to," Missy objected. "I don't like the beach."

"You never want to do anything," Robby said scornfully. "If you don't want to go by the beach, you can stay on the road by yourself."

Missy's eyes widened with indignation. "You can't leave me here. Mommy says we're supposed to stay together."

"But she didn't say we're always supposed to do what you want. Come on." He started across the road, but Missy stayed where she was. When he got to the other side, Robby turned around and glared at his sister.

"Are you coming, or not?"

Missy felt torn. She didn't want to go through the woods, didn't want to walk on the beach. For some reason the beach scared her, even though she knew it didn't scare Robby. Most of all, though, she didn't want to walk home by herself.

She wondered what her mother's reaction would be if she showed up by herself. Mommy might punish Robby for leaving her alone, but she also might punish Missy for not staying with her brother. She made up her mind, on the theory that being a little bit scared was better than being punished.

"Oh, all right," she said, and hurried across the highway to catch up with Robby, who was already hunting for a path into the forest.

Harney Whalen pulled as far up the narrow driveway as he could and still leave room for the Randalls and the truck to get in ahead of him. He switched off the engine but didn't leave the car immediately.

He was still bothered by what had happened. He had tried to act as if it had been the children who had been careless. But he knew they hadn't been.

He knew that he had seen them in plenty of time.

He had frozen at the wheel.

He had nearly killed them both.

And he didn't know why.

For a moment it had been very much like the few seconds before he went into one of his spells. Time seemed almost to stand still, and something happened to his muscles—he lost control of them, as if his body were a thing apart from himself, operating under its own volition.

But always before it had been all right: usually he was alone when something like that happened. Alone, where no one could get hurt.

This afternoon two children had almost been killed. He decided it was time to have the talk with Doc Phelps that he had been postponing for so long.

The decision made, he got out of the police car and walked over to the Randalls, who were waiting for him together with Jeff Horton.

"Something wrong?" Brad Randall asked him.

"I'm okay. Just thought I heard something in the engine."

Without further words, he led the way along the path that took them out of the forest and through the tangle of driftwood. He opened the kitchen door, surprised that it wasn't locked, then handed the key to Brad.

"There's only the one key," he said. "It fits both doors, and I have the only copy. If you want another one you'll have to get Blake to cut it for you."

"I doubt we'll ever lock the place," Brad said.

"Suit yourselves," Whalen said noncommittally. "City people always seem to think they're a lot safer in the country than in town. But there's nuts all over the place." His eyes went to Jeff Horton, and Jeff felt himself flush with anger, but he kept silent.

Whalen led them through the house, halfheartedly apologizing for the mess, but not offering to have it cleaned up. "Sometimes I think I ought to just tear the place down," he muttered.

"Why don't you?" Brad asked. Harney looked surprised, and Brad realized the chief hadn't intended to speak out loud.

"I don't know," Whalen mused. "Just never get around to it, I guess. Or maybe I just don't want to. I come out here every now and then. Gets me out of the house." He started to leave, then stopped and turned back to face the Randalls once more.

"I'm going to tell you folks something," he said heavily. "Clark's Harbor is an inbred town. We're all related to each other, and we don't take kindly to strangers. And it isn't just that we're not friendly. It's something else—whenever strangers come to town the whole place seems to get sort of out of whack, if you know what I mean. So don't expect things to be any good for you here. They won't be."

"Well, if we don't go looking for trouble, I can't see that it's going to come looking for us," Brad said.

"Can't you?" Whalen replied. "Better ask around, Randall. What about Horton here? He and his brother came and trouble found them in a few hours. With the Shellings it took fifteen years, but trouble found them too. And there's your friends the Palmers. They damned near had a peck of trouble just about an hour ago. Well, nothing I can say will convince you." He glanced at his watch. "Better be getting back to town. There isn't any more I can do here. The place is all yours. Rent's due on the first of every month."

Then he was gone.

"That bastard," Elaine said almost under her breath.

"Is that any way to talk about your landlord?" Brad asked. Then he chuckled. "I think he enjoys playing the voice of doom."

Jeff Horton shook his head. "I agree with your wife," he said. "He's a bastard."

Before the discussion could go any farther, a burly form appeared in the kitchen door.

"You people want this stuff unloaded, or do we take it back to Seattle?"

* * *

From their hiding place in the woods, Robby and Missy watched Brad leave the house. They had been watching everything, watching the movers haul carton after carton into the old house, watching them leave. Now Brad was leaving too.

"I thought he was going to live here," Missy said plaintively. "That's what you said."

"Well, who says he's not?" Robby asked. "He's probably just going into town for something. Why don't we go say hello to Mrs. Randall?"

"I don't want to," Missy complained. "I don't like that house."

"You always say that," Robby pointed out. "What's wrong with it?"

"I don't know. Bad things happen there. They happen all over this beach. I want to go home."

"So go home."

"Come with me."

"I don't want to. I like the beach."

"It's late," Missy pointed out. "Mommy's going to be mad at us."

"Oh, she isn't either," Robby replied. But despite his brave words, he wasn't sure that Missy wasn't right; his mother had been acting very strange lately and Robby couldn't figure out why. Ever since that woman had killed herself, his mother had seemed worried. He gave in to his sister.

"All right," he said. "Come on."

He started out of the woods but again Missy stopped him.

"Let's go through the woods for a while."

"Why?"

"This is the part of the beach where that man washed up," Missy said.

"How do you know?"

"I just *know*, that's all!"

"You don't either," Robby said angrily.

"I do too!" Missy insisted. She began walking away from her brother. "You can go that way if you want, but I'm going through the forest."

Robby decided his sister was a royal pain, but he followed her anyway, obeying his mother's edict that the two of them should stick together. A few minutes later Missy clutched his hand.

"What's wrong?" Robby asked wearily.

"I'm scared. Let's run." She tugged at Robby's arm and almost involuntarily he began running with Missy. When they were near the cabin Missy suddenly stopped.

"It's all right now," she said. "I'm not scared anymore."

"That's because we're almost home," Robby pointed out. Missy looked up, and sure enough, there was the cabin, just visible through the trees. As they walked the last few yards to the house, Missy took Robby's hand and squeezed it hard.

"Let's not go on the beach anymore," she pleaded softly.

Robby looked at her curiously, but said nothing.

Brad pulled up in front of the gallery and made sure he wasn't parked on the pavement, remembering the ticket Harney Whalen had written him the last time he had been here. Then he went to the gallery door and stuck his head in.

"Glen? You here?"

"In back," Glen called.

As he made his way to the rear of the building Brad looked around, surprised at the progress that had been made. He was even more surprised to find that Glen wasn't alone in the back room.

"You mean you finally got some help?" he asked.

Glen straightened up from the drafting table where he was working on some sketches and grinned.

"Did you meet Chip Connor when you were out here?" he asked.

The deputy put aside the saw he was holding and extended his hand to Brad. "Glad to meet you," he said with a smile. "You must be Dr. Randall."

"Brad," Brad corrected him. He gazed quizzically at Chip. "Are you on duty?"

"Not for the last hour," Chip said. "But if anybody in town wants to charge me with neglecting my duties, they could probably make it stick."

Now Brad's gaze shifted to Glen, and when he spoke he sounded genuinely puzzled.

"I don't quite understand," he said. "When you called this morning you sounded horrible. I expected to find you huddled in a corner or worse, not happily at work with the deputy sheriff." He glanced at Chip. "You *are* Whalen's deputy, aren't you?"

"Also his nephew, more or less," Chip said. As Brad shifted uncomfortably Chip's smile faded. "You want to talk to Glen alone?"

"That's up to Glen," Brad countered.

"It's all right," Glen said. "Chip knows what's been

going on. As a matter of fact, he's been helping me out with more than just this."

Brad looked at the nearly finished gallery. "It certainly seems to be coming along," he said. "Now why don't you fill me in on whatever else has been going on?"

Glen opened three cans of beer and they sat down, making themselves as comfortable as possible on the makeshift furniture. Brad listened quietly as Glen and Chip explained what had happened over the last few days, and Harney Whalen's unreasonable insinuations that Glen was somehow involved in the death of Max Horton, and possibly even Miriam Shelling's. When he was done Brad shook his head sadly.

"I don't understand that man," he said. "At first I thought he simply didn't like strangers. But I'm beginning to think it's something else. Something much more complicated—"

"More complicated?" Chip asked. "What do you mean?"

Brad didn't answer, didn't even seem to hear what Chip had asked. Instead he asked Glen an apparently irrelevant question.

"What about Robby?"

"Robby? What's he got to do with all this?"

"I don't know," Brad said, trying to sound casual. "But we know something's happened to him out here, and now things are happening to other people too."

Glen's eyes narrowed as he recognized the implication. "Are you trying to say you think Robby's involved in whatever's happening?"

"I'm not trying to say anything," Brad replied. "But

things that seem to be unrelated often aren't. I think I better have a look at Robby."

The three men fell silent. Suddenly there was nothing to say.

21

Chip Connor sat at the bar of the Harbor Inn that evening sipping slowly on a beer, trying to sort out his thoughts. He was confused and upset; things seemed to him to be getting far too complicated. He drained the beer, slammed the empty glass down on the bar, and called for another one. Merle Glind appeared next to him.

"You want a little company?" he asked, rubbing his hands together. Chip smiled at the little man.

"Sure. Let me buy you a beer."

Glind scrambled onto the stool next to Chip. He carefully added a dash of salt to the beer he had drawn, tasted it, and nodded happily.

"Nothing finishes off the day like a good salty beer," he chirped. Then he looked at Chip inquisitively. "You want to tell me what's on your mind?"

"I'm not sure anything is," Chip replied evasively.

But Merle Glind was not to be put off. "It's written all over your face. I know—I can tell. Now why don't you tell me about it?"

"There's not much to tell," Chip said uncomfortably. "It's just a bunch of things, all added together. I guess I'm worried about Harn."

"Harn? Harn Whalen?" Merle Glind's voice was filled with disbelief, as if it were incomprehensible to him that anyone could be worried about the police chief.

"That's what I said," Chip repeated sourly, but Glind seemed not to hear.

"Why, I just can't imagine that," he clucked. "There isn't anything wrong with him, is there?"

Chip shrugged, almost indifferently. "Not that I know of," he said slowly. "It's just a lot of little things."

"What kind of little things?" The innkeeper's eyes glistened with anticipation, and Chip Connor suddenly decided he didn't want to confide in Glind.

"Nothing I can put my finger on," he said. He finished the beer that had just been put in front of him and stood up. "I think I'll go for a walk. I'm probably just nervous."

"It's starting to rain out there," Glind pointed out, his lips pursing and his brows knitting as he realized he wasn't going to find out what was on Chip's mind.

"It's always starting to rain out here," Chip replied. "Or if it isn't starting, it's stopping. See you later." He tossed a couple of dollar bills on the bar and grinned as Merle scooped them up. Then he patted Glind on the shoulder and left.

It was a light rain, the misty kind of rain that makes the air smell fresh and doesn't require an umbrella. It felt cold on Chip's face, and he liked the feeling. It was almost like sea spray, but softer, gentler, almost caressing.

He started for the wharf, thinking he might check the moorings on the boats, but as he stepped out onto the pier he realized someone was already there: a small light bobbed in the darkness.

"Hello?" Chip called. The bobbing light swung around. Chip instinctively raised a hand to cover his eyes as the light blinded him.

"Chip? That you?" Chip recognized the reedy voice immediately.

"Granddad?"

"Well, it's not the bogeyman, if that's what you were expecting."

Chip hurried out onto the wharf. "What are you doing out here in the rain? You'll catch pneumonia."

"If I were going to catch pneumonia I'd have caught it years ago," Mac Riley groused. "I'm checking the boats."

Chip chuckled. "That's what I was going to do."

"Well, it's done. Everything's secure, tight as a drum." Then he frowned at Chip. "How come you were going to check? You don't usually do that."

"I was at the inn and I felt like taking a walk—"

"Something on your mind?" Riley interrupted.

"I'm not sure."

"Of course you're sure," Riley snapped. "Give me a ride home and let's talk about it. I've got some scotch that I've been saving just for a night like tonight."

"What's so special about tonight?" Chip asked.

"You. I don't get to see you as much as I'd like. Well, that's grandsons for you. Only come around when they have a problem. I can sit around jawing with Tad Corey and Clem Ledbetter all day and it doesn't do me any good at all. They think I'm a senile old man."

"You?" Chip laughed out loud. "The day you get senile will be the day you die."

"Thanks a lot," the old man said dryly. "You wanting to stand here in the rain all night, or do we get going?"

They returned to the inn, where Chip's car was parked, and drove the few blocks to Mac Riley's house in silence. "You ought to sell the house or buy a car," Chip remarked as they went into the large Victorian house that Riley had built for his bride more than sixty years earlier.

"I'm too old," Riley complained. "Can't get a driver's license, and can't learn to live anyplace else. Besides, I don't feel lonely here. Your grandmother's in this house."

As Chip's brows rose in skepticism, Riley snorted at him.

"I don't mean a ghost, or anything like that," he said impatiently. "It's just memories. When you get to be my age you'll know what I'm talking about. Every room in this house has memories for me. Your grandmother, your mother, even you. But mostly your grandmother."

They were in the tiny sitting room just off the entry hall, and Chip looked at the portrait of his grandmother that hung over the fireplace.

"She looks a lot like Harney Whalen," he commented.

"Why shouldn't she?" Riley countered. "She was his aunt."

"I know. But for some reason I never think of it that way. I always think of Harn as kissing kin, rather than blood kin."

"Around here there ain't much difference," Riley

said. He found the bottle of scotch, poured two tumblers full—no ice, no water—and handed one of them to Chip.

"That who's on your mind? Harn Whalen?"

Chip nodded and sipped at the scotch, feeling it burn as it trickled down his throat. "I'm worried about him," he said. He was thoughtful for several minutes. Then he explained, "It's a lot of little things. But mostly it's the way he feels about strangers."

"We all feel that way," Riley said. "It goes back a long time."

"But there doesn't seem to be any reason for it."

"Maybe not now," Riley replied. "But there are reasons all right. Tell me what's going on with Harney."

"He's been going after Glen Palmer."

"Palmer? I didn't know you even knew the man."

"I didn't up until a few days ago," Chip said. "The day after Miriam and Pete Shelling's funeral."

Riley nodded briefly. "I was there, with Corey and Ledbetter. Other than us and Harn Whalen, the Palmers were the only ones who came."

"That's what Harney said. He made me go out and talk to Palmer. He wanted to know why Glen was there."

"That doesn't seem unreasonable," the old man said. "Did you find out?"

"Sure. It wasn't any secret really, except Glen didn't think it was any of our business."

"In a town this size everything is everybody's business," Riley chuckled.

"Anyway," Chip went on, "Glen told me why he and his family went to the funeral, and I told Harney.

Then he did something I just can't account for at all. He tried to wreck most of Glen's work."

"Wreck it? What do you mean?"

Chip told his grandfather what had happened. "I felt rotten about it," he finished. "I stayed around and gave Glen a hand, and he's really a nice guy. I've been spending quite a bit of time with him. It's funny—he can draw anything, but put a saw in his hand and it's all over." He smiled at his grandfather. "Wait'll you see that gallery. With him designing it and me building it, it's really going to be something."

"You getting paid for it?" Riley inquired.

Chip squirmed. "Not exactly," he said. "Glen doesn't have any money right now. But I'm still getting paid. I'm finding out a lot of things I never knew about before. Nothing terribly important, I guess, but it's the first time in my life I've ever really gotten to know anyone who wasn't born right here. And the more I get to know Glen, the less I understand Harney's attitude. If he'd just take the time to get to know him too, I don't think he'd be so down on him."

"I wouldn't bet on it," Riley said.

"Well, I can understand him being suspicious of strangers, but it's getting out of hand. He won't do anything to find out what happened to that guy Horton, except that he seemed to think Glen had something to do with it—God only knows why—and the whole thing's getting to me. I keep telling myself it's only my imagination, but it seems to be getting worse. I'm thinking of quitting my job."

Riley frowned and studied his grandson. Finally he appeared to make up his mind about something.

"Maybe I'd better tell you a little about Harney," he said. "Life hasn't been too easy for him, and most of the rough times were caused by strangers. It was a long time ago, but things like what happened to Harney when he was a boy stay with a man. And sometimes the old memories are stronger than the new ones, if you know what I mean." He leaned forward confidentially. "Don't tell anybody, but sometimes I can remember things that happened sixty, seventy years ago better than I can recollect things that happened last month."

He handed his glass to Chip and asked him to refill it. While the younger man did, Riley's gaze drifted away, focused somewhere beyond the room and the rainy night. When Chip gave him the full glass, his eyes seemed to be almost closed. But as he took the glass, he began talking.

"When Harney was a boy he lived with his grandparents. His mother—your grandmother's sister—died birthing Harn, and his father took off a little after that. He came back, but he was never quite the same. So it wound up that Harn's grandparents took care of them both. Anyway, Harn's granddaddy owned a whole lot of land around here, most of it forest. He never did much with it, just sort of sat on it, but eventually some of the big lumbering boys from Seattle came out here and tried to buy it.

"Old Man Whalen wouldn't sell, so then they tried to get him to lease the timber rights to them. That didn't work either, and it looked for a while like that would be the end of it. But then something happened."

The old man stopped talking and his eyes closed

once more. For a few seconds Chip thought his grandfather had fallen asleep, but then Riley's eyes blinked open and he stared at Chip.

"I'm not sure I ought to tell you the story—it happened a long time ago and it isn't very pleasant. But it might help you to understand why Harn feels the way he does about strangers."

"Go on," Chip urged him.

"Well, it was a night very much like this one," Riley began. "There was a storm brewing, but when Harney—he was only seven or eight at the time—went to bed, it hadn't really hit the coast yet. Then, late at night, it came in, blowing like crazy.

"Nobody ever found out exactly what happened that night, but during the storm there were terrible things done. It was the next morning that all hell broke loose. Harney woke up and the house was empty. He looked around for his grandparents but they weren't there. So he started searching for them." Riley closed his eyes, visualizing the scene as he talked. "He found them on the beach. Sod Beach, about halfway between where the houses are now. Neither of them was there back then—the beach was just a beach. Anyway, Harn went out there and at first he didn't see them. But they were there: buried in the sand up to their necks, drowned. It was just like the old Klickashaw stories, but that time it wasn't a story. It was Harn's grandparents. I saw them myself a little while later. The whole town went out there before they even dug the Whalens up. Awful. Their eyes were all bugged out, and their faces were blue. And the expressions—you wouldn't have believed it."

"Jesus," Chip said softly. "Did they find out who did it?"

"Nah," Riley said. Disgust edged his voice. "Everybody had suspicions, of course, and what happened after that didn't help any."

"Something else happened?"

"About a week after the funeral, Harney's dad gave in and signed a lease with the lumber people. The old man wouldn't, but Harney's dad did. And then he leased the beach to that guy Baron, who built the house out there that Harney owns now."

"How'd Harney get it?"

"He grew up," Riley said flatly. "He just waited around. The lease wasn't a long one—only about ten or fifteen years—but by the time it was up his dad had died too and Harney owned the land. He just refused to renew the lease. Baron was mad—real mad. Claimed there'd been an unwritten agreement, some kinda option, I think. But Harn got some fancy lawyer from Olympia to go to work on that. Anyway, he ended the lease, and that was it for Baron. He stayed around for a while and tried to fish, but that didn't work either. Got himself drowned, he did. Nobody around here gave a shit—they all thought he'd been in on killing Old Man Whalen and his wife." The old man chuckled then. "Funny how I always think of him as Old Man Whalen—he must have been twenty years younger than I am now when he died."

He stopped talking for a few minutes, then grinned at his grandson. "Funny thing. I was telling Tad and Clem about Baron the other day, but I couldn't remember his name then. I know it as well as I know my own but it just slipped right on away. Anyway, like I told Tad and Clem, same thing happened to Baron's wife as happened to Miriam Shelling. Hung herself in the woods. Might even have been the same tree for all I know."

Chip stared at his grandfather. "She hanged herself? After her husband drowned?"

"Yup. Just like Pete and Miriam. Funny how things like that happen. I guess the guy who said history repeats itself wasn't so far off, was he?"

"Funny Harney didn't tell me about it," Chip commented.

Riley made an impatient gesture. "Why would he? What happened to the Barons was thirty-five, forty years ago, long before you were even born. Anyway, that's why Harney hates strangers so much. A couple of them killed his grandparents, even if no one ever proved it."

Chip swirled the half-inch of scotch that still remained in his glass and stared thoughtfully up at the portrait of his grandmother. Her dark face had a stoic, almost impassive look, as if life had been hard for her but she had survived it. As he studied the portrait Chip realized that the resemblance between her and her nephew, Harney Whalen, was not so much a physical thing at all. It was the look. The look of impassivity.

Chip began to understand Harney Whalen, and his sense of worry deepened.

Missy Palmer lay in bed asleep, her hands clenched into small fists, her face twisted into an expression of fear. The rain pattered on the roof, and Missy began to toss in the bed. At the sound of a twig snapping outside, her eyes flew open.

She was suddenly wide awake, the memory of her nightmare still fresh in her mind.

"Robby?" she whispered.

No sound came from the bunk above.

Missy lay still, her heart thumping loudly in her ears. Then she thought she heard something. A snapping sound, like a branch breaking.

Her eyes went to the window and the thumping of her heart grew louder.

Was there something at the window? Something watching her?

Her dream came back to her. In it the . . . something at the window was chasing her. She was on the beach with Robby, and it was chasing both of them. They ran into the woods, trying to hide, but it followed them, looming closer and closer. Her legs wouldn't move anymore. Try as she would, she couldn't run. Her feet were stuck in something, something gooey, that sucked at her, trying to pull her down.

Then she fell, and suddenly the shape was above her, towering over her, reaching for her.

She screamed.

She felt her mother's arms go around her and began sobbing, clinging to Rebecca.

"There, there," Rebecca soothed her. "It's all right. It was a dream, that's all. You had a dream."

"But there was someone here," Missy sobbed. "He was trying to get us. Robby and I were running from him but he was after us. And then I fell . . ." She dissolved once more into her sobbing, and Rebecca stroked her hair softly.

313

Robby, awakened by the scream, hung over the top bunk, a look of curiosity on his sleepy face.

"What's wrong?" he asked groggily.

"Nothing," Rebecca assured him. "Missy had a nightmare, that's all. Go back to sleep."

Robby's head disappeared as Glen came into the doorway.

"Is she all right?" he asked anxiously.

"She's fine," Rebecca told him. "Just a bad dream."

Missy's head stirred in her mother's lap. "It wasn't a dream," she cried. "It was real. He was here. I saw him outside the window."

"Who did you see, darling?" Glen asked.

"A man," Missy said. "But I couldn't see his face."

"You were dreaming," Rebecca said. "There isn't anyone out there."

"Yes there is," Missy insisted.

"I'll have a look," Glen said.

He threw a raincoat on over his pajamas and opened the door of the cabin, shining his flashlight around the surrounding forest. There was nothing.

Then, as he was about to close the door, Scooter dashed between his feet, his tiny tail wagging furiously, barking as loudly as his puppy voice would allow. Glen reached down and scooped him up.

"It's all right," he said to the puppy, scratching its belly. "Nothing's out there."

Scooter, soothed by the scratching, stopped barking. But Missy kept on crying.

Two miles away, while the wind rose to a vicious howl, the back door of Glen Palmer's gallery flew open. The horror began.

22

Early the following morning Glen Palmer put on his slicker, opened the cabin door, and let Scooter out. The puppy scuttled around the corner, and when Glen followed, he found the dog sniffing under the window of the children's room. He squatted down, picked up the wriggling puppy, and carefully examined the ground. There was a slight depression, obscured by the still-falling rain, that might have been a footprint.

Or it might not.

Glen frowned a little and tried to find another, similar depression, but the ground was rough, soggy, and covered with pine needles.

"Well, if anything was there, it isn't now," he muttered to Scooter, then set the puppy down again. Scooter, having lost interest in whatever he had been sniffing at, trotted happily off into the woods, looking back every few seconds to make sure he hadn't lost sight of Glen. Clumsily he lifted a leg next to a bush, then ran back to the front door, where he began yapping to be let in.

As Glen followed the puppy into the house, Rebecca looked curiously at him from the stove, where she was frying eggs.

"Find anything?"

"What makes you think I was looking for anything?"

"You were. Was there anything to find?"

"Not without a liberal dose of imagination. There's a dent in the ground outside the kids' window, and I suppose I could claim it's a footprint if I wanted to, but I don't think anybody'd believe me. *I* certainly wouldn't."

Rebecca put down the spatula she was holding and began setting the table. "You want to get the kids going?" she asked.

"Let them sleep a few more minutes. I'll take them in when I go and drop them at school."

"What's the rush this morning?"

"There isn't any really. Except that Chip might show up and I don't want to miss him."

"I like him."

"So do I," Glen grinned. "I especially like the way he works. We'll have the place open by the end of the week. And I'm going to give him that painting."

"Painting? Which one?"

"The one of the old house where the Randalls live. He really likes it. It seems like the least I can do."

They fell silent, but it wasn't a comfortable silence.

"Something's bothering you," Glen said at last. Rebecca nodded.

"I keep having a feeling something's happened, or is about to happen."

Glen laughed. "Maybe you'd better go see Brad Randall along with Robby."

"Robby?" Rebecca said blankly. "What about Robby?"

"Nothing, really," Glen replied, trying to pass it off.

"He just asked me if he could look Robby over. I think he wants to try to figure out what happened to him when we came up here. But if you ask me, he's wasting his time." Then his voice grew more serious. "What about you? This feeling you have?"

"Oh, it's probably nothing," Rebecca said, though her tone belied the statement. "Just nerves, I guess." She paused a moment, then: "When was the last time Missy had a nightmare?"

Glen frowned, trying to remember. Then he saw what Rebecca was getting at. "Never, I guess. But that doesn't prove anything."

"Except that she said someone was outside last night and you found a footprint."

"I found something that *might* have been a footprint," Glen corrected her. "Let's not make a mountain out of a molehill. One nightmare doesn't mean anything."

"But she thought she saw someone outside before, remember?"

"That happens to all kids. They have vivid imaginations. You know that as well as I do."

Rebecca sighed. "I suppose so," she said reluctantly. "But I still have this feeling." Then she forced a smile. "I suppose I'll get over it. Why don't you get the kids out of bed?"

Glen dropped the children off at the tiny Clark's Harbor school an hour later, then went on to the gallery. He knew something was wrong as soon as he opened the door.

The display cases, finished only the day before, had been smashed. All the glass was shattered, and the framing had been torn apart and scattered around the room. The shelves, securely anchored to the walls by Chip Connor only a few days before, had been ripped down.

The back room was even worse. The shelves on which Rebecca's pottery had been stored were empty; the pottery itself was on the floor, heaped against one wall, every piece smashed beyond recognition.

And the paintings.

They were still in their frames, but they too had been destroyed, viciously slashed. Every canvas was in tatters, made even more grotesque by the undamaged frames.

Glen stared at the wreckage, first in disbelief, then in grief, and finally in rage. He felt the anger surge through him, felt a towering indignation take possession of him. He turned away from the wreckage, walked through the main gallery and out the front door. Without pausing at his car, he started walking into the village, staring straight ahead.

Fifteen minutes later he stalked into the police station.

Chip Connor looked up when he heard the door open. At the look on Glen's face, his greeting died on his lips and he stood up.

"The gallery—" Glen began. Then he choked on his own words and stopped. He stood quivering in front of Chip, trying to control himself, trying to force himself neither to scream nor to cry. He breathed deeply, sucking air into his constricted lungs, then let it out in an immense sigh.

"Someone broke into the gallery last night," he said at last. "They wrecked it."

"Come on." Chip grabbed his hat and started out of the office.

"Where are you going?" Glen demanded.

"I want to see it," Chip said. There was an icy quality in his voice that Glen had never heard before.

"Not yet," Glen said. "Let me sit down a minute." He felt suddenly weak, and let himself sink into a chair. "Do you have any coffee around here? Or maybe even a drink?"

The coldness immediately left Chip's manner. He closed the office door, poured Glen some coffee from the huge percolator that was always ready, and sat down at the desk again.

"Sorry," he said. "I guess that wasn't very professional of me. What happened?"

"I don't know. I walked in and the place was wrecked. Both rooms. And Rebecca's pottery. And my paintings."

"Shit," Chip cursed softly. "How bad is it?"

"The pottery and the paintings are completely ruined. As for the gallery, you'll know better than I. Frankly, I didn't take time to really look. I walked down here as soon as I saw what had happened."

"You walked?"

"I was so mad I could hardly see straight, and I didn't even think about getting into the car. If I had, I probably would have run it into a tree." Then he frowned slightly. "Where's Whalen?"

"Not here. He's over to Doc Phelps' this morning."

"Well, I'm just as glad he isn't here," Glen said wearily. "I probably would have blown it completely if I'd had to talk to him. Is there more coffee there?"

"Help yourself." He waited, chewing thoughtfully

on his lips, while Glen refilled his cup. When Glen was seated once more, Chip spoke again. "Can I ask you a question?" he said.

"Sure," Glen said tonelessly.

"Did you come over here to report what happened, or to yell at Harney Whalen?"

The question caught Glen by surprise and he had to think about it. "I don't honestly know," he said finally. "Both, I guess. I had to report it, of course, but I was going to to vent some anger on Whalen too." He smiled weakly. "I guess it's just as well he isn't here."

"I guess so," Chip agreed. "You about ready to go over to the gallery? I'll make out a report there, and we can decide what to do next."

"Do? What's there to do? Everything's ruined."

"Maybe," Chip agreed. "Maybe not. Let's go find out."

"Holy Christ," Chip said as the two of them entered the gallery. "It looks like someone let a bear loose in here."

He pulled out his notebook and began writing down a description of the damage. When he was finished in the front room he went into the back and repeated the process.

"They came in here," he said, starting at the back door. It hung grotesquely, one hinge completely torn loose from the frame.

He made a few more notes, then put the notebook away. Glen was staring at the shreds of the paintings, his face expressionless.

"Is there any way to repair them?" Chip asked.

Glen shook his head. "You can fix a small tear sometimes, but nothing like this," he said tonelessly.

Chip couldn't bear the look in Glen's eyes. "I don't know if it'll do any good," he said, "since there doesn't seem to be anything to sell. But we can fix the gallery."

"It's all broken up," Glen said dully.

"Not that bad. We'll have to get new glass, but the cases can be put back together again." He smiled briefly, then added, "It isn't as if the shelves haven't been torn off the walls before."

"It will just happen again," Glen pointed out.

"Not if we put in an alarm system. And not if we find out who did it."

"Oh, come on, Chip. We're not going to find out who did it, and you know it."

"We might," Chip said. Then he decided he might as well be honest. "No, you're right, we probably won't. Hell, we don't even know *why* they did it."

"I guess you know what I think," Glen said.

"Can I make a suggestion?" Chip asked, deliberately ignoring Glen's comment. Without waiting for an answer, he went on. "Take the day off. Go home and tell Rebecca what happened, then decide what the two of you want to do. We'll start cleaning up tomorrow. I'm off duty."

"Okay. The mess has to be cleaned up anyway." Glen's face clouded as a memory came back to him. "Rebecca said something was going to happen," he said. "Just this morning, when we got up. She said something's happened or is about to happen. I guess she was right."

They had walked from the back room into the gallery, but suddenly Glen returned to the workroom. A minute later he was back.

"They didn't get everything," he said triumphantly. "There was one picture I put away and they didn't find it."

Chip looked curiously at him as Glen turned the picture he held. It was the canvas depicting Sod Beach and the weathered old house with the strange presence in the window.

"I'm glad it was this one," Glen said. "I put it away because I was saving it. But you'd better take it now, Chip. It might not be around much longer."

"Take it? What are you talking about?"

"I was going to give it to you the day we finished the gallery," Glen explained. "So I put it away, just so I couldn't be tempted to sell it. But I think you'd better take it now, just in case."

"I can't take it," Chip protested. "My God, it's all you've got left."

But when they left the gallery a few minutes later, Chip was carrying the painting and planning where to hang it.

Harney Whalen sat in Dr. Phelps' cluttered office, and described what had happened the previous afternoon. Phelps listened patiently. When Harney finished he shrugged his shoulders.

"I don't see why you came to me," he said. "You froze at the wheel for a couple of seconds. Everybody does that now and then."

"But it's more than that, Doc." Harney hesitated. "I have spells."

"Spells? What do you mean, spells? Sounds like a little old lady's symptom."

"It's the only way I can describe them. It's almost

like blacking out for a while, I guess. They don't happen very often, or at least I don't think they do, but when they start my hands start to twitch and I feel funny. Then there's nothing until I wake up."

Phelps frowned. "When was the last time you had one?"

"Last night," Whalen admitted. "I was watching television and I felt it coming on. I don't remember anything until this morning. I was in bed, but I don't remember going to bed."

"Hmm," Phelps said noncommittally. "Well, we'd better look you over." He took Whalen's blood pressure and pulse, tested his reflexes, and went over him with a stethoscope. Then he took a blood sample and had Whalen produce a urine sample as well.

"I'll have to send these down to a lab in Aberdeen, but we should find out if there's anything there in a couple of days. Apart from the 'spells' how do you feel?"

"Fine. Same as ever. When have I ever been sick?"

Phelps nodded. "Well, everything looks normal so far. If nothing turns up in the samples, how would you feel about going into a hospital for a couple of days?"

"Forget it," Whalen said. "I've got too much to do."

Phelps rolled his eyes. "Oh, come on, Harn. You and I are the most underworked people in town. Or we were until recently."

"It's the strangers," Whalen murmured. "Every time strangers come we have trouble."

"You mean the Palmers?" Phelps asked.

"Them and the new ones. Randall's the name. They moved into my old house out at the beach."

Now Phelps's interest was definitely piqued. "The Baron house? I thought you weren't going to rent it anymore."

Whalen smiled bitterly. "I wasn't. But it seems I did." He frowned, searching for the best way to explain what had happened. "I guess I had one of my spells while I was showing the place to Randall and his wife. Anyway, they showed up with a signed lease, and I don't remember signing it." He stood up, and began buttoning his shirt. "Well, what about it? Am I going to live?"

"As far as I can tell," Phelps said slowly. "But what you just said bothers me. I have a good mind to send you to Aberdeen right now."

Whalen shook his head. "Not a chance. If you can't find anything wrong, that's that. Never been in a hospital. I don't intend to start now."

"Suit yourself," Phelps said. "But if you won't follow my advice, don't ask me what's wrong with you."

"Maybe nothing's wrong with me," Whalen said amiably. "Maybe I'm just getting old."

"Maybe so," Phelps replied tartly. "And maybe something *is* wrong with you and you just don't want to know about it."

"What you don't know can't hurt you."

"Can't help you either," Phelps countered. "And what about other people? You might hurt someone— you almost did yesterday."

"But I didn't," Whalen reminded him. "And I won't."

As Harney Whalen left his office Dr. Phelps wished he were as confident as Whalen seemed to be. But he wasn't. The idea of Harney Whalen having "spells" worried him. It worried him very much.

* * *

Glen Palmer arrived home to find the cabin deserted. A note from Rebecca said she had gone down to the Randalls' to see if she could give them a hand. He could fix his own lunch or come and get her. Since it was still early Glen decided to walk down the beach.

The leaden sky showed no signs of clearing; the sky to the west was almost black, and near the horizon storm clouds were scudding back and forth, swirling among themselves as if grouping for an attack on the coast. The light rain that had been coming down all night and all morning still fell softly, soaking into the beach immediately, leaving the sand close-packed and solid. The tide was far out, and the level beach, exposed far beyond its normal width, glistened wetly.

Glen walked out toward the surf line, then turned south, moving slowly, almost reluctantly. He was trying to decide how to break the news to Rebecca and what her response would be.

She would give up and demand that they leave Clark's Harbor. Or she would be angry. Or prepared for a fight, ready to do anything to show that she could not be frightened off. The last, he thought, would be typical of Rebecca.

He was wrong. Rebecca saw him coming when he was still fifty yards from the old house on the beach and went out to meet him.

"It happened, didn't it?" she asked softly.

Glen looked up, startled. He hadn't seen her coming—he'd been staring at the sand at his feet, preoccupied. He nodded mutely.

"What was it?"

"The gallery's been vandalized," Glen told her.

"Vandalized? You mean someone broke in?"

"They broke in, they wrecked the gallery, they smashed all your pottery, and they shredded all but one of my canvases."

"Which one?" Rebecca asked irrelevantly, and Glen realized that she was shutting out what he had said. Of all the possible reactions, this was one Glen hadn't considered.

"The one I gave Chip," he said softly. Rebecca turned slowly and gazed at the old house that was the subject of Glen's only surviving canvas.

"Somehow that seems right," she commented. Then she slipped her arm through Glen's and stared up into his troubled eyes. "Let's not worry about it now. Not this minute anyway. If I have to decide what to do right now I'll make the wrong decision. So let's wait, all right? We'll talk it over with Brad and Elaine, then pretend nothing's happened for the rest of the day. And tonight when we're in bed we'll make up our minds."

Glen pulled her closer and kissed her softly. "If we decide in bed I know what we'll do: we'll stick it out here. When we're in bed anything seems possible."

"Then so be it," Rebecca murmured. "But let's not talk about it right now, all right?"

The chaos in the Randalls' house was only slightly more orderly than that in the gallery, and Glen tried to sound cheerful as he made the comparison. But as he listened to Glen's story of what had happened the night before Brad wondered if Robby had stayed in bed last night: Glen's description of the gallery sounded all too much like the havoc the boy had been known to create in the past. So when Robby and Missy arrived, scrambling over the driftwood on their way home from school, Brad quickly found an excuse to take Robby for a long walk on the beach.

"Pretty out here, isn't it?" he said casually when they were out of earshot of the house. Robby nodded non-committally.

"Your dad tells me you love it out here," Brad prodded gently.

"It's all right. But I like it best when it rains."

"Why's that?"

Robby turned the question over in his mind. Nobody had ever asked him that before, and he hadn't ever thought about it. Now, with the openness of childhood, he began thinking out loud. "I guess I feel excited when the storms come up," he said slowly. "But it's a funny kind of excited. Not like Christmas, or my birthday, when I know something good's going to happen. It's more like a feeling in my body. I get sort of tingly, and sometimes it's hard to move. But it's not a bad feeling—it's more like it's what's supposed to happen. It's exciting and relaxing all at the same time. Sometimes when I'm out in the storms I feel like lying down on the ground and letting the rain fall all over me."

"You go out in the storms?" Brad tried to keep his voice casual but there was a note of concern in it that Robby detected immediately. He stared up at Brad, his eyes large and frightened.

"Don't tell Mom and Dad," he begged. "They

wouldn't like it. They'd think I was still sick, but I'm not. The storms make me well."

"I won't tell anyone," Brad reassured the boy. "But I'd like to know what happens when you go out in the storms."

"Nothing, really. Missy thinks she sees things when we're out together, but nothing ever happens. Sometimes I go by myself, but sometimes Missy comes with me," he explained, though Brad hadn't voiced the question that was in his mind. "But Missy never wants to go and I always have to talk her into it. She's a scaredy-cat."

"What about the night I met you on the beach? Missy wasn't with you then."

"I was looking for Snooker and Missy wouldn't come. She said he was gone and wasn't coming back and there wasn't any use looking for him." Robby looked dejected. "I guess she was right," he said softly, as if the admission hurt him.

"Do you ever see anyone else when you're out in the storms?"

Robby thought about it and decided that the only time he'd actually *seen* anyone was a few weeks earlier. "We met Old Man Riley once. He told us stories about the Indians, and how they used to kill people on the beach and hold ceremonies and all kinds of stuff. But that's all."

They walked in silence for a while as Brad tried to make sense out of what Robby had said. It seemed, on the surface, as if nothing particularly unusual was happening. And yet, Brad was sure there was something else just beneath the surface. He decided to ask one more question.

"Aren't you ever frightened when you're out by yourself and the storms are blowing?"

Robby Palmer looked bewildered. "No," he finally said. "Why should I? I belong here." Then, before Brad could absorb what he had said or question him about the previous night, Robby turned and began running back to the house. Brad watched him go and wondered what he had meant. Wasn't Robby, like the rest of his family, a stranger here? How could he "belong"?

As soon as Brad returned to the house Glen drew him aside, his expression a mixture of curiosity and concern. "Well?" he asked expectantly.

"I don't know," Brad said slowly, wishing he could come up with an easy explanation for the events that were ensnaring Clark's Harbor. "It has something to do with the storms. Robby says they 'excite' him. And if they excite him they must do the same to other people. Only they don't calm the other people down. The storms must turn them into monsters instead."

Brad didn't tell Glen what Robby had said about Missy. For the moment, he decided, he would keep it to himself. At least until he had a chance to talk to Missy directly.

As the afternoon light began to fade Dr. Bradford Randall stared out over the Pacific Ocean and tried to keep the dogs of fear that were nibbling at the edges of his consciousness at bay.

There was an explanation for what was happening around him. He could find it.

But even if he found it he wasn't sure he could do anything about it. He remembered the old adage:

everybody talks about the weather, but nobody does anything about it.

Maybe there was nothing that *could* be done about it.

23

Elaine Randall hadn't slept well. She was uneasy in their new surroundings, but there was something more —what Brad had told them the night before. It hadn't sounded logical. And yet she knew that weather could affect people. Ionization, the Santa Ana winds, that sort of thing. But here, in Clark's Harbor? It may not have made sense, but it was frightening. So she had lain awake most of the night, listening to the steady roar of the surf. And thinking.

Twice she had gotten up, both times without disturbing Brad, and stared out at the beach. It was clear and she had seen the Big Dipper glowing brightly in the black sky. A half-moon had turned the beach a burnished pewter tone.

Near dawn she had finally drifted into a fitful sleep.

Now she was up, battling with the recalcitrant wood stove, poking at the remains of a dead fire. Rebecca had showed her how to bank the fire last night, but Elaine wasn't sure it had worked. She grasped a poker in her right hand. A small bellows sat on top of the stove, ready for her to use in the unlikely event a spark should appear. She jabbed viciously at the largest chunk of wood remaining in the firebox, and was surprised when it broke in two and exposed its glowing interior.

She crammed a wad of newspaper into the firebox, picked up the bellows, and began frantically pumping. She heard Brad come into the kitchen but was too intent on getting the fire going to offer more than a muttered "good morning."

Brad watched her for a few minutes, then took the bellows out of her hands.

"You're working too hard," he said. "You'll blow the fire out as fast as you feed it. Do it slowly." He worked the bellows easily and a moment later a tiny flame leaped to life, igniting the paper. Brad put the bellows aside and tossed some chips of wood onto the tiny blaze, then some kindling. The fire grew steadily.

"Nothing to it," he announced.

"Beginner's luck," Elaine said. "It was all set to go when you took over. Hand me the coffee."

She carefully measured out the coffee, then placed the basket inside the aluminum percolator that stood waiting on the stove. "I could learn to do without coffee at this rate," she complained. "Any idea how long it's supposed to perk, assuming it ever starts?"

"Till it's done," Brad replied just as there was a knock at the kitchen door, followed by a voice.

"Anybody home?" It was Rebecca Palmer, and she didn't wait for a reply before coming in. She was carrying a thermos.

"I thought you might be able to use this," she said cheerfully. "The first couple of days we were here I couldn't get the coffee to perk at all." She pulled the top off the thermos and the room filled with the aroma of fresh, strong coffee. Elaine poured three cups and immediately took a sip from one of them.

"I may live," she sighed. Then she looked questioningly at Rebecca. "Did you see Jeff?"

"Jeff? Isn't he here?"

"I thought I heard him go out just before I got up," Elaine replied. "I think he was going out to look for wreckage."

"He's not on the beach," Rebecca said.

"Probably went the other way," Brad suggested. "But I don't think he'll find anything."

Chip Connor found Harney at his desk, sourly going over the report Chip had left there the night before. The chief looked up at him and pushed the file aside.

"You expect me to do anything about that?" he asked.

"It's our job," Chip pointed out.

"Anything stolen?"

"Not as far as Glen could tell. But you should see the place," Chip added. "It's a mess."

"Well, that's the way things go sometimes," Whalen said, unconcerned. "If nothing was stolen then what's the big deal?"

"You mean you aren't going to do anything?" Chip couldn't believe what he was hearing.

"No," Whalen said heavily, "I'm not."

Chip's eyes narrowed angrily. "I don't know what's going on with you, Harn. It seems like lately you just don't give a damn what goes on around here."

"I don't give a damn about what happens to outsiders," Whalen corrected. "And I have my reasons."

"I know about your reasons," Chip replied. "Granddad told me all about it. But the past is the past, Harney. All that happened years ago. Things change."

"Some things change. Some don't. Some things can be forgiven, and some can't. I haven't forgotten what happened to my grandparents. Never will. And as far as I'm concerned, I don't want any outsiders hanging around this town. They're dangerous."

"It seems to me that this town's more dangerous for them than they are for us," Chip countered.

"That's the way things are here." A hatred came into Whalen's voice, a tone that Chip had never heard before. "When my grandparents first came here it was dangerous for them. The Indians didn't like what was going on and they did their damnedest to get rid of all the whites. But my grandparents hung on and they learned to live here. My daddy even married a girl who was part Indian, but I guess you know about that, don't you?"

Chip nodded, wondering what Whalen was getting at.

"Well, the Indians went away after a while, up north, and left us alone. But they always said the place would be no good for strangers. And it hasn't been. The lumbermen tried to come in here, but it wasn't any good for them."

"That was your doing," Chip said. "First your grandfather's, then yours."

"I didn't renew a lease, that's all," Whalen said mildly. "But they should have gone away then. They didn't. They tried to stay and fish. And it didn't work."

"I heard," Chip said dully.

"Well, it's been that way ever since," Whalen said.

"Every now and then strangers come, and they always bring trouble. But it's just like the Indians said. The trouble always flies back in their faces. And you know something, Chip? There's not a damned thing we can do about it."

"You don't even try."

"Not anymore, no," Whalen agreed. "I used to but it never did any good. So I live with it. Can't say it bothers me particularly." He picked up the folder containing Chip's report on the vandalism at Glen Palmer's gallery. "So don't expect me to do anything about this. I won't find anything—anybody could have done it and there's nothing to look for. If I were you I'd forget it. You just tell Palmer, if he wants to stay in Clark's Harbor, he'd better expect things like this."

Chip nodded his head absently and started to leave. But before he got to the door he remembered something and turned back.

"Did you see Doc Phelps yesterday?"

"Yeah." Whalen said the word tonelessly, as if there were nothing more to add, but Chip pressed him.

"Is anything wrong?"

"Nothing he could find. I just didn't feel very well the other night, so I decided to have him take a look. Must have been indigestion."

Whalen wondered briefly why he was lying to Chip, why he didn't want to tell Chip about his "spells," then decided it was just none of Chip's business. Besides, the spells weren't serious. If Phelps couldn't find out what was causing them there wasn't any point in talking about them.

"Well, if you need me call me on the radio. I'm

going to give Glen Palmer a hand today, but I'll leave the radio open."

Whalen scowled at his deputy. "I don't suppose it's any of my business what you do on your days off, but I think you're wasting your time. You get involved with Palmer and you'll get in trouble."

"I don't see how," Chip said, annoyed at Whalen.

"That's the way it happens, that's all," Harney said flatly. He pulled a file from the top drawer of his desk, and opened it, as if to dismiss Chip.

But as the door to his office closed behind his deputy, Harney Whalen looked up from the file he had been pretending to be reading. His eyes fastened vacantly on the closed door but he didn't really see it. Instead he saw Chip's face, but it was not quite the face he knew so well. There was something different about the face Harney Whalen visualized.

Something strange.

That was it, he thought to himself.

Chip's become a stranger to me.

Then he put the thought aside and returned to the file in front of him.

"Want a beer?" Glen asked as Brad came through the front door. He and Chip were leaning against one of the display cases admiring their work. The mess was gone, the shelves were back up, and all but one of the display cases had been repaired.

"I thought you said it was destroyed," Brad said, puzzled.

"I guess it wasn't as bad as I thought," Glen replied a little sheepishly. "Not that I could have fixed it myself, of course."

"He's been fussing around, getting in the way all day," Chip said. "I told him to go out and paint a picture but he wouldn't."

"Well, if you can get along without him I'll drag him down to the library with me."

"The library?" Chip asked. "What's at the library?"

Brad glanced at Glen and Glen nodded his head. "If he doesn't think I'm crazy," he said, "he's not likely to think you are." He turned to Chip. "Brad has a theory about what's going on around here."

"It has to do with the storms," Brad said. "They seem to affect Glen's son and I'm wondering if they might be affecting somebody else too."

Chip frowned, puzzled. "I don't get it."

"I'm not sure I do either," Brad said. "But it just seems as though too many 'accidents' have happened out here. I'm just trying to find out if they really are accidents."

"You mean the drownings?" Chip asked.

"Not just the drownings," Glen answered. "There's also what happened here, and Miriam Shelling, and my dog. It all just seems like too much."

"I don't know what you think you'll find out," Chip said. "Harney Whalen sure doesn't seem too interested."

"What does he think is going on?" Glen asked carefully. He'd learned to be careful with Chip on the subject of Whalen.

"He seems to think it's some kind of fate, or an old Klickashaw curse or something. He says whenever strangers come to Clark's Harbor trouble comes with them, but that it always turns back on them."

"Makes things simple anyway," Brad commented.

"Yeah," Chip said, a little uncomfortably. He glanced around the gallery and set his empty beer can down. "Tell you what," he suggested to Glen. "If Brad wants you to help him, why don't we call it a day? I'll go down to Blake's and pick up what we need to finish this off and we'll do it tomorrow."

The sky had turned black by the time they locked up the gallery, and Chip glanced at the western horizon. "Looks like a storm's getting ready to hit." The three men shuddered, keenly aware of what a storm could mean in Clark's Harbor.

Jeff Horton had spent the entire day walking the beach, tramping north aimlessly, telling himself he was looking for wreckage from *Osprey* when in fact he was trying to sort out the pieces of what had happened.

He had been awake all night, and several times he had heard someone else downstairs, also awake. Twice he had been tempted to go down and tap at the Randalls' bedroom door, just for the company. But it wasn't company he needed. He needed to understand what was happening.

He had left the house early in the morning, telling no one where he was going—he was sure the Randalls would understand, and besides, he wasn't sure where he *was* going. Or what he was looking for.

He knew that storms could kill people, but they did it simply, straightforwardly. They came down on you if you were at sea, tossed you around, terrified you, then, if the spirit moved them, hurled a gigantic wave at you and crushed you.

If you were on land you were safer, though a storm

338

could still smash your house, drop an electrical line on you, or cut you down with a bolt of lightning. But could a storm make someone cast a boat adrift? Could it send someone into an art gallery to destroy its contents? Could it hang a woman from the branch of a tree in the middle of the woods? All Jeff Horton's sensibilities told him it could not. And yet, as the wind began to blow and the dark clouds began to lower over the horizon, he turned south and started back toward Clark's Harbor. The surf began to build and the tide began flooding in, the storm on its heels.

Missy and Robby were on Sod Beach when the storm struck the coast. As the first drops of rain fell Missy gave up her search for a perfect sand dollar and called out to her brother.

"It's starting to rain."

"So what?" Robby said, not looking up from the patch of sand he was carefully searching. So far he had found five undamaged shells, and Missy none, and he was sure she was just trying to spoil his fun. Besides, the beginnings of the storm made the beach exciting. He glanced up at the clouds, then grinned happily at the sight of the churning surf. He was only vaguely aware of Missy's complaining voice.

"I want to go *home*," she insisted. "I don't want to stay out here and get soaked!"

"Nobody's home," Robby pointed out. "Dad's still at work and Mom's down at Dr. Randall's."

"Then let's go there," Missy begged. "We can go through the woods." She started across the beach, determined not to look back, not to give her brother a chance to cajole her into staying on the unprotected sand. She wanted to turn around when she got to the reef of driftwood that lay at the high water line but was afraid to, afraid that if Robby wasn't coming along behind her she would give in and go back toward the angry sea and the growing storm. Not until she was safely into the forest did she risk a look.

Robby was no longer on the beach. Missy had a moment of panic, then decided that her brother was teasing her, trying to scare her. Well, she wouldn't be frightened. And she wouldn't go running around looking for him, the way he wanted her to. She would stay right where she was, in the safety of the forest, and watch. Sooner or later, Robby would come looking for her. . . .

Jeff Horton arrived at the north end of Sod Beach in a shadowy half-light, a dark gray dusk made heavy by the now-raging storm. The beach looked deserted, but as Jeff passed the Palmers' cabin he paused, a curious sense of apprehension sweeping over him. When he began walking again he had an urge to run but fought it off, telling himself there was no danger, nothing to be afraid of; he only had a few hundred yards to go before he would be comfortably inside the Randalls' house.

But as he moved through the storm Jeff began to feel an odd sensation: the lightning flashing around him seemed to slow him down, drain his energy. He wanted to run but found he could only walk, and with each step his stride became slower.

He tried to force himself to hurry but it did no good. And as his pace slowed he came to the realization that he was no longer alone on the beach. Something else was there, something terrifying. Something that had come out of the storm. . . .

From her vantage point in the meager shelter of the forest Missy could barely make out the shape moving steadily down the beach. At first she thought it must be Robby, but then she realized it was too big. It was too dark for her to recognize who it might be; indeed, as the light faded into darkness the figure began to disappear entirely. But as night closed around her the full force of the storm struck, and the beach was lit up by sudden flashes of lightning. Each time the beach became momentarily visible, Missy looked fearfully around for her brother. He was nowhere to be seen.

A few minutes later she lost her courage and crept away into the woods when the white flash of pent-up electricity suddenly revealed not one, but two figures on the beach. They were close together, and as she watched they suddenly merged. . . .

Jeff Horton felt the attack before it came. The hair on the back of his neck tingled and stood on end, and his feeling of apprehension changed suddenly into a sense of danger. He was turning to face whatever enemy was behind him when he felt the massive arm slide around his neck and a force on the back of his head pushing forward. He felt his windpipe close under the pressure of the opposing forces and began to struggle, his arms flailing in the rain. Once he got a grip on his unseen assailant, but his hands, slick with wetness, slid loose. Before he could break free he began to lose consciousness. His last memory was of a sound, a cracking noise from just below his head. He wondered what it might have been, but before he could find an answer the blackness closed in on him and he relaxed. Seconds later he lay alone on the beach, the rain pounding down on him, the surf licking at him like a beast sniffing at its fallen prey.

Missy ran along the trail through the woods, her heart pounding, her small voice crying out to her brother. And then he was there, standing on the trail ahead of her, waiting for her.

"I was looking for you," Robby said softly. "How come you hid?"

Missy stopped running and stared at her brother, her breath coming in great heaves. She tried to speak through her gasps of exhaustion and fear but couldn't. She sat heavily on a log and began crying. Perplexed, Robby sat beside her and put his arm around her.

"I—I saw something," Missy stammered. "I was waiting for you, but you didn't come, and I saw something. On the beach—there was someone on the beach, and then someone else—and I—oh, Robby, let's go *home*," she wailed.

Robby took her hand and pulled her to her feet. "You didn't see anything," he assured her. "It's too dark." He began leading her along the path, his step sure, his pace fast. The excitement of the storm swept over him. He wished it would never end.

At nine o'clock that evening the librarian at the tiny Clark's Harbor public library—two rooms in the town hall—tapped Brad Randall on the shoulder. Brad stopped writing in the notebook he had nearly filled in the five hours he and Glen had been working and looked up.

"It's closing time." The gray-haired woman whispered, though there was no one else in the area. "You'll have to come back on Monday."

"That's all right," Brad said. "I'm almost finished." He smiled at the woman ruefully. "I hope we haven't put you through too much."

"Oh, it's all right," the librarian assured him. "Most days I just sit here. It's nice to have something to do now and then. Though what you want with all those papers is beyond me, I'm sure."

"Just checking some things out," Brad said mildly. "Sort of a research project on the history of the town."

"Not much history," the librarian sniffed. "We live and die and that's about it."

"That's what I'm interested in," Brad said mysteriously. The librarian's eyes widened, but before she could ask any questions Glen Palmer came in from the other room.

"That does it," he said. "We've gone as far back as the records go."

"That's all right. We've got enough information, I think."

As Brad and Glen left, the librarian began putting away all the old newspapers they had gone through. She was puzzled. She made a mental note to talk to Merle Glind about it. If something was happening he would surely know what it was.

The storm had closed in and rain was coming down in sheets as Glen and Brad made a dash for Brad's car. As they started toward the main highway the wind, blowing at close to gale force, pulled at the Volvo, and Brad had trouble keeping it on the road.

"Why don't we leave your minibus at the gallery?" he suggested as they turned onto the highway. Glen shook his head.

"Not in weather like this. If there's anything to your theory, this is the kind of night that something could happen to it."

Brad chuckled appreciatively, and pulled as close to the ancient Volkswagen van as he could get. "You want to stop at our place on the way? I wouldn't be surprised if Rebecca and the kids aren't there, keeping Elaine company."

"Fine," Glen replied. "See you there."

They found Rebecca and Elaine in the living room. The two women rose to greet them with worried faces.

"It's all right," Brad assured them. "We're here and we're safe. You don't have to look like tragedy struck."

His grin failed to wipe the frowns from their faces and they glanced at each other nervously. It was Elaine who spoke.

"The children came in a while ago," she said quietly. "About half an hour after the storm struck. Missy thought she saw something on the beach, but she isn't sure what."

"Where are they?" Brad asked.

"We put them to bed," Rebecca explained. "They were soaked and Missy was frightened."

Missy thinks she sees things. Robby's words echoed in Brad's mind but he decided not to say anything. Not yet anyway.

"Did you find anything at the library?" Elaine asked softly, almost hesitantly.

Brad nodded. "Something's going on all right," he said. "We went through a lot of papers this evening. Every time something's happened out here, there's been a storm blowing. And it's funny, it seems as though the worse the storm is, the worse the things that happen." He was warming to his subject now, oblivious of the stricken look on his wife's face. "For instance," he went on, "did you know the Shellings weren't the first case of a couple dying here?"

"What do you mean?" Rebecca asked, suddenly pale.

"The people who built this house died the same way," Glen said quietly. "Baron fell off his fishing boat and got caught in his own nets. A few days later, Mrs. Baron hanged herself. It happened during a three-day storm."

"I wish you hadn't told me that," Elaine said softly. "Things like that scare me." Brad moved to put his arm around her shoulder but she pulled away suddenly as a thought struck her. "Where's Jeff?"

Glen and Brad looked at each other blankly. "Jeff? He wasn't with us. We haven't seen him all day . . ." Glen's voice trailed off as he realized what he had just said. Jeff must have been on the beach.

And a storm was blowing.

A bad storm.

He grabbed his coat and began putting it back on. "Let's get going," he said to Brad. He picked up a flashlight from the dining-room table and was gone. disappearing into the blackness. The wind-driven rain quickly blotted out even the faint glow from his light.

345

24

They almost stumbled over Jeff.

The young fisherman was lying in the sand, and if they hadn't been walking at the water's edge they would have missed him entirely.

"Oh, Jesus," Glen whispered as Brad's light played over Jeff's face. The mouth was twisted in a grimace of pain. Dead, Glen thought. Oh, my God, he's dead. But then his eyelids fluttered and Glen fell to his knees, touching Jeff's arm. The eyes opened.

Jeff's mouth began to work, but no sound came out. His eyes closed again, tightly this time, as he winced in pain.

Brad wanted to move him, to pull him further up the beach so the surf couldn't get at him, but as he played the flashlight over Jeff's body he realized something was terribly wrong.

Jeff's head lay at a strange angle. His neck was broken.

That Jeff was alive at all was a miracle.

Then Jeff's eyelids fluttered again and once more he tried to speak. Glen leaned down, close to Jeff's lips.

"What is it, Jeff? What happened?"

Jeff tried hard but no sound would come out of him.

He used the last of his strength to take a deep breath, then made a desperate effort to speak. But before the words could be formed the breath turned into a soul-shaking rattle and was expelled in a long, slow sigh.

Jeff Horton, like his brother, lay dead on Sod Beach.

Elaine Randall paced between the kitchen and the living room, pausing every few seconds to stare futilely into the blackness of the night. Several times she forced herself to sit down in front of the fire, but it was useless. A moment later she was on her feet again, her nerves jangling, a knot of fear twisting her stomach.

Her eyes flicked around the room and she wondered briefly what she was looking for. Then she knew.

The float.

The glistening blue glass ball she had found on the beach—how long ago? It seemed like years, though it had been only weeks.

She picked the sphere up from its place on the mantel, and stared into its depths.

It was no longer beautiful.

What she had thought of as an omen for good now seemed evil to her. She turned it over in her hands, wondering what to do with it.

She decided to return it to the sea.

Without giving herself time to change her mind, Elaine put on her pea coat and hurried out of the house. She moved directly across the beach, and when she neared the surf line she stopped. She looked at the float once more, curiously, then raised her arm and hurled it into the pounding waves. As it left her hand Elaine felt a tingling—almost electric—in her arm.

Suddenly terrified, she turned and fled back into the house.

Glen Palmer lurched unsteadily through the kitchen door, his face pale and his hands trembling.

Elaine stood at the stove stirring a pan of hot cider. As soon as she saw Glen she knew.

"You found him, didn't you?" she whispered.

Glen nodded mutely and sank into a chair at the kitchen table, cradling his head in his hands.

Missy saw it, Elaine thought. *She saw it happen.* She touched Glen gently on the shoulder. "Just sit here. I'll get Rebecca." She frowned. "Where's Brad?"

"He went to town," Glen muttered. "He went to report what we found." Elaine, not yet wanting to hear exactly what they had found, went to the living room and gestured Rebecca to the kitchen. "I'll check on the kids," she whispered. Rebecca hurried toward the kitchen as Elaine stepped into the room where Missy and Robby were occupying her bed.

Robby was sleeping quietly but Missy was wide awake.

"Where's Daddy?" she asked.

"He'll be in in a little while," Elaine whispered. "He had to go out on the beach."

The little girl seemed to shrink before her eyes. "He shouldn't have done that," she whispered. "The beach is a bad place."

Missy's words sent a shiver up Elaine's spine but she said nothing. Instead she merely tucked Missy in and kissed her on the forehead. "Now go back to sleep. I want to be able to send your daddy in to kiss you, not scold you for staying awake. All right?"

Missy made no reply, but her eyes closed tightly and she squirmed further into the bed.

Did she really see it? Elaine asked herself. *Dear God, I hope not.*

She carefully checked the window, then pulled the door closed behind her. A moment later she was in the kitchen, listening as Glen tonelessly told them what had happened on the beach.

Merle Glind was pouring a third beer for Chip Connor when the telephone tucked away at the end of the bar suddenly began ringing.

"They never let you alone," Merle clucked, setting the half-empty bottle on the bar next to Chip's glass. "If it isn't one thing it's another."

Chip grinned as Merle bustled down to the telephone, but his smile faded when the fussy little man held the receiver up and called out to him.

"It's for you but I don't know who it is."

"Hello?" Chip said into the phone a moment later.

"Chip? It's Brad Randall. Are you still sober?"

"I'm on my third beer," Chip replied. "What's happened?"

"Jeff Horton. Glen and I found him on the beach a little while ago. He's dead."

"Shit!" Chip said. Then: "Did you call Harn?"

There was a slight pause before Brad spoke again. "I decided to call you instead," he said almost hesitantly.

"All right," Chip said. "Where's the body?"

"Still on the beach. We didn't want to move it."

"Okay, I'll be right out." Then he paused and frowned slightly. "Where are you?"

"Pruitt's gas station. It was the nearest telephone. You want me to wait here for you?"

"No, I can meet you at your place. I'll have to call Harney and tell him what's happened."

"I know," Brad said. "If I hadn't been able to find you I'd have called him myself."

"Okay," Chip grunted. "Go on back home. I'll get there as soon as I can." Almost as an afterthought, he added, "Is Glen all right?"

"A little shock but he should be out of it by the time you get there."

"Will he be able to answer questions?"

Now there was a long silence, and when Brad finally answered his voice was guarded. "It depends on what kind of questions. That's why I called you instead of Whalen, Chip."

Chip bit his lip thoughtfully and wondered what would happen if he simply handled it himself and didn't notify Harney until morning. He'd get his ass chewed, that's what would happen, he decided. "I have to call him," he told Brad. "He's the chief."

"I know," Brad said tiredly. "All right. See you."

Chip replaced the receiver on the phone under the bar and wasn't surprised when he found Merle Glind hovering behind him, his eyes wide and curious.

"What is it?" he asked. "What's happened?"

"Jeff Horton. He's out on Sod Beach, dead."

"Mercy!" Glind said. Then he clucked his tongue, his head wagging sympathetically. "I knew he should have gone. I just knew it."

But Chip wasn't listening. He had the phone in his hand once more, and was dialing Harney Whalen's number. On the tenth ring, just as Chip was about to give up, Whalen's voice came onto the line.

"Did I get you out of bed?" Chip asked.

"No," Whalen replied, his voice sounding a little vague. "I was watching television. I guess I must have dozed off."

"Well, you'd better get down to Sod Beach right away. Jeff Horton's out there and he's dead." There was a silence and Chip wasn't sure the chief had heard him. Then, as he was about to repeat himself, Whalen's voice grated over the line.

"I warned the son-of-a-bitch," he said. "Nobody can say I didn't warn him. Take care of it, will you, Chip?"

The phone went dead in Chip's hand. Harney had hung up on him.

By midnight it was all over. Chip Connor and Brad Randall had brought Jeff Horton's body in out of the storm. It lay in the dining room, covered by a blanket, until an ambulance could be summoned to take it away. Rebecca and Elaine, chilled by the closeness of death, avoided the dining room as if whatever had killed Jeff might still be lurking there.

Chip hovered near while Brad examined the body, going over it quickly but expertly. When he was finished he drew the blanket over Jeff's face and spoke quietly to Chip.

"His neck's broken. That's all I can find. Of course a full autopsy will have to be done, but that's not my business. And I doubt they'll find anything else. It's almost incredible that he was still alive when Glen found him."

"Why?"

"The way his neck was bent. He should have been dead just a minute or two after his neck was broken."

"Then how did he stay alive?"

Brad shook his head doubtfully. "I'm not sure. Pure will, probably. His windpipe must have stayed open, but his spinal column is a mess."

"Did Glen's touching him have anything to do with him dying?"

"It might have but he'd have died anyway. If anything, all Glen did was put him out of his misery. There was no way he could have survived what happened."

"What did happen?" Chip asked. "Can you tell?"

"From the bruises on the back of the neck, it looks like someone hit him with something—hard enough to crush the bones in his neck—then jerked on his head to make sure the job was done."

"Christ," Chip groaned, feeling a little sick at his stomach. "Why would anyone want to do that?"

"I wish I knew." He looked curiously at Chip. "Isn't Whalen coming out?"

"No. He told me to take care of it for him. I guess he still isn't feeling well."

"What do you mean?"

"He took yesterday off," Chip said. "When I talked to him this morning he said something about indigestion. I guess it must have hit him again tonight."

"Indigestion?" Brad repeated. "He doesn't seem the type. He looks strong as an ox."

"He is," Chip agreed. "But he's sixty-eight years old, even though he doesn't look it."

"Sixty-eight? I'd have thought he was in his late fifties."

"Nope. He'll be sixty-nine in August."

Brad shook his head admiringly. "I should look that good when I'm his age," he said, but his mind was no longer on Whalen's appearance. It was his age that Brad had focused on. Something about his age that made some kind of connection. But before he could sort it out the ambulance arrived, and by the time they had finished attending to Jeff Horton's body the elusive connection had slipped away.

Brad closed the kitchen door against the rain as the ambulance disappeared into the storm. "You still on duty, or can I offer you a drink?"

"I'd better not," Chip replied. "I have to get down to the station and write up this report so Harney will have it in the morning." He closed his notebook and prepared to leave. Then, just as he was about to open the door, he turned to Brad. He had one last question.

"Brad, do you have any idea what's going on out here? What's causing all this mess?"

Brad shook his head sorrowfully. "I wish I did. All I can tell you is that I think it has something to do with the storms."

"The storms?" Chip repeated. "But we've always had storms."

"I know," Brad said softly. "And it seems like you've always had a mess too."

Chip stared at him, then tried to laugh it off. "Maybe it's the Indians. God knows they did terrible things out here." Then he put on his hat and disappeared into the blackness outside.

25

The storm had not let up by morning.

As Brad and Glen drove into Clark's Harbor the rain buffeted the car, flooding the windshield faster than the wipers could clear it away.

"I've never seen anything like this," Glen commented. "I thought the worst storms hit during the winter."

"You never know," Brad said as they pulled up in front of the town hall. "Sometimes I think they gave the Pacific the wrong name. This one looks as though it could blow for days."

Several people lounging in the lobby looked up as they came in, examining them with speculative expressions. Something new in Clark's Harbor, Brad thought with some irony. Ignoring the inquisitive stares, they hurried down the hall to the police station.

Harney Whalen glared balefully at Glen as they came into his office. Before either of them could say anything, Whalen set the tone of the conversation.

"Seems like every time there's trouble around here you're right in the middle of it, doesn't it, Palmer?"

Glen felt the first pangs of anger form a knot in his

stomach and silently reminded himself that losing his temper wouldn't accomplish anything.

"It seems like every time there's trouble it happens on Sod Beach," he countered.

Harney Whalen snorted and tossed a folder toward Glen and Brad. "You want to look that over and tell me if it's accurate?"

Glen scanned the report, then handed it to Brad. When both of them had read it, Brad returned it to Whalen.

"That's about it," Brad said.

"You want to tell me about it?" Whalen asked Glen, ignoring Brad.

"There's nothing to tell. We went out looking for Jeff and we found him. He died almost immediately."

"Why were you looking for him?" The curiosity in Whalen's voice was almost lost in the hostility. "He's a grown man—*was* a grown man."

"It was getting late—there was a storm blowing in. We just didn't like the idea of him being out in it," Glen replied.

"I think it was something else," Whalen said coldly.

"Something else? What?"

"I think you killed him," Whalen said. "Maybe one of you, maybe the other, maybe both. But I sure as hell don't believe the two of you just went for a walk on the beach and found a dying man. Something makes men die and it's usually other men."

Brad and Glen gaped at the police chief, unable to comprehend what they were hearing. Brad recovered first.

"I'd be careful what I said if I were you, Whalen."

"Would you?" The sneer in Harney Whalen's voice hung in the air, a challenge. But before either of them could take it up Whalen went on. "How about this? The two of you were at the library last night, right? Well, let's suppose that while you were gone Horton wasn't staying home taking care of your wives like a good guest. Let's suppose he was just taking care of them. And you two walked in on it." He eyed first Glen, then Brad, looking for a reaction.

Glen Palmer stood quivering with rage, staring out the window at the downpour, saying nothing. But Brad Randall returned Whalen's icy look, and when he spoke it was with a calmness that Whalen hadn't expected.

"Are you charging us?" he asked calmly.

"I haven't decided yet," Whalen growled.

"Then we're leaving," Brad said quietly. "Come on, Glen." He turned and forced Glen to turn with him. Before they reached the door Whalen's voice stopped them.

"I'm not through with you yet."

Brad turned back to face the police chief. When he spoke his voice was every bit as cold as Whalen's had been.

"Aren't you? I think you are, Whalen. You aren't questioning us at all. You're accusing us. Now I'm not a lawyer, but I know damned well, and I suspect you know it too, that there's no way you can talk to us if we don't want to talk to you. Not without a lawyer here anyway."

Once more he started for the door with Glen behind him. This time Harney Whalen didn't try to stop them. He simply watched them go, hating them, wishing they had never come to Clark's Harbor, wishing they would leave him and his town in peace.

His fury and frustration mounting, Whalen put on his overcoat and rain hat and stalked out of his office. As he passed through the door of the police station, the loiterers quickly scattered, reading his ugly mood.

He started toward the wharf, unsure of where he was going or why. When he got to the wharf he turned north and began walking up the beach. The tide had peaked and was on its way out, and as he walked in the rain, the wind licking at him, his anger seemed to recede.

He walked the beach all morning and well into the afternoon.

He walked alone, silently.

As he walked, the storm swelled.

Robby and Missy sat on the floor of their tiny bedroom, a checkerboard between them. Robby stared sullenly at the board. No matter what he did, Missy was going to jump his last man and win the third straight game.

"I don't want to play anymore," he said.

"You have to move," Missy replied.

"I don't either. I can concede."

"Move," Missy insisted. "I want to jump you."

"You win anyway," Robby said. He stood up and went to look out the window. "Let's go outside," he said suddenly. From the floor Missy stared at him, her eyes wide with fear.

"We can't do that. Mommy said we have to stay in today. It's raining."

"I like it when it rains."

357

"I don't. Not when it rains like this. Bad things happen."

"Oh, come on," Robby urged her. "It's not even six o'clock. We can climb out the window, like I did last time. We'll go down to the Randalls' and come back with Daddy."

"I don't think we should."

"Scaredy-cat."

"That's right!" Missy exclaimed. "And you should be too!" Her mouth quivered, partly from fear but more from embarrassment at having admitted her fear.

"Well, I'm not afraid. I like it out there!" Robby pulled their raincoats out of the closet and began putting his on.

"I'm not going," Missy insisted.

"Who cares?" Robby asked with a show of unconcern. "I'll go by myself."

"I'm going to tell," Missy challenged, her eyes narrowing.

"If you do I'll beat you up," Robby threatened.

"You won't either."

Robby pulled on his boots. "Are you coming or not?"

"No," Missy said.

"All right for you then." He opened the window and clambered out. As soon as he was gone Missy ran to the window, pulled it shut, and latched it. Then she went into the other room, where Rebecca was sitting in front of the fire, knitting.

"Robby went outside," she said.

"Outside? What do you mean, he went outside?"

"He put on his raincoat and climbed out the window," Missy explained.

Rebecca dropped her knitting and ran to the tiny

bedroom, hoping her daughter was playing a joke on her.

"Robby? Robby, where are you?"

"I *told* you, he went outside," Missy insisted.

Rebecca ran to the door, pulled it open, and started to step outside, but the storm drove her back in. She shielded her face and tried to see into the growing darkness.

"Robby? Robby!" she called. "Robby, come back here." But the wind and the pounding surf of the cresting tide drowned her words.

She thought desperately, wondering what to do, and immediately knew she would have to go find him. If only Glen were here, she thought. If only he hadn't gone down to the Randalls'. But he had. She would have to find Robby alone.

"I'll go get him," she told Missy. "You stay here."

"By myself?" Missy asked. She looked terrified.

"I'll only be gone a few minutes," Rebecca assured her. "Only until I find Robby."

"I don't want to stay by myself," Missy wailed. "I want to go too."

Rebecca tried to think it out but she was too upset. Her instincts told her to make Missy stay by herself, but the thought of having both her children alone frightened her even more than the idea of taking Missy with her.

"All right," she said. "Put on your raincoat and your boots, but hurry!"

Missy darted into the bedroom and came back with the coat and boots that Robby had already pulled from the closet. Rebecca pulled her own coat on, then helped Missy. A minute later, clutching a flashlight with one hand and Missy with the other, Rebecca left the cabin. A sudden gusting of the storm snuffed out the lantern just before she closed the door.

The wind whipped at her and drove the pounding rain through every small gap in her raincoat. Before they were a hundred feet from the house, both Rebecca and Missy were soaked to the skin.

"I want to go home," Missy wailed.

"We have to find Robby," Rebecca shouted. "Which way did he go?"

"He said he was going out on the beach." Missy was running now to keep up with Rebecca.

They stayed as close to the high-water line as they could, hurrying down the beach. The flashlight was almost useless, its beam refracting madly in the downpour, shattering into a thousand pinpoints of light that illuminated nothing, but made the darkness seem even blacker than it was.

Suddenly Missy stopped and yanked at her mother's hand.

"Someone's here," she said.

Rebecca flashed the light around with a shaking hand. "Robby?" she called. "Roobbeeeee!"

She turned so that her back was to the wind and called out again. There was no answer, but she suddenly felt the sharp sting of an electrical shock as a bolt of lightning flashed out of the sky and grounded itself in the nearby forest. And, she was sure, there was something behind her: an unfamiliar presence.

A presence she knew was not her son.

She dropped Missy's hand.

"Run, Missy! Run as fast as you can."

And then, as she watched Missy dash off into the

darkness, she felt something slide around her neck.

It was an arm, a strong arm, and it was choking her. She tried to scream but her voice wouldn't respond. She tried to batter at the arm with the flashlight, but the pressure on her neck only increased.

No, she thought. *Not like this. Please, God, no . . .*

Missy ran into the darkness, not knowing which way she was going. She only knew she was going away.

Away from her mother.

Away from whoever was with her mother.

Then she stumbled and fell into the sand, crying out into the darkness.

"Missy? Is that you?" She couldn't see who was calling to her but she recognized the voice.

"Robby? Where are you?"

"Over here. Come on."

She scrambled toward his voice and found herself blocked by a log.

"Climb over," Robby urged.

Then she was beside him, crouched down behind the log, peering over the top of it into the darkness. In the distance the beam of the flashlight danced crazily, then suddenly fell to the ground and went out.

"What's happening?" Robby asked.

"It's Mommy," Missy sobbed. "Someone's out there—"

A bolt of lightning split the darkness, and the two children saw their mother. She was on her knees and there was a shape behind her, looming over her, holding her neck, forcing her head forward . . .

A shiver of excitement made Robby tremble, and

he could feel every muscle in his body tense with anticipation.

The light faded from the sky and the roar of thunder rolled over them, drowning the scream that was welling from Missy's throat. It was as if the storm was clutching at Robby, immobilizing him.

"Let's go home, Missy," Robby whispered. He forced himself to take his sobbing sister by the hand and lead her into the woods. Then, as the beach disappeared from their view, he began running, pulling Missy behind him.

Rebecca's struggles grew weaker. She was blacking out. Time began to stretch for her, and she thought she could feel her blood desperately trying to suck oxygen from her strangled lungs.

Then she heard a crack, sharp, close to her ear, and she realized she could no longer move. It was as if she had lost all contact with her body.

My neck, she thought curiously. My neck is broken.

A second later Rebecca Palmer lay dead on Sod Beach.

26

The Coleman lantern on the dining-room table began to fade, and Glen Palmer reached out to pump it up just as the bolt of lightning that had illuminated Rebecca's death a hundred yards away also flooded the Randalls' house with light. Reflexively, Glen snatched his hand away from the lantern, then chuckled. Brad Randall looked up from the chart he was poring over.

"Maybe we should give it up for today," Brad said. "I don't know about you but my eyes are getting tired. I'm not used to lantern light."

They had been at it all afternoon, charting the various events that had occurred in Clark's Harbor, from the deaths of Pete and Miriam Shelling all the way back to the frighteningly similar demise of Frank and Myrtle Baron years earlier. Over the years there had been several fatalities in the area, usually in the vicinity of Sod Beach, always on stormy nights when the coast was battered by high winds. And as far as they could tell, most of the victims, if not all, had been strangers to Clark's Harbor. Strangers who had come to the Harbor for various reasons and intended to settle there.

"It's like the Indian legends," Glen commented as

they stared at the charts. "It's almost as if the beach itself doesn't want strangers here—as if it waits, gathers its forces, then strikes out at people."

"Which makes a nice story," Brad said archly. "But I don't believe it for a minute. There's another explanation but I'm damned if I know how to go about finding it."

Glen thought a moment. "What about Robby?" he asked.

"Robby?"

"You said that the beach affects him. If that's true, couldn't it affect someone else too?"

Brad smiled wryly. "Sure. But it doesn't help the problem. Until I know *how* the beach affects Robby, how can I figure out who else might be affected? So far I don't have the slightest idea what the common denominator might be."

Elaine appeared in the doorway. "Getting anywhere?" She looked drawn and tired.

"I wish we were," Brad said. "But so far it's nothing but dead ends. Apparently the storms are killing people, which is, of course, ridiculous."

"What about Missy? Hasn't anybody talked to her?"

The two men stared blankly at Elaine, wondering what she was talking about. A memory suddenly flashed into Brad's mind, a memory of Robby, talking to him on the beach.

"Missy thinks she sees things."

Did Elaine know something about that too?

"What about Missy?" he asked quietly. The tone of his voice, the seriousness with which he asked the question, frightened Glen, but Elaine's answer frightened him even more.

"I think Missy saw Jeff Horton get killed," she said. There was a flatness to her voice that somehow emphasized her words. "I haven't talked to her but she said something last night. I—I told her that her daddy had gone out on the beach, and she said, 'He shouldn't have done that. Bad things happen there.' That's all she said, but I got the strangest feeling that she'd seen what happened to Jeff, or at least had seen *something*."

Glen sat in stunned silence, but Brad was nodding thoughtfully. "Robby told me awhile ago that Missy thinks she sees things on the beach," he murmured.

Glen suddenly found his voice. "Things?" he asked, his word edged with hysteria. "What kind of things?"

"He didn't say," Brad replied quietly. "I was going to talk to her about it but then everything started happening, and . . ." his voice trailed off, his words sounding hollow.

Glen stood up and pulled on his coat.

"Then we'll talk to her now. I'll go get Rebecca and bring her and the kids back here."

Brad glanced out into the blackness of the storm. "You want me to drive you? It's getting pretty dark out there."

"No thanks," Glen replied. "I'll walk along the beach. It doesn't look so bad out there now." He finished buttoning his coat and opened the door. The wind caught it and slammed it back against the kitchen wall.

"Sure you don't want me to drive you?"

Glen grinned crookedly. "You mean because of last night? They say if you fall off a horse the best thing to do is get right back up and ride him again. If I don't walk the beach tonight I never will."

He pulled the door closed behind him and disappeared into the rain.

Glen leaned forward into the wind, his right hand clutching the collar of his coat in a useless attempt to keep the rain out. His left hand, plunged deep in his coat pocket, was balled into a fist, and he kept his eyes squinted tightly against the stinging rain.

He made his way slowly, keeping close to the surf line, keeping his head down, watching the sand at his feet. Every few seconds he looked up, searching the darkness for the soft glow that should be coming from the cabin windows. Then, as the glow failed to appear out of the darkness, he began to worry and picked up his pace.

When he had walked nearly a hundred yards and felt the cabin should be clearly visible, he stopped and stared into the darkness, as if by concentrating hard enough he could force the dim light of the kerosene lanterns to appear in front of him. But still there was only blackness, and his concern turned to fear.

He began to run, no longer watching his steps, but straining his eyes to find the cabin, the cabin where Rebecca and the children would be waiting for him.

He tripped, sprawling headlong into the sand, his right hand only partially breaking his fall, his left hand, suddenly entangled in his pocket, useless.

He tasted brackish salt water in his mouth and felt the abrasive scraping of sand on his face. As he thrashed around, wiping his mouth on his sleeve and trying to get his left hand free, his foot hit something.

Something soft.

He felt the numbness begin in his mind—the same numbness that had fallen over him last night. He moved slowly, almost reluctantly.

He touched Rebecca gently, caressing her face. Even though she was still warm, he knew she was dead.

Her head, cradled in the sand, lay at the same unnatural angle as had Jeff Horton's the night before.

It was as if his mind refused to accept it at first. Glen crouched beside her, rocking slowly back and forth, no longer feeling the wind, the rain funneling unheeded down his collar.

"Rebecca," he said softly. Then he repeated her name. "Rebecca."

The pain hit him, washing over him with all the unexpected intensity of a tidal wave, and he threw himself onto her, wrapping her in his arms, sobbing on her breast.

"Rebecca," he moaned. "Oh, God, Rebecca, don't leave me."

She lay limply in his arms, her head rolling gently from side to side, her unseeing eyes staring up into the night sky.

Glen's pain changed from the wracking misery of the moment of discovery into a dull ache, an ache he was sure he would bear for the rest of his life.

Why had Rebecca been on the beach at all?

He thought of the children.

Where were the children?

He should look for them. They must have left the cabin, and Rebecca must have gone to look for them; she would never have left them alone, not Rebecca.

He stood up and looked uncertainly toward the forest, a black shadow set deep in the darkness of the night. If they were out here they would be in the woods.

But he couldn't leave Rebecca, couldn't leave her lying cold in the rain and the wind, the surf lapping at her feet. Before he went looking for his children he would have to attend to his wife.

He picked her up and began carrying her toward the cabin, his fogged mind wondering with each step at his need to care for the dead before tending to the living.

Where Rebecca had lain, there was now nothing but sand—and the darkly glistening form of a blue glass fisherman's float.

When he got to the cabin he paused, something preventing him from going inside. At first he wasn't sure what it was, but after a moment he knew.

The cabin wasn't empty.

There was nothing about it that told him it was occupied, only an intangible feeling. Though there was no sound, he was sure his children were there.

He laid Rebecca's body gently on the porch, then opened the door.

"Robby? Missy? It's Daddy."

He heard a scrambling sound, and then the children threw themselves on him.

"Daddy, Daddy," Missy sobbed. "Something awful happened."

Glen sank to his knees and drew the children close. "I'm sorry, Daddy, I'm sorry," Robby kept repeating, over and over.

"There's nothing for you to be sorry about," Glen

told his son. "Nothing that happened is your fault. Nothing at all."

"But I went out," Robby insisted. "I wanted to go outside, so I did. And Mommy and Missy came to look for me, and then—then—" he choked on his words and began sobbing helplessly.

"We were on the beach," Missy said. "Something grabbed Mommy, and Mommy told me to run, and I did, and—and—"

"Hush," Glen whispered. "You don't have to tell me about it now. I have to take care of Mommy, and I want you to do something for me."

He disentangled himself from the children and lit the small lantern that should have been lighting Rebecca's work as she waited for him to come home, but instead had remained cold and dark as night fell over the beach. As the flame flickered to life the room seemed to warm slightly, and Robby and Missy began to calm down.

"Robby, I want you to take Missy into your bedroom. Put some clean clothes in a bag. For both of you. Can you do that?"

Robby nodded gravely.

"All right. Then wait for me. In the bedroom. Don't come out until I come for you, all right?"

"Are you going somewhere?" Missy asked, her eyes wide and her mouth quivering.

"No, darling, of course not. I'll be right here."

Missy started to ask another question, but Robby grabbed her hand and began pulling her toward their tiny bedroom. "Come on," he said.

"Stop pulling," Missy cried. "Daddy, make him stop."

"Don't pull her, Robby," Glen said. "And you stay in there with your brother," he instructed Missy.

As soon as the door separating their room from the main part of the cabin was closed, Glen opened the sofa bed he and Rebecca had shared and pulled one of the blankets off it. Then he carefully reclosed the bed and went back to the front porch.

He moved Rebecca to the end of the porch farthest from the door and carefully wrapped her in the blanket. When he was finished he went back to the front door, then turned to survey his work. If he got the children across the porch fast enough, they wouldn't notice that something was lying there only a few feet away. Struggling to maintain his self-control, Glen went back into the cabin.

Robby and Missy were sitting quietly on the edge of the lower bunk, their faces serious, their hands folded in their laps. Between them was a brown bag stuffed with clothing.

"Mommy's dead, isn't she?" Robby asked.

"Yes, she is," Glen said steadily.

"Why?" It was Missy, and her face looked more curious than anything else. Glen realized for the first time that Rebecca's death had no meaning for them yet. While it was painful beyond bearing for him, for his children it was still an abstract event.

"I don't know," he said gently. "Sometimes things like this happen."

"Do we have to go away?" Robby asked.

"Go away?"

"Is that why I put our clothes in the bag? Because we have to go away?"

"I'm going to take you down to stay with Brad and

CRY FOR THE STRANGERS

Elaine tonight," Glen said. "I'll stay there too, but I have to do some things tonight and I don't want to leave you alone."

"Are we going now?" Missy asked.

"Right now," Glen replied, forcing himself to smile. "Now it's pouring rain outside, so I want you two to see who can get to the car first, all right?"

The two children nodded eagerly.

"I'll open the door, and you two race. The first one to the car gets a surprise."

"What is it?" Robby demanded.

"If I told you it wouldn't be a surprise anymore, would it?"

He led them into the other room and made them stay back from the door while he opened it. Tears were streaming down his face.

"On your mark. Get set. Go!" he cried, and the children, intent only on the race, streaked through the door and across the porch, vying to be the first to reach the ancient VW van. Glen picked up their bag of clothing, closed the door, and followed them.

"Oh, Jesus," Brad Randall moaned as he opened the door for Glen Palmer and the children. The look in Glen's eyes and the tear-streaked faces of the children told him something terrible had happened. He could guess what.

Hearing his words from the living room, Elaine hurried in to find out what had gone wrong.

"Glen? Is something wrong?" She looked first at Glen, then at the children, and she too knew immediately. She knelt down and gathered the children into her arms. They clung to her, almost tentatively, then Missy, followed by Robby, broke into tears and buried their faces against her. As she held the children she looked up into Glen Palmer's drained face.

"I'm sorry," she said. "I'm so sorry . . ."

Glen swallowed and forced himself to stay coherent. "Can you . . . can you . . . ?" He couldn't finish the sentence, but Elaine understood.

"I'll take care of them. Brad, go with him. Help him."

Brad had been silently standing by but he suddenly came to life, grabbing for his coat. A moment later the two men disappeared into the night.

Elaine steered the children into the living room and settled them on the sofa. Then, before she did anything else, she quickly went through the house, checking all the windows, making sure they were closed and locked. Finally she bolted the doors, rattling each to be sure it was secure.

When she returned to the living room Missy was staring into the fire, lost in some small world of her own devising. But as Elaine sank down beside her the little girl took one of her hands, squeezed it, and smiled up at her.

"It's going to be all right," she said. "Really it is."

For some reason that Elaine never understood, Missy's words made her cry.

Glen and Brad carried Rebecca into the cabin and laid her on the floor. While Glen poked at the dying fire, wishing he could bring life back to Rebecca as easily as he could the coals, Brad began a quick examination.

It didn't take him long. By the time the fire was blazing he had finished.

"She was strangled," he said. "And her neck's broken."

"Oh, God," Glen said, shuddering. "It must have been terrible for her."

"That's something we don't know," Brad replied quietly. "I like to think the body has ways of dealing with things like this. We know we go into shock immediately when something happens to us suddenly and unexpectedly. I should think it would be the same with dying. Some automatic mechanism takes over and makes us comfortable. Anyway, that's the way it should be. But we'll never know, will we?"

"How long has she been dead?" Glen asked.

"Not long. An hour. Maybe two at the most."

"If only I hadn't stayed so long," Glen said. "If only I'd left a little earlier. Just a few minutes maybe—"

"Don't," Brad said. "Don't start that or you'll wind up blaming yourself for what happened. And you aren't to blame."

"I brought her here," Glen said.

"And it could as easily have been you out there tonight," Brad said roughly. "Now come on. We'd better get into town."

Glen looked around the little room.

"I hate to leave her here, all alone . . ."

"No. You're coming with me. I'm not leaving you with her. Not tonight, not here. Put on your coat."

They were about to leave when they suddenly heard a sound from the children's room.

A small sound, barely a whimper.

Then, as they were about to investigate, Scooter, his small tail tucked between his legs, crept out into the living room.

He stopped, peered vacantly up at the two of them; then his tail began to wag and he stumbled clumsily toward Glen. Glen stooped, picked the puppy up, and scratched its belly. By the time they were in the car Scooter was fast asleep.

Chip Connor was alone in the police station when Brad and Glen arrived.

"It's Rebecca," Brad said.

The muscles in Chip's face tightened and he sank back into the chair behind Harney Whalen's desk.

"Is she dead?"

"Yes."

"Where?"

"On the beach."

"Shit." Then: "I'll have to call Harn."

"I know," said Brad. "But before you do I should tell you that I'm not going to let Glen talk to him tonight. As a doctor I'm putting him under my care."

"Of course," Chip said. "I don't think anyone would expect anything else."

"Don't you?" Brad said mildly, almost tiredly. "I wish I could share your thought."

If Chip even heard what Brad said he gave no sign. Instead he called Harney Whalen and quickly reported what had happened.

"I'll meet you out at the Palmers'," he said as he finished. Then he hung up the phone and looked at Glen, who had not yet spoken.

"Glen, can I ask you something, as a friend?"

"Sure," Glen said dully.

"Did you do it?"

Brad was about make an angry reply but Glen put a hand on his arm, stopping him.

"No, Chip, I didn't." The two men stared into each other's eyes, and finally Chip stood up and came around the desk.

"Try to take it easy, Glen. I'll find him for you, so help me." Then he turned to Brad.

"Can you give him a pill? To make him sleep?"

Brad frowned slightly. "I'm not sure he needs one."

"Well, if it won't hurt him give him one, will you?" There was a pause, then Chip shook his head sadly. "You were right about what you said before. Harney does want to talk to him."

"I've just changed my mind," Brad said. "What this man needs more than anything else is a good night's sleep."

But it wasn't a good night's sleep. Before dawn Glen Palmer woke up and reached for Rebecca.

She wasn't there. She would never be there again.

Quietly, Glen Palmer began to cry.

27

There was a quality in the air the following morning, a numbing chill that lay over Clark's Harbor like an invisible fog, shrouding the town.

The people of the village went about their business, tending their shops and boats, greeting each other as they always had. When they spoke of Rebecca Palmer, and of Jeff Horton, it was not with the worried clucking of tongues and expressions of concern that might have been expected, but rather with the knowing looks, the almost lewdly arched eyebrows of people who have finally witnessed that which they had known would come to pass.

When Glen Palmer arrived at the police station in midmorning, he was not stared at, not subjected to the hostile glares he had been expecting. Nor were there any expressions of sympathy at the loss of his wife. Rather—and to Glen even more frightening—it was as if nothing had changed, as if what had happened to him was not a part of Clark's Harbor at all, not an event that touched the lives of the Harborites.

Only when he was inside the police station, inside Harney Whalen's office, did reality intrude on the sense of surrealism that surrounded him.

Harney Whalen sat impassively at his desk, staring at Glen.

"Are you ready to talk about it now?" The words were more a challenge than a question. Glen braced himself. He knew what was coming.

In the old house on Sod Beach Elaine Randall did her best to keep Missy and Robby occupied, to keep them from dwelling on the loss of their mother. After Glen left the house, insisting on going alone to see Whalen, the children had wanted to go out on the beach.

Elaine had refused, not so much out of fear that anything would happen to them, but out of her own inability to face the beach that day.

She was not sure she would ever again be able to enjoy the beauty of the crescent of sand. For her it was permanently soiled.

Around noon she set the children to work on a jigsaw puzzle, then went to the kitchen to fix lunch.

"Keep an eye on them, will you, honey?" she asked Brad as she passed through the dining room. Brad glanced up from the charts he was poring over.

"Hmm?"

"The kids," Elaine replied. "Keep an eye on them for me while I put lunch together."

"Sure," Brad muttered, and went back to work. Elaine smiled softly to herself and continued into the kitchen. The house could fall down around him without his noticing. She poked halfheartedly at the fire in the ancient stove and decided a cold lunch would do just fine.

377

Fifteen minutes went by, then Robby appeared in the kitchen.

"When are we having lunch?"

"In about two minutes. Are your hands clean?"

Robby solemnly inspected his hands, then held them up to Elaine for approval. She looked them over carefully and nodded.

"Okay. Take these into the dining room and see if you can get Brad to make room for us." She handed the little boy a tray of sandwiches, then followed him a few minutes later with napkins, silver, and a jar of pickles. The table, she noted, had miraculously been cleared, and Missy and Robby sat flanking Brad, all of them patiently awaiting her arrival.

"Isn't Daddy coming?" Missy asked as Elaine sat down.

"He'll be back as soon as he can get here," Elaine explained.

"Can I save my sandwich for him?"

"What'll you eat?"

"I'm not hungry," Missy said softly. "I'll just drink some milk."

"I'm sure your—" Elaine began, then stopped short. She had been about to say "mother," but quickly changed it. "—father would want you to eat your lunch," she finished.

"No, he wouldn't," Missy assured her.

"He would too," Robby said. "He'd say the same thing Mother would say—'you eat what's put in front of you!' Even if it *is* liverwurst," he added almost under his breath. He determinedly bit into his sandwich, and a moment later Missy did the same. The children munched in silence for a moment, then Robby put the remains of his sandwich down and looked quizzically at Elaine.

"Are we going to have to go away?"

"Go away? What do you mean?"

"Are we going to have to move away, after what happened to Mommy?"

"Well, I don't know," Elaine replied carefully. "That depends on your father, I suppose."

"Do you want to move away?" Brad asked. Robby shook his head emphatically but it was Missy who spoke.

"Yes! I hate it here! Mr. Riley told us a long time ago that there are ghosts on the beach, and he's right. I've seen them. They killed Mommy and they killed Mr. Horton and they'll kill everybody else too."

Elaine half-rose from her chair, intent on calming the child, but Brad signaled her to stay where she was. "Ghosts? What kind of ghosts."

"Indians," Missy said sulkily. "Mr. Riley told us they used to kill people on the beach, and sometimes they come back and do it some more. And I've seen them. I saw them the day Mr. Riley told us about them, and I saw them the night Mr. Horton got killed, and I saw them last night." As she spoke the last words Missy fled sobbing from the table. Elaine immediately followed her.

Robby seemed unperturbed by Missy's outburst. He picked his sandwich up again, took a big bite, and munched on it thoughtfully. Brad watched the boy eat, sure that he was turning something over in his mind. He was right, for Robby suddenly put the sandwich down again.

"Maybe she really does see things," Robby suggested hesitantly.

"Could be," Brad offered.

"I mean, the beach is a weird place during the storms."

"Oh?" Brad could feel something coming and wanted it to come from Robby undisturbed, uninfluenced by his own feelings.

"I like the storms," Robby went on, "but it's funny. I can't really remember what happens when I'm on the beach. It used to be fun, before all the bad things started happening. It was like I was all alone in the world, and it felt good. Even though it was raining real hard, I didn't feel it. I didn't feel anything, except inside myself." His brows knotted in sudden puzzlement.

"What is it?" Brad prompted him.

"It's funny," Robby said. "I can remember how I felt but I can't remember what I did. I mean, I can't remember going anyplace or doing anything, but I guess I must have." His voice dropped, and he seemed about to cry. "I wish I hadn't gone out last night. If I hadn't nothing would have happened."

"Robby," Brad assured him, "it isn't your fault."

But Robby looked unconvinced.

Glen Palmer came back to the Randalls' in the middle of the afternoon, but when Brad asked him how the talk with Whalen had gone he was uncommunicative.

"I'm going to go up to the cabin," he said. "Is it all right if I leave the kids here?"

"Of course," Elaine agreed, watching him worriedly.

"But wouldn't you like one of us to go with you?"

"I'd rather go by myself. I have some thinking to do and I think I can do it best there."

Brad nodded understandingly and accompanied Glen to the door. When he was sure they were out of range of the children he put his hand on Brad's shoulder and spoke softly.

"If it's any comfort, I don't think that whoever killed Rebecca and Jeff knew what they were doing."

Glen paled slightly and stared blankly at Brad.

"I had a talk with Robby a little while ago," Brad explained. "He doesn't remember what he did on the beach last night. He only remembers feeling good."

"What does that mean?" Glen asked dully.

"Well, whatever happens to Robby must be happening to someone else. But with the opposite effect: Robby feels good, someone else goes crazy. He probably doesn't even know what he's doing. Jeff and Rebecca just happened to be there." In his own mind Brad had dismissed Missy's story as childish imagination, not worth mentioning.

"Oh, God," Glen groaned. "It all seems so—so futile!"

"I know," Brad replied sympathetically. "But we'll find out what's happening, and we'll stop it."

"I wonder," Glen said. "I wonder if it really even matters anymore." He started out onto the beach but Brad called him back.

"Try to get back before dark, will you? Let's not have anything else happening."

"Okay," Glen agreed. Then he turned and started up the beach, his shoulders slumped, his steps slow, uncertain. A few moments later, he disappeared around the corner of the house, and Brad stopped watching. While Glen walked and thought, Brad would work.

Chip Connor arrived at the Randalls' at five thirty that afternoon and hesitated nervously before knocking at the front door. When Elaine opened it a few seconds later she found Chip twisting his hat in his hands and looking very upset.

"Chip!" she said warmly. "Come in."

"Thanks," Chip replied automatically. "Is your husband here?"

"Yes, of course," Elaine said, her smile fading. "Is something wrong?"

"I'm not sure. But I need to talk to Brad."

"He's in the dining room. Come on."

Brad was at the dining-room table surrounded by stacks of books as he searched for an explanation for the madness around him. He looked up distractedly when he heard Elaine come into the room, then put his book aside when he realized who was with her.

"What brings you out here? If you're looking for Glen I think he's up at his place."

"I need to talk to you." Chip sank into one of the chairs around the table and Elaine quickly left the room, sensing that whatever Chip had to say, he wanted to say it only to Brad. When she was gone Brad gave Chip a searching look.

"What is it? Has something else happened?"

"I don't know," Chip said unhappily. "In fact, I'm not even sure I should be here. But I had to talk to someone and you were the only person I could think of."

"What is it?" Brad urged him again. "Is it about Glen?"

"Only indirectly," Chip replied. "I guess mostly it's Harn—Harney Whalen."

"What about him?"

"I'm not sure," Chip said, squirming in the chair. Then, almost as if to change the subject, he said, "Did Glen tell you about what happened today?"

"No. He came in a couple of hours ago, but went right out again. He said he had some thinking to do."

"I'll bet he did," Chip said. "I wish I knew what he was thinking."

"Well, you might go ask him," Brad suggested dryly. "You two seem to get along pretty well."

"Maybe I will after a while," Chip agreed. A silence fell over the two men.

"You said you wanted to talk about Whalen," Brad said at last.

Chip nodded glumly. "I think something's gone wrong with him."

"How do you mean, wrong? You mean physically?"

"I wish it were that simple," Chip hedged.

Brad's fingers drummed on the table and he decided to wait Chip out, let him get to the point any way he wanted to. He wasn't surprised when Chip suddenly stood up and started pacing the room.

"Something's been nagging at me for quite a while now," he said finally. "Harn's attitude, I guess you might say."

"You mean the way he feels about outsiders?"

"That's it," Chip agreed. "But up until today I've always been able to convince myself that it wasn't

383

anything particularly serious—that it was sort of a quirk in his personality."

"But something happened today that changed your mind?"

"Glen Palmer. He came in to tell Harn what happened last night."

"And—?"

"And Harn didn't give him a chance. Instead he told Glen what happened."

"I'm not sure what you mean."

"It was crazy," Chip said. "I've been thinking about it ever since and the only word I come up with is crazy. Harn didn't ask Glen any questions at all. Instead he accused Glen of killing Rebecca himself."

"Just like that?" Brad asked.

"Close enough so that it doesn't make any difference what the exact words were. He must've spent most of the night last night dreaming up a story about how Glen found Rebecca and Jeff Horton making love and killed Jeff, then Rebecca. Apparently you're out of it," he added, smiling humorlessly. Brad ignored the comment.

"What did Glen have to say?"

"What could he say? He said it was ridiculous but Harn wasn't even interested in hearing what happened last night. He just kept after Glen, repeating his idea over and over, as if he were trying to convince Glen. I think he wanted Glen to confess."

"I hope he didn't."

"Of course not," Chip said. "And even if he had it wouldn't have made any difference. The way Harney was acting, any court I've ever heard of would disqualify the whole thing."

"But why? Why would he want to put the whole thing on Glen?"

"I don't think it has anything to do with Glen personally," Chip said. "For a while I thought it did, but I talked to my grandfather a few days ago, and he told me some things that made me wonder."

"What sort of things?"

"Stories. Stories about things that happened around here a long time ago. Long before I was even born. For instance, he told me why Harn hates strangers so much."

"You want to tell me?"

"It's a pretty ugly story." He paused a moment, then swallowed. When he spoke again, his voice was strained.

"Harney watched his grandparents being murdered when he was a little boy."

Brad's eyes widened. "Say that again, please?"

"When Harn was a little boy—maybe seven, eight years old—his grandparents were murdered on the beach. Harney watched it happen."

"Holy Christ," Brad muttered. "Who did it?"

"Nothing was ever proven but everyone seemed to think it was a group of people who were interested in lumbering the area. Maybe even the man who built this house."

"Baron? I thought he was a fisherman. He died by getting caught in his own fishing nets."

"Just like Pete Shelling," Chip agreed. "But he only became a fisherman after Harn canceled his lumbering lease. Anyway, whoever killed Harn's grandparents, they were strangers, and Harn's hated strangers ever since. Only now it's getting out of hand."

"What can I do?" Brad asked.

"I was wondering if maybe you could talk to him," Chip replied.

"Me? Haven't you forgotten something? I'm a stranger here too, and yesterday he as much as accused me of murder. What makes you think Whalen would talk to me?"

"I don't know," Chip said nervously. "I just thought maybe if you could go down there—maybe to talk about something being wrong with the house—and sort of draw him out. Maybe you could tell if he's all right or not."

Brad turned the idea over in his mind, wondering if it could possibly work. If the chief were obsessive, as Chip seemed to think, Whalen certainly wouldn't open up to him. But on the other hand, his refusal to talk just might tell him something too.

"Well, I suppose I could try," he agreed without much conviction. "But I can't promise you anything. Don't expect me to go down and talk to him for five minutes, then be able to tell you if he's sane or not. It just isn't that simple. Besides, he'll probably throw me out of his office."

"But you'd be able to tell if he's reasonable or not, wouldn't you?"

"I can tell you that right now. I don't think Whalen's reasonable, and I never have. But what I think doesn't constitute either a medical or a legal opinion. All it means is that as far as I can tell he's a rigid person with some pretty strong prejudices. That doesn't make him crazy. All it makes him is difficult."

"But what about Glen? What about what Harney's doing to him?"

"So far he hasn't done anything except make a lot of wild accusations. And he hasn't even done that on the record. I mean, he hasn't charged Glen with anything. Or has he?"

Chip shook his head. "No. But I think he's going to."

"Do you? I don't. I don't think Whalen has the vaguest idea of what's going on, and he certainly doesn't have anything to use against Glen Palmer, or anybody else. And I'll tell you something else—I don't think he's ever going to make sense out of this mess. I'm not sure there *is* any sense. All I know is that the storms around here do something to Robby Palmer, and my best guess is that they're doing something to someone else as well."

Something stirred in Chip's mind—a connection only half-made, but he was sure it was an important connection.

"What happens to Robby?"

"I'm not sure exactly," Brad confessed. He made a gesture encompassing the books around him. "I've been trying to find something similar, but so far there isn't anything. Even Robby isn't sure what happens to him. The storms excite him but he doesn't remember what he does during them."

The connection clicked home in Chip's mind. Whalen's visit to Doc Phelps. Was it really indigestion? And other things, little things. The day he had worked with Glen, undisturbed. It had been stormy that day and Whalen had never called him. And that night the Hortons' boat had gone on the rocks. He searched his mind frantically, trying to remember where Harney Whalen had been each time something had gone wrong in Clark's Harbor. And he couldn't remember.

All he knew was that usually Harney had been home. Except ... who knew if he was at home or somewhere else?

Chip made up his mind to have a talk with Doc Phelps. Then, and only then, would he talk to Brad Randall. After all, Randall was a stranger, and Harney Whalen was his uncle.

In Clark's Harbor the natives stuck together.

28

The leaden skies over the Olympic Peninsula were dropping a soft mist on the small graveyard that overlooked Clark's Harbor, but there were no umbrellas raised above the heads of the tiny group of people who watched as Rebecca Palmer was laid to rest.

Lucas Pembroke closed his bible and began reciting the prayers for Rebecca's soul from memory, his eyes closed not only in reverence, but so that no one would see the sorrow he was feeling for Rebecca.

"Ashes to ashes, dust to dust . . ."

As the words droned automatically from his lips the minister wondered how much longer he would continue to come to Clark's Harbor, how much longer he would be able to tolerate the coldness that emanated from the village, how much longer, and how many more deaths, it would take before he turned his back on the little settlement nestled by the harbor.

Glen Palmer, holding Missy and Robby close, stood bare-headed in the rain, with Brad and Elaine Randall flanking him. They stood at the end of the open grave, and as the coffin was slowly lowered into the pit Missy began sobbing quietly. Elaine immediately knelt beside the child and gathered her into her arms. Robby, his face frozen in stoic acceptance, watched impassively, but as the coffin disappeared from his view a tear welled in his eye, overflowed, and ran unnoticed down his cheek.

A few yards away, his hands fingering his gloves nervously, Chip Connor stood with his grandfather, Mac Riley. Every few seconds Chip glanced at Glen, nodding slightly, as if to encourage his friend. The gesture went unheeded. Glen's eyes remained fastened on his wife's casket, his features a study in confusion and anguish.

At the fringe of the group, not really a part of it but observing everything, Merle Glind and the village librarian stood clucking together under the protection of a newspaper, their inquisitive eyes darting from face to face, filing away the reactions of everyone there for future discussion and reference.

As the Reverend Pembroke finished his prayers and picked up a clod of earth to sprinkle over the casket, he noticed a flash of movement in the trees beyond the graveyard. But when he looked more carefully, hoping to see who—or what—was there, there was nothing. Pembroke bit his lip, crushed the lump of earth, and dropped it into the grave.

It was like pulling a trigger. Missy Palmer, her quiet tears suddenly bursting forth into loud sobs, clung to Elaine Randall; and Robby, his hand tightening in his father's, suddenly looked up.

"I—I—" he began, but his words were choked off as he began to tremble and sob. Glen quickly sank to the ground beside him and held him.

"It's all right, son," he whispered. "Everything's going to be all right."

Then he scooped up a handful of damp earth, put it in Robby's hand, and led him to the edge of the grave. Together, father and son bade farewell to Rebecca.

"I'm so sorry, Glen," Chip said softly when it was over. "If there's anything I can do—anything at all—"

"Find out who did it," Glen pleaded. "Just find out who killed her."

Chip glanced quickly at Brad, who just as quickly shook his head slightly. Neither of them had yet told Glen of Brad's suspicion, and this was not the time to do it.

"We're working on it," Chip assured him.

"Thanks for coming," Glen said then. "I can't really say I expected you to be here. Not after what Whalen put me through yesterday."

"What Harney thinks is up to Harney," Chip replied. "I asked you what happened Sunday night and you told me. I haven't had any reason to change my mind."

There was a sudden silence and Elaine picked Missy up, then tried to smile cheerfully. "Why don't we all go out to our place," she suggested. "I'm not sure what we have but I'll scrape up something."

Mac Riley, his ancient sensibilities serving him well, took up the suggestion immediately.

"You figure out how to make that old stove go yet?"

"I'm working on it but it still gets to me."

"Nothing to it," Riley quavered. He began leading Elaine away from the graveside, sure that the others would follow. "I been using one of those things all my life, and the trick's in the wood. You got to have small pieces, and lots of different kinds. Some of 'em burn hotter than others. Once you know what's going to burn how, it's a lead-pipe cinch."

Moments later they had reached the cars. The cortege drove slowly away from the graveyard, leaving Rebecca Palmer at peace under the protection of the earth. Glen Palmer glanced back once and for a split second almost envied Rebecca. For her, the horror was truly over.

He wondered if it would ever be over for him.

The gathering at the Randalls' was a quiet one. Chip had begged off almost immediately, pleading business in town. While Elaine wrestled with the stove, encouraged only a little by Mac Riley's advice, Glen and Brad stood nervously in the kitchen, trying to explain to the old man what they thought might be happening.

Riley listened patiently as they told him about the strange effect the beach and the storms had on Robby, and how they had come to the conclusion that Robby was not the only one to be affected by the storms. When they finished Riley scratched his head thoughtfully and turned the whole matter over in his mind.

"Well, I just don't know," he said at last. "Sounds to me like craziness, but then this beach has always been full of craziness. Maybe that's what all the old legends were about." Then he shook his head. "Afraid I can't buy it though. I'm too old for these new-fangled ideas. If you ask me it's the sea. The sea and the past. They always catch up with you in the end. No way to get around it."

"You think the sea is breaking people's necks?"

Brad asked incredulously. Riley peered at him sadly.

"Could be," he said. "Or it could be the Indians. Some say they're still here, out on the beach."

"If they were we'd have seen them," Glen objected.

"Maybe you would, maybe you wouldn't." Riley's ancient voice crackled. "Only a few people can see the spirits, and even them that can, can't always."

Brad decided to play along with the old man. "Missy seems to think she sees things on the beach."

"Wouldn't surprise me a bit," Riley replied calmly. "Children have better eyes for things like that."

"And better ears for old men's stories?"

"Think what you like. Someday you'll know the truth." He glanced over the window. "Rain's starting up again. Big storm coming," he observed.

Involuntarily, the Randalls and Glen Palmer shuddered.

Chip Connor spent the afternoon with Harney Whalen. It was a difficult time for both of them: Chip tried to pretend that all was as it had always been between them, but Whalen was not fooled. Finally, in midafternoon, he accused Chip of staring at him and demanded to know what was wrong.

"Nothing," Chip assured him. "Nothing at all. I'm just a little worried about you."

"About me? I should think you'd be worried about your pal Glen Palmer. He's the one who's gotten himself in a peck of trouble."

Chip ignored the gibe, wanting to steer the conversation as far from Glen Palmer as possible. "I was just wondering how you're feeling," he said solicitously. "You look a little off color."

"I'm fine," Whalen growled. "Nothing wrong with me that won't be cured by a little peace and quiet around here." There was a pause, then Whalen went on. "Tell you what—why don't you take off for a couple of hours, then come back around dinnertime, and spell me for a while."

Chip couldn't think of a good reason not to, so he left the police station—reluctantly—and went looking for Doc Phelps. He found him at the inn, sitting on the stool Chip usually occupied, a half-empty beer in front of him. He started to get up when Chip came in, but Chip waved him back onto the stool.

"Order one for me and I'll fill yours up," he said cheerfully, sliding onto the stool next to Phelps.

"What about me?" Merle Glind piped eagerly from the stool on the other side of Phelps.

"You could buy your own just once," Chip teased. "But what the hell. Might as well be a big spender."

The beers were drawn and set up in front of them when Phelps asked about Harney Whalen.

"Whalen?" Chip said carefully. "What about him?"

"Well, I ordered him to come in for some tests, but he hasn't showed up. I guess he must be feeling better."

"What kind of tests?" Chip asked, trying to keep the eagerness out of his voice.

"Oh, just some things I'd like checked out," the doctor replied cautiously. "He hasn't been feeling too well, you know."

"Told me it's just indigestion."

"Indigestion?" Dr. Phelps gave the word a sarcastic twist that riveted Chip's attention. "Damnedest kind of indigestion I ever heard of. Most people remember indigestion."

Chip felt his heartbeat skip and a knot of anticipation form in his stomach.

"You mean he's having memory problems? Like blackouts?"

"That's what he told me," Phelps said. "Wanted me to keep it to myself, and I suppose I ought to. But if he isn't going to obey doctor's orders, seems to me something ought to be done."

Chip didn't hear what Phelps had just said—his mind was racing.

"Doc, tell me about the blackouts. It might be important. Very important."

Phelps frowned at the young man and tugged at his lower lip. He didn't like these kids trying to push him around.

"Well, I don't know," he hesitated. "Seems to me like I've already broken Harn's confidence—"

"The hell with Harn's confidence," Chip snapped. "Dr. Phelps, I *have* to know what you know about those blackouts."

"Well, I don't really know much at all," Phelps grumbled. He still resented being ordered to talk by Chip, and yet there was a note of urgency in the young deputy's voice that struck a chord in the doctor. "He didn't really tell me much. Mostly he was upset about something that happened the other day while he was driving out to Sod Beach. It was the day those new people moved in—the Randalls?—and I guess Harn was taking them out to their house. Anyway, he froze at the wheel, I guess, and almost ran over those two kids who live out there."

"Robby and Missy? The Palmer kids?"

"Those'd be the ones," the doctor agreed. "Anyway, it upset Harney enough so he came to see me. Told me he'd been having what he calls spells. His hands start twitching, and then he doesn't remember anything for an hour or so."

"Do you know what's causing it?" Chip asked anxiously.

"Haven't any idea at all," Phelps shrugged. "I wanted him to go down to Aberdeen for some tests, but you know Harn—stubborn as a mule!"

"And you didn't try to make him?" Chip demanded unbelievingly. "For Christ's sake, Doc, he might have killed somebody!"

"But he didn't, did he?" Phelps said blandly.

"Didn't he?" Chip muttered. "I wonder."

He slid off the barstool and headed back to the police station, intent on confronting the police chief. But when he got to the station, Harney Whalen's office was empty.

Chip glanced around the office and saw that Whalen's raincoat still hung from the coat tree in the corner. Wherever he had gone, and for whatever purpose, he hadn't bothered to take his coat with him.

The storm outside, so gentle this morning, was raging.

And it was getting dark. Tonight high tide would be an hour after dusk.

As dusk began to fall Elaine took Missy and Robby into the downstairs bedroom and began putting them to bed. The storm had increased, and the sound of rain battering against the window seemed menacing to

Elaine, but she was careful not to communicate her feelings to the children. As she tucked them into the big bed Missy suddenly put her arms around her neck.

"Do we have to sleep here?" she whispered. "Can't we sleep at home?"

"Just for tonight, dear," Elaine said. "But don't you worry. We'll all be in the next room. Your father, and me, and Brad. Everything's going to be fine."

"No, it isn't," Missy said, her voice tiny and frightened. "Nothing's ever going to be fine. I know it isn't."

Elaine hugged the child reassuringly and kissed her on the forehead. Then she kissed Robby too and picked up the lantern by the bed.

"If you need anything you just call me," she told them. Then she pulled the door closed behind her as she left the room.

They lay in bed, listening to the rain beat against the window. For a long time they were quiet, but then Missy stirred.

"Are you asleep?"

"No. Are you?"

"No." Missy paused a moment, then: "I miss Mommy. I want to go home. I don't like this house."

"It's just a house," Robby said disdainfully. "It isn't any different than any other house, except that it's better than ours."

"It's creepy," Missy insisted.

"Oh, go to sleep," Robby said impatiently. He turned over and closed his eyes and tried to pretend that he was sleeping. But he heard the sounds of the rain and the wind and the building surf of the flowing tide. The sounds seemed to be calling him, and try as he would, he couldn't ignore them.

"If you really want to, we can go home," he whispered.

Missy stirred next to him, and he knew she'd heard him.

"Could we go through the woods?" she whispered.

"All right," Robby agreed. The beach would be better, he thought, but the woods would be all right. At least he'd be near the storm. . . .

A few moments later Robby raised the window and the two children crept out into the night.

29

Harney Whalen sat behind the wheel of the patrol car, his knuckles white with tension, his face beginning to twitch spasmodically. The windshield wipers, almost useless against the driving rain, beat rhythmically back and forth in front of his eyes, but if he saw them, he gave no sign. He was watching the road in front of him, and there was an intensity in his look that would have frightened anyone who saw it. But he was alone, driving north toward Sod Beach.

As he approached the beach he began to hear voices in his mind, voices from his childhood, calling to him.

Floating in the darkness ahead of him, just beyond the windshield, he thought he saw faces—his grandmother was there, her face twisted in fear, her eyes reflecting the panic of a trapped animal. She seemed to be trying to call out to Harn, but her voice was lost in the howling tempest—all that came through was the faint sound of laughter, a laughter that mocked Harney, taunted him, made the chaos in his mind coalesce into hatred.

He turned the car into a narrow side road halfway up Sod Beach and picked his way carefully through the mud until the forest closed in on him, blocking him. He turned off the headlights, then the engine, and sat in the darkness, the rain pounding on the car, the wind whistling around him, and the roar of the pounding surf rolling over him, calling to him. Beckoning him.

Listening only to the voices within him, unmindful of reality, Harney Whalen suddenly opened the car door and stepped out into the storm. A moment later the police car stood lonely and abandoned in the forest.

Harney Whalen had disappeared into the night.

When the pounding on the front door began Brad Randall's first impulse was one of fear—the sudden, gripping fear that always accompanies an unexpected sound in the night. But when he heard a voice calling from outside, his fear dissipated and he hurried to the door.

"I can't find him," Chip Connor cried as he came in out of the storm. "He's gone, and I think it's going to happen again!"

"Can't find who?" Brad asked. "For Christ's sake, calm down! You're not making sense."

"It's Harney Whalen," Chip gasped. "I'm sure of it. He's been sick lately, then he got mad at me today. So I went and found Doc Phelps." Chip dropped into a chair and tried to catch his breath.

"Phelps?" Glen asked. "What the hell does he have to do with anything?"

"He told me about Harn," Chip said. "He told me that Harn's been having blackouts."

"Blackouts?" Brad repeated. "What kind of blackouts?"

"The same kind Robby has. He doesn't pass out—he just can't remember what he was doing. As soon as Phelps told me that I went back to the station, but he was gone. His raincoat's still there but he's not."

"Maybe he went home," Glen suggested, though he was sure it wasn't true.

"That's the first place I went," Chip said. "He's not there. So I figured I'd better come out here and warn you. If what you think is true, he's probably prowling around the beach somewhere."

"My God," Elaine moaned. "Is the house locked up?"

"It's been locked up all evening," Brad said.

"I'm going to check anyway." She picked up a lantern and started toward the dining room, intent on circling the main floor.

"We've got to find him," Chip said as soon as Elaine was out of the room.

"Maybe not," Brad replied. "As long as we're all here there isn't much chance that Whalen will find anyone on the beach. Not tonight."

As if to confirm what he said, a bolt of lightning struck, briefly illuminating the room, then the clap of thunder shook the old house, rattling the windows.

As the thunder died the sudden void was filled by Elaine Randall's scream of horror. A second later she appeared at the bedroom door. "They're gone," she cried, her face pale and her voice strangled. "The children are gone."

Glen Palmer started for the bedroom and Elaine stepped aside to let him pass. He looked frantically around the icy room, then went to the open window, the cold, wind-driven rain stinging his face.

"Please," he prayed silently. "Leave me my children."

When he returned to the living room, Chip and Brad were waiting for him, their coats on, flashlights in their hands. Next to the fireplace, Mac Riley stood uncertainly.

"I think I should go too," he said. "I've known Harney since he was a baby. If something's happening to him . . ."

"No, Grandpa," Chip replied. "Stay here. You can't move as fast as you used to, and Mrs. Randall shouldn't be left alone."

"Please," she begged. "Please stay with me. If I have to wait by myself I'll go out of my mind. I know I will." Sobbing softly, she sank into a chair. Brad started toward her, but Mac Riley held up his hand.

"Go on," he said. "Find the children. We'll be all right, I promise you."

As Chip, Brad, and Glen went out into the night, Mac Riley poked at the fire, then began one more circuit of the house, checking the doors and windows. When he came back to the living room he tried to comfort Elaine.

"They'll find the kids," he said softly. "Don't you worry."

But inside, the old man was worried.

30

The maelstrom crashed around them, the high keening of the wind screaming in the treetops providing an eerie counterpoint to the roar of the surf as the tide came to full flood. The beach had shrunk to a narrow ribbon of sand between the roiling sea and the tangle of driftwood that creaked and shifted in the storm.

"I can't see anything," Missy cried out, clinging to her brother's hand, stumbling blindly along after him as he moved quickly through the night.

If he heard her Robby gave no sign. The excitement of the beach was upon him, and his senses took in the wildness of the elements, absorbing the unleashed energy of the tempest. His body was filling with a strange exultation, exciting him, yet at the same time calming him. It was a feeling he didn't quite understand, but he accepted it and was grateful for it.

Missy stopped suddenly and Robby nearly lost his footing as she jerked on his hand.

"Something's here," Missy whispered, pulling close to Robby and putting her lips to his ear. "I can feel it."

"Nothing's here," Robby said. "Only us."

"Yes there is," Missy insisted. "Something's in the woods looking for us. Let's go back. Please?"

"We can't go back," Robby told her. "Not anymore."

He started forward again, pulling Missy with him, and she began sobbing, her terror overcoming her. As they moved along the beach she began to see shapes, strange glowing figures, moving along beside her, in front of her, behind her, coming closer, reaching out for her.

She began screaming.

Harney Whalen crouched behind the pile of driftwood that separated the beach from the forest and listened to the sounds in his head. The laughter was getting louder and the screams of his grandmother seemed to be fading away.

There was a flash of lightning and he saw two figures coming toward him across the beach. They were small figures but he knew who they were.

They were strangers.

Strangers had killed his grandparents while he had helplessly watched.

He wanted to run, wanted to go away and hide, as he had done so many years ago.

But he couldn't. He felt something gripping him, forcing him to stay where he was. He turned and there was someone beside him in the night. His grandmother, her strong, chiseled features gleaming in the night, her dark eyes flashing, was beside him.

While the rain slashed at him and the wind tore through his clothes, chilling him, she whispered to him, her words echoing against the pounding of the surf.

Don't run away. Avenge. Avenge.

Harney waited behind the log, waited for them to come near.

He crouched lower, huddled in upon himself, and listened to the words of the old Klickashaw at his side. She spoke to him of ancient wrongs. . . .

On the beach Robby and Missy, the wind whirling around them, hurried along, unaware of the danger waiting for them in the forest.

Far down the beach, Chip Connor, Brad Randall, and Glen Palmer hurried through the storm, their flashlights playing over the sand, nearly useless in the rain.

"We'll never find them," Brad called out, raising his voice against the wind. "Not if we stay together. Let's spread out."

"You take the surf line," Chip yelled. "Glen, stay in the middle of the beach. I'll go up by the forest. And call for them. They might hear and it will let us keep track of each other. I don't think we should get too far apart."

They spread out, and the three dots of light scattered themselves across the beach, visible for only a few yards but lighting the way for the searchers. They began calling out the children's names.

Robby began pulling Missy toward the forest but she hung back, her terrified eyes seeing nothing but the strange figures closing in around her, reaching for her. A faint sound drifted through the night, nearly lost in the storm. Missy pulled Robby to a halt.

"Someone's calling us. I can hear my name."

Robby glared at his sister, tugging on her arm. "We have to go into the woods. We'll be safe there," he hissed.

Once more the faint sounds echoed through the night: "*Missy . . . Robby!*"

The children crouched uncertainly in the sand, straining to hear better, but it was useless. The wind increased, howling in from the ocean, carrying the acrid smell of salt water with it.

They began climbing over the pile of driftwood.

Harney Whalen also heard the voices calling. But stronger in his mind was his grandmother's voice, whispering to him, urging him on, reassuring him.

We are with you. We will help you. You are a child of the storm. You belong to us.

He stood up, facing the storm, and exultation swept through him. His grandmother cried out to him. *Vengeance! Vengeance!*

The lightning flashed.

The instant of electric brightness seemed to last an eternity, and the three figures froze, staring at each other across the driftwood.

And Missy knew.

"It's him," she screamed. "He's here, Robby. He's going to kill us."

Harney Whalen didn't hear the words Missy cried out—only the sound. He peered malevolently at the two figures, seeing not two small and frightened children, but two faceless figures from the past, two unidentifiable forms, laughing at him, laughing at what they had done to his grandparents.

He had to destroy them.

He started over the driftwood.

The two children, suddenly coming to life, began running up the beach.

The lightning faded and the roll of thunder began.

"I see them," Brad cried as the night closed around him once more. "North. They're north of us, right near the woods."

On either side of him, the pinpoints of light that were Chip and Glen suddenly began bobbing in the darkness as all three of them broke into a run. Then they began hearing Missy's frightened cries, leading them through the night.

The children tore through the night, hearing the pounding of feet behind them. Then Robby stumbled and fell, and Missy tumbled on top of him.

Harney Whalen, his breath coming in fitful gasps, caught up with them, towering over them, glowering down upon them like a furious giant.

Missy saw him first and her eyes widened in terror as she screamed out into the night. Then she felt a hand clamp over her mouth and her scream was cut off.

Robby scrambled free from the tangle of limbs, but his mind was confused and nothing was making any sense to him. He moved aside, staring helplessly at his struggling sister, then began to scream.

"My God, he's got them," Glen shouted as he heard first Missy's choked-off scream of terror, then

Robby's mindless howling in the night. The three men were running together now, shining their lights into the darkness, praying that they would get to the children before it was too late.

And then they found them. Chip Connor hurled himself onto Harney Whalen's back, grabbing the chief by the neck. Whalen let go of Missy and began struggling with Chip, desperately fighting off his unseen assailant.

Glen grabbed Missy and held the sobbing child close to him, stroking her head, patting her, trying to calm her. Then Robby too flung himself onto Glen, and the three of them held each other, unmindful of what was happening around them.

Brad stood helplessly, wanting to come to Chip's aid but unsure if it would do any good. Then, before he could make up his mind, Whalen broke free of Chip's grasp and ran.

Chip started to follow him, but Whalen disappeared into the darkness.

"Which way did he go?" Chip cried. "I can't find him."

"Toward the water," Brad called.

They began running, Brad shining his light ahead, the wind clutching at them.

And then they saw him.

Harney Whalen was in the surf, wading out to sea.

Chip started in after him, but Brad stopped, holding his light steadily on the retreating figure of the police chief.

"Let him go," Brad called.

Chip stopped, instinctively obeying the command. As the two men watched, an immense wave swept in from the sea, breaking over Harney Whalen's head.

He struggled against the force of the water for a moment, his arms waving ineffectually in the air.

Then he was gone, taken by the sea.

Chip walked slowly back to where Brad stood, still playing the light over the spot where Harney Whalen had vanished.

"Why did you stop me?" Chip asked softly.

"It's better this way," Brad answered. "This way we know it ends."

Then they turned away from the sea and started back toward Glen Palmer.

Behind them the tide turned and began to ebb.

An hour later the storm broke.

Sod Beach was quiet.

Epilogue

"It's over," Chip Connor said as he walked into the Randalls' living room.

Brad and Elaine looked at him expectantly, but Glen Palmer didn't seem to care.

Two weeks had passed, two weeks during which the strange story of Harney Whalen had passed through Clark's Harbor in whispers, two weeks during which the people of the village had come to accept what had happened.

Today it had been finished. The coroner's inquest had been held. It had been a strange inquest.

There were few facts to be discussed. Much time had been spent on speculation, on trying to decide exactly what had happened to the police chief.

In the end it had been decided that Harney Whalen had died a suicide. Nothing was said about the other deaths in Clark's Harbor, the deaths that dotted its history like a pox. But outside the inquest the people talked, and wondered, and clucked their tongues in sympathy.

Sympathy for those who had died—and for Whalen, who apparently had killed them.

"They want me to take over Harney's job," Chip

said when he had finished telling them the results of the inquest.

"Are you going to?" Brad asked.

"I don't know," Chip said uneasily. "It makes sense, I suppose, but I don't know if I want the job."

"You'd be good at it," Glen Palmer offered.

"That's not what worries me," Chip replied. "It's the memories. Too many memories. I'd probably do too many things differently from Harn."

"Would that be so bad?" Elaine asked.

Chip shook his head. "That's what I don't know. Harn wasn't all bad. For a long time he ran things very well. If it all hadn't gone wrong for him . . ." He let the thought go, then turned to Brad. "What happened?" he asked. "Isn't there any explanation?"

"A theory," Brad said. "But I'll never be able to prove it. There was a connection between Robby and Harney Whalen."

"I don't understand—" Chip began, but Brad stopped him.

"I'm not sure I do either. It has to do with bio-rhythms, and bio-rhythms are elusive things. We know they affect us, but we don't know why. For that matter, we aren't even sure what they are. Everyone has a set pattern of rhythms that begins the day he's born, and the pattern only repeats itself every fifty-eight years and sixty-seven days. As it happens, that's exactly how much older Whalen was than Robby. Both of them, apparently, had a bio-rhythmic pattern that's affected by the storms out here. For Robby the effect is good. For Whalen—well, coupled with the trauma he had when he was a boy, the effect was disastrous."

Chip stared at the psychiatrist. "How come you

didn't think of that before?" he demanded. "If you knew something like that could happen, Harn could have been—"

Again Brad cut him off. "I'm sorry, Chip," he said gently. "There's nothing that could have been done. In fact, I don't even know if my theory is right. All it is is a theory, but it fits the facts. And with bio-rhythms that's most of the story. You can't predict what's *going* to happen, but they often explain what *did* happen. You might call them a good tool for hindsight," he added wryly.

But what about the future, he wondered to himself. His eyes wandered to the window, and came to rest on Robby Palmer. The boy was walking slowly along the beach, studying the sand at his feet.

Again the words came into Brad's mind. *What about the future?* With Harney Whalen gone, what would the beach hold for Robby?

As if reading Brad's mind, Chip Connor suddenly stood up. "I think I'll go for a walk," he said, almost too casually. "One thing about this beach—it was always a good place to think." As he pulled on his coat, Chip gazed out at the calmness of Sod Beach. On the horizon, as often was the case, a storm seemed to be building, but it no longer posed a threat, no longer induced a fear of something horrible about to happen . . .

And yet, far down the beach, he could see Robby Palmer, standing still now, staring at the darkening horizon, his puppy frisking at his feet.

A chill crept through Chip's body, and he buttoned his coat snug around his neck.

* * *

He left the old house and started north, not stopping until he reached the point where Harney Whalen had disappeared into the surf.

Chip's eyes scanned the sea, unconsciously searching for the police chief's body.

It had never been found, never washed up on the sand, either here or on the beaches to the north and south, all of which had been patrolled regularly.

Chip turned away from the sea and started toward the woods. As he made his way to the top of the driftwood tangle the wind began to blow.

Two weeks ago the blowing of the wind would have frightened him.

He sat on a huge silvery log and tried to sort things out in his mind, tried to separate his memories—tried to categorize them, keeping the good memories and discarding the bad ones.

He wanted to create two Harney Whalens: the one he had known so well, the one he had grown up respecting and admiring; and the other one, the recent one, the Harney Whalen whose mind had been twisted, partly by his ancient memories, but also apparently by the same elements that had twisted the log on which Chip sat. Maybe, Chip reflected, his grandfather was right—maybe it was the sea that got to Harney.

As the sun began to go down and the wind blew harder, Chip shivered. He watched the sand dance across the beach, driven on the wind.

He saw something, something that had been buried on the beach but that was being revealed by the storm.

Curious, he climbed down from the driftwood and uncovered the object.

He recognized it instantly. It was Scooter, Missy and Robby Palmer's tiny puppy.

It was still warm.

Its neck had been wrung.

As the storm broke upon him, Chip turned to the woods, suddenly frightened. Carrying the tiny body of the puppy, Chip once again climbed the driftwood, but this time he crossed it and went into the woods.

Robby Palmer felt the first drops of rain splash on his face and was glad. He'd been waiting for the storm all afternoon and now it was here.

With the storm would come the excitement.

And with the excitement would come the shapes and the voices.

He hadn't told anybody about the things he saw on the beach now. He was sure they wouldn't believe him—none of them except Missy, but they hadn't be-believed her, either.

He still wasn't sure exactly who the people on the beach were, or why they were there.

Usually they danced strange dances that always ended with them burying someone on the beach— someone who didn't belong. But it didn't frighten Robby because he knew he belonged. He was part of the beach and the beach loved him.

It was the strangers who didn't belong.

The strangers who came and took the beach from the people who belonged and betrayed them.

As the storm grew the dance began, and Robby

414

watched it from the forest. Then the voices began, telling him to join the dance.

But he didn't know how.

You will know, the voices said.

Robby suddenly became aware of a figure making its way over the driftwood.

Betrayal, the voices whispered. *Betrayal.*

The figure came closer, and the voices whispered again.

Vengeance. Vengeance.

Robby didn't quite understand the word, but he knew what to do.

He picked up a heavy stick and crept behind a tree.

He waited, and listened to the voices.

The full force of the tempest broke over the coast, lashing at the trees as the tide surged forth, marching before the thunderheads like a harbinger of death.

As the surf crested, Robby Palmer, his eyes seeing nothing of the storm, emerged from the forest to pick his way carefully over the bleached bones of driftwood littering the beach.

He was among them now, and as their ceremony came to its climax the storm dancers reached out to him, sang to him, pled with him to join them in their cry for the strangers.

Uncertainly at first, but then with a sense of all things being right, Robby Palmer gave himself up to them.

Born in Whittier, California, John Saul is a former actor who now makes his home in Seattle, Washington. His first novel, *Suffer the Children*, published in 1976, was a national best-seller and was followed, one year later, by *Punish the Sinners*, also a *New York Times* best-seller. Mr. Saul is currently at work on his fourth novel.